Thomas Rhys Evans, Hans Lassen Martensen

Jacob Boehme

His Life and Teaching

Thomas Rhys Evans, Hans Lassen Martensen

Jacob Boehme
His Life and Teaching

ISBN/EAN: 9783337166243

Printed in Europe, USA, Canada, Australia, Japan

Cover: Foto ©Raphael Reischuk / pixelio.de

More available books at **www.hansebooks.com**

JACOB BOEHME:

HIS LIFE AND TEACHING.

OR

STUDIES ·IN THEOSOPHY.

BY THE LATE
DR. HANS LASSEN MARTENSEN,

Metropolitan of Denmark.

TRANSLATED FROM THE DANISH BY
T. RHYS EVANS.

London
HODDER AND STOUGHTON,

27, PATERNOSTER ROW.

MDCCCLXXXV.

Printed by Hazell, Watson, & Viney, Limited, London and Aylesbury.

AUTHOR'S PREFACE.

WHEN during my younger days I was absorbed in the study of mediæval mysticism, and listened, with the deep attention of a seeker, to the discourses of Master Eckart and Tauler, now in their quiet cloisters, and again under the arches of their churches, I was led forward, almost inevitably, from mysticism to theosophy, and, consequently, to Jacob Böhme. The first impression was not attractive. It was true that the light of the Reformation was here, shining with its great and universal energies; but this light had to force its rays into the narrowness and obscurity of a shoemaker's room, where there was very much to obstruct the illumination. Böhme's style and method of treatment struck me as intolerable and not to be entertained. A longer acquaintance with him and closer attention could not, however, but convince me that his works contained very attractive passages,—passages, indeed, of fascinating beauty combined with surprising depth, vivid and revealing lightning, and new light. I read several of his chief treatises, and, notwithstanding the hard nuts that had to be cracked, it seemed to me not wholly improbable that the result of a more protracted study would be, that youthful love would lead me to attempt a work that should have Böhme as its subject. Nothing, however, came of this; and, so far as I was personally concerned, the undertaking would certainly have been premature. Other tasks imposed their claim upon me; my immediate relation to Böhme gradually faded away, although modern philosophy and theology still kept me in contact with his ideas, during the whole of my life. It is now for the first time, at the eleventh hour, so to speak, when my whole journey draws near its close and must shortly be completed, that I again find myself in direct relation with Böhme and his writings. A point in Böhme which has formed the subject of much philosophical discussion, and with which I had long been occupied, compelled me to return to the fountain head, to seek for myself grounds of more solid and independent conviction. I, therefore, undertook the perusal of his complete works,—no insurmountable task, seeing that they comprise only seven volumes in Schiebler's edition. I was induced, in consequence of this, to record my interpretation of Jacob Böhme as a whole.

I have given the name of *Studies* to this volume, in order to indicate that it was composed especially for my own instruction, and that it urges no claim to exhaustiveness and completeness. I have called them *theosophical studies*, to imply that my main object of interest has not been Böhme as a simply historical phenomenon, but the actual problems to the solution of which he has offered so remarkable and world-renowned a contribution, and which he has so powerfully stirred into activity.

However great may be the interest that I feel in Böhme as the highly-enlightened layman, the great prodigy in the spiritual and intellectual world, the unexplained psychological enigma, the pious soul who, with all his profound knowledge, made it his single aim to advance in earnest, practical Christianity, in the appropriation of " the pearl of great price, and the gracious lily,"—far greater than my interest in purely historical reminiscences is that which I feel in the great subject for which he lived, the subject which belongs to every age, and will always shape itself in souls that are able and willing to devote themselves to it. I am interested in the fountains from which he drew, and which still flow for us, when we are willing to heed them, and thus to gain deeper comprehension of Divine things and greater earnestness in our religious life. Under these circumstances it will scarcely be thought unpardonable that, in these studies, I have frequently developed my own view, my own conviction of the truth.

The method of treatment pursued by Jacob Böhme presents this difficulty, that it is impossible to delineate him by mere quotations, seeing that they contribute little to our comprehension of him ; but that one is bound to reproduce him with a certain degree of freedom. And here the objection is obviously close at hand that this plan is very perilous, and that it is to be feared that the narrator will introduce something of his own, and give the subject an admixture of his own subjectivity ; that, instead of an interpretation, one may give a mosaic of one's own ; as, for instance, has so often been urged against the innumerable commentaries on Faust and on Dante's " Divina Commedia." There is certainly a measure of truth in this objection ; but it cannot be helped ! No one can interpret an intellectual subject unless through the medium of his own consciousness, which is, so to speak, the mirror in which one is compelled to behold and to interpret what shows itself, with regard to which, however, it can by no means be asserted that all mirrors are equally good.

But to the man who has no confidence in a specific interpretation, and is afraid of missing what he calls the pure objectivity, no other counsel can be given than that he himself should go to the fountain head, and then reproduce it for himself. For, if he wishes to understand what he has read, to say nothing of expounding it to others, we believe we can answer for the fact that he will be compelled to reproduce it!

And, herewith, I entrust this volume to the circle of benevolent readers, capable of these inquiries, into whose hands it may fall. And I append a reference to the words of the Apostle: "Prove all things: hold fast that which is good!" (1 Thess. v. 21).

TRANSLATOR'S PREFACE.

ENGLISH readers are already in possession of Bishop Martensen's treatises on "Christian Dogmatics" and "Christian Ethics." It would be superfluous to mention the profound esteem in which these treatises are held, or the immense stimulus which they have given to thought upon the subjects with which they deal. Their value is confessedly European. "Jacob Böhme" completes the triad of the author's most important works, and was his own favourite production. It is, however, simply a fragment of that larger history of Protestant mysticism which Martensen often thought of writing, but which the world will never see from his pen.

The value of the present work consists partly in its clear and comprehensive summary of Böhme's views, and partly in the keen and thoughtful criticism to which those views are subjected.

Theosophy is, at present, a somewhat discredited term, but it is needless to say that, in the case of Jacob Böhme, the term involves no suspicion of chicanery, juggling, or crazy eccentricity. Dr. Martensen wisely deprecates the hostile attitude so frequently adopted by dogmatic theologians towards those who work along freer, or at least less formal, lines. Professional soldiers have often distrusted irregular troops and guerilla chiefs who, nevertheless, have rendered extraordinary service to the common cause. Thus, also, men destitute of all formal scientific training have often generated fresh and powerful ideas which became the parents of the great discoveries which enriched succeeding centuries. In like manner, a just appreciation of the constitution of the human mind, and of the action upon it of the Spirit of God, will render it easily explicable that a man who simply surrenders himself to devout meditation upon Divine things, may be enabled to recover truths that had been long in abeyance, to kindle a deeper practical devotion, and valuably to enlarge the field of our religious knowledge. The delightful freshness, the rapid flashings of a genius never separated from reverence, and the profound belief in the living voice of God which characterise many of these thinkers, appear to be elements which the Church of Christ can never too gratefully recognize.

These are some of the reasons which induced Dr. Martensen to offer to the public his generous but impartial estimate of the great sixteenth century mystic.

The reader may disagree with individual points of Böhme's teaching, and may still find portions of it unintelligible ; he may find himself occasionally at variance with Dr. Martensen's speculative opinions. But the books with which we most absolutely agree do not always form our most profitable reading, and, in the humble opinion of the translator, the circumstances just alluded to will not impair the suggestive and practical value of this treatise.

It only remains to add, that the quotations from Böhme's own works have been taken from William Law's curious and valuable edition of Böhme's works (4 vols. quarto, London, 1781). The quaint and antique flavour of Law's substantially accurate translation seems more in harmony with its subject-matter than would be the case with any attempt to give it a more modern dress.

T. RHYS EVANS.

BRIGHTON, *Sept.* 1885.

CONTENTS.

I.

GOD AND THE UNCREATED HEAVEN.

CRITICAL RETROSPECT.

II.

GOD AND THE CREATED WORLD.

JACOB BÖHME was, as is well known, a shoemaker. But, in addition to this, he was a theosophist—indeed, the greatest and most famous
of all theosophists in the world,—and has gained the
cognomen ; *philosophus Teutonicus.* An attempt
will be made in the sequel to explain the meaning
of theosophy. Here we simply observe provisionally,
that theosophy signifies wisdom in God, in the
Spirit of God (not in the spirit of the world), an
intuitive apprehension of Divine and natural mysteries, on the basis of God's revelation in Holy
Scripture and in the book of nature. Jacob Böhme,
who applied himself to this kind of wisdom, has had
to pass, not only during his lifetime, but also after
his death, through honour and dishonour, good
report and evil report. Many have regarded him
as a visionary, and have placed his teaching in the
history of human follies. In many libraries his
writings are to be found under the rubric " *Fanatici.*"
Others have extolled him to the skies, and have
believed that they have found in him all the treasures
of knowledge and all enigmas solved. Others again,
who recognise and admire his greatness, are still
of opinion that a query and a corrective must be
applied to many passages in his discourse concerning

the Divine mysteries, and that his precious pearls
and pure gold need to be cleansed from adherent
shells and scoriæ. But he always remains one of
the most remarkable phenomena in the history of
the human mind. A humble peasant, without learning or scientific education, who combined with
simple Christian faith and piety the most profound
philosophical speculation ; who was upborne and
encircled by a gigantic imagination ; whose works
may, it is true, be called chaotic and shapeless, but
in which, as one roams through their labyrinths, one
is constantly and irresistibly persuaded that a stream
flows through them, which has its source in the
eternal hills ; labyrinths in which one is surprised,
amid the obscurity and gloom, by lightning which
now gladdens and anon appals by the glimpses it
affords us of Time and Eternity, of the Divine,
human, and demonic depths. Among the great
spirits of mankind Böhme occupies, it is true, a
lonely and isolated place. His defective education
excludes him, as it were, from polite society, and
exposes him to a degree of contempt. It would be
a mistake, nevertheless, to suppose that Böhme has
exercised no influence whatever upon intellectual
development. During his lifetime he endeavoured
to recall the clergy of the State Church, who had
entered arid paths, to a deeper and more living
apprehension of the doctrines of the faith ; he
sought to promote a true and practical Christianity
which should not be confined to the " sphere of the
letter " : in this he coincides with the nobler pietism.
However futile, in many respects, his attempt may
have been, and however much the theologians of

a later period may have tried to exclude him, our own nineteenth century, no less than the eighteenth, exhibits theological works which bear direct or indirect testimony that their authors have not found it beneath their dignity to learn of the unscientific but highly-enlightened layman. Philosophy also, in so far as it has entered into the realities of life—by which we mean not only the sensible and tangible, but the super-sensible realities which this science sometimes, and by no means least of all in our own day, ignores or regards as non-existent (" I do not see them ; therefore they do not exist ! ")—philosophy also shows the influences of this " powerful mind," as Hegel calls him. We may especially mention Schelling and Franz Baader, different as these thinkers are from one another, and different as is their relation to Böhme. There is also the important French author St. Martin, himself a theosophist and a disciple of Böhme.

Although Böhme's doctrine, at his own epoch, and during the following century, found no slight echo even beyond the limits of Germany—*e.g.*, in England, where the unfortunate Charles I. was greatly interested in it,—still it has never become the foundation of a religious sect. Böhme himself adhered to the Lutheran Church, and died in its communion. But, without becoming the founder of a sect or a partisan—things utterly abhorrent to his spirit, he has often gathered round him a quiet congregation which has rejoiced in the light that he kindled in the Divine mysteries, and has been edified by his exhortations on the way of salvation and the practice of earnest Christianity. And it is undeniable that there are few men whose life and thought so pregnantly express the saying of the Apostle, that " in God we live, and move, and have our being " ; and that whether we regard him on the side of mind or temper, the lines of Angelus Silesius are applicable to him :

> " In water lives the fish, the plant in the earth,
> The bird in the air, in the firmament the Sun.
> The salamander must subsist in fire,
> And the Heart of God is Jacob Böhme's element."

It is this man who has exercised, and will continue to exercise, a quiet attraction over speculative minds and religious dispositions, although it must be admitted that his special fascination will be experienced only by those who are at the same time religiously and speculatively constituted.

We will now relate the usual particulars concerning Böhme's life, following the biography of Frankenberg, which consists, in large measure, of information from the mouth of Böhme himself. A few points are added from Böhme's writings. Although these particulars are tolerably well known, they ought not to be omitted here.

Jacob Böhme was born in 1575 at Old Seidenberg, a village near Görlitz. His parents were poor peasants, who were only able to procure for him the usual religious school teaching, together with some instruction in reading and writing. At an early age he was compelled, with other boys, to watch the cattle in the fields. He was a quiet, introspective lad, whose face bore somewhat of the dreamy expression which is frequent in poetic natures. Indeed, when very young, he was marked by a certain visionary element, by inward visions, which for himself assumed the character of outwardness and reality. Thus, when a shepherd boy, he once climbed to the top of a mountain called the " Land's Crown " ; and here he saw a vaulted entrance composed of four red stones, and leading into a cavern. When he had toiled through the brushwood that surrounded the entrance, he beheld in the depth of the cave a vessel filled with money. He was seized with inward panic, as if at something diabolical, and ran away in alarm. Subsequently he often returned to the spot, accompanied by other boys. But entrance and cavern had alike vanished !

As he was not well qualified for agricultural and rural pursuits, he was apprenticed to a shoemaker. Here also something remarkable happened to him. One day, when the master and his wife were out, and he was alone in the house, a stranger entered the shop and asked for a pair of shoes. As Jacob did not consider himself empowered to conclude a bargain, seeing that his master had given him no express authority for this, he tried to release himself from the dilemma by demanding a high price for the shoes, in the hope that the man would be disinclined to buy. But the man paid the sum required, and, when he had gone out into the street, shouted, " Jacob, come forth ! " Surprised that the stranger should know his name, Jacob obeyed the call, and now the stranger looked at him with a kindly, earnest, deep, soul-piercing gaze, and said, " Jacob, thou art as yet but little, but the time will come when thou shalt be great, and become another man, and the world shall marvel at thee. Therefore, be pious, fear God, and reverence His Word; especially read diligently the Holy Scriptures, where thou hast comfort and instruction; for thou must endure much misery and poverty, and suffer persecution. But be courageous and persevere, for God loves, and is gracious unto thee." Thereupon the stranger clasped his hand and disappeared. Whether all this is to be accepted as an actual occurrence or partly as a vision, we leave an open question.

After this experience Jacob became even more pensive and serious, and devoted himself to pure morality and devout meditation; nor could he refrain from words of confession and admonition when the other journeymen on the work-bench indulged in loose conversation about sacred things. Naturally, they would not listen to his exhortations; and to make an end of the disputes that followed, his master dismissed him, saying that he would have no "house-prophet" to bring discord and trouble into the house. And thus Böhme was compelled to go forth into the wide world as a travelling journeyman. During his wanderings, he discovered that the period was full of theological conflicts, and that the Evangelical Church was split into parties that mutually vilified each other, and made on him the impression of a Babel. He was afflicted with profound solicitude, and fell into manifold doubts, against which he had to struggle by seeking for himself in Holy Scripture some firm foundation on which he might stand and have full assurance. In addition to the reading of the Scriptures, he was diligent in prayer, and clave especially to Luke xi.: "How much more shall your heavenly Father give the Holy Spirit to them that ask Him !" And thus it befell him when, during his wanderings, he was again engaged by a master that, amid the labour of his hands, he was lifted into a condition of blessed peace, a Sabbath of the soul, that lasted for seven days, and during which he was, as it were, inwardly surrounded by a Divine light. Outwardly, there was nothing noticeable about him. But "the triumph that was then in my soul I can neither tell nor describe. I can only liken it to a resurrection from the dead." It was a foretaste of the tranquillity that was to be vouchsafed him in contemplation.

In the year 1594 he returned to Görlitz, became a master-shoemaker in 1599, and married a tradesman's daughter, with whom he lived in happy union for thirty years, and who bore him four children. In the year 1600 he had another remarkable experience. Sitting one day in his room, his eye fell upon a burnished pewter dish, which reflected the sunshine with such marvellous splendour that he fell into an inward ecstasy, and it seemed to him as if he could now look into the principles and deepest foundations of things. He believed that it was only a fancy, and in order to banish it from his mind he went out upon the green. But here he remarked that he gazed into the very heart of things, the very herbs and grass, and that actual nature harmonized with what he had inwardly seen. He said nothing about this to any one, but praised and thanked God in silence. He continued in the honest practice of his craft, was attentive to his domestic affairs, and was on terms of good-will with all men.

Ten years later (1610) he again had another

remarkable inward experience. He suddenly discovered that what he had previously seen only chaotically, fragmentarily, and in isolated glimpses, he now beheld as a coherent whole and in more definite outlines. He felt an inward yearning, a fire-like impulse to write it down. It was, however, by no means his intention to publish it, for he regarded himself as far too simple and illiterate to write books for the learned world. He simply wished to write it down for himself, as a " Memorial " for his own use. For it happened that his visions occasionally vanished from him, and that he could not afterwards recall what he had thought. He sought to obviate this by composing a " Memorial " ; and he wrote it in the morning before the toil of the workshop began, and in the evening when he could no longer fit his last. The work that sprang from this was his famous " Morning Redness," or, as a friend entitled it, "Aurora," " the Root or Mother of Philosophy, Astrology, and Theology on the proper basis, or description of Nature." He was not completely master of himself when he wrote it ; it was like a heavy shower that sweeps past ; what it strikes, it strikes. It was not until his later years, as he himself says, that he acquired greater clearness · and a better style.

But even before this book was finished—according to his own statement it still lacked some thirty sheets, it was destined to bring heavy persecution upon him. A nobleman, Carl von Endern, who possessed religious and philosophical tastes, happened to see the manuscript at Böhme's house, borrowed it for a few days, and, seized with great enthusiasm, had some copies made of it, which came into circulation. A copy also fell into the hands of the parish clergyman at Görlitz, Pastor-Primarius Gregorius Richter, a man who was full of hierarchical arrogance, had only an outward apprehension of the dogmatics of that age, and was incapable of understanding Böhme's "Aurora." And inasmuch as he was antagonistically disposed towards Böhme on private grounds, he felt peculiarly called to attack him. In a sermon on false prophets he assailed him by name, and invoked the action of the authorities against him, as otherwise the Divine chastisement would fall upon the town. Böhme, who, being a regular churchgoer, was himself present in the church, stationed himself by the door at the close of the service, and humbly asked the clergyman wherein he had erred, saying that he would willingly receive instruction. But the Primarius threatened to have him arrested, unless he instantly took himself away. On the next day Böhme was summoned before the magistrates, who had suffered themselves to be overawed by Richter. He was ordered to leave the town, and was not even granted time to set his house in order. Böhme, who had the deepest reverence for authority, replied : "Yes, dear sirs, it shall be done ; since it cannot be otherwise, I am content." But as the magistrates meanwhile began to reflect that they had gone too far, they called him back on the next morning. He was obliged, however, to deliver up the manuscript of "Aurora," was forbidden to write books in future, and was given to understand that, as a shoemaker, he must stick to his last.

There now consequently came a pause in Böhme's literary activity. But the persecution had given fame to his "Aurora," and many thoughtful men began to notice him, and came into personal relations with him. He gained learned and influential friends, especially chymists and physicians, noblemen also, who sought his acquaintance, because they felt themselves attracted by his spirit; they supported him with corn and money, as his shoemaking business gradually declined. Among his learned friends may be particularly mentioned the director of the Chymical Laboratory at Dresden, Dr. Walther, who had made many journeys to the East, and who once spent three weeks in Böhme's little cottage, in order to have the opportunity of undisturbed conversation with him, also the physician at Görlitz, Dr. Tobias Kober. Intercourse with these learned friends exercised a refining influence upon Böhme himself, and he learned from them many Latin technical terms, which he afterwards employed in his writings. He was far from despising culture; he greatly lamented that he was not acquainted with the ancient languages, and that he had not mastered the art of dialectic. But, as a compensation for this deficiency, his friends often marvelled at his spontaneous natural sense. During his walks with Dr. Kober, who was a disciple of Paracelsus, Böhme could often, when Kober put him to the test, divine from the form and colour of a plant its hidden properties, and infer the meaning of a foreign word from its mere sound. When he once heard the Greek word *Idea*, he became as if electrified, and exclaimed: " I see a pure and heavenly maiden!" This pure and heavenly maiden plays a great part in Böhme's writings, where she is also designated as the heavenly Sophia or Wisdom, who reflects the glory of God, of the world, and of man.

The five years during which Böhme felt himself compelled to obey the injunction of the authorities, and not to meddle with book-writing, were very grievous years for him. He often fell into deep melancholy, for he thought that his conscience accused him of obeying man rather than God; he also thought that the light which had been kindled within him was in danger of being quenched, because he did not let it shine before men; and he often meditated with dismay on the parable of the talents, and the servant who wrapped his pound in a napkin. His friends continually admonished him not to set his light under a bushel, but upon a candlestick, that it might give light to all in the house. At length he gained courage to break silence. He says himself: "I had resolved to do nothing in future, but to be quiet before God in obedience, and to let the devil, with all his host, sweep over me. But it was with me as when a seed is hidden in the earth. It grows up in storm and rough weather, against all reason. For in winter-time all is dead, and reason says: It is all over with it! But the precious seed within me sprouted and grew green, oblivious of all storms, and, amid disgrace and ridicule, it has blossomed forth into a lily!"

Between 1619 and his death in 1624, he composed a series of writings, which, however, were not published by himself. Among the most remarkable of these, in a *speculative* respect, we may mention : "Concerning the Three Principles," "Concerning the Three-fold Life of Man," "Concerning the Birth and Designation of all Existences (*Signatura Rerum*)," "On the Election of Grace," "Mysterium Magnum" (which contains an exposition of the Book of Genesis, through which he develops his own ideas) ; "Forty Questions on the Soul," proposed by Dr. Walther, and answered to his satisfaction by Böhme, to which is added an appendix ; "The Inward Eye." The whole forms an outline draught of a Psychology (*psychologia vera*) ; moreover, "Concerning the Incarnation of Christ." Other of his writings have a predominantly *practical* and edifying character,—*e.g.*, " Dialogue between an Enlightened and an Unenlightened Soul." We may also mention his polemical works against Balthazar Tilken, a Silesian nobleman, in which Böhme redargues the false view of Predestination ; "Two Scruples " against Esaias Stiefel and Ezekiel Meth, citizens of Langensalze, who had been led astray into a naturalistic and visionary pantheism, and who boasted of their (false) identity with God and Christ ; also a pamphlet against Gregorius Richter, which will be noticed below. Finally, we must mention his Theosophic Epistles, which treat of the occasion of his writings, and of his personal relations. For the rest we refer the reader to the edition of Böhme's " Collected Writings," by Schiebler, 7 vols., 1831. Literary-historical sketches of the works will be found in Fechner : " Jacob Böhme, his Life and Writings," a prize essay, 1857.

Yet once again before his death Böhme was to be subjected to a new ordeal. His book, "The Way to Christ," had been printed by his friends, and the approbation with which it was widely received stirred up once more his irreconcilable opponent, Gregorius Richter. Richter not only attacked him from the pulpit, but published an Invective, full of abuse and anathema. Amongst other things occurs this passage: "There are as many blasphemies in this shoemaker's book as there are lines; it smells of shoemaker's pitch and filthy blacking. May this insufferable stench be far from us. The Arian poison was not so deadly as this shoemaker's poison," etc. This time, however, Böhme did not remain passive, but published a written defence to the magistrates against the accusations in question, and wrote a special controversial pamphlet against Gregorius Richter, in which he refutes his libel, point by point, and does it, as Hamberger remarks, with an earnestness that inspires holy awe, and, at the same time, with a most hearty gentleness and love which stream forth from the depths of his nature. The magistrates, who had again allowed themselves to be influenced by Richter, did not accept Böhme's defence, but notified him that he had made himself liable to be treated as a heretic by the Emperor, and that it would be most expedient for himself, the country, the town, and the magistrates, that he should go into voluntary exile.

Böhme remained at Görlitz for two months, and then proceeded to the Electoral Court at Dresden, where for a considerable time attention had been fixed upon him, and whither he had been invited to repair.   Here a conference took place between Böhme and several eminent theologians, among them the great dogmatist John Gerhard.   Böhme excited the admiration of all.   Dr. Gerhard said : " I would not take the whole world, and help to condemn this man!"   And his colleague Meissner said: "My good brother, neither would I !   Who knows what stands behind this man ?   How can we judge what we have not understood ?   May God convert the man if he is in error.   He is a man of marvellously high mental gifts, who at present can be neither condemned nor approved."   Thus these learned and upright theologians declared themselves incompetent to judge Böhme.   When the Elector asked their opinion, they begged for indulgence and patience until the spirit of the man should express itself more plainly.

In August 1624 Gregorius Richter died, and before his death had to lament that one of his sons had become a zealous adherent of Böhme, and had transcribed and circulated his writings.   But Böhme himself was very shortly to follow his antagonist to the grave.   While he was staying in Silesia at the house of one of his noble friends, to whose estate he had journeyed in order to spend a few months, he fell into a burning fever, which developed into mortal gastric disease.   He had a presentiment of his approaching end, and, at his own request, was carried back to Görlitz, where he was attended by Dr. Kober.   After an illness of about a fortnight he asked for the sacrament, which the new clergy-man, who trod in Richter's footsteps, would only administer on condition that Böhme subscribed the Lutheran Confession of Faith,—a wholly superfluous demand with which Böhme was able in all sincerity to comply. He awaited death with composure. On Sunday, November 21st, shortly after midnight, or early in the morning, he called his son Tobias, and asked him if he did not hear that sweet, harmonious music. As Tobias heard nothing, Böhme begged him to set wide the door that he might the better hear it ; then he asked what was the hour, and when he was told that it had just struck two, he said : " My time is not yet ; three hours hence is my time." After some silence he exclaimed : " Oh, Thou strong God of Sabaoth, deliver me according to Thy will ! " and, immediately afterwards : " Thou crucified Lord Jesus Christ, have mercy upon me, and take me to Thyself into Thy kingdom ! " A little later, he gave instructions where some of his manuscripts would be found, and expressed the hope that the noble friend whom he had visited in Silesia would provide for his widow, but also assured her that she must speedily follow him (as indeed took place, for she died of the plague in the very next year). At six in the morning, he suddenly bade them farewell with a smile, and said : " Now I go hence into Paradise," whereupon he yielded up his spirit.

Frankenberg writes of him : " His bodily appearance was somewhat mean ; he was small of stature, had a low forehead but prominent temples, a rather aquiline nose, a scanty beard, grey eyes sparkling into heavenly blue, a feeble but genial voice. He was modest in his bearing, unassuming in conversation, lowly in conduct, patient in suffering, and gentle-hearted. He was accustomed to write in his friends' albums :—

> " To whom Time and Eternity
>   Harmoniously as one agree,
>   His soul is safe, his life's amended,
>   His battle's o'er, his strife is ended."

As a proof of his loving disposition, an incident, which is recorded in one of his letters, deserves to be emphasized. He had a dead brother who had left a little girl, of whom Jacob took tender care. Absorbed though he was in his works and deep speculations, it was his habit to walk out, once a week, to the village where the little girl was living, that he might have a glimpse of her.

His friends placed upon his grave a cross with significant symbols : a lamb (" veni "), an eagle (" vidi "), a lion (" vici "). The inscription is: " Here rests Jacob Böhme, born of God, died in Christ, sealed with the Holy Spirit," to which are appended his dying words. The cross was soon removed from the grave by orthodox fanaticism and the wantonness of the rabble. But in 1875, the tercentenary of his birth, a monument was erected to him, and a great festival was held, which was attended by an assembly not only of scholars, but also of laymen, amongst them a great number of shoemakers, who desired to honour the memory of their famous brother of the last. On this occasion one could not but be reminded that God is no Respecter of persons, and that He often selects His chief instruments from the humbler classes of society.

Hamberger has written a short and popular reminiscence of this event.

From the outward let us now turn to the inward, and contemplate Böhme as a Theosophist.

BÖHME AND THEOSOPHY.

I.

THEOSOPHY, as we have said, is wisdom in God, a wisdom which has God not only as its subject, but as its principle ; it has for its basis the Divine revelation in Scripture and in nature, and it springs from an inward illumination by the Spirit of God, which makes the contents cf the revelation apprehensible. Its form is not that of reflective thought, although this is not excluded, but, first and foremost, that of intuition, immediate perception, central apprehension of God and existence. Theosophy might thus seem to be a branch of Speculative Theology. But although, under certain narrower limitations, this may be true, Theosophy seeks to embrace far more than Theology. Out of the idea of God it seeks to apprehend the world, in all the circles of the universe to see things as they are in God ; it seeks to be a *philosophia sacra* in contradiction to a *philosophia profana*. It embraces nature and history ; seeks to present a philosophy of nature in the light of the Divine idea, just as it also strives to give a philosophy of history, a representation of the principles of the kingdom of God, as these are developed from the first super-historical commencement of the kingdom of God, from the creation and fall of the angels, and of man throughout the various periods of time,—a persistent struggle between the light and the darkness,—until the final judgment and the consummation of all things. In its interpretation of Christianity, it does not limit itself to its practical ethico-religious import for man, but seeks to apprehend its cosmical meaning, its significance for the universe, and to prove that the principles of Christianity are identical with those by which the world itself subsists, and on which the foundation of the world is laid,—that Christianity is the focus for all world-forces and world-powers.

In so far as Theosophy is assigned a place in the history of philosophy, and is not excluded as an unscientific or super-scientific vagary, it belongs to that department of philosophy which Schelling has styled *positive* philosophy, in contrast to a *negative*, purely rational, non-postulating philosophy, which seeks its principle out of reason itself. The difference between Theosophy and purely rational Philosophy may be thus indicated, in terms borrowed from Leibnitz: " Theosophy pursues the path of light " (" In Thy light we shall see light ") ; "while purely rational Philosophy pursues the path of gloom, because it simply roams among dim shadows with its own faintly-glimmering light."

II.

ALTHOUGH Theosophy has been broadly described as mysticism, it must be more rigorously defined as objective, theoretical mysticism as contrasted with subjective practical mysticism ; it is the mysticism of the mind as distinguished from that of the heart. Mediæval mysticism, by which Luther also was influenced, is subjective and practical, is the mysticism of the heart, although in some of the great mystics, like Eckart, it passes over into Theosophy.

Practical mysticism starts from the soteriological standpoint, seeks the union of the individual soul with God, and immediate communion of love with God by means of the absorption of prayer, and detachment from the world ; it often manifests hostility to nature. Tauler passed once through the convent garden, and drew his cap over his eyes, in order that the flowers might not disturb him in his abstractly spiritual meditations. Theosophy, on the contrary, is eagerly attracted towards nature, and Böhme often says how pleasant it is to wander among the flowers on a fine summer's day, because it is then clearly perceptible how everything sprouts and grows, blooms, and emits fragrance in the living and all-replenishing power of God. As the mysticism of the mind, Theosophy is attracted, not only to the microcosm, but to the macrocosm, to the universe and universal life in all its multiplicity, but in all this multiplicity it beholds only one—God, the Living and Triune.

But, on the other hand, it must be emphasized, that there is no genuine theosophy which is not qualified by the mysticism of the heart, by a regard for the salvation and perfection of the individual, and by personal relation to God in believing and prayerful love. Genuine theosophy cannot rest satisfied in its interpretation of the macrocosm, with a reflection like that which the poet places in the mouth of Faust, when he beholds the sign of the macrocosm :—

" Here all things live and work, and, ever blending,
　Weave one vast whole from Being's ample range !
　Here powers celestial, rising and descending,
　Their golden buckets ceaseless interchange ;
　Their flight on rapture-breathing pinions winging,
　From heaven to earth their genial influence bringing.
　Through the wide whole their chimes melodious ringing."*

A view like this, which is also met with among pantheists, very inadequately characterizes Böhme. In the macrocosm and its harmonies—which he regards as interrupted by the discords of sin—in this great All, he seeks, beyond all else, to see the Living God Himself. But only the pure in heart can see God. Theosophy is, as St. Martin and Franz Baader so often repeat, a philosophy of prayer, a philosophy which is contingent not only upon intellectual toil, but upon prayer. This personal life in God, as the qualification for philosophizing, is very frequently emphasized by Böhme. He admonishes all who desire to peruse his writings, that they must not do so with naked if never so acute speculation (which seeks only abstract knowledge devoid of religious and ethical interest), because in this spirit they must remain outside them, and will only succeed in catching a glimpse of one detail and another, of no kind of utility in themselves, but only to make a boast of. He writes only for the children of God and for sincere seekers ; for to

---

* *Faust.*　Miss Swanwick's translation.

such alone belongs the pearl. For his own part, he has often prayed God that He would take this knowledge from him, unless it might tend to the Divine glory and to the edification of himself and his brethren. He testifies that, from the outset, he did not seek to know anything concerning the Divine mysteries. He has, from the first, sought only the Heart of Jesus Christ, that he might there hide himself from the wrath of God and the malice of the devil. Then met him the gracious Maiden from Paradise, and offered him her love, and showed him the way to Paradise. And first he must needs pass through the world, and the Kingdom of Hell. This gracious Maiden, who plays so great a part in his apprehension of God, is the Eternal Idea, the precious Sophia, the heavenly Wisdom, who not only reveals to him the Divine mysteries, but espouses his soul, reforms him by leading him to God and Christ, consoles him in all his anxiety and distress, and conducts him to peace and salvation.

III.

IF, then theosophic knowledge is knowledge in God, and is founded upon Divine illumination, it is of prime interest to inquire whether, as has often been alleged, it claims to be inspired and infallible? This charge is not altogether without foundation. Unequivocal passages are to be found in Böhme in which he expounds his doctrine in a prophetic tone, and says, for example: "It is not I who know this. It is Christ who knows it in me." Or, as where he says to his opponents, "You say truly enough that I was not present at the creation of the world, and that I consequently cannot describe it ; but the Spirit who is in me was present, and now reveals it at this time." A vague and fermenting prophetic tendency has often displayed itself in the Church, and something of this may be found in Böhme and he, and particularly his adherents, unquestionably speak at times as if he had inaugurated a new period of revelation, which was described by the Church theologians as a period of enthusiasm and visionary reliance upon the inward light. But, on the other hand, it should not be overlooked that in Böhme this never developed into sectarianism, and that he says in other passages of his writings that several of his works, and particularly the "Aurora," present the doctrine imperfectly, but that he gradually attained greater clearness ; that he had striven after a better style ; that he does indeed behold the Truth within him, but as if in a chaos, where everything lies in a complication which he finds it excessively hard to disentangle into shape.

On the whole, the essential proposition of theosophy—and also of Böhme—may be said to be this : that it is only in the Spirit of God and in His Wisdom (Idea) that we can search the depths of God, and that it is as unreasonable to seek to apprehend God without God, as to seek to see the sun except by means of the sun itself, by the aid of the light that issues from the sun. But, most assuredly, we should be unable, either in the sensible or in the spiritual world, to see the sun by means of the sun itself, unless our eyes were fashioned for the sun, and were kindred with the sun. This capacity of ours to see the sun,—to apprehend God,—is based by Theosophy upon the fact that *man is created in the image of God.* Theosophy certainly admits that man's standpoint in the world has been dislocated by the Fall, that man has been thrust out of his original place at the centre of the creation, has been banished from its centre to its circumference, a fact which is fraught with the most serious results for human knowledge in the natural and sinful state. Just as when I wish to survey a region in the physical world, but am unable to do so, if I am placed in a position where the view is obstructed, so also in the spiritual world. The natural man has been placed by the Fall, in a position where he has lost the right view-point and the true horizon, where he cannot but see many things confusedly, and is inevitably deceived by optical illusions (a doctrine which Baader has enforced with reference to the Kantian antinomies of Time and Space). That philosophers imagine that they occupy the standpoint from which truth is apprehensible proves nothing. The optical illusions still remain, and simply change their character *ad infinitum.* For, no matter how persistently the knowledge of the natural man may change its standpoint, it never escapes from the worldly and circumferential. It is only by a new creation, by regeneration in Christ, that this dislocation is removed, and man is led back to his proper *locus*, to the place where he is truly set right, because he regains his true horizon. Only here can he acquire the spiritual central perception, when the Spirit of God is pleased to bestow it upon him. For the spiritual gifts are various, and the revelation of the Spirit is given to every man for him to profit withal.

Moreover, Theosophy pins itself to Holy Scripture. Certainly, with regard to Böhme, we must here again make an admission to the orthodox theologians who charge him with handling the Scriptures arbitrarily. Thus, we find passages in which he says : " The dear Moses has here a veil before his eyes." Or : " Moses indeed writes quite correctly, but who understands him ? " Whereupon he himself gives a novel exposition, wholly irreconcilable with the text, but suitable to his own purposes ! Again, his typical treatment of Scripture exposes him to no little censure. Still, it must be confessed that he lives and breathes in the fundamental perception of Scripture, and that his soul is a soil in which the seed of the Word sprouts and grows, becomes green, and bears abundant fruit, a soil in which the Divine Word, to use an expression of his own, has happened to *qualificere, i.e.,* to unfold its properties and powers, has become active and productive. The chief aim of his investigation of Scripture, as it is the aim of all theosophy, is not to cling to the letter, or to the merely historical, but to press through the letter and the history to the eternal postulates for the word and the history, the eternal principles which are active in them : to effect a cohesion between the historical and the metaphysical. The same remark applies to his relation to church doctrine. The individual theosophist can be a believing professor of the Church Creed, just as Böhme, for instance, sincerely confessed his adherence to the Lutheran Church. Theosophy, as such, is

super-confessional, precisely because it moves in
super-historical principles, in the radical conceptions
which Scripture postulates rather than expresses, or
from which it only partially lifts the veil in isolated
passages. For this reason, Franz Baader, although
a Catholic, was able to call Böhme, with whom he
was congenial, his real teacher.

POSTULATES FOR BÖHME'S THEOSOPHY.

IV.

IT is not with Böhme that Theosophy makes its first appearance in history. It dates back to pre-Christian times, and is found already among the Hebrew people. " Not only salvation, but also wisdom comes from the Jews," says Franz Baader. We are alluding to the Jewish Kabbala, a theosophic tradition, which has propagated and developed itself by the side of the historical revelation. It dates back to the patriarchs, to Moses, who must have had a deeper knowledge of the mysteries of God than was entrusted to men in general ; and it has been augmented throughout the ages. The writings themselves belong, for the most part, to a later period. Some of the books were not composed until the time of Christ. One important work, " Sohar," or " Lustre," which contains the theosophical conversations of Rabbi Simeon with his disciples, was commenced in the second century after Christ, and was not completed until the twelfth century. But it must here be observed that from the composition of the books at a later period no certain conclusion can be drawn as to the antiquity of their contents. A doctrine may be orally transmitted for long periods of time before being committed to writing, although in the Middle Ages it was liable to be coloured by more distinctly Christian influences.

The Kabbala has a theoretical and a practical division. The theoretical portion consists of traditions with regard to the Being of God, Trinity, the Fall of the angels and of the devil, the origin of darkness and matter, the Mosaic history of creation, which the Kabbala regards not as a history of creation in the most absolute sense of the term, but as the history of a renovated cosmic order, a restitution of the world which had been transformed into chaos (Tohu Vabohu) by the Fall of the angels. It treats of the creation and fall of man, of Redemption, and of the consummation of the world by the Messiah. The practical portion has for its subject the cleansing of souls, sanctification, and union with God.

The religious philosophy of Philo of Alexandria may also be classed with Jewish theosophy.

Although some have regarded the heretical Gnosticism, with which the early Church had to contend, as a species of Christian theosophy, we must maintain that these systems are rather to be viewed as caricatures of Christian theosophy, as rank offshoots, which have not borne, nor can bear, any fruit for the Christian spirit. They are medleys of Greek and Oriental Paganism with the admixture of distorted Christian and Kabbalistic ingredients.

The germs of a genuine theosophy are to be found, however, in the Middle Ages, in the great John Scotus Erigena, blended, it is true, with Neoplatonic and Areopagitic speculation, also in Thomas Aquinas. But the Middle Ages were more propitious to the culture of subjective mysticism than to that of Theosophy properly so called, although the latter is not left without witness among the more speculatively-gifted Mystics. We must mention as special forerunners of Böhme the whole band of German Mystics, Eckart, Tauler, Suso, and the author of the " Theologia Germanica," who may also be said to have contributed to the Reformation. Impossible as it may be to ascertain whether Böhme had read their works, still, an indirect influence from mediæval Mysticism, as well as from the Kabbala, which about the time of the Reformation had come into more general knowledge (Pico of Mirandola, Reuchlin), can scarcely be denied.

V.

BUT a leading postulate for Böhme is his *epoch* itself, and the multifarious agitation that was taking place in the minds of men, an agitation that had begun long before Luther, and which continued after him. Not only the religious consciousness, but the general consciousness of man, had been emancipated. And, simply to lay stress upon what relates to our present subject, the human mind was not only searching the Holy Scriptures, for the contents of which a new sense had been revealed ; it was also searching the book of nature with new and vigorous scrutiny, which indeed may be done in various ways. Here, then, must be mentioned the great Bacon of Verulam, who gave such powerful impulses to the whole natural science of modern times, which is based upon the inductive method, upon observation, and experiment. Still, it is not Bacon who must be regarded as a presupposing cause for Böhme, whose contemporary he was, and to whom he furnishes the most pronounced contradiction. Böhme had a quite different postulate for his interpretation of nature. During the period of transition to the Reformation, and subsequently, there had sprung up a natural philosophy, which assumed, among many of its votaries, a theosophic stamp, and remained in cohesion with ideas that had arisen during the Middle Ages. This mystical natural philosophy, which is strongly influenced by the Kabbala, busies itself with subjects which, as a rule, wholly evade experimental and exact research, on which account they are usually regarded as chimerical by natural inquirers of the Baconian school. One characteristic feature of this Natural Philosophy is *Magic*, on which subject Agrippa of Rettesheim wrote a large treatise, " Philosophia Sacra." What Mysticism is with regard to the soul's relation to God, Magic is with regard to the mind's relation to Nature. Just as Mysticism seeks to place itself in relation to God *without means,* so Magic would set itself in relation to the *penetralia* of Nature *without material means.* Magic is a Nature-Mysticism in which man places himself in immediate relation with the spirit in Nature, with the mysterious Divine forces, and, indeed, with God Himself, whose mystery is the innermost thing in Nature.

There is a will, an energy which, in virtue of a higher spiritual relation, is enabled to produce real effects in Nature, without the agency of material means. By magic man is enabled partially to regain that dominion over nature which was lost at the Fall, and which must assuredly be conceived as something far more and far higher than the Baconian *imperium in naturam.* There is both a *white* magic and a *black* magic, according to the good and evil spirits with which man has placed himself *en rapport.* There is a *perceptive* and an *active* magic (*i.e.,* a *visio et actio in distans*). The magical operations which transcend the usual conditions of our perception and activity closely depend upon powers which exist in all of us, but which, in our habitual state, are fettered. According to Paracelsus, they depend upon an inward corporeity, which, in his opinion, we bear within us and carry with us after death. In contrast to our *elemental* body (composed of the four elements), which is dissolved in death, he accepts a *sidereal* body, which attracts to itself the influence of the stars, and from which, even in this life, effects of power may proceed. In combination with this, the magical operations depend upon an energetic strength of will and a vigorous imagination. He often mentions. as magical means, prayer with seeking and knocking, faith which moves mountains ; nor can he sufficiently emphasize the value of strong imagination when it is kindled in a moral disposition, and can thus produce the most marvellous effects.*

---

* Rocholl, '' Beiträge zu einer Geschichte deutscher Theosophie,'' §.93; Carrière, '' Die philosophische Weltanschauung der Reformationszeit,'' 83. Many researches of modern science prove that magic is not in every sense to be viewed

The mystical natural philosophy, which embraces *Magic*, also includes *Alchymy*. An attempt is made to transmute metals by chymical processes, to separate the impure and pure in order, through continuous transmutations, finally to arrive at the precious essence (residuum). The Alchymists, who seek the Philosopher's Stone, prosecute their work with prayer and invocation of the "holy Name." The legitimate Alchymist practises his art not for the sake of worldly emolument, but in order to pierce more deeply into the mystery of nature. He regards it as closely akin to the transmutation which is to be effected in man by Regeneration in Christ ; and, indeed, views it in connection with the history of the Kingdom of God, the consummation of which is brought about through processes of *Digestion*, *Fermentation*, *Putrefaction* (corruption of all that pertains to the old, dead, sinful nature), and *Sublimation* (refinement and exaltation of the good that had been buried beneath the earthly cerements). An attempt is also made to discover, by the aid of chymistry, a universal specific for the healing of disease.

This natural philosophy also embraces *Astrology*, and knowledge of the influence of the stars and constellations upon human fortunes, upon the innate character and temperament of men.

The elements of all this are found in Böhme. He is particularly influenced by Paracelsus, the celebrated physician, who has greatly injured his

---

as visionary. Cf. what J. H. Fichte (in his " Anthropology and Psychology ") has said with regard to the inward corporeity and the plastically-working imagination.

historic fame by his insufferable boastfulness, but who, after all, was far higher than a common charlatan. Franz Baader calls him the " Eagle " among physicians. Böhme was influenced not only by his ideas, but by his certainly barbarous terminology. From Paracelsus he derives the three fundamental categories, Salt, Mercury, Sulphur, which are not, however, to be understood as the salt, mercury, and sulphur that are to be found at the apothecary's, but as the spirit within these (" for there is no body without a spirit "), which is also able to manifest itself in a higher corporeity than this gross and material one. From him Böhme derives also the term " Tincture," which again does not mean an artificial drug in fluid form, but a *substantia intra substantiam*, a mediating nature between spirit and corporeity, a more subtle volatile energy, which works both physically and spiritually. It is the *Tincture* which gives to metals their lustre, and to flowers their pleasant colour and fragrance. When the *Tincture* vanishes, pallor and decay supervene. A poem, we may say, in harmony with this view, may be excellently composed and elaborated, but, if it lacks the *Tincture*, it produces no effect. In addition to *Tincture*, we may also specify the words *Limbus* (the procreative power), *Matrix* (the conceiving power), etc., etc.

VI.

BUT what we must specially invite attention to is the fact that, in this natural philosophy, Böhme is confronted by *a living intuition of nature*. The universe is regarded as a total organism, of which man is the microcosm—the epitome—or concentration of the universe ; the universe, or macrocosm, is an extension and development of that which exists in man in a state of concentrated unity. " The philosopher," says Paracelsus, " finds nothing else in heaven and earth save what he also finds in man ; the physician finds nothing in man except what is also possessed by heaven and earth." There is a living unity, cohesion, and reciprocal influence between the microcosm and the macrocosm. " If thou eatest a piece of bread," says Paracelsus, " thou dost taste therein heaven and earth, and all the stars ; " viz. : in so far as all these have co-operated to produce the bread, and their effects are in the bread ; consequently, in the very simplest things we stand in relation to cosmical potencies. All existing things in nature are encircled by a magical band ; they influence one another by attraction and repulsion, sympathy and antipathy. Nor is nature a mere *object*, in such a manner as that man alone —as microcosm—is to be regarded as *subject*. No! a universal subjective life is diffused throughout nature. Will and imagination are everywhere at work, although not self-conscious, but plastically-working will and imagination. The whole of nature is pervaded by magic. The higher seeks the lower, in order to impart itself to it ; the lower craves the higher, in order to participate in it ; the sun desires to bestow itself upon the earth, the earth yearns for the sun and opens its matrix to it. Nevertheless, there exist in nature, not only sympathetic, but also antipathetic forces. There is conflict and hostility. Theosophical natural philosophy recognizes that a disturbance has entered nature, in consequence of the revolt of the creation against God, whereby the *Temperature, i.e.,* the harmonic concord, of the forces has been disorganized, and forces that were once united have now become mutually antagonistic. It is true that other thinkers of this period, standing outside the Christian consciousness of sin and redemption, interpret nature as a total organism, but as an organism which is *purely harmonious* (*e.g.,* Giordano Bruno). But Theosophy is not exclusively optimistic ; it recognizes in the macrocosm not only harmonies, but also discords. It is by redemption that all things are finally to be restored to "Temperature." And this is the object of the world's development until the consummation of all things.

We have now endeavoured, in a very brief and cursory way, to give a sketch of this natural philosophy, which certainly conflicts with modern science at very many points, and the weaknesses of which are so often complained of, when it attempts the task of explaining *details* in nature. Confessedly, it will be useless to seek to give a philosophical explanation of individual natural phenomena, or, as Böhme says, " to explain them according to the spirit," unless one is in possession of the natural science which has its starting-point in Bacon. But, at the same time, we venture to observe that, with all due recognition of experimental physical science, one is under no necessity of accepting the metaphysical conclusions which some students of nature deduce from their researches. And however visionary this old mystical natural philosophy may be, and however fruitless and untenable many of its results, it has given powerful expression to one idea, the validity of which can be questioned only by death and soullessness. We refer to that idea of *Life*, both in the macrocosm and the microcosm, which was of such high significance for Jacob Böhme. It is true that he possesses this idea, so to say, *à priori*, and in an eminent degree. But when we search for the predisposing causes and suggestions of his theory, we are bound to repeat that this idea, kindled in his inward man, was strengthened and developed by the view which confronted him in this philosophy. If we wish to understand Böhme, we must fix our attention upon this idea of *Life*, for it is the radical condition for the comprehension of his theosophical fundamental-problem.

THE PROBLEM.

VII.

THE fundamental task which Böhme has set him-self is to apprehend God, and in this light to apprehend the world. The God whom Böhme seeks to know is not any kind of a God, an unknown God, such as is sought after the fashion of earthly philosophers, without any presuppositions whatever, while the thinker, like Robinson Crusoe, speculates in perfect isolation, gazing out from the solitary island of his own thought into the abstract infinity of the ocean and horizon. The God, whom Böhme seeks to know, is the God of Christianity, the God of revelation and of the Church, in whom he believes, the God who is Holiness and Love, whose mani-festation he is absolutely certain of, but whose depths he desires to explore. It has been said that it was Böhme's fundamental task to know God as the Triune, and to apprehend the similitude of the Trinity in the whole creation. This, indeed, it is admissible to urge, and we may add that his eminent significance for Protestant theology is shown by this very fact, that whereas the Reformation had contented itself with reviewing and refashioning the dogmas that belong to practical soteriology, Böhme took up the speculative dogmas which the

Reformation had passively accepted from Catholicism, at the head of which stands the doctrine of the Trinity. In this respect, Böhme pointed back to the Eastern Church which has absorbed itself in the mysteries of the Trinity and of the Incarnation. Nevertheless, Böhme's original individuality is attested by the fact that to assign the Trinity as his fundamental problem, without more minute qualifications would be to characterize him with extreme inadequacy. The problem which is of cardinal importance for Böhme is : *the apprehension of the God of Revelation as the Living God.* The idea of *Life* is his fundamental idea, which he tries to work out both in the conception of God and in the conception of the world ; and his theosophical follower *Oetinger* was moving very closely along his master's path when he wrote his "Theologia ex ideâ vitæ deducta." It will, therefore, be well for us provisionally to look away from the subject of the Trinity, and, undisturbed by Trinitarian conceptions, to think only of Life and the Living God.

If we endeavour to form a conception of life, we must necessarily conceive unity in a multiplicity which is not *reduced to* unity from without, but which unfolds itself from an internal unity, and must consequently, from the very beginning, be enveloped in it, as an undeveloped πλήρωμα, *e.g., a seed-corn.* Of that empty unity which is barren, and out of which nothing can be born, Böhme seeks to know nothing, and he here agrees with the poet, who says :—

> " Kein Lebendiges ist ein Eins,
> Immer ist's ein Vieles."

The more fully Life corresponds to its name, the more will this unity in multiplicity manifest itself as a self-productive unity, as self-movement, self-evolution by its own native powers ; it will reveal itself as its own cause, its own effect, its own goal. The movement of Life is teleological, or full of design, for Life is a will, a tendency which, through the medium of its own properties and powers, seeks to produce itself as its own object, as self-consistent and harmonious unity. For Böhme, the idea of Life is inseparable from the idea of Manifestation. Life is an unfolding from darkness to light, from the hidden, indefinite, and unknowable to the manifested, definite, and knowable. But Life and Manifestation can only be conceived of as a movement between contrasts, and as the mediation of these. Without contrasts, there is neither life nor manifestation. Without contrast, without *another*, there is only eternal immobility, stillness, and repose, in which nothing can be distinguished or perceived. Inasmuch, then, as Böhme seeks to know God as the Original Life and the Source of Life, he, at the same time, seeks to know Him as the Spirit that manifests Itself to Itself, by means of its own inward contrasts, seeks to apprehend, separate, and combine the momenta in the process of the Divine Life and Manifestation, which has no beginning in time nor any end in time, but in which God produces Himself, from eternity to eternity, in a blessed and incessantly self-renewing cycle.

The conception of God which is sought by Böhme thus presents the most direct contrast to the conception of the Mystics. While Mysticism, from

Dionysius Areopagiticus down to Schleiermacher, defines God as the unvarying nameless One, for whom every designation is inadequate, and who transcends every conception, because every conception contains contrasts, while God is above all contrasts, Böhme demands a God who manifests Himself in differences, in contrasts, in definite relations ; and only this God is to him the true God. And while Mysticism excludes from the Being of God the faintest trace of corporeity, demanding that all symbolical images must be swept far from God (wherein, however, it is inconsistent, seeing that it designates God now as pure Light, and again as pure Darkness !), Böhme teaches an eternal nature in God, and ascribes to God *Fancy*, or, as he terms it, Imagination (*imago*), an image-shaping, form-fashioning energy, of which more will be said below. A more definite opposition between two views would not be possible.

VIII.

BÖHME is conscious that when he seeks to apprehend the Being of Beings, in Life and Manifestation, everything that applies merely to the created and finite life which is fettered in limitations, and the vital source of which is only derivative, must be excluded. Whether he has always succeeded in this exclusion is another question. But it is with this intention that he seeks to apprehend what has been termed the theogonistic process, the eternal Generation and Self-production of God. He seeks in this nothing but what the Church has sought, and has effected in its doctrines of the Trinity, of the eternal generation of the Son from the Father, and of the Procession of the Spirit from the Father and the Son, doctrines of which the Athanasian Symbol is the great memorial. But Böhme seeks it in his own way! He cannot confine himself to the conception of the Trinity which is presented to him in church-tradition, although he sincerely subscribes to this. The Church representation moves only in abstract conceptions, in scholastic formulæ, and although it alludes to Generation, Birth, and Procession, it is not clearly perceptible that we have here, in any full sense, the Living God. The doctrine of Scripture and the unanimous Church doctrine is that God is a Spirit (John iv. 24). But if Spirit is to exist in life and power and luminous manifestation, it must hold within itself its *other*, its contrast. But the contrast of Spirit is Nature, the unconscious, but nevertheless self-moving, instinctively-working principle. Only when there is in God an eternal Nature can we know Him as the absolutely-perfect Spirit. Böhme's problem is, consequently, not only a problem of unity and triplicity (problem of Trinity), but a problem of unity and duality (of Spirit and nature, seeing that God must be conceived of as at the same time Spirit and Nature), and this is the problem which for Böhme occupies the first rank. In the Divine Unity there must be an original and eternal Duality, in which nature is the medium and instrument for Spirit, is, indeed, a resisting and counter-principle, so that the Spirit, through the conquest of this counter-principle, may succeed in manifesting its own energy. It is only when the theogonistic process moves through a reciprocity of relation between these two principles,—the principle of Spirit and the principle of Nature—that we dare hope to realize a Living Trinity. With the postulate of the eternal Nature in God, Böhme promises us an apprehension of the Being of all Beings, an apprehension which will not consist simply of abstract and lifeless conceptions, as in the Church Theology, but will be an apprehension " in the highest sensuousness," *i.e.*, in keenest perception, wealth of colour, and rich fulness of tone.

IX.

NATURE in God! Many who have been accustomed to the idea of the pure spirituality of God will be appalled, and will fear that we wish to introduce materialistic views, especially as at the same time they hear mention of Salt, Mercury, Sulphur, the Sour, the Bitter, etc. But we would call attention to the fact that these definitions are figurative and symbolical, and that when Nature is affirmed in God, it is, in comparison with what *we* call Nature, something infinitely more subtile and super-material, is not matter at all, but rather a source for matter, a plenitude of living forces and energies. Nor is the idea of Nature in God so foreign as may appear at first sight. The religious consciousness believes in the Almighty God. Should it, therefore, be so alien and remote a thought, that in the depth of the Omnipotence there lies a $\pi\lambda\dot{\eta}\rho\omega\mu\alpha$ of Nature, a totality of forces which the Almighty Will can place outside Itself in what assumes the aspect of a certain separate independence, even prior to the creation of this world ? Readers with any degree of philosophical knowledge will certainly be familiar with the thought that in every existing thing there is a distinction between an ideal and a real aspect. The ideal is that which we can absorb in our consciousness, in our thought ; the real is that which is never thus absolutely merged in thought, but which at the same time is inseparable from thought, if thought is to gain figure and plastic shape. Thought gives things their form ; but the form demands matter, material, *substratum*, in order that it may be able to impress itself upon this, as it is often illustrated by the example of a work of art, which never achieves perfection by the mere form alone, or by the mere material alone, but by the happy wedding of both.

It is the constantly repeated endeavour of philosophy to reconcile idealism and realism, the world of thought and the world of things, idea and reality. An un-ideated reality is as unsatisfactory to our mind as is an unreal and amorphous idea. It is Böhme's intention to reconcile idealism and realism in the conception of God, to apprehend in God at the same time an ideal and a real side, an aspect of spirit and an aspect of Nature, an inward and an outward. For, inasmuch as it holds true of every being that this dualism is found within it, must not this also apply in the most eminent degree to the Being of Beings, to God ?

Moreover, other thinkers besides Böhme have held this idea of a Nature in God, although with modifications. That is to say, they interpret Nature in God as the Nature which is known to us, this material universe in which we live. The personal

God is thus the ideal principle of the world, and the world itself is God's *real* aspect, His body. Although this doctrine is not simple pantheism, it must be defined as semi-pantheism, or as a pantheism of personality. For, on this view, God, as Spirit, is only the self-conscious centre of the world, is only the self-conscious unity in a world, that is mapped out in time and space. Thus in *Giordano Bruno*, who holds that there must be *matter* in God, as that wherein God fashions out His ideas. But he interprets this "fashioning" as the same that manifests itself to us in our well-known material universe. In this connection *Schelling* claims special notice, in his celebrated "Treatise on Human Freedom" (1809), which vividly recalls Böhme, while, however, Schelling takes his own path, and one very different from Böhme's. God is here the ideal-principle of the world, is self-conscious, self-reflected, self-equipped · Intelligence; but He requires an eternal Nature as His *substratum*, a Nature which, as a blindly-working, resisting medium, is destined to be overcome and transfigured in Spirit, and which Spirit requires in order that it may manifest itself, actualize itself, and acquire reality and shape. According to Schelling, the Deity proceeds from eternity under two *initia :* an *ideal* beginning as the self-conscious Spirit, and a *real* beginning as the obscure Nature-basis. Through this permanent reciprocity of relation between the Spirit and the obscure basis (in which latter evil has its root, although not as, *ab initio*, evil), the various stages of natural life are developed, the various periods of history are evolved with the contrast between Sin and Redemption; a self-

unfolding epic or drama with its crises and conflicts ; a cosmogony, prosecuting itself throughout
all time ; a cosmogony which is also a theogonistic
process. For although, viewed upon His *ideal* side,
God is certainly, from the very beginning, self-
conscious Intelligence, still He does not become a
complete living and actual Personality until the close
of the development. It is as the result of this
development that the " Becoming One " becomes
realized Love. This view was stated and defended
by Schelling with strenuous polemic [in his famous
" Denkmal "] against the attack of Jacobi. Schelling
affirms that a Theism without Naturalism, the doctrine of a Natureless God, is a sapless, powerless,
marrowless Theism ; while Jacobi, for his part, continued to protest against a *developing* God, and to
maintain God as, from all eternity, self-complete and
free from the world, without, however, being quite
able to confute Schelling.

In one respect all who occupy the Christian
standpoint will agree with Jacobi ; viz., in protesting
against a God who develops through temporal existence, and who needs to pass through a history in
order to become actual. Christianity cannot admit
that the temporal world is necessarily indispensable
to the Being of God, but proclaims a God who is
perfect and blessed in Himself from all eternity, and
whose love is not the *result* of the world's development, but its *postulate.* It is the God of Christianity whom Böhme is desirous of apprehending,
and he consequently states the problem in much
higher terms than does Schelling in his " Treatise."
But, inasmuch as Christianity does not teach a sapless

and powerless Theism, a natureless God (a fact to which Holy Scripture testifies on every page), Böhme supposes an eternal Nature in God, prior to the Creation. True, the difficulty here presents itself that this eternal Nature in God lies outside our experience, and thus cannot become the object of our immediate perception, much less of so-called exact natural research. And natural research takes this convenient opportunity of lodging the charge of visionariness,—a charge, however, which shows at once that those who make it do not at all comprehend what is here being discussed. Those whose line of thought is Christian or, in any degree, consistently theistic, will, when they have gained a general grasp of the gist of the problem, feel the necessity of conceiving God as the God who lives not merely in the temporal world, but also in Himself, will be formally compelled to think in God an analogon to what we call Nature, although this by no means involves their agreement at all points with the mode in which Böhme has worked out the problem.

We are well aware that Böhme's doctrine has been variously interpreted, even by thinkers of considerable repute, a circumstance which has been partly occasioned by the defects in Böhme's mode of statement, inasmuch as he constantly speaks in symbols drawn from this present world. *Hegel* has interpreted Böhme in a purely pantheistic sense. But it has become very generally known that Hegel, notwithstanding his admiration for Böhme's speculative power, had but a very superficial acquaintance with his writings, and, moreover, was disposed to " Hege-

lianize" him, and to make him a herald of his own.
Others interpret Böhme's doctrine as a pantheism of
personality, and suppose that his view of Nature in
God was essentially the same as Schelling's, in the
above-mentioned "Treatise." For our own part, we
maintain that careful study of Böhme will establish
Franz Baader's conclusion that Böhme's God (as
stated above) is the God who is perfect in Himself,
prior to creation and the world. We base this
view, not so much upon isolated passages, as upon
Böhme's general train of ideas. Still, if individual
passages are demanded, we may quote the well-
known paragraph in the "Signatura Rerum" (16. 2),
"For God has not brought forth creation that He
should be thereby perfect, but for His own manifestation, that is, for the great joy and glory. Not that
this joy first began with the creation. No! for it
was from Eternity, in the great Mystery, yet only
as a spiritual melody and sport in itself. The creation is the same sport out of Himself, an instrument
of the Eternal Spirit, a great harmony of manifold
instruments which are all tuned into one harmony."
Or, in another passage, where it is asked : "What
was, prior to the existence of the angels and the
creation ?" and the reply is : "God was, alone with
light and fire ; or God was, alone with two fire-
centres (the lucid and the dark fire-centre). And
the angels and the souls of men and all creatures
lay in an idea or spiritual model in which God from
eternity beheld His works."

X.

BUT while Böhme seeks to apprehend God in

His inward life of manifestation, he also seeks to apprehend Him in His manifestation in the world ; out of the Self-Perfect God he desires to grasp and to explain the created world with all its contrasts. What most afflicts his soul, as he contemplates the world, is the pervading conflict of everything with all else, one thing struggling with, buffeting, biting, pushing, crushing another. Evil, not only in the human world, but in the whole world, evil in its cosmical sense, is the burden that so heavily weighs upon his mind. He is incessantly struggling with this "dark point." "For it cannot be said that fire is in God, much less that air, water, and earth are in Him ; only it is plain that all things have proceeded out of that Original. Neither can it be said that Death, Hell-fire, or Sorrowfulness is in God; but it is known that these things have come out of that Original. For God has made no devil out of Himself, but angels to live in joy. Therefore, the source or fountain of the cause must be sought ; viz. : what is the *prima materia*, or first matter of evil ? and that in the originality of God as well as in the creatures. For all is out of God" ("De Tribus Princip.," 1, 5). Böhme fell into deep dejection and gloom, when he saw that there was good and evil in all things, and that the ungodly as well as the pious prospered in this world. No Scripture could console him, and he fell into heathenish thoughts. Finally, however, he penetrated, "through violent tempests and through the Gates of Hell, to the innermost Birth or Geniture of the Deity" ("Aurora," 19, 4-13). And he discovered the Foundation of Hell, not indeed manifested but in mystery, not as a reality but as a possibility. He searches the depths of wickedness and of Satan, but also the depths of the Redemption, whereby the world, which had lost its " Temperature " by reason of the fall of Lucifer and of Adam, is once more to be restored by Christ to " Temperature " (or proper arrangement and harmony of powers), restored to that proper place which is well-pleasing unto God.

XI.

As it is our purpose in the following pages to attempt a sketch and a criticism of the solution of this problem which has been given by Böhme, we do not forget that, in the solution of a philosophical problem, account must be taken not only of the subject matter, the result to which the inquiry has led, but also of the form, the scientific basis. It is tolerably well known that in a formal and dialectical respect Jacob Böhme is exceedingly imperfect, although it is also known that on points of detail he has a firm dialectical grip. This pervading defect is largely occasioned by the fact that Böhme is in an ecstatic condition, in which he is overwhelmed by his subject, by its vast riches, which he cannot succeed in appropriating by any calm and deliberately reasoned process of thought, for which reason his mode of treatment often becomes unintelligible and chaotic. He sees everything, as it were, in a complexity which it is extremely hard to unravel. He is himself a theogonistic nature, who desires to give birth to the conception of God, which stirs and throbs and travails within him, revolves within him like an incessantly-whirling wheel, a wheel of Ezekiel which seeks to escape from within him to the light of day, and often causes him grievous birth-pangs.

He himself is conscious of the inadequacy of his representation, and, accordingly, is for ever repeating himself, and explaining over again what he has explained many times before, while the reader is impatient for the argument to advance. But amid his diffuse explanations and descriptions the reader gains only too frequently the impression of a vast, wind-swept, and roaring forest, wherein he can neither understand nor hear a word. Still, among these defects, we must not ignore what he has actually given us. When it is said of him that he is a nature that seeks to give birth to wisdom, but cannot do so because he is unable to struggle out of the chaotic and extreme abundance that over-whelms him, and at the mercy of which he lies (Schelling), this criticism must be qualified by the fact that it was not a *system*, but an *idea*, which he brought to the birth, and that by this birth something was placed in the intellectual world which was not previously present, and without the presupposition of which it would be impossible to explain some of the most profound intellectual movements of modern times. But what, undeniably, makes the comprehension of these ideas difficult, is the fact that Böhme constantly employs physical categories (like salt, mercury, sulphur, etc.), where mental categories,—either logical or ethical,—ought to have been used ; and that his great wealth of poetic imagery and symbolism continually conceals his

thought, instead of revealing it. It is absolutely
necessary to fasten upon certain recurring main
thoughts, abiding thoughts that keep their place
and, so to speak, light up the multiplicity of the
ever-changing phantasmagoria of thoughts and
figures, which, as so many have complained, so
often glimmer before one's eyes and beat tumul-
tuously about one's head, while at the same time
it is impossible to grasp them firmly. There is
in Böhme's writings a twofold light : the restless,
flickering, and fancifully-glittering which often dazzles
the eye, and the calmly-beaming light which shines
through the former, and to which the lines may be
justly applied :—

> " Wie durch des Nordlicht's bewegliche Strahlen
> Ewige Sterne schimmern ! "

It is these " eternal stars," breaking through the
dazzling confusion of splendour, to which one must
look ; or, to change the illustration, it is upon these
notes, these voices from a higher spiritual world,
which at certain intervals ring so clearly through the
roaring forest, that one's attention must be fixed.

It is one conspicuous excellence in Böhme's mode
of treatment that by philosophizing in his mother
tongue, by the side of the " barbaric," he has enriched
the former with no small number of highly expressive
words, which have been adopted by later thinkers.
The readers of *Schelling's* above-mentioned " Treatise
on Human Freedom," in 1809. were surprised and
enraptured by a wealth of new and previously-
unheard expressions and turns of speech in their
mother tongue. But all of these belong to Böhme,

or are fashioned on the model of his symbolic language. Böhme himself lays great stress upon the fact that he philosophizes in his mother tongue. He laments over those who have really beheld nothing of the truth, but in whom pride has spoiled everything, because they will not use their native speech, but fancy that they must paste and lard their discourse with foreign words, to prove that they are learned men! He thus apostrophizes the mother tongue: "But hearken, thou simple mother who dost bring into the world children that are ashamed of thee and despise thee! Thus saith the Spirit who is thy Father: 'Be not discouraged! I am thy strength and thy might, and I will give thee a comforting draught in thine old age. Because all thy children, whom thou hast brought forth and nursed, despise thee, and will not cherish thee in thine extreme old age, I will console thee in thine age, and will give thee a young son; he shall abide in thy house as long as thou livest, and shall nurse thee and comfort thee against all the uproar and boastfulness of thy proud children.'"

Finally, we will venture to remark, in Böhme's favour, that *logic*, however great the value that may be assigned to it, is by no means the chief thing in philosophy. It is the *secondary* thing, the medium by which perception is made clearer. The first thing, upon which all true philosophical progress depends, is speculative, intelligent perception, *Intuition*, without which all logic is barren, as experience amply proves. The keenest inquiry of a critic of Böhme will, therefore, not be " Has he *reasoned* correctly?" but "Has he *seen* aright?" Meanwhile however, if any should hold that Böhme's standpoint must be defined, on account of its defective form, as a pre-scientific standpoint, that is, a standpoint which lies in advance of science properly so called, and that he is simply a precursor of Christian science, we shall offer no contradiction. Ancient philosophy presents similar phenomena ; *e.g., Pythagoras.* But the main question is, whether philosophy and theology can avoid taking notice of his ideas.

As we are now about to describe the solution which Böhme has attempted of the all-embracing problem, we refer the reader to the original treatises in Schiebler's edition ; to Hamberger's well-known and excellent work : " Systematic Epitome of Böhme's Doctrine ;" and to Franz Baader's collected works, especially his " Lectures on Jacob Böhme." Other works will be occasionally cited, as they may bear upon the matter in hand. A synopsis of Böhme-literature lies beyond our present field.

Our discussion will fall under two main sections :

I. GOD AND THE UNCREATED HEAVEN.

II. GOD AND THE CREATED WORLD.

I.

GOD AND THE UNCREATED HEAVEN.

XII.

BÖHME frequently repeats that, in order to understand and to represent the Generation of God (the Theogonistic process), one must always keep it in mind that this does not take place in a temporal manner, in *Succession*, but in an eternal manner, in *Simultaneity*, or, all at once, in an infinite cycle or circular movement. But this is precisely where the difficulty lies for our human thought, which is chained to the fragmentary and piecemeal, and to that which advances in succession : " If I had the tongue of an angel and thou the intelligence of an angel, we should understand one another very well. But now I must speak in an earthly fashion with my half-dead understanding, and since I am only a spark, a particle of the whole, I cannot describe to thee the whole Deity in a circle all at once. I must set one thing after another, that thou mayest at last behold the whole. Yes! I must even speak sometimes in a diabolical manner, as if the Light were kindled out of darkness, and as if Deity had a beginning! Otherwise I cannot instruct thee. But it is not so ; God has no beginning ; or more truly,

He has an eternal beginning and an eternal end. Therefore, I exhort the reader not to understand me in an earthly sense, but to interpret everything in a high and supernatural way."

When one reads Böhme's description of the theogonistic process, it undeniably appears as though God passed through a *history*, marked at many points by tumultuous and chequered scenes, a history with crises and conflicts between light and darkness, with appalling throes and bursts of apprehension, but also with brilliant victories and spoils. It should, however, be remembered here that Böhme thinks, like a poet, in figures and symbols, and cannot think in any other way ; that he is compelled to write, as Oetinger says, "opticè et phœnomenologicè." He does not mean that God *becomes* through a temporal history ; but he wishes to consider and point out the eternal momenta in the Divine Life-movement, and in the process of the Divine Self-consciousness, where all is, at one and the same time, Being and Self-production. Without an eternal life-movement, God would be only dead existence ; for it is only death that is without " process." And without eternal existence and unchangeable self-resemblance, God would be only mere movement that had reverted to time and history. Therefore, inasmuch as Böhme desires to point out the various momenta in the Being of Beings, he isolates and separates the individual " moment," seeks to apprehend this in and for itself and to show what condition and quality belong to this " moment " when it is conceived of, as severed from its cohesion with the whole, and, as it were, left to itself.

But he also demands that, in contrast to this isolation, this "moment" shall be placed in that rhythmic movement and harmony of the whole, in which it has often an entirely different character from that which it possesses when it is viewed in abstract isolation. "Just as a sour or bitter apple is constrained by the sun, so that it becomes pleasant to eat, thus also does God retain His attributes, but they manifest themselves in a pleasant manner. When the sour or bitter is viewed in itself, when it is isolated (separated) for the taste, it is viewed abstractly; in reality, when it is subjected to the constraining power of the sun, and is in combination with other qualities, it does not express itself *quâ* sour or *quâ* bitter, although these elements are contributory to the whole. The bitter quality also certainly exists in God, not, however, like the gall in a man, but as an everlasting power, a triumphant fountain of joy." One must always keep in mind, while reading Jacob Böhme, that he continually moves, with a stream of metaphors, in the representation of isolated (severed) momenta, which representation, however, has significance only for our thought, because it has no corresponding reality. It is necessary, on this account, constantly to correct and supplement his description by transposing the successive into the simultaneous, by referring the separated and specially prominent elements back to the whole, to the circular movement (from which they have been separated for our instruction), and by seeing what part they play in the whole. It will then often appear that that which, on an abstract consideration, was tumultuous and chequered is, in reality, in the

deepest calm, is only in latency, in concealment.
(A thought which applies very forcibly to his
description of the seven natural properties or fundamental forces.)   If we neglect this, as many neglect
it, and pay the penalty by falling into hopeless confusion, we do not comply with Böhme's stipulation,
which is, that he is not to be interpreted in an
earthly, but in a high and supernatural manner.

XIII.

THE ABYSS AND THE ETERNAL WILL.—THE IMAGINATION AND THE ETERNAL IDEA.— THE POTENTIAL TRINITY.

THE first link in Böhme's theosophic train of
thought is the unit which he designates as the *Abyss*,
where all as yet is in indifference.   Here as yet
there is no ground, cause, or basis, no centre, no
principle, nothing defining or defined, because
ground, cause or basis, can only appear when the
different, the definite appears.   Here there is neither
light nor darkness, light nor fire, neither good nor
evil ; here there is neither height nor depth, great
nor small, thick nor thin.   Here is everything and
nothing.   For all is stillness, in which nothing
actual stirs.   In this stillness lies the whole Trinity,
Father, Son, and Spirit, who have not yet come
forth.   Böhme "must speak in diabolical fashion
as if God had a beginning, or else he cannot instruct
us ; " here lies the whole creation, with everything
that is in heaven or upon earth.   This abyss, which
is everything and nothing, Böhme often designates

as the "*mysterium magnum,*" and also as the Eternal Chaos, with regard to which it must be observed that chaos, in Theosophy, does not signify disorder and confusion, but a complex $\pi\lambda\acute{\eta}\rho\omega\mu\alpha$, which has not yet developed itself. An egg, for example, from which a bird comes forth, is called in Theosophy, the chaos of the bird.

But in the recesses of this abyss, this *mysterium magnum*, there is a *bottomless unoriginated Will*, which Will, however, we are not to explore more closely, because it would disturb us, and fill us with confusion. We can readily comprehend that it would disturb us to search into this Night of Indifference, to seek conditions and varieties where no such things exist. On the other hand, it is precisely this Will which Böhme desires to explore when it steps out of the night, determines itself to its own manifestation, and assigns to itself progressive conditions or determinations. In connection with this Will, Böhme also often speaks of a great, enormous Eye, in which all marvels, all shapes, colours, and figures lie concealed. But this Eye sees nothing, because it only looks out into an undefined, illimitable infinity, where it meets with no object.

XIV.

" A WILL is thin or obscure, as it were nothing ; therefore, it is desirous, it willeth to be *somewhat*, that it might be manifest in itself." But still, this Will demands or desires only itself, for there is nothing else for it to desire ; it seeks to possess itself and its $\pi\lambda\acute{\eta}\rho\omega\mu\alpha$, and to manifest itself in itself. The first thing it does is to fashion for itself a *Mirror*, in which it can behold itself. Of what quality, now, is this Mirror? One would be most readily disposed to think of it as a reason-mirror, a thought-mirror ; and there are those whom this mirror has reminded of the eternal, universally-valid, and necessary laws of thought, without which God cannot see Himself and His real side, the ontological determinations which form the main subject of Hegel's logic. Or one might, *per oppositionem*, think of Kant, whose entire theoretic philosophy is a doctrine of the mirror,—certainly only a miniature mirror in comparison with Böhme's,— viz. : the doctrine of the forms of thought and intuition in which not God but *man* beholds himself and the whole world of experience (with which Kant combines the thought· or " thing unthinkable," that the mirror can never show us things as they are in themselves, but only their surface or phenomenon, which, indeed, certainly applies to the earthly, material mirrors we have upon our walls). We cannot, however, pronounce any of these explanations to be satisfactory. Böhme's mirror is not only a reason-mirror, a thought-mirror, but also a mirror of imagination and of fancy, a combination of reason and imagination ; and, if philosophical parallels be demanded, one must immediately think of Schelling's intellectual intuition, transferred to God. Böhme's mirror shows infinitely more than mere logical forms. To the imaginative Eye that looks into the mirror, it reveals the whole πλήρωμα,—shapes, colours, and figures ; indeed as we shall find in the sequel, it reflects an image of the Triune God

Himself. There is nothing either in heaven or upon earth which did not, at the beginning, become manifest in this mirror. Böhme designates this mirror as God's visibility, or as the eternal Wisdom, the eternal Idea. And he also calls this idea a *Maiden.* One must be prepared for very frequent shiftings of metaphor and symbol in Böhme! What just now was a mirror, is now a maiden who stands, in the dawn of eternity, before the God who gives Himself up to Self-manifestation, and who, so to speak, allures Him to manifest Himself, by showing Him the exceeding riches of His glory. The eternal Idea, or Sophia, is described as a maiden, because it engenders nothing, but only receives and reflects the image. Although co-eternal with God, it is not God of God, but simply the friend of God. It is, however, impersonal and selfless, because it is only an instrument for God's manifestation. We shall see in the sequel that it furnishes a contrast to the eternal Nature (which is also God's instrument, although subordinate to the idea), and that it will manifest itself to us, in union with the eternal nature, as the Glory of God, wherein the mirroring first finds its consummation.*

---

* " For the nothing causes the willing that it is desirous, and the desiring is an Imagination wherein the Will in the Looking-glass of Wisdom discovers itself, and so it imagines out of the abyss into itself, and makes to itself in the imagination a ground in itself, and impregnates itself with the Imagination out of the Wisdom, viz. : out of the virgin-like looking-glass, which, there, is a mother without generating, without willing."

" If the looking-glass of Wisdom were not, then could no fire or light be generated ; it all takes its original from the looking-glass of Deity."—" Incarn. Christ.," II., cc. ii., iii.

XV.

THE mirror in God is not complete at the outset, but fashions itself during the very process of mirroring.

What first takes place is only this, that there arises an abstract outline of that which, in the sequel, is to become full of vivid life and wealth of colour. The bottomless incomprehensible Will, which only is one, is nothing and yet everything, apprehends and discovers itself, and the unity beholds itself as trinity, and the trinity beholds itself as unity. Thus, the first only Will, without beginning, which is neither evil nor good, generates in itself the one eternal good as a comprehensible Will, which is the Son of the abysmal, bottomless will, wherein this primal Will apprehends and finds itself, and which is co-eternal with the unoriginated Will (God of God) ("Election," I., c. x.). And the unsearchable bottomless Will goes forth through its eternally found or invented Will, and brings itself into an eternal Visibility of itself. And that first bottomless Will is called Father, and the second, the conceived or generated Will, is called Son. And the exit of the bottomless Will, through the conceived Ens, or Being, or Son, is called Spirit, for it drives out the conceived Ens, or Being, forth from itself into a moving or life of the Will, as a life of the Father and the Son ; but that which is gone forth, or, as Böhme also calls it, the fourth effect (or operation), is called the Wisdom or Visibility of God, wherein Father, Son, and Spirit (not one individual of these, but the whole triad) ever behold and discover themselves. Böhme develops this more fully by sayingthat al the energies or forces of the Father are concentrated in the Son ; but the Spirit breathes them forth and diffuses them,—"just as when the sun's rays shed themselves out of the sun's magick fire, and manifest the power, virtue, or influence of the sun:" In the Divine Visibility or Wisdom, the Spirit of God plays with the radiated powers as with one single power (wherein the multiplicity is consequently restored to unity). The Wisdom is neither great nor small, has neither beginning nor end, but is infinite, and its form is inexpressible. It stands before God as a Virgin, is still and speechless (and, therefore, must not be confounded with the Son, who is the Word). Nor is it to be confounded with the Spirit, for it is passive, while the Spirit is active. In this mirror the Holy Trinity beholds itself and all the wonders of eternity (the riches of the Glory of God), which have neither beginning nor end.

XVI.

BUT in all that has been hitherto considered, in this first mirroring, we have not yet reached the Living God. " It is a life, and still it is no life, a figure of life and an image of life" (" Six Theosoph. Points," I., vii.). God beholds Himself thus far only as a potentiality of becoming Trinitarian, and He beholds in the mirror only a wealth of potential glories or miracles, which are not yet realized. He is also absorbed in an immediate mystic contemplation,

wherein the distinctions are only self-entangled, but
are not yet actual and separate contrasts, on which
account, moreover, Böhme expressly asserts that as
yet there are only three operations, but not three
Persons, which means, in clearer language, that,
hitherto, we have no real self-consciousness. For
real Trinity and real thinking Self-consciousness are
inseparable conceptions. Here are no Divine attributes, for attributes can be found only where there
is *another*, a contrasted, by which they can be
qualified. Here as yet everything is only a *Magia*,
the simple mirrored image without reality. This
mirroring, which is a life and yet no life, a Spirit
and yet no Spirit, is consequently as yet no actual
personal self-consciousness; it is but a dim and
dreamy self-consciousness. The Maiden stands
before God as if in a vision, a morning-dream of
Eternity, which prophetically reveals to Him what
He *can* become, what He *can* make Himself.

How then does God become the living and actual
Triune? According to Böhme, this happens only by
means of the eternal Nature, which, as a medium of
manifestation, provides a contrast to the Maiden,
the eternal Idea. When God, in the tranquil delight
of contemplation, beholds Himself and His wonders,
as the Maiden displays them to Him in the mirror,
the Will grows eager, and desires that what it sees
in the mirror shall become something more than
an image, shall become actual, as when an artist
longs to realize the vision, the image that reveals
itself to him in his inward soul. And not only
does the Will become eager, but the Wisdom,
Sophia, surges about it, and yearns for the mani-

festation of the marvels of Wisdom, although she herself *is* all these marvels.   In this union of the joy of contemplation and of desire, of imagination and desire, the eternal nature hidden in God is aroused, and now comes forward as the contrast or *Contrarium* of the Idea.   The generation of the eternal Nature depends upon the magic of the desire, and is the power of summoning non-existence into existence, without the use of material means. All effective magic depends upon desire and imagination, and whatever is born and comes into being arises, in the last resort, from desire and imagination.

XVII.

IT is one of Böhme's most characteristic features that he interprets Spirit—even the absolute Spirit of God—as desire and imagination, will and fancy. He is here in diametrical opposition to those who entirely exclude fancy from God.   A God, destitute of fancy, who is only pure reason, pure thought, bare and blank intelligence, is, for Böhme, an abstract being and not an actual living Spirit.   And undoubtedly, a God destitute of fancy could not have produced a world like the world we know, like the world in which Böhme lived and had his intuitions, inasmuch as this world, both in nature and history, is moulded and everywhere influenced by fancy, is actively pervaded by the *principium individuationis*, which manifests. itself in an inexhaustible wealth of individual forms that are incapable of being merged in general conceptions.   But there could not have been

Fancy in God unless there were Nature in God, and Böhme, by the very fact that he speaks of a mirror of Imagination, already points to Nature as a potency in God Himself. For Fancy is precisely, in the form of ideality, the connecting link between Spirit and Nature.[*] Precisely because God is the unity of Spirit and Nature, not merely reason, but also fancy, must be ascribed to Him, which fancy, however, is certainly to be conceived of as illuminated and irradiated by Wisdom.

We notice in passing that we get here the root of Böhme's psychology. According to Böhme, the *Will* is the inmost thing in man, the principle of our personality ; and,—*Fancy* the form-fashioning and image-shaping energy, not excluding but presupposing reason and wisdom,—is the necessary complement of the Will. It is impossible to will, or to hate, or to love the purely abstract, but only that which presents itself in an image and shape. No act of the Will is possible without imagination. A Will must have an object ; but an object that is posited by the Will lies in the future, must be pictured by the imagination, and must hover before it. A Will must determine itself according to motives, love or hatred, hope or fear, good or evil, and all of these things are *imaginations*. The difference between human characters depends upon this,—wherein do they set their imagination or their desire, their aspiration, their will, which is inseparable from the imagination ? "Where thy

---

[*] Portig, " Religion und Kunst," ii., 273 ; Froschhammer, " Die Phantasie als Weltprincip."

treasure is, where thy spiritual and volitional image is, there also will thy heart be!" Now, if man is created in the image of God, it follows, from Böhme's train of thought, that a corresponding relation must also be found in God (on the scale, however, of eternity and absolute perfection).

XVIII.

CONSEQUENTLY, the Nature which is hidden in God is aroused and bursts into activity, [through the medium of] desire and imagination. This eternal Nature must not be interpreted as Matter in God. For matter is nothing original, but is simply a product. We grasp Böhme's meaning more accurately when (with St. Martin and Franz Baader) we define nature as *a spirituous potency*. This spirituous potency is impersonal and selfless, yet, according to Böhme, it is a Will that has issued forth and separated itself from unity, a Will that multiplies itself in an infinite plenitude of powers, a living fountain of forces, that pour forth in an infinity of many thousand times ten thousand particular wills. For life consists of many wills. Each of the forces in the eternal Nature has its own will, and each of these wills is against the other. And life would be sheer hostility, unless all these powers of life gained a gracious Lord, under whose control they may abide, and who is able to break their strength and their will. But in Nature there is merely a blind, not a self-conscious Will.

With the bursting forth of the eternal Nature there occurs an obscuration, which furnishes a contrast to the pure light and spirituality. But this obscuration is a necessary condition, in order that the light may succeed in manifesting its splendour. We may also say that, with the eternal Nature, the *thick* presents itself in contrast to the *thin*. The *thin* is mere ideality, pure spirituality ; the *thick* is Nature, the condition in virtue of which the thin, viz., the Spirit, can gain life and fulness, sap and power. And now, for the first time, we get actual contrasts and actual manifestations.

Böhme is never weary of enforcing the necessity of contrasts in order to life and manifestation. All things, not merely earthly and diabolic, but also heavenly and Divine, consist of *Yes* and *No*. The Eternal Will of Unity is the eternal *Yes ;* but this *Yes* cannot be manifested without the eternal *No*, which provides a contradiction to the Unity, and posits multiplicity and variety. And yet we cannot affirm that the *Yes* and *No* are sundered, that they are two things by the side of one another. They are only one thing, but they separate themselves into two beginnings, into two *centra*, each of which wills and energizes within itself. The eternal Will must pass out of itself, and lead itself into particularity, otherwise there were no shape or intelligibility, and all powers would be simply one power. Intelligence is based upon multiplicity and variety, wherein the one property beholds and tests the other. A thing has nothing in itself that it can will, unless it doubles itself. It cannot perceive itself in mere unity ; it can perceive itself only in duality. Where there is no contrast, there is only a perpetual issuing forth, but no ingoing and retrocession into self.

XIX.

MANIFESTATION THROUGH THE ETERNAL NATURE.
—THE SEVEN NATURAL PROPERTIES.—THE
ACTUAL TRINITY.—THE GLORY OF GOD.—
THE UNCREATED HEAVEN.

IN order to become manifest to Himself as the Living God, God has consequently been obliged to found an eternal distinction, an eternal contrast in Himself. The Divine Will has had to divide itself into two, has been compelled, if we may so speak, to contraposit an anti-Divine Will (that is, a Will derived from, and yet sundered from Unity) as a condition for its Life of Manifestation. We have, accordingly, two *centra* in God, the Nature-Will and the Spirit-Will. The Nature-Will may be more closely defined as the Particular Will, the *Self-Will* in contrast to the Universal Will, which wills the one and the whole, as the *No*-Will in contrast to the *Yes*-Will, as the Will of Dissimilarity in contrast to the Will of Similarity. The object of the process of Life and Manifestation which we are now to consider is that the Nature-Will may be sub-ordinated to the Spirit-Will, as its obedient instrument and medium of manifestation. The first part of the process shows a relation of contrast, indeed, a hostile relation between Nature and Spirit; the second part, on the contrary, shows Nature as the willing servant of God and of the Idea, for the shaping forth of the Glory of God. The process is more clearly defined by the seven fundamental Forces, or *Natural Forms* or *Properties*, by which last expression Böhme means the form-giving, nature-fashioning energy. Nothing can gain shape in nature without the aid of these seven forces. In these seven Natural Properties we shall perceive two ternaries or triads: the first, the negative, dark ternary, where Nature shows what it is capable of by itself, shows that, notwithstanding all its power, it remains an unsatisfied hunger, and an anxiously eager restlessness; the second, the positive, bright ternary, in which Nature has surrendered its independence, and is transfigured into the Light, in order to the fashioning of the eternal harmonies. The fourth Natural Property, or the Lightning Flash, is the central point, or the transition from the darkness to the light. *Four* is the centre of *Seven.*

XX.

THE *first* Natural Property is the introspective Desire which demands only itself. "It has harshness, sharpness, hardness, cold, and substance," and finds its symbolical expression in *Salt.* To adopt a scientific phrase, we call it *Contraction.* It is the austere, self-contained, and gloomy property which desires to be alone, and will not endure anything outside it, but seeks to absorb everything into itself, and to have everything for itself, as when we say of a man, that he has a gloomy, self-contained temperament, and that he hardens himself in austerity and rigour against everything that is outside him.

The *second* Natural Property is the outward-looking Desire or Movement, which seeks to go forth into multiplicity; the symbolic expression of which is *Mercury*, but which we call, scientifically, *Expansion*, the tendency to self-diffusion and self-propagation in all directions. These two Properties are now in dead antagonism to each other. The one tends outwards ; the other tends inwards. The one seeks to compress itself, and to compress everything into itself ; the other seeks to manifest itself, and to outpour itself on every side. The more the one tends inwards, the more does the other tend outwards. The one seeks to be still ; the other is loud and noisy. The one seeks to draw itself back into itself ; the other seeks to run, to go forward, and to fly out into the wide and remote. These conflicting forces are inseparable, cannot escape one another, but are inevitably forced into collision. This conflict finally becomes an oscillation or whirling, the revolution of a wheel, a movement that cannot come to an end, but which, nevertheless, leads to no goal, and there ensues an appalling restlessness and *Anguish*. This restlessness and anguish is the *third* Natural Property. "One cannot remain in oneself, and yet can go nowhither!" Both of the two opposites desire to go their own way, but they cannot get loose from one another. They desire to be separated, but their union is indissoluble, and they continue to oscillate about, in company, in wild confusion; and in a kind of frenzy. *Anguish* is here a symbolic expression which designates the unsolved dispute, dissension, and tension ; this again is symbolized by *Sulphur*. We call this Property *Rotation*. The first ternary is, thus,—Contraction, Expansion, Rotation, but unharmonious ; a contradiction which Nature itself cannot solve.

How then is Nature to be liberated from this torture? Nature, in its own strength, is powerless (Natura quaerit se, sed non invenit). The contradiction can only be removed by that which is higher than Nature, by that which is above and outside of Nature, by God, the Eternal Freedom. Nature's inmost essence is need of God, " indigentia Dei, indigentia gratiae," a hunger and restlessness, which can only be stilled, satisfied, and calmed by freedom. There is aroused in Nature an anxious yearning after freedom. On the other hand, freedom yearns after Nature, in order that, through Nature, it may manifest itself. God is Holiness and Love, but before Holiness and Love can be manifested, there must be something that needs love and grace, something that needs to be released from its torture. The higher desires the lower ; the lower desires the higher. Nature, however, will not, immediately, give up its unruliness, and subordinate itself to the Idea. A conquest must take place here, when Freedom, the Spirit, lets its light stream into the darkness and confusion of Nature, and a tremor, terror, and shock passes through the whole of Nature. The Lightning, which is the *fourth* Natural Property, the first contact of Spirit and Nature, breaks forth as, at once, a joyous and appalling surprise. By the Lightning that which is gross, dark, and selfish in the desire of Nature is consumed. The Natural Properties, so to speak, faint away, sink out of their selfishness, and become quite meek and gentle. They accept the Will of the Light, wholly surrender themselves to it, become as those who have no power of their own, and desire only the power of the Light. The Lightning itself becomes altogether terrified, and is transformed into a light which is absolutely white and mildly beaming. Here, for the first time, we notice a doctrine that pervades Böhme's writings, and is full of very profound practical applications, viz. : that every life must be born twice, in order that Nature may traverse the path to the light and to freedom through the lightning, as the kindled fire. Hence the old maxim, which so often recurs in theosophy: *Per ignem ad lucem ;* or, since the Lightning, as the *fourth* Natural Property, has for its theosophic-symbolical designation a *Cross—per crucem ad lucem—*a thought that has such significance for created Nature, and especially for the Christian Life (" We must through much tribulation enter into the Kingdom of God "). Böhme constantly insists that every life is born in fear, is enjoyed in freedom, and again perishes in anguish. We have defined the first ternary as the *dark* ternary, and may, when we view it as a unit, describe it as the Dark Principle in God, but also as the Fire-Principle. For there is, already, Fire in the Darkness, but it is latent ; it is first kindled by the inbeaming of the Light, by the Lightning, as at the collision of flint and steel. Fire is Böhme's symbol for the Nature-Will, the rigid, strong, consuming power ; the Light, the Spirit-Will, the mild nourishing power is Love and Gentleness. Böhme, however, speaks, in many passages, of a heavenly Fire, which is bright and gentle, and fundamentally different from the dark, dry, and consuming Fire.

XXI.

WITH the conquest and clarification of the dark, anti-Divine Principle or Property, begins the positive, the good and bright ternary. The same three Natural Properties that we find in the dark ternary (Contraction, Expansion, Rotation) repeat themselves in the bright ternary, but are now transfigured. The savage, refractory, and formless have vanished. Life has now gained shape, goal, and definite limits ; or, as Böhme expresses it, all now is Gentleness. The bright ternary begins with the *fifth* Natural Property. Here the powers are concentrated into the unity of Wisdom. This Natural Property Böhme also designates as the gentle Love, the clear Water-Spirit, under whose peaceable dominion the powers are now collected ; hostility has vanished, the one power rejoices over the other. They gain a liking for each other, and rejoice with each other over the violent transition that has taken place, and " because the dear child is now born." Water and Spirit, Water and Light are designations for this principle or property, which subdues, ripens, and moulds the severe and sharp element in nature. And as Böhme's metaphysic is pervaded by practical applications, we must here recal that even upon earth there occurs a birth of Water and Spirit, and that the fire of concupiscence and of the passions, the wild emotions that spring from the dark fire-root in our nature, need to be quenched and subdued by the cooling streams of heavenly gentleness and love, which release us from the torture of the fire.

The *sixth* Natural Property is intelligible Sound. The powers that are concentrated in the fifth natural property are now led forth into intelligible separation ; they become distinct and audible. When the Psalmist (xix. 4) says of the manifestation of the Glory of God in created nature : " Their line is gone out through all the earth, and their words to the end of the world," and when the Apostle (Rom. x. 18) gives this a higher application, Böhme already discovers something analogous to this in Eternity, in the Divine life of inward manifestation. There is here a great concord of intelligible sounds, of tones ; and the audible has in correspondence with it the visible ; sound-figures and light-figures. But in comparison with what are called tones upon earth, are called song and sound, which are very coarse, the heavenly tones are extremely subtile, as when the soul inwardly sports in itself, and hears within pleasant and sweet tones, but outwardly hears nothing. No human ear can perceive the heavenly tones that sound and play before God in His Life of inward Manifestation. The angels alone can perceive anything of this. But this their perception or hearing is determined by the character of their world, the peculiarity of their dwelling-place. The *seventh* Natural Property is the concluding one. All the foregoing powers and energies are here gathered into a harmonious whole. This seventh and last Natural Property Böhme calls the *Essential, e.g.*, Wisdom shaped into reality, life, and corporeity. The Wisdom, the Image which God beheld from the beginning in the Mirror, in His eternal Imagination, and which He desired to behold

in actuality, is now realized. Böhme also designates
this as God's *Corporeity* (His aspect of reality, His
encircling periphery), the Heavenly *Salnitter*, the
Abode of God, the House of the Holy Trinity,
the Uncreated Heaven, the Kingdom, in regard
to which Böhme agrees with the Kabbala, which
asserts in God seven Natural Properties, the last of
which is the Kingdom (*Malkuth*). The Uncreated
Heaven possesses unspeakable beauty. " To describe it I have neither pen nor tongue. Even if
this Maiden (Wisdom) happen to lead anything of
it into our heart, yet the whole man is too cold and
dark for us to be able to utter of it even so much as
a vestige (*scintilla*)."

XXII.

IN order not to misunderstand this doctrine of
the Seven Natural Properties, it will be needful to
keep in mind Böhme's frequently reiterated declaration, that this process takes place not in time, but
in eternity. It is only our feeble mind which is
compelled to place one thing after another, because,
otherwise, we could not comprehend it. But the
real state of the case is different. In eternity there
is no temporal succession, but everything is in
circular movement ; nothing is first, nothing last
in point of time; but everything is simultaneous,
and each individual natural property presupposes all
the others, because there is here a constant reciprocity
and mutual influence. And in eternity one thing
does not stand outside another, as in our relation
of material space, but the one thing is in the other,

and yet is different from it (*v.* "Aurora," x., 40). The *reality*, in contrast to the abstract momenta, is here only the seventh natural property—wholeness, the complete, the Uncreated Heaven, the Kingdom, or harmony. If we were permitted to gaze in immediately upon these regions, we should behold nothing but the seventh natural property, or the Glory of God. All the rest lies in concealment. But it must be noted, on the other hand, that if we wish to understand this harmony, we must, for the purposes of contemplation, analyse the individual momenta in this movement each by itself, just as we pay attention to the individual tones and transitions in a musical composition or a painting ; and then we discern a variety of deeper, higher, stronger, and more gentle tones, or of darker and lighter colours, and, indeed, discover even discords, which are most admirably fused into ineffable harmony. It is this analysis, this separation of momenta which Böhme has attempted in his doctrine of the seven Natural Properties. The Natural Properties, or fundamental forces, are, as would not otherwise have been expected, the same as those which we know in created nature. Created nature, according to Böhme, is a *derivatum* of the uncreated, and ultimately consists (however numerous may be the intermediate links) of these uncreated principles. Thus, we have Contraction, Expansion, Rotation ; we have the Lightning and the Light ; we have sound and tones with figures and colours—the elements of a natural world, in which are found intelligibility, severance, and separation. A natural world, whether uncreated or created, would certainly be unthinkable if God were only the thin "spiritus" which Deism imagines ; if He were only pure Thought ; if He had no fancy, and could not perceive ; if He had no "sensorium" (as also Newton has emphatically urged) ; or if God, as Böhme expresses it, were only an all-knowing, but not also an all-seeing, all-hearing, all-tasting, all-feeling, all-smelling God (*v.* "Aurora," c. 3). In the next place, we have this natural world in its consummation as the Uncreated Heaven, the riches of the Glory of God, a pattern of the Glory of the Creation when it is brought to perfection. We have, finally, what we have hitherto been debarred from expressing, because it belongs to the Trinitarian process : the Living Word of God as the Word of Power.

XXIII.

THE Self-manifestation of the actual, living, and triumphant Trinity is effected through the process here described. We must not, however, leave the Nature-process before dwelling on one single point of it, which may be called, in more senses than one, *the dark point.*

The reader will doubtless have discovered that the most difficult point, but also the point which peculiarly rivets attention, is what we have called (following Baader) the first, negative ternary, but what Böhme calls "centrum naturæ." In order to comprehend this phrase, it must be observed, that by "centrum" Böhme means not simply the mid-point in a circle, but also the whole circle, not a mathematical circle, nor a mathematical mid-point,

but a circle the mid-point of which is everywhere,
" cujus centrum ubique," active at all points, domi-
nating and penetrating the whole region.   The
contrast of the Nature-centre is the Light-centre,
or Life-centre.   There are in God two " centra,"
or two regions, of which, however, only one, the
bright region, is manifested, while the other remains
in the deepest concealment.   The two centra repeat
themselves in the creation.   But in one half of
the creation, as we shall see in the sequel, only the
dark centrum and the dark region has come into
manifestation, and the bright centrum has retired
into concealment, by reason of sin.

" Centrum naturæ " is thus, in Böhme, the first
thing in nature, that original variance and conflict
between opposing forces with which life begins, and
which cannot lead it farther than anguish, a tension,
vibration, or gyration of the forces, which is designated
now as an apprehensive darkness, now as a fire
which is not yet kindled, but smoulders in the
depths, and which only the Lightning is able to
bring out of this restlessness into subordination to
the higher principle,—the Light which shines into
it—in which subordination it finds rest.   This
" centrum naturæ " Böhme also calls the " Wheel of
Nature," the " Wheel of Life," the " Wheel of
Anguish."   By this he means what that apostle, to
whom, on the score of his doctrine of faith and
works, Luther assigned a very low place, but whom
Oetinger regards as the most profound of all the
apostles, and whom Schelling mentions as one
who was highly privileged to gaze into the first
beginning of Nature, and the primal sources of life,

—what the Apostle James calls the "Wheel of Birth" ($\tau\rho\sigma\chi\delta\varsigma$ $\tau\hat{\eta}\varsigma$ $\gamma\epsilon\nu\acute{\epsilon}\sigma\epsilon\omega\varsigma$, James iii. 6). The "Wheel of Birth" does not mean simply the revolving of life and of the forces of life in general, which is so justly comparable to a circling wheel, and which is liable to be brought into disorder by sin. The "Wheel of Birth," in a stricter sense, is the "Wheel of coming into existence," the "Wheel of Becoming;" the first magical life-circle, which is the beginning of all natural and creaturely Birth and Becoming; the first restlessly circling movement, which is the womb and basis of the life that is working itself into shape. It is a secretly-burning wheel, because "life is fire" (ignis ubique latet). In Böhme, image succeeds image, and metaphor metaphor; he, therefore, designates it by another symbol as the Dark Fire-root, which never dares to catch fire and to burst into fierce flames (whereby the whole of life would be brought into confusion), but is destined to remain in latency, in concealment, in subordination to the higher principle. It is only by means of this subordination that the Dark Fire-root itself can be calmed and maintained in that order which accords with the harmony of the whole. What is called the "Wheel of Birth" may be described, under another figure, as the Hearth of Life, or the Mother and Nurse of Life. But the child, *i.e.*, the Life, which, arising from this dark womb of fire, presents itself in its appointed forms and shapes, is far nobler than the mother, whose function is simply ministerial.

The "Wheel of Birth," which never stands still, does not occur simply in God as a foundation for the eternal Nature-process ; it is also present in the whole created universe, and, indeed, in every single creature, in harmony with the character of this creature. In Nature it is Fire ; in the world of souls and spirits it is Desire. Fire and Desire are, at bottom, one and the same thing. We are taught by experience that in proportion as fire gains unrestricted power and scope, it grows fiercer, becomes increasingly a consuming and devouring fire, and finally, indeed, may become unquenchable.

Among the ancient heathen sages, Heraclitus was aware of this Wheel in the universe, when he spoke of an unwearied incessantly-coursing Fire (ἀκάματον πῦρ), by the quenching of which the universe was produced. But this " Wheel of Birth " in the whole creation was viewed far more clearly, and in a great and holy connection, by the prophet Ezekiel, when he was permitted to behold the Glory of God in the vision which is recorded in the first and tenth chapters of his book,—passages which are so vitally important in Theosophy. Ezekiel gives us the ideas, says Oetinger, only we must remember that Holy Scripture shows us the Glory of God in that aspect of it which is turned towards the Creation. The prophet first saw or heard a whirlwind out of the north (which may suggest to us the Almighty Will of God as the impelling power), and he beheld a thick cloud, and a fire infolding itself, circling and whirling about itself. We must think of this cloud as quivering with flame, and as if made one with the whirling Fire. In this Fire, which runs and whirls in itself, we have the " Wheel of Birth." It must also be observed that the self-infolding Fire had a "brightness about it," and there was the appearance as of burning brass (amber?) out of the midst of the fire. The brightness that the prophet beheld round about the whirling fire is the splendour of light into which the fire is to be transfigured, and the "burning brass" out of the midst of the fire betokens the lightning, and the transition of the fire into the light. Out of the midst of this whirling and self-circling Fire, this "Wheel of Birth," this "centrum naturæ," proceed the actual forms of life, the living creatures or cherubim, who represent the creation and the powers of the creation, and who have, themselves, a glowing and radiant appearance. The prophet observes that each of them has four faces, those of a lion, ox, eagle, and man, emblems of all that is strong and royal in creation; and he beholds "their wings full of eyes" (Ezek. x. 12). Two of their wings were stretched upward; with the other two they veil their creaturely nothingness. The noise of their wings was as the noise of great waters, as the Voice of the Almighty. He beholds the marvellous four wheels that move by the side of the cherubim, and his vision inspires a holy awe. For in each of the wheels there was another wheel equally large, so that each wheel could, without turning, direct itself towards the four corners of the earth, and could always go forward; and their felloes were full of eyes, as a sign that these wheels, which are emblematic of the circularity of movement in the Divine cosmical order, are intended to serve the living, omniscient, and wise God. The cherubim go round about between the wheels, and these princes of life stretch out the hands which they have under their wings, and take coals out of the fire, coals from the Hearth of Life, from the " centrum naturæ," in order to execute the Lord's Will, whether it be to make alive, or to perform the judgments of the Lord, and to afflict the sinful world with great outbursts of the terrible power of God. Nevertheless, all that has been mentioned thus far is but the *substratum*, the basis for the highest, is simply the *Vehicle* (*Merkabah*). Far above all this, the prophet beholds a Firmament, and above the Firmament a Throne, and, upon the Throne, the Lord in the appearance of a man, with a brightness round about Him, like the appearance of the. bow that is in the cloud in the day of rain. We have only imperfectly recalled the vision in question. A more minute description and exposition would lead us too far, and into a quite different line of meditation. We simply wish to emphasize the fact that here, once more, we find Böhme's fundamental categories : Darkness, Fire, and Light, the last of these as the gentle brightness, which encircles the whirling fire, and the brightness of the rainbow. In Ezekiel, moreover, the Fire proceeds out of the Darkness, and the Light out of the Fire.

What Fire is in the outward region, Desire is in the inward. Thus, from the intellectual and spiritual standpoint, the " Wheel of Birth," or the " centrum naturæ," is the restlessness of Desire. Modern thinkers disagree with Böhme on this point, assigning *instinct* as the deepest root in natural life, and restricting *desire* to self-conscious life. Böhme, on the contrary, speaks of a blind desire, which turns both inwards and outwards, and is in continual restlessness, a thought which reminds us of what Schopenhauer, who at many points agrees with Böhme, only, however, immediately to forsake him and to pursue a totally different path, calls "the tendency towards, or struggle for life." For if we ask what is it that this blind craving, which does not desire this or that, but is the mother and the nurse of all desire, really seeks in its restlessness, the only reply is, that it desires itself, desires to be satiated and filled; it desires life (" vehementer cupio vitam "). Desire is the foundation of Egoism, of *Self-ness*, of that in us whereby we separate ourselves from everything else, centre in ourselves, establish ourselves as mid-point, and exclude all else. Egoism gathers itself into itself, but is soon impelled to go forth again from itself, to spread itself in the manifoldness of life, but in a selfish manner. In none of these movements can it find satisfaction, but it is in perpetual restlessness—a fact of which every man can convince himself in proportion as he lives in his own egoism, separated from a Higher One, in whom he may, as it were, forget himself. This restlessness and torture can only be quieted and subdued when freedom, wisdom, love, and light descend into it ; and then it becomes the helpful basis for life and for the activities of love. For love cannot exist without a powerful egoism which surrenders itself to it, and denies and sacrifices itself. Without the astringent and contractile force of Egoism the self-imparting power of love would lead only to a vague absorption in, and fusion with, the illimitable. Without the austere and sharp ·

element in Egoism, the gentleness of love would degenerate into vapid and effeminate sentimentalism. Life is wholesome and sound only when the restlessness of Egoism, with its keen, sharp, vehement, and passionate element, its hungering and thirsting, is subordinated to higher forces and powers by which it is permanently quieted, and which it helps to nurture. In the normal condition, this restlessness of Desire and Egoism is only like the pendulum of a clock, or like the beating of our pulse, which is not noticed unless we expressly direct our attention towards it ; whereas we are compelled to notice it in fever, because the fire then makes itself plainly perceptible. It is this Desire and Fire, in the sense here referred to, that the apostle is thinking of when he admonishes us, in a series of practical precepts, to keep our tongue in check, to guard ourselves against sins of the tongue, because an impure tongue, kindled by hell, can set on fire the " Wheel of Birth," introduce disorder into the natural foundation and root of life, can produce a pernicious inflammation in the orbit of these blind forces, which may then spread itself into the whole life of the soul, penetrate the entire intellectual and spiritual constitution, and throw it into confusion, and indeed, we might add, can also set on fire the whole body, as when we picture to ourselves a man who is disturbed, overwhelmed, and dominated by blind passions. It is Desire and Fire that Böhme is thinking of when he traces in the " centrum naturæ," not only the Foundation of Life, but also the Foundation of Hell.

XXIV.

DESIRE and Fire, according to Böhme, form the foundation of Hell, as well as of Life. The possibility of the origin of evil here confronts us in the midst of the theogonistic process. This is the problem which, at an earlier period, made Böhme so melancholy. Evil cannot exist in God *as evil*, nor can it be congenital with man, or with any other creature ; these ideas must be rejected as impious and monstrous. And yet, in one form or another, everything must have its origin in God, and it remains eternally true that " all is God's ! " Here now is displayed a " centrum naturæ " in God, that *contrarium* in God, that blind nature-will, with conflict and tension of the forces, which cannot lead beyond an unappeased restlessness and anguish, but which has, nevertheless, issued forth from Unity, and is necessary in order to the manifestation of Light and Love. In God, this dark will is continually vanquished and outshone by the Light, and simply remains at bottom as a tendency, which is continually vanquished and willingly allows itself to be vanquished ; for the Life of God is an endless and uninterrupted life ($\zeta\omega\dot{\eta}$ $\dot{\alpha}\kappa\alpha\tau\alpha\lambda\dot{\upsilon}\tau\sigma\varsigma$. Heb. vii. 16), in which all the forces are bound together by an incorruptible and indestructible bond, which can never, to all eternity, be broken, in which all disorder is unthinkable, in which every mediation of the forces, at every transition, must necessarily succeed. In creation, on the other hand, life is a disintegrable life. Here, the forces may fall into disorder, for a rupture of their bond is possible—a rupture, indeed, that can only take place in an intelligent creation, which, in a false desire, seeks to centralize itself in itself, instead of in God, makes that which ought to be subordinate supreme, and makes what should be the servant the ruler. Accordingly, there is a "periculum vitæ" for the intelligent creation, viz., the danger of allowing itself a false and negative combination of the forces, and of suffering that which ought to be repressed to spring up and to come forth. For the unfallen creation, this dangerous moment is the moment of choice and temptation. When, therefore, such a creation, instead of sacrificing its abstract independence, and constituting itself a servant of God and of the Light, sets itself up as Lord, and places itself in opposition to the Light, there occurs a pause and a stoppage in the process of Life. The higher Divine principle, the principle of Life, which ought to stream freely into the lower created life, is now arrested and pushed back, and thus a process of obscuration takes place ; for the creation, resisting the light, and desirous of centering in itself, is compelled, more and more, to gather itself together in itself, the result of which is, that it only becomes darker and darker, and inevitably sinks into itself, as into an abyss, for now it can nowhere find foundation or solid footing.

Moreover, in addition to the obscuration, there occurs a false "kindling." For when the greedy egoism is minded, now and again, to rise out of its abyss, and to ascend, in order to outstretch its dark huge wings over the illimitable, it becomes inflamed (in consequence of the pause and confusion that has occurred in the process of Life), it becomes more and more fiery and fiercely-flaming, and moves in a whirl of sparks and devouring flames. Then the "Wheel of Birth" is set on fire, and the Light from above, which has been forced back, and the free shining of which is prevented by unrighteousness, flashes amidst this *turba* with judicial and punitive lightning. The "Wheel of Birth" now becomes, in the most literal sense, a "Wheel of Anguish." Instead of the anguish, tension, and collision of the forces being soothed and tranquillized by the Light, instead of the anxious restlessness forming a simple point of transition to the birth of the higher life, the anguish, which was intended to be simply a "momentum," now becomes chronic, the restlessness becomes a permanent condition, a perennial birth-pang and a perennial death-pang, without attaining actual birth or actual death. This is what Franz Baader calls "the Wheel of Ixion." According to the legend, Ixion was a king who, for his arrogance and presumption, was hurled by the lightning of Zeus into Tartarus, where he was bound to an eternally revolving wheel, a wheel, however, which paused, when Orpheus appeared in the lower world.

The Devil and Hell, consequently, make their appearance when the negative ternary, in separation from the light, becomes actual in an intelligent creation, and happens to work in false independence, instead of remaining in obedient concealment, latency, and potentiality. We now understand what Böhme means when he repeats so often in his writings, that the man who would follow him must be well equipped, and that he will assuredly discover that the matter is serious. "For we must pass through the Kingdom of Hell; and I myself should sometimes have fainted unless God and the gracious Wisdom had kept by me." He tells us again and again, that what has been described above became actual in Lucifer, when he fell from God. Lucifer opened his "centrum naturæ," instead of keeping it eternally closed. He sought to rise above God, and, therefore, his light was quenched, and he became a spirit of darkness, a horrible fire-spirit, a spirit of stinking sulphur, and was cast out into exile. The same thing happened to Adam, although, God be praised! not in the same manner as to Lucifer (this difference we shall not be able to explain until later), because for Adam and his children there is still grace and succour. "O ye children of men," says Böhme so often, "this is earnest and serious! Hell is quite near, indeed, it is within you! Repent and seek the new Birth! Live circumspectly, and let the Spirit be Lord, so that the fire may not be kindled. O worldly security and confidence, the devil waits for you! O pride, thou art the fire of Hell! O self-reliance and revenge, thou art the terrible wrath of God! O power and longing after worldly honour, Hell hath made thee blind! O beauty, thou art a dark valley!" etc., etc., etc. Böhme very frequently designates this "centrum naturæ" as the *Fire-pregnant Triangle.* We are to conceive of this Triangle as quite dimly burning, not as flaming. The Triangle, moreover, includes precisely the same momenta as the "Wheel of Birth." This dangerous Triangle

exists in the eternal Nature of God ; but in God it is
eternally outshone and covered up by the Light.
It exists in every creature, in every man. But it
should be our aim to let the Spirit be Lord, so that
the Triangle may be kept in concealment, and may
not come to light, and that the fire break not out.
As in God, so also in every true Christian, the
Triangle is to be quenched by the Light, by the Love
of Christ, the wisdom, gentleness, and humility of
the Holy Ghost. We shall be in complete harmony
with Böhme if we give a deeper meaning to the
refrain of one of our old watchmen's songs : " Watch
Light and Fire ! "

Another designation for the " centrum naturæ "
is the Life-Worm. *Omnis vita a verme.* The
Worm is the same as the " Wheel of Birth." Viewed
objectively, it is the Fire, viz., the self-infolding Fire
which Ezekiel beheld in his vision. Viewed sub-
jectively, it is the restlessness of Desire. As long
as the Worm is held in subjection by the power of
the Light, as long as it ministers to the Life, its
restlessness furnishes the contrast, by the vanquishing
and ruling of which Life acquires true repose and
harmony internal, just as health and the feeling
of health depend upon the suppression of an opposing tendency, which, if it had free scope, would
disturb the unity of life, and introduce disease.
But if, on the contrary, the Worm emerges from
its fettered and concealed condition, and acquires
self-conscious volition, it becomes terrible. We
have daily evidence of the manner in which a desire
can grow, how, by every indulgence of it, it becomes
stronger and more powerful, *i.e.*, more full of craving

hunger. Moreover, we say of a man, that this or that is his Worm, by which we mean a tendency or inclination within him, in which his Ego is specially conspicuous, and in which he specially seeks satiety for his self-love. In proportion as the Worm, which at the outset is impersonal, becomes a personal entity, the more it reaches the point at which it must be said, that it is not so much the personality that is lord over the Worm, as the Worm that is lord of the individual. And when the Worm attains absolute dominion, it becomes the dark Worm of Hell, or, as it may also be termed, the burning and gnawing Worm of Hell, of which Scripture says that it "dieth not." " Their Worm dieth not, and their fire is not quenched."

But furthermore, to these considerations (to which we have been necessarily led in the midst of the statement of the concept of God and of the doctrine of the Trinity, where it is not usual to discuss the doctrine of Evil) it must be added that Böhme specifies the " centrum naturæ" as not only the foundation of Hell, but also as the foundation of the Wrath of God. By the Wrath of God is generally understood the Divine displeasure against sin. Although Böhme also presupposes this, he nevertheless directs special attention to the physical aspect of the Wrath of God, to the power of the Wrath of God, the contents of the forces which, when they are unloosed, become destructive. As the eternal nature in the first ternary is the *contrarium* of God, is the anti-Divine principle, so this nature, as a principle of power (for nature or fire does not cease to be powerful because it is full of craving and hunger), is the principle, the character of which is severity and rigour ; and it thus provides the " contrarium " to the Love of God, which is His essential definition as God. God, as God, is pure Light, absolute Goodness and Benevolence ; but viewed in relation to His power in the " centrum naturæ," He is a Consuming Fire. In God Himself, in His life of inward self-manifestation, wrath as such never appears. Sternness and severity lie in complete concealment within the harmony of the whole. But, when God comes into relation with the created and sinful world, a severance takes place, and God manifests Himself in duality, both according to His Love and according to His Wrath. And here we may recal the words of the apostle : " The Wrath of God is revealed from heaven against all ungodliness and unrighteousness of men, who hold the truth in unrighteousness." The apostle is here alluding to the power of the Wrath of God, and we cannot but reflect upon the forces that are sent forth to spread destruction and ruin, as a punishment for the sins of men. We may think of the cherubim in Ezekiel, chap. x., who move between the wheels, and take a coal out of the fire, which is to be cast over Jerusalem, as a righteous judgment upon it. We may also recal the words of Scripture, that " we by nature are the children of wrath," words which signify not only that the Divine displeasure rests upon us, or even that the Divine chastisement must ever go forth against us, but also that *within ourselves* there is the power of wrath and rigour, viz., our wild desires and fiery dispositions, whereby we belong to the Kingdom of Wrath. In a little unfinished work of Böhme's, which is called

" Theosophical Questions, or 177 Questions on Divine Revelation," of which, however, Böhme had only answered fifteen before he was removed by death, occurs the following : "Had the Foundation of Hell a beginning in time, or did it exist from eternity ?   Does it endure eternally or not ? " And the answer is, " The Foundation has been from eternity, but not in manifestation, for the wrath of God has existed from eternity, although not as *wrath*, but it has existed, just as fire is latent in a tree or stone, until it is aroused."   The rousing, the kindling, or the opening of the Dragon's mouth took place at the Fall of Lucifer, as in a creature in whom self-will or the " No " turned itself away from the " Yes."   But because this secondary cause has sprung from an eternal foundation, and has an eternal will, it can by no means pass away.   Oetinger, who in his work on the " Princess Antonia's Doctrinal Picture (Lehrtafel)," has attempted a solution of the whole 177 Questions, diverges from Böhme in his reply to this last-mentioned and most difficult eschatological question (whether Hell can ever pass away ?) ; we shall return to it in the sequel.*

----

* Antonia was a princess in Würtemberg (+ 1679), who caused a large picture, representing the Kabbalistic doctrine in episodes, symbols, and metaphors, to be painted and hung in the church at the Baths of Deinach and Wildbad.   The painting has two divisions, a House and a Garden.   The House represents the Old Testament dispensation ; the Garden the New Testament dispensation, with Christ as its central figure.   The princess had this picture set up in the church, in order that it might induce visitors to the baths to seek health for their inward man at the heavenly fountains.

Oetinger (+ 1782) gave an interpretation of this picture, remarking, however, at the same time, that there is a certain

XXV.

As we are now leaving "the dark point," let us not omit to repeat what Böhme reiterates again and again, that God is light, and in Him is no darkness. "But now, thou mayest say, is there in God also a contrary Will or opposition among or between the Spirits of God? I answer: No! though I show here their earnest birth, how earnestly and severely the Spirits of God are generated, whereby every one may very well understand the great earnest severity of God ; yet it does not therefore follow that there is a disunion or discord among them. In God all the spirits triumph as one spirit, and one spirit always mitigates and loves the other, and so there is nothing but mere joy and delight. But their severe Birth or Geniture, which is effected or done in secret, must be so " (" Aurora," ch. x.).

---

incongruity in the idea of representing these things in a painting. A painting is *still ;* but the Divine things are full of life and movement, are in a perpetual process, in a "perpetuo fieri." A far better symbol of the sources and powers of life is to be found in the natural springs themselves, in their great multiplicity and variety, salt-springs and sulphur-springs, sour, bitter, and sweet (James iii. 11), which suggest the contrasts in the eternal Nature in God, and indeed, as Oetinger says, actually include somewhat of that eternal nature, on which account it is that they effect such marvellous results upon our bodies. He whose health is distempered will discover here that which will restore him to "temperature ;" he who suffers from too much acid will find a species of earth which absorbs the acid; he who suffers from an internal stoppage will find the solvent forces, etc.

The Princess Antonia was celebrated for her learning. She read Hebrew fluently, and was deeply versed in the Kabbala.

XXVI.

AND now to return to the doctrine of the Trinity. For the whole natural process, which has been indicated, forms the medium for the manifestation of the Trinity. We began with the Abyss, in which a Will arose. This Will sought and found a mirror (the Eternal Idea), in which it beheld itself as a possibility of becoming three-fold in an infinite $\pi\lambda\acute{\eta}\rho\omega\mu\alpha$. But there were, as yet, no real and actual differences in God. The whole lay simply in a Magia, as a mere image. In order to life, reality, and actual development, there was need of a " contrarium," and this " contrarium " is the eternal Nature. The eternal Will, united with the idea, posits out of itself the eternal Nature, and thereby gains life, actuality, definition, and attributes. Now, in so far as the one eternal Will enthrones itself as Lord over the fire and the might-principle (the primary qualities), God exists as the Father. In so far as the one eternal Will constitutes itself as Lord and Bearer of the Light-principle, which gathers into its unity the plenitude of power that proceeds from the Father, God exists as the Son. Without the Son, the Father would be only a dark valley. But the Father, in His infinite yearning for manifestation and love, begets the Son through the Fire (through the fourth natural property), through the Lightning, begets Him as the Word of Power. In so far as the Father is contemplated without the Son, His character is severity. The Son is gentleness, is the Father's Heart, Love, Light, and Beneficence.

He unlocks a second "Principium," and is, as it were, the Janitor in the Holy Trinity. For it is when the Son unlocks the second "Principium" that Love first becomes a flowing current, and everything is enabled to stand in the fire of pure and heavenly Love. He reconciles the austere and angry Father, and makes Him loving and compassionate. It is only in His union with the Son that the Father is Love and Compassion ; for in the Son's "centrum" there is nothing but pure joy, love, and delight. But from the Father and the Son proceeds the *Spirit*, for, when the light of God is born in the Father, so, in the kindling of the light in the fifth property, there goes forth a Spirit, rich in love, odorous, and of pleasant taste. The Spirit is the eternal Will, in so far as this sets itself as Lord over the principles of Fire and Light in their union, and develops, shapes, and fashions the manifoldness which is contained in the Son, confirms and ratifies the eternal Birth of the Trinity. The Holy Spirit is an Artist (Sculptor, Modeller), fashioning, shaping, and completing. And thus God is one single inseparable Being, but is three-fold in variety of Person, one God, one Will, one Heart, one Desire, one Joy, one Beauty, one Lord, one Omnipotence, one Plenitude of all things, without beginning, without end ("Three Principles," sect. 35).

Böhme consequently implies, that the one eternal Will, which arose in the Abyss, unfolds itself into absolute personality, by means of the eternal Nature. He cleaves to the unity. There is only one God, only one absolute Personality. But in the one absolute Personality, there are three Will-centres, three centres of manifestation, three springs of movement, by which Böhme means what church doctrine calls Persons or Hypostases. Until we have reached the idea of the eternal Nature, we cannot speak of Three Persons or "centra." These are simply beheld in the mirror as possibilities. They can gain manifestation, as "centra," only in the eternal Nature, which implies varieties, and the discharge of its own characteristic function or office by each of the three Persons.

But to God as the one central Being in three centres of manifestation, there corresponds an infinite Periphery, which is a fourth composite part of the Trinity. Böhme teaches that there is in God not simply a Ternary, but also a Quaternary. By "Ternary" we are now thinking of the Trinity, not of the other "ternaries" that have been discussed in the nature-process. But a fourth element belongs to the Trinity, not a fourth Person, but an impersonal thing, which is different from God and is yet inseparable from Him, viz., the eternal product which is developed through the process, and which we have already spoken of as the seventh Natural Property, the Glory of God, the Uncreated Heaven, which Böhme sometimes also designates as the essential, *i.e.*, as Wisdom evolved into actuality, the Maiden that generates nothing, but merely reflects, or beams back the Triune God, His image and His whole developed riches. In the "still mystery" the Maiden stood before God, and displayed to Him all His hidden wonders; and now she shines forth in manifestation. The Maiden, the Wisdom, the Glory, the Uncreated Heaven, the diffused extension of the Power of God is visibly symbolized, in the created world, by the starry sky. Whereas theology usually counts only Three in God,—Father, Son, and Holy Spirit,—and then proceeds at once to the Created World, Böhme says, Father, Son, and Holy Spirit, these Three ; but the fourth is the Glory of God, God's own Uncreated Heaven ; and only *after* this can we begin to speak of the Created World. Böhme (and still more his disciple Oetinger) sharply rebukes the theologians, because they pass immediately and at once from the Triune God to the Creation and the Created World, deal so loosely and superficially with the conception of the Glory of God ($\delta\delta\xi a$), and defraud God of His Heaven, notwithstanding the fact that, in the New Testament, everything points to this, and, so to speak, converges upon it. Böhme and Oetinger remind us that in the New Testament God is called "the Lord of Glory" (Eph. i. 7).   He is not called the Creator of Glory, for the Glory is uncreated.   He is called the Father of lights, from whom cometh every good gift and every perfect gift.   This Light is not created light, it is not stars or created spirits ; it is Uncreated Light, the seven lamps of Fire burning eternally before the Throne, the seven Spirits of God, *i.e.*, the seven eternal fundamental powers that penetrate and illuminate the infinite multiplicity of the riches of the Glory of God.   God energizes in the Created World with the powers of His Glory, and reveals Himself both according to His wrath and according to His love.   In a certain degree, and under various symbols, God revealed His Glory to the prophets. But, as Oetinger strongly emphasizes, no one prophet ever beheld the Glory of God exactly like another, and no two saints have precisely the same vision of it.

In harmony with the above exposition we must draw a distinction, even in the life of the Divine inward manifestation, between an internal and an external, an esoteric and an exoteric, between mystery and revelation. The *internal* is that primal "still mystery" in which as yet God exists, so to speak, only in mystic self-contemplation, and in the magical self-mirroring, the tranquil wisdom, where God, in pure introspection, converses only with Himself, without expressing Himself, or rather, simply ponders within Himself what He can become (λόγος ἐνδιάθετος). The *external* is manifestation through the eternal nature, where the will is active, where God expresses Himself in the Word, as the Word of Power (λόγος προφορικός). When it is said of the created world, in the Psalms, "The heavens declare the glory of God, and the firmament showeth forth His handiwork," this is but a later analogy of what had previously occurred in the Uncreated Heaven, through which the Word and the Spirit resound. God is the true God only as He is the unity of the internal and external, of Mystery and Manifestation. There is here an eternal going-forth and an eternal entering-in. God eternally goes forth out of His inwardness to manifest Himself in externality, and from this externality He again returns, enriched, into the tranquil inwardness. This, however, Böhme does not explain more fully, because it is impossible for us to know God outside nature. Outside nature, the Deity is called Majesty ; but within nature He is called Father, Son, and Holy Ghost ; Wonderful,. Counsel, Power ! " for whatsoever is without nature could in no wise help me. I could not in eternity either see, feel, or find it, because I am in nature and generated from nature (" Dreifaches Leben," iv., cap. 86-88). Böhme can recognise nothing as living, unless it be in nature, in these concrete differences and varieties. He ends, therefore, with an Unutterable, an Ineffable !

Thus far the highly-enlightened layman, whose doctrine of God, the Being of all beings, we have now endeavoured to reproduce ! Let us proceed to inquire how far we can formally accept this doctrine.

CRITICAL RETROSPECT.

XXVII.

THE RELATION TO THE ETHICAL CONCEPTION OF GOD.

IF we compare the doctrine of the Trinity, here set forth, with the Church doctrine, as the latter is presented to us in the Athanasian symbol, we perceive an immense difference.

Let us, however, first emphasize the unity and harmony of the two doctrines. Böhme presupposes the truth of the Church doctrine of the Trinity, wishes to be in agreement with it, and believes himself to be so. He demands One God in Three Persons, unity in trinity, trinity in unity. As it has been objected that the Persons do not attain complete independence in Böhme's scheme, we must repeat that Person and Personality are not the same thing. There is only one God, one Divine Being, one absolute Personality. But the one absolute Personality sets itself in a three-fold form of existence, or of being (Person, Hypostasis). In each of these three forms of existence there is the whole God, the postulate (pre-assumption) of the other two forms of existence or hypostases. The Father is not the Father prior to the Son and the Spirit,

etc., etc. And that this is the sense of the Church
doctrine is evident from the Athanasian symbol,
which expressly states :

> "The Father eternal, the Son eternal, and the
> Holy Ghost eternal, and yet they are not
> three eternals, but one eternal, as also there
> are not three incomprehensibles, nor three
> uncreated, but one uncreated, and one in-
> comprehensible. The Father is Lord, the
> Son Lord, and the Holy Ghost Lord, and
> yet not three Lords, but one Lord. For
> like as we are compelled by the Christian
> verity to acknowledge every Person by Him-
> self to be God and Lord, so are we forbidden
> by the Catholic religion to say : There be
> three Gods or three Lords."

On the other hand, stress must be laid upon the
fact that Böhme nowhere reduces the Persons to
mere forces or attributes. So long as the question
is simply that of abstract harmony with the Church
doctrine, then, whatever defects of detail there may
be in his evolution of the doctrine, it is scarcely
possible to point out any vital contradiction.
But what is characteristic of Böhme, and what
constitutes the chief-interest of his conception of
God, and distinguishes it from many other speculative expositions, is his deviation from the Church
doctrine when he states his acceptance of it in fresh
terms.

For if we compare Böhme's doctrine of the
Trinity with that which is contained in the otherwise so admirable Athanasian symbol, the latter
displays to us the most abstract metaphysic, a God

for mere thought, in whom there is nothing sympathetic for the heart of man and for his religious and ethical consciousness. Böhme, on the contrary, reveals to us a living Trinitarian God, a God in whom there is a Nature, a God who eternally produces not only Himself, but also His Heaven, and in whose Life, independent of the Created World, there is, at the same time, an inward and an outward, an esoteric and an exoteric mystery and manifestation.

And since this God is a Spirit, Böhme shows us that this Spirit is the ethical Spirit, that this Triune God is the God of goodness, is the eternal Love, of which there is absolutely no hint whatever in the Athanasian symbol, which moves exclusively in purely logical categories. By this relation of his to the human heart and affections, Böhme's doctrine of the Trinity is in coherence with the Reformation, and with the Evangelical Church. We have, indeed, affirmed that Theosophy contains a super-confessional element, as is proved, so far as Böhme is concerned, by the fact that his greatest and most congenial exponent, Franz Baader, is a Roman Catholic. Still it must be added that Böhme, notwithstanding the free attitude which he adopts towards all narrowness and literalism of creed, points back, precisely here in his doctrine of the Trinity, to that characteristic form of the religious consciousness which was kindled into activity by the Reformation.

XXVIII.

It has been justly said that the Reformation, in so far as dogmatics are concerned, bequeathed an unfinished task, inasmuch as it only developed from its fundamental principle the anthropologico-soteriological dogmas, *i.e.*, the religious tenets that deal with sin and grace and man's need of redemption, but left untouched the more distinctively theological doctrines. It accepted the doctrine of the Trinity, simply as an inheritance transmitted from the past, and the consequence was that there occurred a "hiatus" between the anthropological and the theological. The new principle penetrated and inspired only the anthropological side, while the theological remained absolutely untouched. Consequently, in the course of time, the doctrine of the Trinity began to stand in foreign relations to human consciousness and was treated with ever-increasing indifference,—an indifference which, in the case of many thinkers, passed over into avowed hostility. If the doctrine of the Trinity is to become actually significant to the religious consciousness, and is to be brought into union with it, the doctrine itself must assume an ethical character, the Triune God must become the God of goodness, must become Love, a fact which had been previously recognized by such mediæval thinkers as Richard of St. Victor. The Apostles' Creed appeals to us to form this conception of God. The pre-assumption is that there is one God who is Saving Love. But this One Saving Love reveals Himself to us in three causalities who effect our salvation: the Father, Son, and Holy Ghost. The problem which Christian faith undertakes is to conceive these Three in unity, and the unity in trinity, to conceive of God as the One who in Himself is Love, amid Trinitarian varieties. Nothing would be more subversive of the faith than to suppose that God only manifested Himself *to us* as Love, revealed Himself to us under three masks, but that *in Himself* He was not Love, was perhaps in His appalling solitude something wholly other than Love. And yet, even among the Reformers themselves, when they discuss the doctrine of Election, one finds a distinction drawn between the revealed Will and the secret Will of God : there is a *revealed* Will, in accordance with which God desires that all men shall come to the knowledge of the truth, and shall be saved, and a *secret, unsearchable* Will, in accordance with which He wills that some men shall be lost, because He does not extend to them the mighty aid of His grace in accepting salvation. Nor is it in Calvin alone that we find this dualism between the revealed Will and the secret Will, which latter Will transcends and prevails over the Will of Love, and is higher than this, an unsearchable, super-ethical Wisdom into which we may not and dare not intrude ; we find the same thing in some passages of Luther. For Luther, who is no friend of speculation, enjoins us again and again to confine ourselves to the God who is preached (Deus praedicatus), to contemplate God in Christ, in the Christ who lies as a child in Mary's bosom, and hangs upon the Cross of Calvary, and to feel absolute confidence that such as we see God in Christ, such is God in Himself. Nevertheless, in his work " De Servo Arbitrio " Luther speaks of the Hidden Will, in the sense above alluded to. But if this painful dualism is to be overcome, it must lead us to strive after the knowledge of the ethical, after the apprehension of

Love as the Being or Nature of God, as God in Himself, who has nothing higher above Him ; it must lead us to strive after a comprehension of the ethical as the ruling factor, the hegemonic, in God, and to view the logical and physical, the Wisdom and the Power, as attributes of Goodness and Love ; it must conduct us not simply to a logical and physical, but to an ethical Trinity.

While the Apostolic symbol already . demands this ethical conception of . God (which does not . exclude, but includes, the logical and physical), this demand is even more firmly defined by the religious consciousness which was evoked at the Reformation. The personality, which is regenerated and redeemed in Christ, and which moves in the contrast between sin and grace, must necessarily behold the principle and eternal pattern of this contrast in God Himself— a fact which certainly does not imply that it must behold sin in God Himself.. But it *does* imply that one must behold the contrasts of the Divine manifestation which stream into human consciousness, and the unison of these contrasts in God's own inward life. It must behold in the inner Life of God the contrast between · Law and Gospel, between the ethically necessitated and the ethically free, between Holiness and Grace, Righteousness and Mercy, and also the unity and harmony of these contrasts. Man is created in the image of God, and must consequently have his eternal pattern in God. But this especially applies to the new man, who is regenerated in Christ, and who is destined to be ever increasingly developed into likeness with God. In proportion as we are enabled to indicate in God Himself the contrasts of manifestation, which constitute the regenerated personality, those of which that personality has the most vivid experience, and in which it lives and moves, and in proportion as we succeed in bringing these contrasts and their union into association with the trinitarian, the triune in God, the doctrine of the Trinity gains in human interest, and is brought more closely home to us, although some mystery will always cling to it, some veil that we cannot lift.   This is the problem which forces itself with growing urgency upon all modern theology and upon all philosophy of religion that really deserves the name.*   And, although under certain limitations, Böhme may be regarded as a pioneer of this endeavour.   The Living God, whom he seeks to apprehend, is none other than the God of the Gospel, in whom he believes as his Rock and his Redeemer.   He is anxious to state a conception of God that may fill that hiatus between the theological and anthropological sides of the dogmatic development which was bequeathed by the Reformation ; he seeks to unite the theological and the anthropological.   It is true that he does not seek this by the method of scientific reflection, but only in an instinctive, immediate, and simple-hearted manner.   He seeks the Living God, but always pre-supposes that this God is the God

---

* Among modern theologians, there is no one who has so clearly and profoundly pointed out that the doctrine of the Trinity must be developed in this direction, if it is to fulfil the principle of the Reformation, or who has himself offered so weighty a contribution to the solution of the problem, as Dorner in his remarkable treatise : "Christliche Glaubenslehre," 1879.

of Christian revelation, whom he knows in his evangelical consciousness. The central point in his conception of God is God as Love. And, as must be very specially emphasized, he rediscovers in the Life of God Himself the very contrast in which the regenerated human personality moves. There is certainly somewhat here that needs clearing up, and that presents itself only in vague fermentation. Close regard must be paid to Böhme's intention. One main contrast, which we have already noticed in God, and which merits the closest attention, is the contrast between the Wrath of God and the Love of God. Böhme speaks of a reconciliation in God; the Son propitiates the severe and wrathful Father. Böhme himself, this devout soul, knows from his own experience, from the conflicts and anxieties of his own inward life, the wrath of God and the power of the wrath of God, the love of God and the might of that love, the severity and the compassion of God; he finds in God the union of these attributes, and gives them a Trinitarian application, inasmuch as the Father is the Bearer of the principle of severity (the Fire-principle); the Son is the Bearer of the principle of gentleness (the Light-principle); and the Spirit is the Bearer of the union of both. In the eternal nature in God Böhme sees a pattern for created nature. But everything that is simply nature must be born twice, must be transmuted. From careful study of Böhme's statements of the conception of God (of which we have been able to give only a brief outline) one gains a prevailing impression that his God is, in His inmost Being, *kindred to man*, as man is kindred to God. And we recognize, throughout, the pulse-beat of a believing man, who is anxious about his own salvation and that of his fellow-men. His speculation streams forth from the deepest practical inspiration, for he has fled to the Heart of God in order to hide himself from the fury and tempest of the Devil. And, in the course of his metaphysical elucidations of the Being of God, he glances aside at the terrible Fall of Lucifer and Adam, and exhorts men to work out their salvation with fear and trembling. This practical momentum, this reference to salvation with which Böhme's speculations are saturated, may be regarded as the mystical element in him. But it is Protestant ethical mysticism, not pantheistic mysticism, as is so frequently the case with the mediæval mystics.

We have, at the same time, serious objections to urge against Böhme's doctrine—objections which, if they are proved to be well grounded, will show that this doctrine is not to be immediately accepted as the truth, but that it needs to be purified and "transmuted." It is true that there are thinkers of considerable reputation who are of opinion that the perfect truth is here presented, and that the fundamental view is correct, simply needing to be restated in a more scientific form. We, however, cannot but maintain that the fundamental view suffers from indistinctness, and this in very important particulars. The limitation in Böhme's theory is, that he postulates the ethical conception of God instead of working it out as his express subject. And the consequence of this is that his gold is mixed with slag. We detect

Böhme's weakness at the very point where he is peculiarly strong,—viz., in his treatment of the eternal Nature as the instrument of the Spirit. Our objection, stated briefly and generally, is this: that although Böhme, in his deepest intention and in harmony with the inmost yearning of his heart, seeks the ethical, and regards Love as the highest thing in God, he is nevertheless so engrossed with the eternal Nature that this, in point of fact, gains undue predominance over the ethical, and improper independence of it. Although the Living God whom he seeks—"My soul thirsteth after God, after the Living God"—is Spirit, ethical Spirit, absolute Personality, still Böhme is so enamoured of the natural form of life, that the Spirit, and the independent life of the Spirit, do not receive their due. He overlooks the fact that, in relation to the Spirit, life is only the secondary thing, only the predicate, although certainly a necessary predicate, and that life, viewed purely in and for itself, is merely a physical category. Thus in St. John's Gospel it is not said: "In the beginning was the *life*," but: "In the beginning was the *Word*," which points to God as Spirit. Not until after this statement do we read: "In this (Word) was the Life." Briefly, according to our judgment, Idealism, or Spirituality, does not receive its full rights in Böhme; Realism, the natural aspect, remains unduly predominant.

Vast as may be the wealth comprised in the idea of *life*, we are not disposed to agree unconditionally with Böhme and Oetinger, that Theology is to be deduced from the idea of life ("theologia ex ideâ vitæ deducta"). For self-consciousness,

spirit, love is not capable of being deduced immediately from life, but is a higher thing, an uncondi-
tional primary, which has life in itself, and takes
shape therein. In any case, spiritual life must not
be deduced from natural life. The idea of "The
Living God" implies not only that there is a nature
in God by means of which He can summon into
existence round about Him a growing and flourishing
life, but also that in God, in His own independent
Life, there is spirituality. To desire the Living God
is to desire the Personal God, the absolute Ego in
the absolute πλήρωμα, which is not, however, to be
so imagined as that the absolute Ego first gradually
evolves itself out of the πλήρωμα as out of a chaos,
but that the absolute Ego, in full independence,
posits and shapes the πλήρωμα out of itself, out of
the depths of its own being. To desire the Living
God is to desire the ethical God, the God who is
not only Might, but Righteousness and Goodness, the
God to whom prayer can be made. The spontaneous
religious consciousness demands this, nor will it give
the name of the Living God either to a God who
becomes in time, or to a God who is deaf and dumb.
And the history of philosophy shows that the same
demands have been made by the men who have
maintained, in this domain, the conception of the
Living God. In the history of modern philosophy
we may allude to Jacobi, as a memorable witness
for the Living God. When Jacobi says to Fichte,
who denied the personality of God : " Blessed is the
man for whom the old simple assurance 'By the
Living God !' is always the highest," he means the
God of goodness and righteousness, who from all

eternity says *I* to Himself, and whose arm is not shortened. Thus it must certainly be recognized, as Jacobi did not recognize, that if the manifestation of the Living God is to be complete, there must also be a *nature* in God, for, otherwise, He would lack organs of manifestation, and we could not speak of "an arm which is not shortened."

We will now consider more closely Böhme's definition of the relation between the Eternal Nature and the Eternal Spirit.

XXIX.

RELATION BETWEEN THE ETERNAL NATURE AND THE ETERNAL SPIRIT.

IT must be admitted that, when Böhme pourtrays God in the Still Mystery, in inward contemplation, and makes the transition to Nature subsequent to and dependent upon this, he ranks Spirit above Nature, and defines it as prior to Nature. But the truth herein expressed is again obscured by the fact that this condition is as yet to be viewed as merely potential, that God possesses Himself only as a possibility, and that the varieties in God are not actual, and, consequently, we have not yet arrived at a Triune God. We cannot as yet, as he says, speak of three Persons, but only of three energies or operations. The varieties and differences are, so to speak, involved and entangled in each other.. We are at present only in the undefined Unity. God, as yet, exists only in a vague "unio mystica" with Himself. It is Life, and yet not life, only a figure or schema of life. God does not become the

Living God until the eternal Nature arises; the general process does not begin until the eternal Nature bursts forth. It is only by means of Nature that God becomes trinitarian. In the Still Mystery and the inward self-contemplation, God is absorbed in mystic introspection, in half-dreamy, half-darkened self-consciousness. What we lack is, that God is not, from the outset, pure and perfect self-consciousness, which is not merely dreamy and imaginative, but meditative and apprehensive in the undarkened clearness of the varieties and separations.

This, then, is our present objection, that Spirit—although Böhme ranks it above Nature, and although it is Spirit itself that posits Nature—is permitted to borrow its life from Nature. Now, while we admit that Spirit cannot attain complete life or perfect energy without Nature, we must still regard the doctrine—that Spirit without Nature is merely potential, a life and yet no life, a shadow and figure of life—as conflicting with the essential character of Spirit. We cannot but maintain that the personal God, even *prior* to Nature (employing the expression *prior* not in a temporal sense, but to denote the relation of superiority and subordination), is the Living God. Life is energy, self-movement, self-mediation, as the result of an inward force, for mechanical movement is not life. Indeed, the more powerful is this inward indwelling force, the more independent and perfect is the life. But the same thing applies to Spirit. Self-movement and self-development with conscious self-determination must be predicated of Spirit; and the greater the indwelling power, the more Spirit moves and energizes ·from within itself and by itself, independent of all else, the greater, mightier, and more living is Spirit. The highest Spirit, the Spirit of all spirits, the absolute Spirit of God is He who, without limitation,. and in perfect independence of aught else, by His own inward power, energizes Himself and all things, and is, consequently, from the very beginning, " primo actu," the Living God, who posits living nature out of Himself, as His medium and instrument.

Böhme repeatedly affirms that Life depends upon contrast (" contrarium "), but the " contrarium " without which God cannot be living and actual is, on Böhme's view, nothing but Nature. We, however, bearing in mind the Christian conception of God, must maintain that the eternal Spirit, purely as Spirit, has its own " contraria "· independently of nature. God as Spirit, or God in the Still Mystery, is, for Böhme, only universal will,. or the will of unity, the mystic freedom which, at root, wills nothing, and can only become a definite Will through the agency of Nature. According to .Böhme, God first acquires His *Egoism* by His ·conquest of Nature. But, from the standpoint of revealed truth, it must be maintained that God, apart from, and outside of, Nature, is self-concentrated Egoism (which is certainly very different from simply natural Egoism with its morbid restlessness), viz., the holy self-harmonious Egoism which is inseparable from eternal Love. God, as absolute Personality, is at the same time Individual Being, distinguishing itself from all else, and He is also Universal and General Being, the Being that in itself is good and true, the

Being whose volition is all-valid, the Universal Will; and this contrast between God as Individual Will and as Universal Will (with its corresponding contrast between God as *Self*-consciousness and *all*-consciousness) finds its harmonious reconciliation in the absolute Spirit.

And if we meditate upon the *ethical* Being of God, is it not true that this ethical Being contains its own immanent contrasts? as, *e.g.*, the contrast between the ethically necessitated and the ethically free, between the Glory and the Love of God, between His Independence and Self-exaltation (which may also be defined as God's righteousness towards Himself) and His Goodness, Self-abnegation, and Self-communication? Does not Scripture point out to us the contrast in the ethical Being of God between the jealous God, who wills and asserts His own Honour, and the long-suffering God, the God of Love, Compassion, and Consolation, the union of Severity and Gentleness in the same God? We will not enter here upon the doctrine of the Divine attributes; but we maintain that God, as Spirit, possesses life and contrasts in Himself, independently of, and prior to, nature. We deny that God, as Böhme teaches, first acquires attributes by the agency of nature, although this denial by no means excludes the fact that each determination in the spiritual and ethical Being of God has, and must have, a corresponding might-or nature-side.

XXX.

OUR objection to Böhme's definition of the relation between the eternal nature and the eternal spirit thus starts more precisely from this :—that God as Spirit is represented as first acquiring His power (for a Spirit that lies in obscure self-consciousness has no power of its own) by vanquishing a nature which, at the outset, confronted Him in antagonism. We have to emphasize the fact that God, as the absolute Spirit, must be self-powerful, self-conscious, and self-defining, *prior* to the nature which He posits out of Himself; and that there can be no single momentum in His being which is not irradiated and encircled in perfect clearness by this self-consciousness. We must insist that God be conceived as *Causa Sui*, or, as it may also be expressed, that He be conceived under the title of *Aseitas* (Self-caused, independent Being) ; otherwise He is not apprehended as the absolute or all-perfect Being. Undoubtedly, every philosophical system demands that God be thought of as Causa Sui ; but, in point of fact, He is so apprehended only in the ethical conception which regards Him as absolute Personality. For *Causa Sui*, or *Aseitas* (which must be construed not as a single attribute, but as the pervading element in all the attributes of God), implies not simply the negative truth that God has not His cause in any other than Himself, and that He exists in virtue of an internal necessity, but also that He posits Himself, produces Himself, as His own absolute operation and His own absolute object. But Self-positing, Self-production is un-thinkable otherwise than as Self-consciousness and Self-determination. It is only when God is con-ceived as the perfect Personality, as the one Good, as the eternal Love, who has Wisdom and Power

as His attributes, that He can be livingly apprehended as Causa Sui, as His own efficient cause
(Causa efficiens), as His own final cause (Causa
finalis), as His own teleological self-movement, which
posits from within itself all the requisite means for
its manifestation, and is, accordingly, of itself, by
itself, and to itself. We are deeply conscious of
the difficulties which hinder us from conceiving the
Aseitas of God, this self-positing, but also eternally
self-presupposing Ego, which is more precisely defined in its threefold relation to itself and to its
πλήρωμα. But however difficult it may be to
apprehend the Divine *Aseitas*, which is the fundamental condition for the Absolute, we must, nevertheless, imagine what we cannot formulate, and what
is lost from our gaze in excess of light. The difficulty of thinking and imagining the Eternal
Self-Existent One, who has life in Himself, and has
power and potency ceaselessly to renew and to restore
Himself, depends essentially upon the fact that we
have to exclude from this conception the element of
time, and that, nevertheless, our thought and imagination cannot dispense with a beginning. The
Self-existent One incessantly produces Himself, but
never produced Himself for the first time. He
incessantly posits Himself as the absolute Ego in
threefold relation, but yet He never said *I* to Himself for the first time. He produces Himself as His
own result, but the result is equally eternal with
the self-production. He lives in an absolute Present,
from which succession, past and future, is excluded;
and yet, as truly as He is the Living God in ceaseless movement, the elements of *time* must be in

Him, although they are eternally abrogated. In His perfect and blessed Life-movement, He never ceases to begin, never ceases to end, never ceases to go out of Himself, never ceases to return into Himself; and in this harmoniously flowing movement He never ceases to be in perfect rest and undisturbed tranquillity,—at once the Living and the Unchangeable God. Even though there be something here which we cannot grasp, and which we hope to approach more closely when we ourselves shall have exchanged time for eternity, and thus, released from our present enthralled condition, shall be more fully able to live and think in the forms of eternity, we are nevertheless under the necessity of conceiving even now (unless everything about us is to slip into confusion) the Self-Powerful, the Self-Existent, the Self-Producing. And for this very reason we ought to guard ourselves most carefully against the admission of definitions which imperil the conception of the Self-Mightiness and the Self-Production.

The final and insuperable word on this subject is the word of the Lord to Moses: "I am that I am! say unto the children of Israel: *I am* hath sent me!" This word, however, must be interpreted in a living sense, and not in a dead one. When a *creature* says: "I am that I am," the phrase merely expresses the simple identical proposition, that this created individuality remains, amid all changes, the same and not another. But, when it is uttered by God, its meaning is infinitely vaster. It implies not only the *identity* of His Being, but that He Himself is the *Principle* of His Being. He hereby defines

Himself as the Absolute, the All-Perfect, the Fundamental Being, as the One who was before all things,
the One who is, and who is to be, and this not
only of necessity, but also with freedom, complete
self-consciousness, and self-determination. That God
is the Being existent from all eternity does not
mean that He happens upon Himself as the necessary Being, prior to His self-determination. Nor
does it mean that He meets with eternal truths,
eternal laws, unalterable by God Himself, as a
necessity imposed upon Him from without (which
would imply the subjection of God to Fate!);
nor does it mean that He arbitrarily ordains
these universally-valid laws. It means that all
the momenta in His Being are free, and have
His absolute Will as their principle; that this
necessity, this universal validity, these eternal laws
are the internal attributes, the internal essential
determinations of His Will. It means that these
laws are not outside God, but in God, inherent in
His nature. Consequently, when we say that His
Being is one with His eternal Self-production, we
imply that God or the Absolute is the Absolute
Personality. For only absolute Personality is sus-
ceptible of these predicates, which are totally inap-
plicable to the creature ; viz., *Causa Sui* and *Aseitas.*

XXXI.

PANTHEISM is unable to apprehend God as *Causa
Sui*, or as the eternally Self-positing and Self-
producing. In Spinoza, Causa Sui is essentially
only a negative conception. It merely asserts that

God has not His cause in another, outside of God. The God of Spinoza is not His own cause, does not energize Himself and produce Himself, but is simply abstract lifeless Being, a blindly necessary substance. Life and process are lacking in Spinoza: in his God there is no living fountain, no spring of self-production and self-renewal. That Spinoza cannot conceive *Causa Sui* is due to the fact that he excludes the idea of teleological cause. For absolute cause, as living and active, must be that which energizes itself, as its own absolute goal. Nor can the higher teleological Pantheism of Schelling and Hegel (whose God is a *becoming* God) define God as Causa Sui, or as efficient or teleological cause. It recognizes only a blind and passive basis, whether it be an obscure nature-basis, as in Schelling, or a logical basis, as in Hegel, from which God comes forth in an infinite process, in which process, however, God never succeeds in actualizing Himself, because there subsists an eternal dualism between the ideal and the real. It is only the ethical conception of God, the conception which views God as the eternally self-realizing, and in Himself eternally realized Goodness and Love, that can hold God to be His own cause (causa efficiens et causa finalis). And, high as Böhme stands above all pantheistic conceptions of God (inasmuch as he defines God as Spirit in inward self-contemplation, independent of temporal existence, and prior to the eternal nature itself), still he is clearly influenced here by the pantheistic *typus*, as is proved by the fact that, instead of beginning with God mighty in Himself, and existing from the very first, instead of allowing self-consciousness and

Love to mediate themselves by their own instrumentality, he begins by defining God as potentiality, as dreamy self-consciousness, which requires the aid of Nature, before it can gain life, reality, and power of its own.

XXXII.

AND in connection with this stands another point to which we cannot assent ; viz., that Böhme regards the first link in the theogonistic process as an Abyss, a Chaos, an undeveloped πλήρωμα, wherein nature and spirit repose as yet in complete indifference, where there is neither light nor darkness, good nor evil, and where all varieties and differences are dormant. We are well aware that Böhme does not hold that this Abyss is to be hypostatized as independent and outside the other momenta ; and we also know that the idea of temporal succession must be excluded. Nevertheless, Böhme demands that we begin by thinking and picturing to ourselves this *mysterium magnum*, this stillness without reality, this indifference of Spirit and Nature, God and the World, because the whole creation is germinally enfolded in this, and Father, Son, and Spirit are here, although at present quiescent. We maintain, on the contrary, that we are not called upon to embark on a train of thought of this heathen, pantheistic, and cosmogonic type, and that we shall gain nothing by doing so. If we would conceive of the ethical God, the God of Christianity, who is Love, we must begin by conceiving of God as the Being who is real and actual from the very outset. In the true

God, actuality is prior to potentiality, and embraces the conception of all potentialities, while in the World, infinitude, potentiality always precedes actuality. Pantheistic thought transfers to God Himself this earthly cosmogonic relation, in which the world springs out of chaos. We shall find it easier to grasp the truth that God is the self-existent Being (*Aseitas*) if we assign to Him a postulate inherent in His very Being, a ground out of which He comes forth (cf. Schelling's " Treatise on Freedom"). But it remains totally inexplicable how a God, who is Love, can come forth out of Böhme's " Abyss." Böhme says that in this Abyss there arises a Will, which proceeds to define itself as eternal Freedom and eternal God. But, here, precisely the same difficulty recurs. Whence this Will? We say : The Abyss with the vague emergence of a Will is not the first thing ; nor ought it to be conceived of as the first. The first thing is the eternally self-predicating Spirit in its supremacy over all its possibilities, a predication and a postulate which is hidden from us in the light of eternity. " Say unto the children of Israel : ' *I am* hath sent me ! ' "

Kant says in his " Critique of Reason : " " The thought is unavoidable, and yet intolerable, that a Being, whom we conceive as the Highest among all possible beings, says to Himself, as it were : ' I am from eternity to eternity ; outside Me there is nothing except that which by My Will has become something ; but—whence am I? Here everything sinks beneath us ! " The *intolerable*, however, consists simply in this, that Kant here makes the Highest Being think in the category of finite causality, in accordance with which whatever exists had a prior cause. He might with equal justice have made the Highest Being think in the category of finite purpose (finite teleology), and ask Himself: "Wherefore am I, and to what end?" For, in the sphere of finitude, we ask such questions as these. The truth, however, is, notwithstanding Kant's un-demonstrated and indemonstrable assertion of the inapplicability of our categories to the Unconditioned, that we have in God the absolute cause and the absolute goal, where all further question of Whence and Whither must cease. For we have here reached that from which everything has its origin, and unto which everything is, that which gives to all else its purpose and its meaning, that precisely which makes it possible for us to ask the questions *whence* and *whither*. But assuredly we have not reached this, unless God is the absolute Personality, the Good, the Eternal Love.

Schelling, in his "Philosophy of Revelation," says that, if our thought is to find its satisfaction, we must venture upon the question: Wherefore is Thought? To what purpose is it? This and all kindred questions will be answered if we are able to point out an absolute Final Cause. This is given to us only in the Good. Thought is not the final end; but Thought, Beauty, Life, Nature, Order, and Design exist *because* of the existence of the Good, which can only be real in a Will; they exist because Love is, and is to be. Here there can no longer be the question: "Cui bono?" for we have named the absolutely valid and valuable, which conditions all other values, or that with reference to which all else is. To ask what lies above this is a contradiction in terms, because it is to ask for that which is higher than the Highest. In the same way, it is self-contradictory to ask what is the cause of that which is the cause of all else. This "Cause of all" is described by Plato as the Good, which in the visible world brings forth light, and in the invisible extends to us the truth. God as the absolute Personality—who, in the teleological cycle of eternity, where beginning and end coincide, is His own efficient cause, His own final cause, and who possesses in Himself all the means that are requisite for His manifestation—is the only Self-Intelligible Being. When the Highest Being asks Himself (according to Kant) : "Whence am I?" the reply (according to Böhme) must be : "I am from the Abyss, and have established or grounded Myself." But if this were the whole explanation, God would not be Self-Intelligible. God can be the Self-Grounded only when, in addition to being His own basis, He is His own Cause. We must, therefore, constantly insist that the delineation of the Christian conception of God does not begin with an obscure depth, in which (as Böhme says) there is neither good nor evil, but that it begins ethically with Love, with the eternal absolutely-perfect Spirit—a doctrine which does not prevent, but rather demands, that, previous to the delineation of the Christian conception, as in the Fore-Court of the Gentiles, a series of preliminary and preparatory inquiries should be instituted concerning the lower conceptions of God, which are, so to speak, only the rudiments ($\sigma\tau o\iota\chi\epsilon\hat{\iota}a$) of the true, and also concerning the relation between the ethical, logical, and physical elements.

XXXIII.

IT may be noticed, from an historical point of view, that Böhme's doctrine of the Abyss is closely related to that of the Kabbala, which also commences with " God in indifference," Ensoph (not anything), out of which the varieties, the Sephirim or Lights, then stream forth. It also reminds us of the Gnostic *Bythos*, the groundless Abyss which is wedded to Silence, the first *syzygy* in the Valentinian system. This *Bythos* ($\beta u\theta\grave{o}s$) the Gnostics designate as $\pi\rho o\text{-}\pi\acute{a}\tau\omega\rho$, Father before Father, and as $\pi\rho o\alpha\rho\chi\acute{\eta}$, beginning before beginning. They thus conceive of God from the outset as *in potentiâ*, an obscure possibility out of which He evolves Himself into actuality. But this is precisely the conception which must *not* be entertained, if one wishes to think the ethical conception of God. The ethical God, or God as the fundamentally Good, as Love, can have neither father nor mother, for Love is the principle of all paternity and maternity ; and it can, consequently, recognize no $\pi\rho o\pi\acute{a}\tau\omega\rho$, from whom the actual God-Father, who is the fountain of absolute goodness, is generated. When Böhme makes God, as the eternal Love, proceed out of an abyss in which there is neither good nor evil, he states what is inconceivable ; for unless the fundamentally good, the holy Will of Love is actual from the very outset, it will never be able to become so. We repeat : The ethical is the highest ontological, the highest and the primal Being, not simply potential, but actual Being. It is utterly inconceivable that the ethical, that Love, should be allowed to rest in the absolute, as a potentiality which does not become a reality until a *later* moment, and that, consequently, a moment should be affirmed in God (even if only in idea) when Love is only a demand, a "shall be," an unfulfilled craving. Love must, on the contrary, be posited as that which, from the very beginning, is the eternally complete reality. The commencement must be ethical. Unless we *begin* with Consummate Love in perfect reality, we shall never find it. Böhme is influenced here by a theosophem which is of Pagan origin, and which clashes with his own most heart-felt and fundamental idea. We can only express our astonishment that Baader and Hamberger seem to approve of this " Abyss in which there is neither good nor evil." With Schelling, it is quite another matter! For this Gnostic theosophem of the " Abyss," the absolute Indifference, and God in potentiality, harmonized, during his earlier period, with his own doctrine of the " Becoming God." But Aristotle long ago attacked those who supposed that God was generated out of the night ($\gamma\acute{\epsilon}\nu\nu\eta\sigma\iota\varsigma$ $\acute{\epsilon}\kappa$ $\nu\nu\kappa\tau\acute{o}\varsigma$). And it is the abiding service of Jacobi to have maintained, in opposition to Schelling's doctrine of the Abyss, that the Personal God, the God of Goodness, is, from the outset, the absolutely real, that He does not develop Himself from incompleteness to completeness, from potentiality to reality, but is absolutely perfect from the beginning. So far as we are concerned, we add : Every philosophy that seeks to conceive the absolute, the unconditioned Primal and Self-Existent, has its unfathomable mystery. Our mystery is the Holy Love which postulates nothing outside itself, but which possesses in and under itself all things both potential and actual ; our mystery is the Light wherein is no darkness, and which streams from eternity. But this Mystery is all-revealing and all-explaining.

Our objections to Böhme's interpretation of the relation between the Eternal Nature and the Eternal Spirit may be thus summarized : (1) that he regards the absolute Spirit as only potential, until nature supplies contrast, life, and actuality ; (2) that the Spirit first acquires its power by vanquishing a nature that previously confronted it in hostility ; and, finally, (3) that his theogonistic process begins with an indifference of Spirit and Nature, of the ethical and the physical (" there is neither good nor evil "). Taken as a whole, our objection is that he ranks Nature too highly, and ascribes to it too great importance, by making it a necessary condition for the self-conscious Life of God. The importance of Nature is, as will be more fully shown in the sequel, more subordinate and limited, inasmuch as it is a condition and a medium only for God's outwardly-directed energy, for the shaping of the Glory of God, for the external and phenomenal aspect of the Life of God, as an outgoing manifestation, a *manifestatio ad extra*, prior to creation, and is, secondly, a condition and medium for Creation and the Created World. The answer to the question whether nature in God conditions the self-consciousness of God, or whether it is, in absolute dependence upon His self-consciousness and will, merely a medium for His activity, lays the foundation of a grave contradiction within Theosophy itself. But, furthermore, we have to urge a peculiar objection with reference to the dark nature-principle in God. We have already alluded to this as the "dark point" in Böhme. Its enunciation formed an episode in the doctrine of the Trinity. It must also furnish a chapter to our critical review.

XXXIV.

THE DARK NATURE-PRINCIPLE IN GOD.

THE dark antagonistic Nature-principle in God, by the conquest of which God first becomes the Living God, and which can only be brought into the proper relation of subordination by means of conflict, can only thus be placed in its right stratum, is the previously-mentioned negative ternary (Contraction, Expansion, Rotation). It has been variously designated as the "centrum naturæ," "the Wheel of Anguish," "the dimly-burning Triangle," "Fire," "Desire," and "the Foundation of Hell." We must here recal Böhme's fundamental view, that without contrast there is no Life and no Manifestation, but simply passive repose. The principle, which Böhme finds in God, makes its appearance in philosophy under a more general heading, as the Principle of Negativity, the "No-" Principle, the Principle of Negation, which is the condition for Spirit and Life, the forward-impelling element in the process, without which the whole world would stagnate, and remain in dead and motionless tranquillity. "Who knows peace," says Böhme, "who has not known conflict? Who knows joy who has not known pain?" and he transfers this same antithesis to God. The principle of Negativity pervades the entire history of philosophy from the earliest times to the latest. It has been revived, in recent times, by Schelling. "Heaven," he says in his letter to Eschenmayer, "rests upon Hell. Heaven is the supreme peace and concord of the forces. Hell is discord and dissension. Real concord is vanquished discord. Heaven would be lifeless without Hell. There is no possible feeling or perception of Heaven without Hell, without the permanent conquest of the Hell of dissension. Just as there is no feeling of health without the conquest of sickness, which is on the point of manifesting itself, but is continually forced back. If God is to live in a man, the Devil must die in the man." In many ways Schelling has urged that gentleness, mildness, and love are useless unless they come forward and arise on the foundation of strength, severity, and wrath, because it is only thus that they can acquire the stamp of definite character; he urges that it is impossible for us to feel respect for the sheepish gentleness which is found in many men, and that we can respect and admire only that gentleness which shines forth out of vanquished and subdued passions. He has often repeated that the noblest manifestation of beauty of soul is that which is afforded by tranquil strength amid the tempest of the passions. Not only in his "Treatise on Freedom," but in many other passages, he reminds us of Jacob Böhme, as when he says that everything that exists is conceived and born in strife, or when he says of God : ".We cannot doubt that the Deity is enthroned over a world of terrors, and that God, so far as concerns what is hidden in Him, must be called, not figuratively but actually, the Dreadful and Terrible." Hegel, akin to Heraclitus, who said that " war is the father of all things," has bestowed the highest eulogy on the Principle of Relativity, and asserts that *Contradiction* is the driving-wheel in the process of life and spirit ; he praises and extols Böhme for having apprehended the principle of Negativity—Contradiction—in God Himself.

But the Christian view can recognize the principle of Negativity as necessary to development only when the Negative is defined as *Contrast*, not as *Contradiction.* In modern philosophy great confusion and arbitrariness is observable in the use of these categories ; contrasts are frequently viewed as contradictions, and contradictions as contrasts. Contrasts are necessary differences which emerge from the essence of the thing, and which mutually demand one another ; *e. g.,* Nature and Spirit, Necessity and Freedom, Self-assertiveness and Self-surrender, Solemnity and Gladness, Severity and Gentleness. But Contradiction is that which ·is repugnant to the essence of the thing, and makes its appearance when the contrast oversteps its limits, assumes false independence, combats its " other," and thereby becomes unlicensed and illegitimate. No moral character can be conceived without inward contrasts. But a character that is full of inward contradictions cannot be approved. A Created World connot be conceived otherwise than as a world of contrasts, but, when a created world displays, like our own, a multitude of contradictions, we infer that disorder has entered this world. If not simply contrast, but also contradiction be necessary to the manifestation of Life, sin and evil must be necessary to the development of the world. This, indeed, is the opinion of Schelling, Hegel, and many others. Evil, it is true, is defined not as the goal, but as the necessary medium for the manifestation of the good. This Evil, this Negative, is itself only a momentum in the process, wherein it is incessantly posited, in order to be incessantly denied and compelled to minister to the manifestation of the light.

The Christian view must indubitably recognize the possibility of evil, if God is to create a world of freedom. But, on the other hand, the actuality of Evil, the real contradiction, can never be acknowledged as reasonable, or as necessarily pertinent to a world brought forth by the Holy God. This would be in diametrical opposition to the nature of the Creator, and of the Creation in the Divine Image.

XXXV.

BÖHME can by no means be accused of teaching the necessity of Evil. But, on the other hand, it is impossible to praise him for consistency in his opposition to the false doctrine. He vehemently defends himself against the view that the Fall of Lucifer and Adam was necessary, and that they could not have resisted the temptation. Again and again he says emphatically, that they fell by their own fault, especially Lucifer, who applied himself to "the selfish art," gave himself to a false imagination, and thereby introduced appalling confusion ("turba") into the world. But we also find passages in Böhme the tendency of which is wholly different, as when he says in his preface to "The Three Principles:" "In all creatures there is a poison and malignity; and it must be so; otherwise there were no life and no mobility, nor would there be any colour nor virtue, thickness nor thinness, or any perception whatever; but all would be as nothing. In this high consideration it is found that all is through and from God Himself, and that it is His own substance, and that He has created it out of Himself. And the Evil belongs to the Forming and mobility, and the good to the Love, and the *austere, severe*, or contrary will belongs to the Joy." We are quite willing to accept the declaration of Baader, Hamberger, and Hofmann, that passages like these, in which Böhme has expressed himself somewhat incautiously, are not to be unfairly pressed, but must be construed by Böhme's predominant view; we readily acknowledge that Böhme's intention was right. Nevertheless, it seems undeniable that Böhme was not perfectly clear upon this point and the great importance of it (which, indeed, is much easier for us moderns, who have encountered so many philosophical stumbling-blocks in the application of this principle of relativity), and that he did not establish a thorough-going distinction between contrast and contradiction, inasmuch as passages are to be found in his works which compel one to say: "The good that he would, he does not; but the evil

which he would not, that he does." The most
erroneous point in Böhme appears to us to be that
in his very conception of God there seems to be a
prelude to the doctrine of the necessity of evil in
order to the manifestation of the Light.

XXXVI.

IF Böhme's conception of God be viewed in its
completeness, and grasped in one intuition, it may
seem as if all on this subject were in due order.
The "Centrum Naturæ," "Wheel of Birth," or
"Worm," which we will now express by the one term
"Nature-Egoity," with its tendency towards self-
centralization, with its yearning after another and
higher than itself, with its consequent self-circling
restlessness, is in its normal bed, and is co-operant to
the manifestation of the Life and the Light. The
multiplicity of powers are all transfigured in the
Light, find pleasure in one another, rejoice over and
bless one another ; and yet each one of them possesses in latency the quality which belongs to it in
consequence of its "sharp birth," and which is concealed in it like a kernel. Just as a sour or bitter
green apple is constrained by the sun so that it becomes pleasant to eat, and still one tastes all its properties, so also in God, in the eternal nature. But
before this harmony is reached, a perilous prelude
has to be gone through.

The "Nature-egoity," in its intrinsic power, places
itself from the beginning in a hostile relation towards
the Light, towards the heavenly Idea which God
desires to shape in Nature. There is an appalling con-

flict, and terrible anguish, and it is only subsequently that a violent transition takes place. Consequently, we have—as the first momentum in the process—a *hostile* contrast in God, which is not different from a contradiction ; and this we cannot but regard as incompatible with the Being of God as the Holy and absolutely-perfect One. Franz Baader, indeed, remarks that Böhme himself has helped to obscure his subject, by beginning his representation with the three first natural Properties, or the negative ternary. According to Baader, one ought to start from the central property, that is, the fourth natural Property or the Lightning, and the three previous ones should be viewed as merely abstract momenta. But even if we begin with the Lightning we begin with a violent breach, with the vanquishing of a hostile contrast. That the contrast at the outset is *hostile* is, moreover, the view of Hamberger, when he says : " Nature as such does not simply furnish a *contrast* to Spirit ; on the contrary, they both stand in contradiction to each other, and are mighty powers which oppose one another with the utmost vehemence." This is the view which we are combating. However far we are from accusing Böhme of Manichæism, we cannot but hold that this doctrine verges upon Manichæism. For this hostile contrast cannot fail to give the impression that something exists by *the side of* God. If unity is to be maintained, God must posit Nature out of Himself ; He may posit as conflicting with Him, as *non*-Divine ; but He cannot posit it as *Anti*-Divine. If it be observed that He posits this contradiction in Himself, in order that He may have something to vanquish ;

that Nature, refractory and insubordinate at the outset, finally yields, first says " No !" and at the next moment says " Yes ! I will subordinate myself, so that I may be liberated from my torture,"—we cannot avoid the conclusion that this supposed episode in God Himself forms a prelude for the doctrine of the necessity of Evil in order to the development of the world.   If it be urged that the blind nature principle in God cannot be called *evil*, since it is only a blind will, not a self-conscious one, we must reply that Nature sustains a relation to the ethical, and must be viewed in its light, and that what is hostile to the ethical cannot be found in the Holy God.   And if it be said that this contradiction of nature against spirit is eternally quenched by the light, we must retort, that it might be said with equal justice that it is as eternally posited ; for we are not discussing a past history in God, but an incessantly self-repeating process.   But this view, that contradiction is posited in order to be eternally vanquished, is precisely the fundamental idea of Hegel and Heraclitus (" War is the Father of all things ").   And on this point it is difficult to distinguish between them and Böhme..

If God, as the Being of all beings, is to be conceived as the Union of Spirit and Nature, He must be so conceived that nature, although it possesses a life of its own, is still absolutely subordinated to spirit, and is its willing servant, instrument, and medium.   It does not begin with rebellion against spirit, but with cheerful subordination.   Böhme says in many passages : " In order that the Holiness and Grace of God may be manifested, there must be

something that needs grace and love." This statement we can readily accept ; and if Böhme had
continued along these lines, there would have been
no ground for opposition. We can illustrate our
meaning more clearly by a reference to Romans
viii. 18, where the apostle speaks of " the earnest
expectation of the creature, and the whole creation
groaning and travailing in pain together." From
this created nature we may transfer our thought
to the Nature in God. Earnest expectation or
longing is the fundamental characteristic of the
creation, even apart from the corruption which has
entered through sin. But this longing would diffuse
itself vaguely in the Infinite (" Expansion "), unless
there were a contrasting force, a force of Egoity
or Self-ness, with a tendency to concentrate itself
and to abide in itself (" Contraction "). But until
the longing has found rest and is tranquillized in the
Higher, Nature, the Creation, is in perpetual restlessness (" Rotation "), because it cannot find peace
and satisfaction in itself. It whirls about itself as
if in travail, because it possesses only a possibility
of the Light, but is itself unable to produce it. The
Light must descend into it from above and quiet its
longing.

We find in the Eternal Nature the same fundamental forces, self-ness, longing, and the unsatisfied,
self-circling, anxious restlessness, which is tranquillized
by the Light that streams into it, and fills the poverty
of Nature with its riches. Nature is eternally
posited as the non-Divine, which needs God, and
the essence of which is *indigentia Dei ;* and this again
repeats itself at a later stage, when God posits

outside Himself a created world and a creaturely existence, and the longing of Nature is eternally stilled. But although Nature's longing is eternally stilled, yet the restlessness of the Nature-Life must continue to circle in the Abyss; for, where there is no perception of the natural self-ness, its poverty and helplessness in itself, and its ceaseless longing, there can be no perception of love and grace, light and peace. We may here recal the " Self-infolding Fire " in Ezekiel, the " Wheel of Birth " in the Epistle of James, Böhme's "Worm," " Triangle," etc., etc., all of which symbols retain their truth when they are kept within proper limits, and present themselves, from the outset, in that legitimate manner which harmonizes with the Being of God.

Where Böhme differs from this is that, in his view, the harmony, the super- and sub-ordination, is only effected by means of a struggle, that the first momentum in the nature process is—or at any rate must be conceived as being—a wild, refractory, titanic effort at independence, which is not checked and changed into longing until a subsequent moment. Our best efforts have not succeeded in gaining any other impression from Böhme's confused and stormy description of the *centrum naturæ;* nor do Baader and Hamberger assist us to any other construction. We find the same train of thought in Schelling, who, independently of Böhme, or without naming him, develops the same idea in his own way, begins with wild desire, and does not suffer longing to enter nature until a later period, and reminds us that the prescient, ancient world expresses this second momentum, this entrance of longing into

Nature by the poetic idea, that the World's Egg, which is born of Night, breaks and parts asunder, and——Eros comes into being.

We venture to remark that longing and egoity, and therewith also restlessness, must be regarded as a single indivisible act, and that, on the pre-assumption of the ethical nature of God, egoity can never (even in idea) appear in the eternal nature in the shape of wild and refractory desire. The Christian conception of God recognises in God only *harmonious* contrasts. In the creation, and in our own life, we certainly perceive nature as a hostile contrast to spirit; for the flesh lusteth against the spirit, and the spirit against the flesh. But this we lament as disorder; we do not regard it as normal. And we see that *in Christ*, from the very first, Nature is the obedient instrument for the Spirit; undoubtedly, He is tempted; the possibility of evil rises in Him; He perceives the possibility of preferring His own Ego to the Father's Will, the cosmical principle to the holy principle. But this temptation, in which the possibility of evil is vanquished and never attains reality, belongs to His development in Humiliation, and finds no place in His Exaltation. When He says to the rich young man: "Why callest thou Me good? None is good save God," He implies that He is subjected as yet to temptation and persecution. But God is not tempted. He is ἀπείραστος κακῶν. In Him there is no conflict; from the very first, His glory consists of eternal harmonies.

XXXVII.

WE maintain that this view of ours is in full harmony with Scripture, which says : "God is Light, and in Him is no darkness at all" (1 John i. 5). Darkness is not the same as natural obscurity or dimness. Darkness is the hostile contrast to Light, and according to the Scripture, Light and Darkness can have no fellowship (2 Cor. vi. 14). Obscurity is not a hostile contrast, just as little as unconscious life is a hostile contrast to self-conscious life, but, on the contrary, is a dim longing after it. There is a pitch-dark night, which is hostile to light and to the day ; and it is this hostile night that is referred to in the old proverb that " the Night is no man's friend," and that, in the night, deeds of darkness are concocted. But there is also a dim and yearning night, which longs for the morning-dawn, and eagerly desires to conceive the light. The opinion of Böhme and his disciples, that they do ample justice to the passage in St. John, by saying that the darkness is eternally quenched by the light, is unsatisfactory. For in order to be eternally quenched, the darkness must either be eternal in itself, or must be eternally posited by God. But Holiness cannot posit that which is hostile to itself, in order to swallow it up. And if there be, from the very beginning, a hostile principle by the side of Holiness, we fall into a semi-Manichæan Dualism, which must be totally rejected. And when, in Böhme's defence, appeal is made to Isaiah xlv. 7 : " I form the light and create *darkness*, I make peace and create *evil*; I, the Lord, do all these things," it must be observed that *darkness*, in this verse, is synonymous with *misfortune*, and that we must understand by it the calamities in which the Wrath of God manifests itself, His punitive righteousness. Compare it with the passage in Amos : " Shall there be evil (trouble) in a city, and I the Lord have not done it ? " Nor do we forget that the words : " I form the light and create darkness ! " may perhaps contain a protest against that Persian dualism which taught two fundamental principles—Good and Evil. The words inform us that everything, even evil, must be deduced from Unity, from the one God ; and this is exactly what Böhme means. But all depends on the answer to the following question : Through what mediating definitions and conditions do we thus deduce it ?

Another form of defence of Böhme is, that the darkness exists in God not actually, but potentially. Here, again, everything depends on the more precise explanation of this assertion. It may certainly be admitted that every contrast, when it is conceived as torn out of the harmony, and allowed to pursue its own one-sided tendency, becomes contradiction, and engenders darkness. Consequently, if the subordinate element in God were able to assume isolated independence, appalling darkness would arise in God. But this is absolutely impossible, for His Life is an indissoluble life. The potential darkness is thus a possibility which can never be realized, and we can only speak of it in the abstract. But if, on the contrary, the meaning be, that the subordinate in God perpetually desires to attain an isolated independence and self-will, and tends ever towards the wild and unrestrained, which is as eternally vanquished, then it is not wholly indefensible to say that God has the Devil in His Life, but perpetually represses him. Then the "Foundation of Hell" is found also in God, even although, as Böhme teaches, it is first manifested in the creation.

In reality, the "Foundation or Possibility of Hell" must be sought in the free creation, yet as a possibility which indeed *can*, but *ought not* to, become reality, and can only become so by the fault and sin of the creation.

XXXVIII.

WE, therefore, return to the position that the ethical conception of God permits the principle of Negativity only as a principle of contrast, not of Contradiction, and that on this point Böhme is not clear. Franz Baader says that Böhme's doctrine may be expressed in the following lines, which are suggestive of Angelus Silesius :—

> " Licht und Liebe sich entzünden
> Wo sich Streng' und Milde finden ;
> Zorn und Finsterniss entbrennen
> Wo sich Streng' und Milde trennen."

["Light and Love catch fire where Stern and Gentle meet ;
Wrath and Darkness burn where Stern and Gentle part."]

But these lines can be brought into unison with the ethical conception of God only when the contrasts are viewed as harmonious. In and for themselves, moreover, the stern and gentle are only contrasts, not contradictions. If we are to accept these lines from our own standpoint, we must maintain that the contrast between stern and gentle is already given in God, when He is viewed purely as Spirit. God, as a Personality, *is* severity and self-exaltation, is holiness and righteousness, is the jealous God who vindicates His own honour, and is also gentleness, self-surrender, and love. The one set of attributes implicates the other. But this ethical element in the Being of God has also a corresponding physical element as its instrument and medium. To ethical severity, holiness, and righteousness, there correspond severe natural forces, which are especially manifested in the relation which God sustains to the world when His wrath is revealed from heaven. Ethical gentleness and love have corresponding natural forces which diffuse blessings in the physical sphere of the created world, give life and growth, and without which barrenness, dearth, and decay would intrude. But, both in the ethical and in the physical sphere, gentleness can only work on the basis of severity. Where there is no severity, strength and might, gentleness—whether conceived ethically or physically—becomes insipid, and dissolves into mawkishness and vagueness. This conception of the union of severity and gentleness in God pervades the whole of Holy Scripture. Thus we find it both in Ezekiel and in the Apocalypse. The vision of Ezekiel, which begins with a whirlwind from the north and a cloud whence fire issues, and which ends with Him who sits upon the Throne in the appearance of a man, with a rainbow about Him, is best interpreted in an ethical sense, as suggestive of the chastising right-eousness and the love of God. Still, it would be a grave error if we failed also to discern in the vision a representation of real physical forces and potencies, both of the creative power of God, and of the power of His wrath. And the delineation of " Him who sits upon the Throne " demands special attention (Ezek. viii. 2). For He revealed Himself to the Seer, "from the appearance of His loins even downward *fire:* and from His loins even upward as the appearance of *brightness*." The brightness indicates gentleness, the fire severity. The same remark may be made respecting " Him that sitteth upon the Throne" (Apocalypse iv. 3 : " And He that sat was to look upon like a jasper and a sardine stone "). Jasper, which is described as crystalline, indicates the Light-side in God, gentle-ness ; and the sardine, which has the appearance of fire and blood, indicates severity. God possesses (to speak for a moment in Böhme's categories) at the same time a Light-side and a Fire-side. He is at once the gentle and gracious, and the severe and dreadful God. " Out of the Throne proceeded lightnings, and thunderings, and voices," which symbolize the severe judgments of the righteous-ness of God ; but " before the Throne there was a sea of glass, a crystal sea," which betokens the waters of Light and of Life.

Here, once more, we discover the same contrast. And before the throne there burned seven lamps of fire, the Seven Spirits of God, which indicate the harmony of the Glory of God, and the consummate unity of the contrasts.

It is only in this sense that we can accept Böhme's doctrine in accordance with the above-quoted lines of Baader.

XXXIX.

THE ILLICIT ANTHROPOMORPHISM.

IF we glance back upon the course of our previous exposition not only of the dark Nature-Principle, but of the general relation between Nature and Spirit in God, we have already stated, as our chief objection, that Böhme assigns too high a position to Nature by making it a necessary condition for the personal self-consciousness of God, instead of placing it in absolute dependence upon the self-consciousness and self-determination of God, as a medium for the Divine energy. We are now prepared to state this objection in another form, which will perhaps conduce to greater clearness. We gather all our objections into this one : that Böhme has been guilty of an illicit anthropomorphism in his conception of God. Not that we reject anthropomorphisms in general ; without them we should be absolutely unable to speak of God. We are perfectly in accord with Böhme when he starts from the position that man is created in the Image of God, and must consequently be able to know God. We must, however, lay emphasis upon the fact, which Böhme has overlooked, that man is not the *direct*, but the *inverted* image of God, which implies that the relation between Nature and Spirit in man is the converse of that relation which exists in God.

Man, the created creaturely being, has to develop

himself from Nature to Spirit, from outwardness to inwardness, from a fixed, and in many respects a fettered, condition to freedom. Our consciousness develops itself out of a prescribed natural basis, an obscure natural ground, as out of an abyss of night, . and out of which we emerge and evolve ourselves by the impulsion of dim instincts. No creature is Sui Causa; every creature is caused, produced, and posited by its Creator. None of us, therefore, can have perfect self-knowledge, because there is always something impenetrable to our sight in the nocturnal abyss of our condition. None of us possess complete self-determination, for we are determined in a multitude of ways both from within and without. This limitation is necessary, if God would produce a creature after His own Image. For there is one thing which is impossible even to God, viz., to bestow upon His creatures *Aseitas*, or original self-existence. He can give His creatures a derivative or deduced independence, an independence which is conditioned by dependence. Only on condition that we subordinate and energize our nature (so far as this can be our legitimate task) in progressive development do we succeed in taking possession of ourselves in an ethical sense. But in God we are impressed by the absolute contrast of this. God, in His absolute autonomic self-manifestation, moves from above downwards, from Spirit to Nature. Man, on the contrary, whose autonomy is an assigned and deduced autonomy, which can only gradually succeed in gaining power, moves from below upwards, from Nature to Spirit, just as he also moves from outwardness to inwardness, from the phenomenal to the essential. That which for God is the last thing, viz., Nature and the phenomenal aspect of His Being, is for man the first thing ; what for God is the first thing, viz., complete spirituality, is for man the last thing, and the goal of his development. We may certainly concede that Böhme has in view the ethical conception of God when he teaches that God, out of pure Love, introduces Himself into Trinity, and that Böhme, prior to his construction of Nature, apprehends God as Spirit in the inward self-mirroring. But this is wholly vitiated by the fact that God, as Spirit, is regarded as potential, not actual, a Life which is not Life, but a mere figure and schema of Life. It is only through conflict with Nature that God first becomes the Living God, and attains complete possession of Himself. In reality, God, according to Böhme's view, unfolds Himself, through Nature and its manifestation, into Spirit ! And this is what we call the illicit anthropomorphism. Nor will it excite much surprise that there are those who have pronounced Böhme's standpoint to be that of an idealized Naturalism (*Sengler, Peip*).

We must, therefore, agree with Molitor (who thus criticizes Böhme, and blames him for viewing man as the direct instead of the inverted image of God), that the difference between the Divine and the human life-process, according to Böhme, is only quantitative, is simply a difference of degree, since what takes place in man under the terms of finitude and temporality take place in God in infinity and in a timeless manner.*

---

* In a letter addressed to Delitzsch, and printed in the "Biblical Psychology" of the latter. Also, in his work

We may also take this opportunity of mentioning Günther, who, in his doctrine of creation, defines the created universe as " the Contraposition of God," by which he means that the creation, which is not of itself, is "Not-God," the contrast of God, that which is not similar in essence to God.

We shall not enter on a criticism of Günther's doctrine, but will simply remark that he urges, with invincible argument, that the Life of God cannot be interpreted in complete accordance with the type of created life, and that we fully agree with him when, in his struggle against pantheism, he steadily points to the *Aseitas* of God, and refers to the Archangel Michael, who warred with Lucifer, because this arch-dragon sought to withstand God, as though he too were of himself and by himself. Michael, with the flashing eye and the glittering sword, demands : " Who is like God ? Who is as the Lord ? Who is like Him who is of Himself ? " Michael points to God as the Only One, the Incomparable. And for this very reason that God is of Himself and that all is of Him, creatures made in the Divine Image cannot bear a direct resemblance to Him, but there must be, in their likeness, a contraposed element, a birth-mark of dependency. It is undoubtedly important that this contraposed element and essential unlikeness should be kept within due limitations, so as not to exclude the true resemblance. The

---

" Philosophy and Tradition." After Baader, Molitor is probably the greatest modern theosophist. His relation to the Kabbala is very similar to Baader's relation to Böhme, " Vorschule zur Speculativen Theologie. Creations-und In-carnations-theorie."

creature must be receptive of God. We are the offspring of God. God will take up His abode with His creatures. Indeed, the Eternal Word of God, the Son, will become man. The doctrine of the Creation must not come into collision with the doctrine of the Incarnation, as might easily happen, unless the contraposition were rightly limited.

That aspect of the relation between Nature and Spirit, which becomes false when Böhme applies it to God, remains true when it is applied within the domain of creation. If we follow Böhme in his roamings through the Kingdoms of Creation, we are often astonished at the appropriate and striking applications which he makes of his principles. And if we descend into our own inward being, we shall also discover that Böhme's theogonistic process is capable of being transferred into a psychological process within ourselves. We evolve ourselves as if out of an abyss, an obscure nature-depth, and *our* higher ideal consciousness is, at the outset, only vague and dreamy, as if in a Magia. But natural Egoity, Desire, is the principle which brings life, movement, and real existence. In the Natural Ego we shall easily be able to discover the negative Ternary, the self-concentrated Egoity, the vague and self-diffusive yearning, and the self-circling restlessness. The Ego seeks, first, to concentrate in itself, to be its own mid-point, to condense itself. But then, because it cannot be self-sufficient, it strives and stretches out beyond itself, and moves in the direction of diffusion. The natural man now seeks to be self-sufficient, shuts himself up to himself, and now plunges out into the manifoldness of universal life ; but not even here can he find satisfaction ; so he returns into himself. And now occurs this *In* and *Out*, this *Up* and *Down*, this *Back* and *Fore*, which Böhme characterises as the vibrating movement, the revolving of the wheel, restlessness. The restlessness is immediately caused by the fact that the higher moral and religious world shines into the soul, that the soul's own yearning urges it to surrender to this, but that the natural Ego will not surrender, is afraid of dying and losing itself ; this restlessness is potentiated into anguish, until a violent transition takes place in the Lightning. In the Lightning the natural obscurity is removed, the clearness of self-consciousness is revealed, and a distinction is marked out between the higher and the lower sphere, between Light and Darkness, Light and Fire. For the created spirit, liberty of choice now emerges, and all now depends on *what I set my imagination upon !* I can imagine back into my Ego, can desire to centre in myself, and be master of myself. Then arises a *Turba*, or confusion, and a false kindling into evil lusts and passions. Or, I can set my imagination upon the higher religious and moral world, upon the Kingdom of God, can resign myself to the travail of the new birth, and to the burning up of my Egoism ; and then the motto is verified : " Per crucem ad lucem." Then, also, the world of light is kindled in me, and the light which is kindled continues to unfold its inward riches through various degrees of sanctification unto perfection. But, even in perfection, the Natural Ego has not in every sense vanished, nor is it destined to do so. The sinful Egoism has been consumed, but *Egoity* must remain, as the obedient basis for the holy life ; as the perception of a self-life, different from that of God, but also of the inadequacy and nothingness of this self-life, and its infinite need of God. The blessed Life in God is not a vague absorption in God without any perception of self and personality. When I say, " It is not I that live, but God liveth in me," I must, nevertheless, be conscious of an Ego, which would be able to live even without God (although assuredly only in unblessedness). The "Wheel of Birth" continues to revolve to all eternity. But woe to the man who in the hour of the Lightning imagines back into himself, and abides in this false imagination, because for him the " Wheel of Birth " is transformed into an Ixion's Wheel ! (Cf. Fr. Baader's treatise, "Vom Blitz als Vater des Lichts.")

What is here stated has also an important application to intellectual production in the departments of Art and Science. An idea may stir in the depths of the mind with fermenting restlessness; its momenta may struggle with each other in mutual attraction and repulsion, unable to escape from one another, and yet not fusing into harmonious unity. And this restlessness may be potentiated into the distinct anguish of production in severe pangs, which are only ended by a violent transition in the shape of the Lightning, out of which the Light-image arises, in order that it may subsequently be fashioned in Light. It is true that easy births sometimes occur. But, in every real production, something can always be pointed out, that corresponds to the Lightning, the happy light-flashing moment, the swift conception of genius at the instant of the Lightning, which is decisive of the whole work. And it is erroneous to suppose that in proportion to the profundity and value of a production is the *tranquillity* with which it is created, as if the stamp of a great masterpiece were that it is created *tout doucement*, without inward fermentation and travail-pangs. It is precisely the deepest thinkers and writers who know most of fermentations and pangs, and of the lightning as the parent of the light. In Fr. Baader, *e.g.*, we get scarcely anything but these lightning flashes ; the light-image appears in his work, but is never elaborated, because new lightnings at once beset him. In Baader's case one cannot help wishing that the lightning flashes had been less frequent, and that the light-images had been more completely worked out and finished. He says himself that the *lightning* quivers and darts in zig-zag erratic courses, while the *light*, on the contrary, shines with steady radiance. It is this that we seek, and it is only in this that we can find peace and tranquillity after inward struggles and anxieties.

Böhme's Natural Properties have also a bearing upon society and history. It is through ferment, conflict, and birth-pangs that human society moves forward to higher organic forms of comparative peace and perfection. There are historical epochs (among which our own may be fairly classed) which stand in Böhme's third Natural Form, that of restlessness and anxiety, inasmuch as contrasting forces clash with each other, resultlessly, and, indeed, without effecting any real progress whatsoever, despite all the toil, whirling, qualm, and tumult. In our epoch

the Lightning has to be long and anxiously awaited.
And when it comes, it will reveal whether it comes
for judgment, for a further "turba," or whether it
will pass over into the tranquillizing light.

XL.

BÖHME deserves our admiration for developing—
in psychological delineations, profound and based
upon living experience—that which he considers
to be the central thing in the creature: *the Birth of
the new man.* He describes natural life and natural
human life as a life of anguish and continual restlessness ; he depicts, in his pious and practical
treatises, the gloomy torture-chamber in which the
soul finds itself, and from which, burdened as it is by
sin, it cannot pierce through to the light ; he speaks
of the sharp transition, and the blessed peace and
joy that come, when the world of light is kindled in
the soul.   But the immediate transference of this to
God is wholly inadmissible. In a certain sense, Böhme
was well aware of this ; but it is not enough simply
to perceive that what in man exists in finitude and
temporality exists in God in an infinite and super-
temporal manner.   It is equally necessary that the
various momenta in the Life of God should be
placed in their due relation to one another, and in
their proper order.   Böhme presents us with all the
momenta of the conception of God ; but in his
evolution and mediation of these momenta, we miss
the due relation, the proper order.

<h1 style="text-align:center">XLI.</h1>

THE GLORY OF GOD.—THE UNCREATED
HEAVEN.

THE fact that, in the preceding pages, we have lodged very serious objections against Böhme's doctrine, by no means prevents us from recognizing in his conception of God some fundamental definitions which, when properly construed, afford valuable fruit for theology and for the philosophy of religion. Among these we reckon not simply the general conception of *Nature in God*, but also the contrast between an *internal* and *external* in God Himself, the contrast between mystery and manifestation. For although Böhme views God, in the still mystery, as mere potentiality (a course that we cannot approve), yet the contrast between an internal and external phenomenal manifestation in God Himself, quite independently of the created world, remains perfectly valid. Connected with this is the fact that Böhme teaches not simply a Ternary, but a Quaternary ; that he does not, like theology, count three, God, the Father, Son, and Holy Ghost, and then posit the created world as the fourth. Böhme posits as the fourth the Glory of God, conceived as an objectivity different from God, and yet inseparable from Him ; prior to, and independent of, the created world ; the first and eternal production of the Triune God ; the mirror from which His riches are reflected upon Him. The Glory of God is a conception which has been greatly neglected by theology. And as we are studying Böhme not merely as an historical curiosity, but, above all, that we may come into contact with his ideas, and appropriate all of them that are valid, although perhaps independently of the forms in which Böhme expressed them, we must be permitted, conformably to the character of this volume as a free study, to take occasion from Böhme to offer a few suggestions as to this conception.

XLII.

WHETHER we speak of the Glory of God, or the glory of man, or the glory of the world and the kingdoms of the world, we always understand by Glory the external and splendid form in which the invisible essence becomes visible and phenomenal. Now, because the being of the world and of man, in its separation from God, is without durability and strength, so is the glory of the world and of man transient as a flower of the field, and always devoured by the worm of death and corruption.

The Uncreated Glory of God, on the contrary, is incorruptible. What, then, do we understand by the Glory of God? The most precise definition that we can offer is: The Glory of God is the splendid manifestation of all the perfections of the Triune God, of all the attributes of God reduced to unity, the corresponding inward reflection of which in God Himself is the Divine Blessedness, the Divine consciousness and enjoyment of absolute perfection. Most theological statements of the conception of Glory are capable of reduction to this view; and thus, at root, the *Glory* of God becomes identical with what is also called the *Majesty* of God. But this does not exhaust the conception. God possesses not merely a subjective personal Glory, which is one with His Being; He also possesses an impersonal objective Glory, in which there is a reflection of Himself, and which throws a splendour back upon Him.

XLIII.

THE difference between what we have here called personal and impersonal glory may be easily illustrated in relation to man. A man's personal glory is his inward perfection, his intellectual endowments, his moral excellence, in so far as these shine forth into the outer world, and display themselves to the spectator as a luminous image. A man's impersonal glory, on the contrary, consists of his possessions, his various property, his houses and fields, wealth, power, and reputation in the world, his costly garments, and the distinctions that are conferred upon him by society. In Holy Scripture, Joseph says to his brethren: "Ye shall tell my father of all my *glory* in Egypt," *i.e.*, my power and honour, the dignities with which I am invested. Job says (xxix. 20): "My *glory* was fresh in me;" and he is thinking of his wife and children, and his former wealth. It is said in Proverbs (xiv. 28): "In a multitude of people is the king's *honour*" (*glory*); and when it is said in the New Testament that Solomon in all his glory was not arrayed like the lilies of the field, the allusion is to the sumptuous character of Solomon's raiment.

And if we mount higher, we shall find this difference between personal and impersonal glory in Jesus Christ. We read in John's Gospel : "We beheld His Glory, the Glory as of the Only-Begotten of the Father." Here it is the personal glory that is spoken of, Christ's inward perfection of being, which shines forth in the form of a servant, unrecognizable by the worldly eye (for the worldly eye was sealed, as we read in Isaiah, " He was without form (glory) or comeliness "), but discernible by the eye of the spirit and of faith. And we behold the personal glory of Christ in a very special sense, when the external becomes, so to speak, a transparent vehicle for the inward. When He says to Martha : "If thou wouldest believe, thou shouldest see the Glory of God," He is referring to the personal glory that God has bestowed upon Him, to that union of the Love and Power of God which is now to be displayed in the resurrection of Lazarus. We also perceive a similar "transparency" in the Transfiguration upon the mountain, when " His face did shine as the sun, and His raiment was white as the light." And we also remark it in the appearances of the Risen Christ, and in His Ascension into Heaven.

But it must not be forgotten that Christ also possesses an impersonal Glory, an external Glory, over which He is Lord. He says of Himself, that He will come in His Glory with the angels, and that He will sit upon the *Throne of His Glory*, and judge the nations. Unquestionably, the " Throne of His Glory " is a symbolical expression ; but, unless it is to be regarded as an empty phrase, it points to a sphere of Power which is assigned to Him, and in which He rules. Is this sphere of Power to be sought simply in the created world? The High-priestly prayer of Christ directs us to a higher world. When He prays: "Father! I will that they also whom Thou hast given me be with me where I am: that they may behold my Glory which Thou hast given me; for Thou lovedst me before the foundation of the world," He is speaking of something more than a personal glory, and of something more than glory in the created world. "To behold His Glory" involves the necessity that they "*must be with Him, where He is.*" And this *where*, this sphere or region in which He is, and in which they are to be with Him, is closely connected with the Glory which they are to behold. This *where*, this *sphere*, this theatre of His manifestation is eternal, uncreated, before the foundation of the world was laid; it is prior to the relations of created space, to these materialized and corrupted space-relations.

And if we ascend to God Himself—and, indeed, we have already reached this supreme conception,—to the Triune God before the foundation of the world was laid, to God's own inward Life of Manifestation, prior to Creation and Redemption, we can again distinguish between the personal and the impersonal Glory. The personal Glory is the majesty of God, for all these perfections belong to Him. But there is also an impersonal Glory, a sphere which Böhme calls "the House and Dwelling-place of the Holy Trinity." We read in Scripture, "God, dwelling in the Light, which no man can approach unto, whom no man hath seen or can see." The immediate reference of this passage is to the Father, but we may also interpret it of the whole Trinity, which the apostle,—here, as in many other passages,—embraces under the potency of the Father. Now are these words intended to tell us nothing else but that God is absolutely incomprehensible to us? This view would wholly overlook the fact that there are no *absolute* mysteries, but that in every mystery there is always some revelation, some light which shines forth upon us, just as St. Paul says that believers see "only through a glass darkly and know only in part." Are we not rather to suppose that these words actually reveal something to us; show us, that God dwells in Light, has a dwelling-place of Light? on which point we may recal the words of the Psalmist: "Who coverest Thyself with Light as with a garment," even although this Light may be impenetrable to us, and far above our understanding. The Light in which God dwells we can only conceive of as an uncreated light. Concerning this Uncreated Light there was much discourse among those monks of Mount Athos, known as the Hesychiasts, who believed that they had beheld it in the moments of their most rapt contemplation. We will not enter into this more deeply, but simply ask: Is this uncreated Light nothing but a purely mystical, indistinguishable unity; or are we to picture it to ourselves as breaking into rays and beams? Scripture tells us that God is the Father of Lights, which is the same as the Father of Glory, and teaches us that there are distinctions in the one Light. Would it be discordant with Scripture to suppose that the Light in which God dwells is a seven-fold Light? an assumption to which we are led by the Seven Lamps in the Apocalypse, of which Böhme says that they do not stand by the side of one another, but are in one another. Would it be discordant with Scripture to suppose that this Light, with its seven beams, its seven fundamental powers, reveals itself in a natural infinity of shapes and forms, and consequently in a world and kingdom of Light, as the impersonal Glory of God, His eternal possession, at once the sphere for His eternal energy and the product of His eternal energy? This, at all events, is the opinion of the theosophists, and is the essential meaning of the Böhme-Baader Quaternary. The eternal uncreated Kingdom of Light is the fourth element of the Holy Trinity, different from God Himself, and yet pertaining to His essence. So far as we are concerned, we conclude that on this point Theosophy is right when we abide by its fundamental idea, and that Scripture here, as in other places, is more theosophical than many suppose. But as we have now to attempt to establish this thought upon our own premises, we will begin by submitting two questions for the reader's consideration.

XLIV.

THE *first* question we propose for consideration is this: "Has God a Heaven?" Now, we say that God is in Heaven, and we pray to our Father ἐν τοῖς οὐρανοῖς. By Heaven we conceive a locality, a sphere or region, where existence has attained absolute perfection ; and when we speak of Heavens, we imagine a system of spheres, higher regions, which God wholly fills with His Presence ; and although God is omnipresent, still we say that Heaven is His proper and peculiar abode, His House, because it is only there that God absolutely dwells in His own, only there does He dwell in the absolute fulness of His perfection, which is not fragmentary and partial, as upon earth, but is in unity, integrity, completeness, and harmony.*

But when we thus ask, Has God a Heaven ? our question means more precisely : Has He an Uncreated Heaven, or merely a Created Heaven ? Does He simply dwell in the company of the holy angels and the spirits of just men made perfect, without possessing a peculiar habitation of His own ? May we not ask whether the allegation that "God must create, in order to prepare for Himself an abode," does not represent God in a state of far too great dependence upon the created world ? and whether it is more worthy and accurate to suppose that God prepares a dwelling-place for Himself, before He prepares an abode for the blessed angels and for man ? This dwelling-place, this Uncreated Heaven, which must be conceived of as prior to the Created Heavens, is what we have defined above as the objective,

---

* Cf. Dante, "Div. Comm.," *Inf.*, i., 130, 131.
> " In tutte parti impera e quivi regge,
>   Quivi è la sua cittade e l'alto seggio."

Translation :—
> " He governs everywhere, and there He reigns,
>   There is His city and His lofty throne."

impersonal side of the Glory of God, an eternal World of Light, different from God, and yet inseparable from Him.

The second question that we have to ask is: "How do we apprehend *Beauty* in God?" We speak of the Good, the True, the Beautiful, the original essence of which qualities must be sought in God. Now, it is not difficult to apprehend the good and the true in God, seeing that He Himself is the Only-Good, and the Only-Wise. But if God, according to the usual conception, is only mere and bare Spirit, Spirit without Nature, Natureless Spirit, it may be very hard to discover *Beauty* in Him. It is true that men have sometimes spoken of a *purely spiritual Beauty.* But however certain it may be that Beauty cannot be imagined without spirituality, it is at least equally certain that Beauty cannot be imagined without corporeity. A merely spiritual Beauty, from which all corporeity, all externality, and all the phenomenal is excluded, is an abstraction which will scarcely commend itself to any man who possesses a keen perception of Beauty. Accordingly, others have supposed that Beauty is absolutely indiscoverable in God, and that it is a conception that belongs only to the finite created world. And inasmuch as this world of the senses is also a world of perishableness, others have held that the Beautiful is to be found only in the perishable, that it only arises when the transient is touched and illuminated by the rays of eternity. In this connection we may quote Goethe's well-known distich :—

"'Warum bin ich vergänglich, O Zeus?' so fragte die
    Schönheit.

> 'Macht ich doch,' sagte der Gott, 'nur das Vergängliche
> schön,' "*

and also the following lines, not by Goethe, which
express the contrast between eternal but abstract
ideas and transient but beautiful forms :—

> " Sage, was sind die gediegenen, kalten
> Göttinnen, welche die Ewigkeit drückt,
> Gegen die blühenden, weichen Gestalten,
> Welche der Reiz der Vergänglichkeit schmückt." †

But we ask whether Christians are prepared to
abandon the claim that there must also be an
incorruptible and imperishable Beauty, which is to
be found in God Himself ; and whether we can relinquish our hope that the Heaven or Heavens into
which the blessed enter will reveal to them an incorruptible beauty ?   In this case, however, we shall
require another conception of God than the purely
spiritualistic.   We shall be unable to find Beauty
in God, if He is merely to be conceived of as
thinking and *willing ;* we shall only find it when
God is also regarded as *imagining, image-forming,
figure-shaping*, and, indeed, when He Himself exists
in a definite shape.   We, therefore, discover the
source of Beauty in the Divine Fancy or Imagination,
a conception which is certainly unthinkable, unless
there be a Nature in God.   We cannot find Beauty

---

* Translation of above :—

" ' Why am I transient, O Zeus ? ' thus asked Beauty.
' Because I made,' replied the god, ' only the transient
beautiful.' "

† Translation :—
" Say what are the pure, cold goddesses
Whom Eternity oppresses
In comparison with the blooming, tender forms
Whom the charm of transience adorns."

in His purely unseen being, but only in the visible and phenomenal element which belongs to His inward Life of Manifestation. Or, in other words, *Beauty must be sought in the Glory of God.* Thus, the Son is called " The Brightness of the Father's Glory, and the express image of His Person "; here it is the personal glory that is referred to. The Son is the Revelation of the Father's hidden perfection ; and, in the eternal generation, the Son shines forth like a radiant image, or, as Delitzsch has expressed it, it is God's supersensuous, spiritual Fire- and Light-nature itself that here rises like a sun. In this there is a phenomenal element, and in this there must be a momentum of Beauty, even although it transcend our faculties of apprehension. But if the idea of Beauty is to be adequately construed, there must also be a Kingdom of Beauty, a world of beautiful individual shapes and forms. This Kingdom of Beauty we find in the impersonal Glory. Although we may hesitate to say, directly and distinctly, *God is beautiful,* while we have no hesitation in saying, God is good, or, God is all-wise, yet no one will shrink from affirming that God's Heaven, the surroundings of God, are beautiful, the Brightness that shines around Him as His garment is beautiful, Scripture, however, does not speak of Beauty, but of Glory. Glory is higher and more comprehensive than Beauty, for Glory includes the Sublime as well as the Beautiful. Having propounded these questions, we proceed to ask : *How do we deduce the conception of the Uncreated Heaven from the ethical conception of God?*

XLV.

WE start from God as Trinitarian Love. That is our postulate, and we shall not here develop it further, because we are not now considering the mutual relation of the Hypostases, but the Glory of God, the fourth element in the Trinity. Now, if we imagine God to be Love, independently of the Creation, there is no object for His Love except Himself. The Trinitarian relation, therefore, is God's relation of Love towards Himself. That this is without egotism, without selfishness in its evil sense, depends partly on the fact that, in the Trinitarian relation, God confronts Himself as another ; partly on the fact that when God loves Himself, He loves the All-worthy, the in itself worthy, which is His substance, loves Himself in a universal manner.

How then are we to conceive of this Self-Love of God ? It will be most accurately regarded as God's intellectual, contemplative Love to Himself, self-contemplation in holy joy. We have here what Böhme calls the *still mystery*, where as yet all exists in inwardness, with this exception, that we cannot follow Böhme in his definition of this "still mystery" as a half-unconscious, dreamlike condition, but are, on the contrary, bound to interpret this still mystery of Love (the primal thing in God) as a state which is fully conscious from the outset.

But if we pierce a little more deeply into this mystery, we shall reach a fourth thing, impersonal, distinct from the Three Persons, and yet inseparable from them. When God recognizes and views Himself with holy delight, He apprehends not only

Himself, but also His contents, His πλήρωμα. This πλήρωμα—which is best thought of as a πλήρωμα of ideas, streaming forth in multiplicity from the Father—is gathered by the Son into intellectual unity, and is shaped by the Spirit into a world of ideas, distinct from God, and yet inseparable from Him. We have here what Böhme calls Wisdom, viz., the impersonal objective Wisdom that displays itself before God Himself, distinct from subjective Wisdom, or Wisdom as an attribute which appears especially in the Son. It is of this objective impersonal Wisdom that Böhme says, that it stands like a maiden before the Triune God, generating nothing, but reflecting all the splendour and riches of Deity. Here already then we have the Glory of God, but only in an abstract and purely ideal sense ; and here already we have the Light in which God dwells, His House, His Heaven, but viewed only from the ideal side. Theosophy has also defined this Wisdom as a Veil enwrapping and encircling God, but a veil on which His self-manifestation is contingent, a splendour that encompasses Him, or, to use Böhme's words, a *mirror* that surrounds Him, in which the Triune God beholds the marvels that lie in the abyss of His Being.

But can we stop short at the view that the Love of God to Himself is a simply intellectual, contemplative, meditative Love? Simply contemplative Love is, even when it is a Living Love, a merely inward, introspective, and ideal thing. But an inward demands an outward, the esoteric requires the exoteric. Even in man we demand that Love shall be practical, not merely contemplative. The conception of ethical spirit carries with it the necessity of being practical, active, productive, and widely energetic. And this must apply pre-eminently to God, as the Ethical Spirit in an absolute sense. An inert, simply meditative, and observant Love is only half Love, is entangled in abstractions. Now, if God is to be conceived of as *Active Love*, there is a very strong temptation to pass over immediately to the creation of the world. To this temptation many thinkers, and indeed Christian thinkers, have yielded. But, upon this view, the Created World becomes essentially necessary to God, and is not created purely out of His free Love ! For then God is independent of the world only in so far as He is Contemplative Love, consequently only in half of His Being. In the other half, He is fettered to the creaturely world, because He *needs* it for the purpose of energizing and operating upon it. But if the creaturely world is metaphysically indispensable to God, if it is a necessary appurtenance of His own Being and His proper Existence, the Love and Grace of God towards the creation are not truly free.

If we shrink from taking this dangerous . step, which is plainly semi-pantheistic, and if we ask : How are we to conceive of God's Love to Himself as practical and energetic, independently of the creaturely world ? the reply is : God's active Love to Himself—in contrast to self-contemplation, to intellectual and meditative Love—is Self-Glorification. This Self-Glorification is evidenced by the fact that God, by the necessity of His Being, eternally produces and energizes an absolutely perfect product, an objectivity which reflects the riches of

His Being. This perfect product is energized by means of the eternal Idea, through the eternal Nature which God posits out of Himself, out of the depth of Omnipotence. This formula brings us back to Jacob Böhme, whose fundamental idea remains valid, notwithstanding the flaws in its detailed development, to which we have already called attention. This thing, which is eternally and incessantly energized, is the impersonal Glory of God, the objectivity that encircles Him, and is at once an ideal world and a natural world in incorruptible beauty. It is God's Uncreated Heaven, not merely in living but in corporeal reality, the externality or corporeity of God, the imperishable garment of light which God eternally produces, and in which He arrays Himself. In this His Heaven dwells God the All-Perfect, who does not need the creaturely temporal world, and, if He creates it, creates it only out of the pure freedom of His Love and Grace.

Self-contemplation and Self-glorification are consequently the momenta in the Divine Self-Love, through which the Uncreated Heaven arises before the Triune God. It is true that to describe this Uncreated Heaven transcends all human faculty. Our own corporeity and that which surrounds us is so grossly material, so clogged by heaviness, darkness, death, and corruption, that we must always experience immense difficulty in conceiving a corporeity which is absolutely penetrated and irradiated by Spirit. No description can possibly be adequate. We have already cited Böhme's words : " Beloved mind ! behold, consider this ; this now is God and His Heavenly Kingdom, even the eternal Element and Paradise, and it stands thus in the eternal original from Eternity to Eternity. Now, what Joy, Delight, and Pleasantness is therein, I have no pen that can describe it ; neither can I express it, for the earthly tongue is much too insufficient to do it. We will defer it until we come into the bosom of the Maiden " (*v.* " Three Principles," xiv., 89). Böhme, notwithstanding this caveat, often attempts very detailed descriptions, so detailed, indeed, that he sometimes falls over into the materialism which has exposed him to so many reproaches. *Rocholl* has certainly hit the truth when he says of Böhme's too adventurous descriptions, that all intrusion into the recesses of the Holy of Holies is "terribly presumptuous," and that every delineation of the mysteries of the Eternal Nature will inevitably invest the subject with something grossly material (just as the purest light seen through a turbid atmosphere becomes a dusky red) ; that our human speech is fashioned to disentangle things from one another, and to place them in relations of mutual outwardness and independence,—a function wholly unadapted to the subject in hand, where all things stand in a magical inter-weaving, inter-cohesion, inter-implication, while earthly descriptions change them into an " outside one another," " by the side of each other," or " after each other," and consequently wrench asunder that which ought to be treated as inseparable unity.

Yet even Rocholl himself, with many other modern thinkers, has tried his hand if not at detailed, still at vivid descriptions, a fact which shows the attractive power which this subject exercises upon us when our minds have once become familiarized with it. We are not, indeed, to attempt an intrusion into the sanctuary; we are incapable of doing so; it is the Light which no man can approach unto. On the contrary, we are enjoined by Scripture to postulate it, and also to point out the necessity of our pre-assumption, whereby we separate ourselves from those who wholly ignore it. We can only speak of it in symbols of more or less perfect correspondence. It will have been observed that, in these symbols and images, it is now the Eternal *Being*, and now the Eternal *Movement* that predominates. The Uncreated Heaven may thus be conceived of as a Starry Heaven, of which the Created Heaven with which we are familiar is but a feeble copy, a shining Firmament (the outspreading of His Strength, *Rakia*). Relatively more perfect symbols of this eternal nature-world which is absolutely transparent to Spirit, God's own Paradise, those symbols indeed may be which vividly express not only the *eternal tranquillity*, but also the *movement* in its exhaustless multiplicity, the symbols which express the process. And Rocholl has quite correctly perceived that the approximately best symbol of the Uncreated Heaven and its harmonious unity is—*Music.** In the evolution of harmonies in the upper and lower notes, and their mutual conflict, in the solution of strife and tension into blessed calm, in the transmutation of the ever-recurring theme into new phases, in the constant re-appearance of the *motif*, of the question

---

* Thus also it was finely imagined by Dante. Music and the myriad gleamings of precious stones form his symbolic expression of the life of the Paradiso.—*Translator's Note.*

which seeks a reply through every evolution of the notes, and which leads the reply into a new process, in this we see a temporal symbol of the eternal Rhythm, the eternal circular movement in God's Heaven, where melodious colours and radiant notes are interwoven with each other ; where nothing lies in stagnant repose, but all is in motion ; where unity and harmony are eternally effected by means of the contrasted movements and actions.

And let us lay special stress upon the " melodious colours and radiant notes." What is separated and parcelled out in the earthly world is in union above. A truth that reminds us of the Vision of St. Martin, of which he says : " I saw flowers that sounded ; I heard notes that shone." The quality of this Nature is quintessential ; it holds in unity all that is parcelled out among the four elements.

This, however, is only a faint symbol, a stammering utterance, a feeble groping. Yet this, at least, may be said, that if we could gaze into this harmony, observe and hear it, it would be the same to our imagination as the Peace of God which passeth understanding is to the heart of the Christian who has received grace. Harmony is a word which Holy Scripture does not know. But what we call *Harmony*, the Bible calls *Peace*.

XLVI.

IF the validity of this conception be granted, the theosophic doctrine, that the Uncreated Heaven forms the pre-assumption and foundation of the whole Created World, will not be judged baseless. The created universe hovers in this Uncreated Heaven, which encircles the created, permeates it, is both within it and without. From this springs everything which, whether in spiritual or physical sense, is called Blessing. If this word is not a mere empty sound, it implies that super-terrestrial, heavenly forces exert an influence upon lower nature, bestowing good, imparting strength, bringing life and prosperity. Every good and perfect gift descends from above, from the Father of Lights, from His Heaven, His radiant Glory. Created life and created light would, both physically and spiritually, fade quickly away and be quenched if they lost connection and communication with the heavenly vital forces and the heavenly Light. This Uncreated Heaven, the Heaven of Heavens,—*Heaven itself* (Heb. ix. 24), as the Scripture calls it, thereby distinguishing it from the created heavens,—is not divided from us by material distances in space ; for it is not subject to the laws of this material world. It is, in its very nature, all-pervading and everywhere at hand, certainly in different modes in relation to the different circles of Creation and the various qualities of created things. God's Heaven and Paradise may be absolutely near us, may invisibly encompass us, as is confirmed by those glimpses into Heaven which have been vouchsafed to individual saints under extraordinary conditions.

But, amid the usual circumstances of earthly life, there is a veil which prevents us from seeing it. This veil is the material world of the senses, this parti-coloured veil with the visible heaven and earth, with flowers and stars, with images, figures, and enigmatical symbols, a *Veil* which is treated by many as if it were the thing itself, the finality to which one must cling, inasmuch as they do not know that the true and abiding realities are first found behind or within the veil (Heb. vi. 20), behind what they term the Laws and Forces of Nature.

It may also be said that the Veil is this flesh of ours, our gross corporeity, which is subjected, like the whole physical world, to heaviness and darkness, corruption, and death, and in which, in rebellion to the glory which encircles us, we move, as it were, with closed eyes and sealed ears.

We must not, however, pursue these conjectures ; they would lead us from the first things into the last things—into Eschatology. And up to this point of our inquiry, we have not yet grasped the idea of the Creation, nor, indeed, even the thought of a created world.

II.

GOD AND THE CREATED WORLD.

XLVII.

CREATION.—THE WHEREFORE AND THE
MEANS OF CREATION.

THAT God creates means not only that He energizes and realizes an eternal object, but that He produces a life outside Himself, places a spirit-world over against Himself in relative independence, and a nature-world as a qualification and presupposition for the spirit-world. That God creates implies further, that He produces a world which is to be developed from imperfection to perfection ; a development which has to proceed through time and temporality, consequently gradually and fragmentarily, quite differently from the Glory of God or the Uncreated Heaven, which is produced by the inward working of God, and stands in absolute perfection from eternity to eternity. The Uncreated Heaven is an indissoluble life ; the Created World is a disintegrable life (but a life which by the Divine aid is to evolve itself into indissolubleness), while decomposableness, disintegrability, lability are absolutely impossible in the Glory of God.

While the eternal inward energy of God depends upon a necessity of His Being, Creation must depend upon a free resolution.   It must have been *possible for God not to have created*, viz., in the sense that creation is not, like His inward energizing, necessary to His own perfect metaphysical Being or Existence.

XLVIII.

WHEREFORE, then, has God created the world, since He did not create it for His own perfection ? Böhme replies : " We can only say in answer to this that it pleased the Trinity to have children in Its own likeness" ("Forty Questions," i., 279). Consequently, God created the world out of love, seeing that He conceived the idea of another existence, which is not God, but which needs God, and is able, through free surrender, to be transfigured into likeness to Him. It is impossible for Glory and Love to be manifested unless there be something that *needs* Glory and Love. This thought, one of Böhme's fundamental thoughts, has already found application in the Inward Life of God, viz., with regard to the *nature* in God which needed to be released from its torture ; but it gains new and more striking application when one thinks of actual creaturely existences in derivative independence over against God, and yet helpless, needy, and poor, hungering and thirsting after the freedom and fulness of life, which God alone can bestow upon them, and by which He, in turn, can acquire a derived self-glorification. God creates the world with perfect freedom. It is the good pleasure of His Will to create it. He is, so to speak, not compelled to create it, although creation harmonizes with His Being, which is Love.

XLIX.

"THE Eternal God in Trinity has created all things
with and by His eternal Word, out of Himself."
Creation *ex nihilo*, in its usual signification, Böhme
rejects. He accepts it, however, in the sense, that
God has not created the world out of any alien
material, has not drawn from any other fountain
but His own. God has possessed in Himself, from
all eternity, *means* for His creation. He has created
the world out of the Eternal Nature, in which there
is a countless multiplicity of forces, and out of the
Eternal Wisdom, in which there is a countless multiplicity of thoughts. "The Wisdom is the true
Divine Chaos, wherein all things lie, viz, a Divine
Imagination, in which the Ideas of Angels and Souls
have been seen from Eternity in a Divine type and
resemblance, yet not then as creatures, but in resemblance, as when a man beholds his face in a
glass." In His eternal Wisdom, God has the *Form*
for the Created World ; in His eternal Nature He
has its *matter ;* not as though there were matter in
God Himself, but rather an energetic potency, which
is the *fons originis* of matter. We may also say
that the world is created, according to Böhme's view,
out of the seven Natural Properties or Forms which
compose the Glory of God, and which themselves
contain the mediation of Idea and Nature.*

---

* "De Triplici Vitâ," iii., 40 : "Now this world, with all
that belongs to it, as well as man, is created as an Outbirth
out of the Eternal Nature ; understand, out of the seven seals
of the Eternal Nature."

The question arises how the Wisdom, in which God beholds the whole created world as future, is related to the essential Wisdom, which we have previously considered, and which is an indispensable condition for the Uncreated Heaven itself, viewed under the ideal aspect. Hamberger says, that the Wisdom in which God sees the created world, *i.e.*, the World's Idea, is the same as what Plato calls "The Divine World of Ideas," and that it is quite possible to distinguish it from the essential Wisdom or Uncreated Heaven. This last is pure life and actuality. The World's idea, the idea of Creation is, on the contrary, "without life and without being," and only gains life and existence by being actualized. Undoubtedly, one must draw a distinction here; for, if the World's idea were immediately one with the Uncreated Heaven, God would have no other substance than the created world—a conclusion which utterly clashes with our premisses. There cannot, however, be a double Wisdom in God; it must be the same Wisdom. On this point, Böhme gives us no further guidance. The only mode, in which we can picture the relation, is, that when God grasps the thought of another existence outside Himself, this must also display itself to Him in inward objectivity. He beholds, in His essential Wisdom or Uncreated Heaven, not merely an infinite wealth of eternal reality, but also an infinite wealth of eternal possibility, possibility of creating, out of this πλήρωμα, a world outside Himself, and of gaining thereby a derivative Glory. The essential Wisdom certainly includes far more than the "World's Idea." God has His own substance and His own Glory, independently of the Glory that He is able to bestow upon Himself in a created world. But the essential Wisdom includes the " World's Idea " as its momentum. The exceeding wealth of Glory in the Inward Life of God also contains resources or means for the creation of a world outside of God. So, we think, in any case, the matter must be viewed. This " World's Idea," this thought of the possibility of a created world, is depicted, in the Old Testament, as an objectivity which displayed itself to God before the times of the actual world. In Proverbs viii. 22, Wisdom is introduced as saying : " The Lord possessed me in the beginning of His way, before His works of old. I was set up from everlasting, or ever the earth was. When there were no depths, I was brought forth, when there were no fountains abounding with water. When He established the clouds above, when He strengthened the fountains of the deep, then was I by Him, as one brought up with Him, and I was daily His delight, rejoicing always before Him, rejoicing in the habitable parts of His earth, and my delights were with the sons of men." Like a maiden child she played, from the beginning, before God upon *His* earth, not this earth of ours, which then was non-existent, but *God's earth.* Before the times of this world, she rejoiced before God in the eternal nature, in the Uncreated Heaven, and revealed to Him, in a circle of visions, all that might become real in a future nature- and spirit-world, if He willed it, if He would bestow His ratification on the as yet shadowy and transient visions that she evoked before Him, if He would call the non-existent existent.

Above all, she revealed to Him the lovely creation which might become His image, the link between Nature and Spirit, and in which she found her highest delight, viz., *Man.* This passage plays an important part in Theosophy. Schelling also speaks of it with the greatest enthusiasm. It impresses him like a breeze from some. sacred morning dawn, and he says that, even if he met with it in a profane author, he would pronounce it to be inspired.

L.

CREATION AND COSMOGONY.—THE UNFATHOMABLE MYSTERY.

IN a certain sense, the whole created world, with stars and elements, men and spirits, pre-existed in God, although not in a palpable and tangible manner. It was in God, as Böhme expresses it, " essentially," but not " corporeally." The whole Universe stood in the Wisdom of God as in a self-entwined, self-implicated Mirror of Love, and the Wisdom rejoiced with itself in virtue thereof. But now, when the Will of God defines itself in the Word, and utters the eternal Fiat, a new thing arises. For that which in God had been implicit and self-entwined in unity now steps out in separation, fragmentarily, and in division. That which is unknown in the Inward Life of God begins now to show itself. Creatures manifest themselves, coming forward *after* one another, and outside one another ; their whole life moving in the relations of succession and mutual independence, *i.e.,* in the forms of Time and Space, while in God and the Uncreated Heaven, everything stands in an eternal " Now " and " Here," in which " near " and " distant " are unknown, where beginning, middle, and end are blended together in the circle of eternity. In the creaturely world, Beginning, Middle, and End fall outside of one another, and need to be harmonized. Consequently, we have here a wholly new form of Existence, which fills us, as we ponder it, with increasing surprise. Not only the seven Natural Properties, but even the Triune God, Father, Son, and Holy Spirit, here manifest themselves in separation, and, as it were, in division ; for God shows Himself in various *times* of revelation, where Beginning, Middle, and End are outside of one another. We are not, however, to suppose that the Inward and Blessed Life of God is disturbed by this revelation outwards, or that, by suffering these innumerable forces and powers to come forward out of Himself, God thereby loses them and is impoverished ; for His depth is inexhaustible. As an analogy, we may think of a man who may indeed impart his thoughts to others, and publish works, and produce external effects, without, on that account, being compelled to lose his thought or productive power. For he may retain within himself the springs of production, and live a secret life of his own.

LI:

CREATION is inseparable from Cosmogony. The World is created by God by the eternal Fiat ; but, nevertheless, it may be said that the world is born "out of God," if only this "out of God" be rightly understood. It must, on no account, be confounded with the Birth of the Son from the Father. The Son is not created; He is God of God, Light of Light. The World, although it is taken out of God, "cannot be called God, but the expressed and formed Word of God, a mirror of the Spirit which is called God, wherewith the Spirit manifests itself."[*]

The World does not arise immediately from God, but from the seven Natural Properties, from that which is the Externality in God. It is summoned forth from non-existence to existence, from possibility to reality. It is generated out of the *Centrum Naturæ* as its matrix, out of the *lower* Natural Properties, and is shaped by the *higher* Natural Properties, while the Creative Will presides over the whole, understands the whole, seeing that the eternal Nature and the eternal Idea are only the instruments of this Will. And as all created things are born and formed, so also do they form themselves, give themselves shapes, and incorporate themselves. God can only create a living thing; every living thing must then develop itself. Thus, then, the life of the created World advances through continuous births. As all the creatures are summoned forth from the eternal "Centrum Naturæ," the Hearthstone of Life, so also every living creature has its own partial "Centrum Naturæ," or "Wheel of Birth," and has to develop itself from this, to grow and elaborate itself, according to the destiny assigned to it by the Wisdom.

---

[*] "Mysterium Magnum," viii., 25.

"The same one only substance of the Divine Operation, which has ever been from eternity, God has comprehended and moved with the Science of His abyssal Will, and comprised it in the Word of His speaking, and expressed it forth out of the first Principle of the painful dark world, and out of the holy light-flaming Love-world, as a Type, Model, or Representation of the inward spiritual world.

"And that is now the outward visible world with the stars and elements, not so to be understood, that it was in a palpable substance *before* in Distinction. It was the Mysterium Magnum, wherein all things stood in the Wisdom in a Spiritual Form in the Science of the Fire and Light, in a wrestling sport of Love.

"It was not in creaturely spirits, but in the science or root of such a Model and Representation, wherein the Wisdom has thus in the Power sported with itself. This Model, Idea, or Representation, the one only Will has comprised in the Word, and let the Science or Root out of the only one Will go free, so that every power in the separation introduced itself into a Self-Will in the Science, which was left free, into a Form according to its property."*

We must, consequently, represent to ourselves that the bond which—in the Inner Life of God—held the forces entwined in unity is unloosed by the Creative Fiat, and that now every power is released and left free to express itself according to its own will. There thus arises, at the creation, a countless

---

* "De Elect. Gratiæ," iv., 21-24.

number of relative "centra," of particular wills, which determine themselves each after its own character. Still, no strife or confusion occurs here. The Unity of Wisdom rules the whole, and at the beginning of the Creation, before the Fall of Lucifer, everything stands as yet in "temperature." We often find in Böhme the symbol of a field full of flowers on a fine summer's day. Each of the flowers has its own distinctive colour. But they are not in conflict with each other; they rather serve to enhance one another's glory. This is an earthly parable of the Creation in a state of temperature. Every creature is fashioned by the seven Natural Properties, but some special Property is paramount in each creature, in each individuality, without necessitating the repudiation of the others.

Some creatures bear more of the stamp of severity, and are most allied to the lower Natural Properties; others bear more of the stamp of Gentleness and Light. But, since the Creation has passed out of temperature, God is revealed in some according to the power of His Wrath, His severe and terrible Might; in others He is revealed in the character of His Love.

LII.

ALTHOUGH Böhme points out the factors of the Creation, and even enters upon a descriptive sketch of it, he is far from supposing that he has fully grasped the meaning of Creation. He regards it, on the contrary, as an unfathomable mystery. He says explicitly: "What is here hidden from us is that we know, not that which first moved God to create ; we know well the making of the soul, but how that which was in its essence from eternity is become movable, we know no ground of that, for it has nothing that could awaken that ; and it has an Eternal Will, which is without beginning and unchangeable."*

What he finds unfathomable is the first movement to Creation in the God who is unchangeable from eternity. When God moves Himself to Creation, a beginning is posited ; but how can anything begin in the Unchangeable, in whom time does not exist ? "How came it," asks Böhme, "that God hath moved Himself, when, nevertheless, He is an unchangeable God ?" This God has kept in His own power. We must not search deeper here, for this confuses us. Böhme also finds unfathomable that which has been called the transition, the leap from the Infinite to the Finite, from the circle of Eternity to temporal division and succession, from circular movement to linear movement. Pantheism treats this matter very lightly, by denying the problem of Creation and accepting simply an eternal Universe, wherein the changeable has existed from eternity together with the unchangeable, the temporal together with the eternal ; by denying the reality of the world, regarding the temporal as a phantasm, which has only a vanishing value for thought. Böhme cannot treat the subject so lightly. The enigma to him is the actual transition, the actual transposition of the essential into the sub-

---

* " Forty Questions on the Soul," i., 344.

stantial, of that which has stood in eternity, destitute of a beginning, into a beginning thing, a moving thing, into actual self-moving, self-incorporating existence. This is the greatest miracle that Eternity has wrought, that it has shaped the eternal into corporeal (actually and, indeed, physically existing) spirits, which no understanding can grasp, no sense perceive, and which we cannot fathom. The core of the mystery is gathered into the creative Fiat. Notwithstanding Böhme's opposition to Creation *ex nihilo*, he seems compelled, in a certain sense, to have recourse to it here. *Ex Nihilo* would then imply: " only by the magic of the Word and Will," not, however, excluding the possibility that there may be eternal essences in God, which undergo a change or transposition by this magic of the Word and Will.

Dr. Walther had asked "whence the Soul proceeded originally at the beginning of the World?" and Böhme replies: " No created spirit can posit itself, nor, therefore, can it fathom itself. We behold, indeed, our Potter, our Maker, but we know not our Making. A child knows its father and mother well, but it knows not how its father made it ; it is also as highly graduated as its father, but it is hidden to it how it was in the seed, in the wonder, a spirit in the wonder. The soul grows like a bough of the tree of humanity ; but the first movement to creation is not to be named. It is a mystery which God has reserved for Himself " ("Questions," 1).

To those who pore over the mystery of Creation, Böhme recommends patience, humility, and obedience, or else " our proceeding from God avails nothing."

By this he implies: Pantheism profits not. Let none climb above the Cross, the unfathomable mystery, or, if he does, he will fall into Hell to the Devil. *God will have children near Him, and not lords.*

In these closing words, Böhme has clearly and simply expressed the canon of theonomic thought, as against all false autonomies. The philosophers, who claim for human self-consciousness absolute autonomy or self-legislation, deny their creatureliness, their created being, seek to be lords instead of children, to place themselves on an equality with God, or even to enthrone their understanding in the place of God. Notwithstanding the authority of ever so many great names, it is palpably absurd to ascribe absolute autonomy to a self-consciousness which is born out of a dim natural abyss, and is continually supported by an obscure natural basis (of which it never becomes master, and which it cannot see through), and which, after having pondered and inquired upon this earth for a number of years, is again to be quenched in the night of death, wholly ignorant whether this night be the end, or a new awakening.

Birth and Death, and the whole night-side of our existence, establish the fact that God will not have lords but children. What these would-be lords lack, and what we all lack, is *Aseitas*, Self-Existent Being, which belongs to God alone. God alone possesses absolute autonomy. Unless one possesses *Aseitas*, one ought, with Jacob Böhme, to possess humility.

LIII.

CREATION AND EMANATION.

IT will be obvious, from what has been said above, that the often-repeated assertion, that Böhme does not really teach Creation, but Emanation,* must be rejected, or, in any case, greatly modified. Emanation means that the World is a necessary effluence or radiation from God. But Böhme teaches very distinctly, that God creates with perfect freedom; if Böhme had taught simply Emanation, he would not have invented a *crux* for the thought in the shape of Creation. The doctrine of Emanation never leads to anything which is really other than God; it raises no question of anything that conflicts with God, no question of physical or moral evil. Thus we find Emanation in Leibnitz, in his doctrine of monads, where the finite monads are represented as radiations, outgleams, effulgences, and corruscations from God, or the Primitive Monad. But by this we never emerge from God Himself, and Leibnitz's doctrine of Monads, viewed from this standpoint, is as pantheistic as Spinoza's doctrine in which the relation between God and the world is simply one between cause and result. Böhme, on the contrary, distinctly teaches that the Creation does not proceed from the pure, clear Deity (the Heart and Light of God), but from the Eternal Nature, or, as it may be more concretely expressed, from the seven Natural Properties, from the Glory of

---

* Stöckl, "Geschichte der Philosophie des Mittelalters."

God, from the Externality in God, consequently from that in God which is not God Himself, and from which it is summoned forth by the Creative Fiat.

And yet one cannot help recognizing that there are passages in Böhme which, when isolated and wrenched from their general context, may be adduced as evidence that he teaches an Emanation or Evolution, an unfolding of the world out of God. Thus he says : " Whatever God is in His eternal un-beginning generation and dominion, of that also is the Creation, but not in the omnipotence and power, but like an apple which grows upon the tree, which is not the tree itself, but grows from the power of the tree." *   In harmony with this illustration, then, the world has grown out of God, as an apple out of the tree, and is the progeny of God. Böhme is more felicitous when he gives us the symbol of a mother, who has seed in herself. So long as she has seed in herself, it belongs to her ; but when a child grows from it, the seed is no longer hers, but becomes the property of the child.†   Here the *otherness*, the independence of the Creation, is more distinctly emphasized. But in many other places, Böhme says, that the creatures have " issued forth " from God ; and it might seem that we have no need of further testimony. We recal, however, a saying of Oetinger's—that to press single passages, incautious expressions of Böhme, which have not been sufficiently hedged and guarded, is simply to prove that one has no proper love for symbolism. Still, we would not quote this remark as if it were a

---

* " Signatura Rerum," xvi., 1.   † " Aurora," iv., 51.

mark of any unimaginative dulness towards symbolism to acknowledge that Böhme (who is a
passionate lover of *Life*, and whose favourite illus-
trations are those of being born, growing, flowering,
and bearing fruit, a lover of the Scripture parables
of the Sower, the Tree and the Branches, and the
welling fountains) has often moved with far too great
partiality in the categories of Life, and has failed
to raise into their proper place the categories of
Spirit ; that he often speaks of the generation of
the world and of the creatures (cosmogony), without
laying sufficient weight upon the fact, that this
generation is conditioned by a determination of
the creative spirit ; that everything stands for him
in a *perpetuo fieri*, while he does not always and
at all points lay stress upon the creative unsearchable Fiat, which, however, he does emphasize in
many passages.   It is undesirable that Böhme's
writings almost everywhere bear the trace of a
turbid ferment, which has not clarified, and that,
in more senses than one, he requires to be rewritten.
But it would be highly unreasonable to overlook his
unmistakable fundamental thought and ground-
intention, which is that of Christian Theism.   The
question, however, finally resolves itself into this,—
whether Creation and Generation, Creation and Cosmogony, are mutually-exclusive conceptions ?—a
position which it is extremely difficult to maintain,
seeing that we are daily encircled by innumerable
births, and that we yet say of the things born that
they are the "creatures of God."   This question
also arises, whether Creation *ex nihilo*, in the usual
sense of the term, is the interpretation which has

unqualified right to be called Christian ? This, it is true, is the opinion of many, but it cannot be substantiated by Scripture. For $\mu\grave{\eta}\ \check{o}\nu\tau\alpha$ (in Rom. iv. 7) is not the same as $o\grave{\upsilon}\kappa\ \check{o}\nu\tau\alpha$; $\mu\grave{\eta}\ \check{o}\nu\tau\alpha$ is not that which in no sense whatever exists, but that which only in a certain limited sense does not exist, is not existent actuality, but only possibility ; while $o\grave{\upsilon}\kappa\ \check{o}\nu\tau\alpha$ implies that which does not exist in any sense whatsoever.

Since Böhme teaches that God, with His unsearchable Fiat, produces the world by means of the seven Natural Properties, which are the creative forces, we must allude to another objection, viz., that the doctrine of the seven Natural Properties is unauthorized by Holy Scripture. Theosophy appeals, however, to the seven Spirits in the Apocalypse. We have, therefore, to inquire how far this appeal is justified, and how far it is not.

LIV.

THE SEVEN NATURAL PROPERTIES AND THE SEVEN SPIRITS IN THE APOCALYPSE.

WE will examine the often-quoted and classical passage Apocalypse i. 4, in which the seven churches are saluted with the following greeting : " Grace be unto you and peace from Him which is, and which was, and which is to come, and from the seven Spirits which are before His throne, and from Jesus Christ, who is the faithful Witness," etc., etc.

Now, what is to be understood by the seven Spirits ? We will not pause to refute interpretations that are clearly preposterous, as that the seven Spirits are *Angels*. For " grace and peace " from *creatures* cannot be brought into immediate relation with that which comes from God and Jesus Christ. In Apocalypse iv. 5, we again discover the seven Spirits, namely, as seven lamps burning before the throne ; and we also find the cherubim and the twenty-four elders, who all worship. But the seven Spirits do not worship ; they are immediately united with God Himself ; they are supercreaturely, uncreated Spirits, although certainly impersonal Spirits. A far more probable interpretation is that the seven Spirits form an expression or designation for the Holy Spirit, whose powers they are, and in whom they have their personal unity. Reference has also been made sometimes to Isaiah xi. 2, which describes the powers and gifts that are to descend upon the Messiah : " The Spirit of the Lord shall rest upon Him, the Spirit of Wisdom and Understanding, the Spirit of Counsel and Might, the Spirit of Knowledge and of the Fear of the Lord." This explanation, however, is inadequate. We must certainly admit that the seven Spirits have an ethical aspect, and that they are conditioned by holiness ; but they must also have an aspect of strength, of Nature. This is clear, when we note the connection between this first salutation and the whole sequel which is to be unrolled in the Visions, and which shows us that the Holy Spirit is here designated, not simply as the Holy Spirit, but also as the Spirit of Glory (1 Peter iv. 14). And why is the Spirit assigned this peculiar place *before* Jesus Christ, instead of being simply suffered to follow Him, if the intention is merely to designate the Holy Spirit *as such*, as the Spirit that works in the Kingdom of grace and redemption, in the Church ? The final goal, to which the Apocalypse points, is the Kingdom of God, not simply as the Kingdom of Grace, but as the Kingdom of Glory and Victory. But the Kingdom of Glory is the union of the Kingdoms of Grace and of Might. And it is the purpose of all the visions in the Apocalypse to show that the Kingdom of Grace and Holiness, which is now subjected to such great persecutions and tribulations, has, nevertheless, at its service world-conquering powers and forces, with which God will establish His cause to His own Glory, and to the Glory of Christ, to whom the Father has given all power in heaven and upon earth. This is what is told to the churches for their consolation, when Grace and Peace are brought to them from Him which is, and which was, and which is to come (wherein we must think especially of the Father, whose power embraces everything, even the future, and who is faithful to His promises) ; and from the seven Spirits, which are not only Spirits of grace and peace, but also strong Spirits, Spirits of Power ; and from Jesus Christ, who cometh with clouds, and before whom all kindreds of the earth shall wail. There can be no doubt but that the Spirit, in whom the seven Spirits have their personal unity, is the same Spirit who addresses the churches in the epistles. But this Spirit, who addresses the churches, is here to be apprehended, not merely in His significance for the Church and for the society of the saints, but also in His cosmical significance. The cosmical significance of this Spirit is disclosed to the reader even more plainly by the fact, that the seven Spirits point back to the seven Eyes in the prophecies of Zechariah, where mention is made of the Building of the Temple, which is to be triumphantly accomplished, and where the seven Eyes are to watch over the sacred enterprise, a symbol of watchful and protective Providence.

When the reader is led back to the Old Testament circle of thought, he is reminded of the activity of the Spirit before the manifestation of Christ. He is reminded of the Spirit of God, who, as the Creative Spirit, brooded over the waters, worked mightily, as the Spirit of Power, in the heroes of Israel, and, as the Spirit of Wisdom, imparted Himself to the prophets. The potencies and powers with which the Spirit of God worked in the Creation and Government of the World, before the manifestation of Christ, are the same with which He works still. He still works as the world-ruling and creative Spirit, who produces new conditions upon the earth, and who, indeed, even when the fashion of this world passes away, will produce, by means of His mighty workings, that which is the final vista of prophecy :— a new Heaven and a new Earth, with the Resurrection of our Body.

This is still more apparent when we consider the seven Spirits in their relation to Jesus Christ. They stand in immediate relation to God and the Father, who is the Father of Glory, the Father of Lights, the Father of the seven Lamps which burn before the throne, and are the fundamental forces in His Glory. But they also occupy an altogether unique relation towards the Lord Jesus Christ. If they are able to bring grace and peace, and to co-operate towards the victorious establishment of the Kingdom of Peace, this is simply because they belong to Christ, and because their energy is determined by Him who loved us, and washed us from our sins with His blood. Jesus Christ is "He that hath the seven Spirits" (Apocalypse iii. 1), because the Father has given unto Him all power in heaven and upon earth. Just as it is He also who sends the Spirit, who will not speak of Himself, but will simply glorify Christ. That these potencies are not merely ethical, but cosmical potencies, is evidenced in the fifth chapter, where Jesus Christ is named as "the Lamb, having seven horns and seven eyes, which are the seven Spirits of God, sent forth into all the earth." The *horns* symbolize the powers by which the hostile powers of the world are crushed, and the *Eyes* symbolize the Wisdom which corresponds to the power ; they remind us of the seven Eyes in Zechariah, which run to and fro through the whole earth, as if searching out and having the care and superintendence of all things. The Lamb—who is also the Lion !—thus holds in His Hand the world-directing, world-ruling potencies, and avails Himself of them as media through which to work. And this same One, who is the Lion and the Lamb, is also the Eternal Logos, "by whom all things are made, and without Him was not anything made that was made." He is "the Firstborn of every creature, by whom were all things created that are in heaven and that are in earth." He must, consequently, have the seven Spirits from the beginning ; He did not first acquire them by His Incarnation. And it is only because, as the Lord of Glory, He possesses these seven Spirits, these metaphysical and cosmical potencies, that He can hold the seven Stars in His hand, and walk in the midst of the seven candlesticks ; only for this reason can He reveal Himself so majestically to the seer, as " He whose eyes are as a flame of fire, and His voice as the sound of many waters." Or, in other words, it is only because He is the Lord of the whole Creation that He can be the Lord of the Church, and that the Church can absolutely rely upon Him. Without the seven Spirits, He would be unable to establish the Kingdom, or to fulfil His mighty promises.

If what has here been advanced be essentially correct, we may proceed to say : *Within*, in the Inner Life of God, the seven Spirits are the uncreated potencies, or fundamental forces, which constitute the Divine Glory ; *Without*, in God's relation to the created world, they are the cosmical, creative, sustaining, and world-governing potencies, the *principia* both of natural life and of historical world-life, principles of which God avails Himself as His instruments, organs, and media. If we stop short at these general considerations, it must be said that this is precisely the idea of Theosophy. This is what the Kabbala implies with its seven " Sephiroth " ; this is what Böhme means by his seven Natural Properties, or fontal spirits of life ; this is what Schelling means (although he takes no notice of the Apocalypse or of the number *seven*) in his " Philosophy of Revelation," with its potencies. For the Schellingian " potencies " are, at the same time, principles in the Inner Life of God, and it is by their emergence, separation, and tension, that they become cosmical potencies. Thus it may be said in general that, on this point, Theosophy by no means lacks Scriptural corroboration. But, undeniably, a difficulty presents itself when it is asked what special functions, what special activities are to be ascribed to each of the seven Spirits? Here Scripture is silent, and gives us no reply. An endeavour may be made to combine the passages in the Apocalypse with the passages in Ezekiel; but the intimations of Scripture still remain imperfect. This, at least, must be admitted, that Scripture itself leads our meditation into a path where it becomes our problem to apprehend more closely the uncreated potencies through which the Will of God works in its manifestation, and to which Scripture itself makes unmistakable allusion. But the validity of this or that conjectural interpretation, which ventures into details, must demonstrate itself by its own internal truth and necessity, and by its harmony with the Biblical view, taken as a whole. Proofs from single passages of Scripture are inadmissible here. That which Scripture, notwithstanding its veiled suggestions, suffers us to lack on these points, the theosophers have attempted to supply by recourse to the Book of Nature.

LV.

IT will be vain to seek in Böhme a thorough-going Natural Philosophy, although he makes some attempt at this. *Oetinger*, who makes free use of Böhme and the Kabbala, has treated Natural Philosophy with greater explicitness.   Although Oetinger desires to hold fast by the naïve and simple physics of " Abel, Noah, and the other patriarchs,"—which he highly recommends to learned natural inquirers in order that they may not be led astray from life and from a living intuition of Nature by their mathematical abstractions,—he was, nevertheless, very conversant with the natural science of his age, and himself made chemical experiments.   In practice, the seven Natural Properties are reducible to a duality, viz., to the contrast between Darkness and Light, Fire and Light, the severer and the milder potencies, a contrast which, as we have seen, may be discerned in Ezekiel.   The same thing is repeated in the Natural Philosophy of Schelling, where the fundamental contrast is that between the Real and the Ideal, between Weight (gravity, heaviness) and Light,—a contrast which is carried, with many transformations, through the various stages of natural life, and thence makes its way into history.   And the more Schelling was induced, on more mature reflection, to abandon his pantheistic standpoint, and to seek a higher unity of Theism and Naturalism, so much the more was he led back to Jacob Böhme.   At this point Franz Baader already stood. Baader's Natural Philosophy is an attempt to develop Böhme's fundamental idea, that every life has a double " centrum," a *Nature*-centrum and a *Life*- or *Light*-centrum ; that it begins with the first, and is consummated in the second ; and that every life, in order to realize its destiny, must be born twice.

THE ANGELS

LVI.

DERIVED ETERNITY AND TIME.

THE Work of Creation unfolds itself through a diversity of circles of creation. The first circle of creation which God produces is the Angelic World, a Kingdom of pure Spirits of Light. Here Böhme specifies the three Archangels,—Michael, Lucifer, and Uriel,—each of whom has his own kingdom with a multiplicity of angels. Michael is the symbol of the Father, Lucifer of the Son, Uriel of the Holy Ghost. They have under them seven other Throne-angels with the heavenly hosts. The Angels dwell in a wonderful natural world, the perfection of which far transcends that of our earth ; it is akin to God's own Paradise, the Uncreated Heaven, and by this it is encircled.

The Angels are created out of Fire and Light, for no creature can come into being without having in itself the fiery Triangle, the obscure nature-basis. They are Spirits, although not destitute of corporeity. Böhme says that some angels are light-brown in colour, that others have the appearance of lightning, that others are of a shining white, others of heavenly blue, others are like clearest crystal, whereby allusion is made to the seven Natural

Properties, and to the contrast between the severer and milder qualities which predominate in the various angelic classes. It is as with the flowers in a meadow : each has its specific colour. So also with the holy Angels. But everything stands in " temperature." The astringent and sharp in their nature is transfigured in the light and love of God.

But what must be specially emphasized is that the life of the Angels is not fettered by the limitations of time and space, as our human life is in this material world ; their existence is temporally and spatially free. They have indeed their *locus*, their proper place and region, but are not restricted to it ; they can exist where they please, and are raised above the contrast between *near* and *far*. They roam among one another in the three kingdoms, and hold communion of love with each other in common joy. And yet each of them retains its own region as its property and possession. In a similar manner, they are free from *time*. Although they may acquire a history by reason of the trial which they have to undergo, and by means of which their relation to God is to be established and confirmed ; and although they may acquire a relation to time by becoming God's fellow-labourers and ministers in later natural creations, and by their participation in the history of man,—they are, nevertheless, from the beginning, without history, and without temporal succession. They live in the circle of eternity, in the undivided $\pi\lambda\acute{\eta}\rho\omega\mu\alpha$ of Life ; the momenta of their life are not parcelled out, but exist in simultaneity. Their life-employment is adoration of God, blessed contemplation of His

glory, and reciprocal love. They live their life in a
derived or derivative eternity.

LVII.

A DERIVED, a deduced Eternity! Jacob Böhme
does not employ the term, but it harmonizes with
his thought; and this thought is not without validity.
Primitive original Eternity belongs only to Him
who alone hath immortality, because He is self-
existent, and "Aseitas" is His attribute. The
creature can only possess an eternal life which is
imparted to it, and is the gracious gift of God; can
live only in an eternity which is deduced from the
eternity of God, and participates in this. We are
certainly able, as Christians, to have eternal life in
faith during this temporal order ; but still, we look
forward, as the phrase is, "to exchange time for
eternity," to exchange this form of existence, where
everything is fragmentary and sundered into succession, for a fuller and richer form of being, where
everything is simultaneous, whole, and undivided.
But this eternity, which for us lies in the future, we
cannot designate otherwise than as a derivative and
communicated eternity, which participates in the
Eternity of God, and receives its contents from
this.

But now, instead of looking forward, we look
back into the morning of creation and ask, When
did the derived Eternity begin? When were the
angels born? Böhme replies, "The creation of
the angels had a beginning ; but the powers of which
they are created had no beginning." Does this

mean that the angels have a temporal beginning, or that they have an eternal beginning? A temporal beginning is very hard to imagine, because the angels were not created to live in the forms of time and succession, but in those of Eternity and Circularity. Not to mention the fact that, if temporal beginning means that they were created in time, time must have elapsed before they were created. Time is nothing in itself, but is only a form for existence; and then it must be asked, What temporal existences preceded the angelic? The whole representation of the angels includes the idea that they were created with the natural world that belongs to them, their heaven and glory, all at once.*

Or does it mean they have an eternal beginning, that they sprang from that movement in the unchangeable God which Böhme regards as unsearchable, but which does not presuppose time, as if a space of time had elapsed in God Himself before He began to create,—a movement which, consequently, was itself eternal? But if we say this, we say, they are not created at any point of time; there has been no time when there were not angels before the throne of God, no time when the Hallelujah of creatures did not ascend to the Eternal One who alone hath immortality. And then it will be asked, Is not this Pantheism? If the world—which here means the angelic world—is thus made co-eternal with God Himself, is not this a denial of the concep-

---

* We are thinking here only of the primitive Hierarchies; for it is certainly conceivable that later hierarchies might have arisen.

tion of creation ?   We are unable to perceive this. Creation is an act of the freedom of God, who does not need a world, but wills it out of pure love ; and this freedom and love are not impoverished by the supposition that no time elapsed in God before the world was created ; nor are they magnified by the supposition that God, whose resolution to create must certainly have been eternal, arbitrarily postponed the execution of His design.

The main point here, in a metaphysical respect, is this, that the Eternity of the Angels and the Eternity of God are essentially dissimilar.   The eternity of the angels is posited, assigned by God ; they lack " Aseitas ; " and this is the important point if a fundamental distinction is to be drawn between God and the angels.   These created beings, the angels, know themselves to be in absolute dependence upon God, as brought into existence by Him, although they have no recollection of a temporal origin.   We cannot avoid calling attention to the fact that Dorner, in his excellent dogmatic treatise, has been led to the same view, independently of Böhme, and, following his own train of thought, he expresses himself thus :—

" We have no right to say that there may not have existed, prior to this palpable world which is subjected to time, a world which stood in the light of Eternity, a world of pure spirits, even although they had not entered into history, and were as yet exempt from succession, but who stood in the simultaneity of all the elements that pertained to their existence, and surrounded the throne of God ; —a kingdom prior to the creation of our world, in which the creative love of God, which would not endure to be without a world, had always its abode ; a kingdom of which it cannot be said that there was a time when it was not, because there was no time before it was, and because for this kingdom itself there had as yet arisen no Time, no Succession, no Becoming."*

Dr. Dorner reminds us that many passages of Scripture seem to point to such a heavenly world which belongs to the throne of God ; *e.g.*, the living creatures ($\zeta\hat{\omega}a$) in Ezekiel and in the Apocalypse, the representatives of created life, Cherubim and Seraphim. We may add the seven Angels who stand before God (Apocalypse viii. 2), and are not to be confounded with the seven Spirits who, as we have seen, are uncreated. With respect to the throne we note that Jewish Mysticism regards it as the point of transition from the Divine to the creaturely. †

Can one imagine the throne of God as coming into existence in time ?

LVIII.

BUT in whatever manner one may interpret Böhme, and answer the question as to the temporal or eternal origin of the angels, it remains clear that, for Böhme, the fundamental type of the angelic life is not that of time, but of eternity ; that for

---

* Dorner, " System der christlichen Glaubenslehre," I., s. 471.

† Molitor, " Philosophie und Tradition," ii., S. 183.

him the primal circle of creation is a Spirit-world, standing in derivative eternity in which there is as yet neither time nor history. It is incontestably his view that the angels are prior to man, indeed, prior to this earth ; and here he is in harmony with the declaration of Scripture (Job xxxviii. 7) that, when the corner-stone of the earth was laid, "the morning stars sang together, and all the sons of God shouted for joy." The creation of the angels is certainly included in the general description : " In the beginning God created the heaven and the earth." But it is altogether arbitrary to assign the creation of the angels to the Mosaic creative days. The angels were prior to the whole history of the creation of this earth of ours, which Moses narrates, while he maintains absolute silence with regard to the angels. When the morning-stars and the angels are compared in Job, it must be remembered that, according to Scripture, there is a mysterious connection between the angels and the stars.

If we take our standpoint with Böhme in this beginning, we gain the best position with regard to this temporal world, and acquire a living view of the unity of the universe. Thus, the first circle of Creation is a spirit-world in a derived Eternity. The final circle of Creation into which the whole pours itself,—Perfection, the Future World,—is also a derived Eternity, but one far richer than the former, because it embraces the heavenly Jerusalem with the Church of Christ. But in the midst lies the temporal world, the region where means and object, where beginning, middle, and end, past, present, and future are outside one another, while in eternity all these are within one another; where the predominant feature is not rhythmic circulation, circular movement, but linear movement, progressive serial movement; where that congeries of events and actions occurs which we call history. This middle world, accordingly, has not always existed, nor will it always continue to exist. Its significance is simply that of being an intermediate world, a world of transition to eternity. This theory releases us from the dreary and nebulous conception of the infinity and boundlessness of the world. The current ideas of the infinity of the universe with unlimited time without beginning or end and illimitable space are only valid in a purely abstract view of the world, when one looks wholly aside from its teleological, purposeful, and conditioned elements, and regards this abstract conception of the world exclusively through logical, mathematical, and physical categories, as, for instance, when one discusses the infinite divisibility of matter. But if we are to apprehend the living, actual, teleologically-defined world (the characteristic of which is to be not only a natural world, but a world of spirits and souls), we need finiteness and limitation, we require a *terminus a quo* and a *terminus ad quem*. We demand of every work of art that it shall be finished and symmetrically rounded off in itself, and that therein it shall have its own inward infinity. Should then the universe,—which must, most assuredly, be the most consummate work of art,—lack this symmetrical self-completeness, be without object or limitation, begin and end in mist? We ask with

Schelling : " Which is the more perfect, an endless series of worlds, an eternal circle of existences with no goal of perfection, or a universe which issues forth into something definite and consummate ? " *

Böhme expressly teaches, and is here in close accord with Scripture, that the Universe begins with something definite and perfect, and issues into something definite and perfect ; and that, for this reason, it must be self-limited. But how, then, did this temporal world, this middle world between two eternal worlds,—which may be well compared to an island floating in a vast ocean with eternity behind it, before, above, beneath, and around it,—how did this world come into being ? That, in some mode or other, Time must have proceeded out of Eternity is obvious, for whence else could it have come ? The clearest conception that we can frame is, that it arose by a new creative determination, a new creative act, in relation to which the angelic world, in its derived eternity, would then be placed as an *antecedent* world, and would thereby receive a qualification of time. According to Böhme, this process did not take place so peacefully and harmoniously as one might be disposed to imagine, or as, indeed, it would have done if the work of creation had advanced along strictly normal lines. He points to the suggestions which are presented to us in Revelation itself, and teaches that time originated in a Fall from Eternity. This temporal world arose, at the outset, as an Eternity broken and shattered, flung into confusion and disorder. Böhme

---

* Schelling, " Werke," i., book 9, 97.

directs our attention to a great catastrophe in the
morning of creation,—a rebellion in the Spirit-
world! And this forms the starting-point of a
long history.

LIX.

THE FALL OF LUCIFER, AND THE APPALLING "TURBA."

LUCIFER, in the angelic world and amongst the
primitive hierarchies, was a mighty Spirit of Light;
he was, indeed, the mightiest of all created spirits:
he had above him only the Son of God, and he
ruled over a domain of natural worlds, which for us
is indeterminable, but of which this earth of ours
formed a part, standing then in marvellous beauty
and glory. But Lucifer did not maintain himself
as a Spirit of Light, did not continue in the truth;
he conspired against God, and a multitude of his
subordinate angels shared his fall, the effects of
which also extended to the natural world that was
subject to him.

We here face the mystery of the Origin of Evil;
and the first thing on which we must fix our
attention is the Temptation. Böhme certainly
indicates the possibility of temptation more profoundly than other thinkers have done by his
doctrine of the two *centra*,—the Nature-centrum and
the Light-centrum, Egoism and Love. A being
that can be tempted must have within himself two
contrasting principles, according to either of which

he may determine himself. It is necessary that even the angels should be tempted and proved, in order that their holiness may not be simply nature, but may be conditioned by their own free-will. Temptation takes place in the fourth Natural Property, where Fire and Light, Darkness and Light are separated. It is the will of God that the creature shall sacrifice the Fire-principle, Egoism and Selfishness, to the Light-principle; shall sacrifice the Fire-life, the " Own "-life, by absolutely surrendering it to the Light, to the Life of Love. With this Will Lucifer would not comply. He beheld his beauty, for he was marvellously beautiful ; he regarded his power, for he was a most powerful Lord ; and he passed into the realm of false imagination. Instead of setting his imagination upon God, and serving Him in obedience and meekness, he fixed his imagination upon himself, envied the Son of God, who was even more beautiful and mighty than he ; he looked upon the created world and understood its foundation. Then he fancied that he also could become a God, and rule over all things by the power of fire, that he could become a Fire-Lord with a Fire-régime ; and that, by bringing his own thoughts into shape, he could destroy what God had made, and replace it by something altogether new. The Fire-ground burned within him and sought to be manifested, and the darkness in him sought to become creaturely. He opened his "centrum naturæ," and thereupon his Light was quenched. The beautiful star was wholly darkened. The foundation of Hell, hidden from all eternity, was now revealed. He aroused in himself Hell and the principle of the Wrath of God ; the three first natural properties that now have dominion over him. His torment consists in this : that he perpetually climbs up to destroy the Heart of God, but, as often as he reaches the height, he is plunged back into the deepest abyss. ("He that exalteth himself shall be abased ! ")

Exhaustive knowledge of the Temptation and Fall in the angelic world is certainly impossible for us, because the angelic world and that potent angelic prince, whom we firmly renounce in Christian Baptism, is too high for our comprehension, particularly as we can form but a very imperfect conception of the power that was bestowed upon him by the Creator. But the general metaphysic which is here necessary is accurately given in Böhme's doctrine of the *two centra.* It might certainly seem incredibly absurd that a creature could desire to undertake a conflict against its Creator, and to enter upon an utterly hopeless opposition. But if we reflect upon all the absurdities, all the hopeless revolts against God and His world-order, and all the illusions of possible victory to which highly-gifted human spirits so often abandon themselves, we cannot deem it incredible that a corresponding event, on a higher scale, should have taken place in the angelic world. "Lucifer," says Böhme, " knew well that he himself was not God, and he foresaw the judgment of God ; but he had no sensible perception of it, but only a bare knowledge (something merely theoretical) ; his sensible perception was only of the Fire-ground that burned within him, and incited him to wish something altogether new, to uplift himself above all kingdoms and above the whole Deity." *

In additional explanation of the illusion to which he abandoned himself may perhaps be adduced the fact on which we have previously touched, viz., that the angels stand in derivative Eternity, and that thus the illusion lay ready to Lucifer's mind, when the Fire-principle tempted him, *that he was not created;* that a primitive eternity was also his possession ; and that he might enter, as a veritable God, an Anti-God, into conflict with the Most High. This is a feature, at all events, which the great poets have ascribed to Lucifer. Thus, for instance, Byron, whose Lucifer in *Cain* distinctly says that " he does not believe that God created him," whereupon he proceeds to question and argue away all moral attributes in God, and grants validity only to the conception of might. Another trait which the poets have assigned to Lucifer is his confidence in his own immortality, his belief that God cannot annihilate him ; and that thus he may enter into conflict with God with impunity. In Milton, Satan says : " What tho' the field be lost ? All is not lost ! Since, by fate, the strength of gods and this empyreal substance cannot fail ! "

Already in the pre-Christian world, a similar Titanic thought is expressed by the Promêtheus of Æschylus. It is the consciousness of being spirits, —for to be a spirit is to be immortal, imperishable, and unquenchable,—that emboldens the devil and the demons in their defiance. In their spiritual

---

° " Mysterium Magnum," ix., 9 ; " Aurora," xiv.

consciousness, by which they are certainly in kinship
with God, they delude themselves into the idea that
an absolute autonomy belongs to them, and they
reject all Theonomy. They simply forget that they
are not self-existent, that they do not possess the
attribute of " Ascitas," that their Eternity is not
primitive but derived ; and that the final meaning
of their unquestioned deathlessness is merely this,—
" their Fire is not quenched."

LX.

ACCORDING to the view that predominates in
Böhme, the reality of evil must be traced back
exclusively to the free-will and choice of the
creature. He insists again and again that the idea
that it was impossible for Lucifer to have resisted
temptation, is inadmissible. Lucifer, like the other
Throne Angels, had the light of the Majesty of
God before him. If he had centred his imagination upon this, he would have continued to be an
angel. But he withdrew himself from the Love, and
passed into the Wrath of God. It is true that God
foresaw his fall, but He was unable to prevent it.
True also that the realm of imagination had existed
from all eternity, and that it provided him with the
opportunity of falling. It was, nevertheless, absolutely and entirely of his own free-will, and without
constraint, that Lucifer entered the realm of false
imagination. The pervading thought in Böhme's
doctrine of the Election of Grace is that the intelligent creature possesses in itself the "centrum" in

which good and evil originate. It is false to suppose that it is not the will of God to admit all into heaven. It is His will that all should be assisted. But every being arouses Heaven or Hell within itself. What thou stirrest up within thee, whether it be Fire or Light, is accepted by its like, either by the Fire of the Wrath of God, or by the heavenly Light-Fire of Love. If one *will* be a devil, the wrath of God will have him; if one *will* be an angel, God chooses him to be an angel. If a man has entered into wickedness and selfishness, the wrath of God judicially confirms him in his choice. If a man has entered into the word of the Covenant, God confirms him to be a child of Heaven.

It follows from this view that what has been called the Mystery of Evil, or the Sinful Fall, is one with the Mystery of Freedom of Choice. No other reply than this can be given to the question why Lucifer placed himself in hostility to the Will of God. Because he willed it so, because he willed to centre in himself. The same reply must be given when the question of Adam's Fall is proposed. No other reason for this can be assigned except the will itself; it cannot be supposed that outside the will some other cause is to be sought, which is hidden only from us, which we do not know, but which we may perhaps discover some day. The fact is that there is absolutely no other cause. Shakspeare felt this when he made Julius Cæsar say : " The cause is in my will " (*Julius Cæsar*, Act ii., sc. 2), and placed the same reply in the mouth of Shylock in the *Merchant of Venice*. For, if the cause were outside the will, a will-coercing cause, then will were not will, were not the power to initiate a new beginning, were not a primal thing and a principiating element.

At the outset, the electing will lies in indifference ; it has not yet characterized itself, is impelled by no motive. It is certainly necessary that various motives should present themselves to the will, in order that it may choose from amongst them. Here, now, the great significance of Fancy or Imagination displays itself. Every motive presents itself to the electing will as a phantasmal image of the good, be it a real good or only an apparent good. The image on which the free-will dwells with pleasure assumes more and more magic of colouring, grows definitely into shape, and becomes magically influential. And when, at length, the free creature wholly fixes his desire upon it, surrenders himself to it, and takes it to himself, this image becomes a fructifying and impelling power for life or death. If the will has chosen, it is no longer free. The motive for Lucifer was the phantasmal image of his own greatness and glory, and of the novelty which he desired that his revolution should introduce into God's world.

We have said that this is Böhme's *fundamental* view ; for it is undeniable that isolated expressions are to be found which suggest that Evil *could not but* become actual. These utterances harmonize with Böhme's conviction of the necessity of contrasts for the manifestation of life, wherein, as we have already pointed out, he sometimes fails to distinguish between contrast and contradiction, between possibility and reality. But if we dismiss from our regard these contradictions and inconsistencies (which must be viewed as partly casual expressions), and keep to Böhme's distinctly-marked and general meaning and intention, we cannot but admit that no philosopher has given a truer and more profound explanation of Evil. *Evil* is, as is well known, the weakest point in philosophical systems ; it is, so to speak, their " partie honteuse." The majority of philosophical systems regard evil and sin as necessarily attached to finiteness—a view by which God is made the origin of Evil, or by which Evil is abolished as *Evil*, and, from a higher standpoint, is resolved into defectiveness and mere semblance. According to Böhme's doctrine, rightly understood and cleared from its obscurities, it is not the reality of Evil, but simply its possibility which is associated with finiteness, and with the conception of a free creature. According to Böhme, Evil is not a semblance, but an actual abnormality which has entered the creation ; for it is the result of a real separation, an actual rending asunder from unity and wholeness ; it depends upon the perversion of the originally moral and good powers, a perverted relation of supremacy and subordination ; depends upon the fact that the creature is in antagonism to God, and posits itself as a false *centrum*, which seeks to gather about itself, both from within and from without, a multiplicity of forces, which constitute its sphere of power.

Nevertheless, in spite of all the disturbances it occasions, Evil continues, in the main, to be powerless ; continues to be only an effort which never achieves its purpose ; continues to be merely sub_ jective, and can never bring itself into objectivity

The devil, notwithstanding all his disturbing power, is still only the slave of God ; is compelled in the Divine economy to be the instrument of God, and, in self-despite, to contribute to the Glory of God.

LXI.

WHEN Lucifer, by his self-kindling, loses his normal relation to God, he drags down with him in his Fall his subordinate Nature-world, which has its centre in this earth. The then-existing Natural World was, according to Böhme, thin and subtile, and there was a magical connection between Spirit and Nature. Spirit is the unity of Nature, the uniting dynamic centre of the Natural forces; and when a disturbance, an explosion so to speak, takes place at the centre, it is transmitted throughout the whole circle. There now occurs in Nature an appalling *Turba !* The bond of the forces is broken ; and, instead of harmoniously co-operating, every force is now left to itself, and seeks to effectuate itself in a particularistic fashion. Thus arises a state of Chaos, which bears the fundamental stamp of the wrath of God, with the fierce consuming fire, materialization, darkness, and death. But it is not the Will of God that confusion should be the final condition ; He, therefore, introduces a reaction. God submerges the whole under water, and begins a new creation. This forms the subject-matter of the Mosaic history of Creation, which describes the new creation of the earth. The various stages in the advancing history of Creation, the Days of

Creation, are to be interpreted as the stages of a progressive struggle between God and the Powers of Darkness, whereby the fettered Light-forces are restored to their former relation, until the whole work culminates in Man.

It is now that what we call Time, successively-advancing Teleology, makes its appearance. According to Böhme, Time begins at the Fall of Lucifer, and the Divine reaction that was then induced. The fundamental meaning of Time is the struggle of the Light against the Darkness, both in the spiritual and physical world, until the perfect triumph of the Light. In the same way, *Daub*, in his *Judas Iscariot*, has viewed the origination of Time and Space as a consequence of the Fall of Lucifer. On which point we observe, what Daub omits to notice, that other normal relations of Time and Space would have arisen if Lucifer, and subsequently Adam, had not fallen. Time would then have been the form for a rhythmic evolution, and Space the form for corporeal relations, conditioned, strictly and throughout, by idea and spirit.

LXII.

TOHU VABOHU. THE MOSAIC HISTORY OF CREATION.

IF we ask whether Böhme's interpretation of the Mosaic history of Creation has any foundation in Holy Scripture, it must be with the understanding that we do not expect to find in Scripture other than isolated and obscure suggestions upon this subject. It is well known that Scripture is very reserved in its information with reference to the devil and the demonic kingdom. This especially applies to the Old Testament. It is in the New Testament, when Christ appears, and when men can endure a fuller explanation of the powers of darkness, that the demonic kingdom first comes more distinctly into the foreground. The interpretation of the Mosaic history of the Creation, now to be stated, can be spoken of only as a hypothesis, which can be imposed upon no one as an article of faith, but which relies upon data of Holy Scripture combined with the conclusions of Natural Science. The question is whether this hypothesis can explain what, otherwise, we should be unable to explain.

If, with Lindberg and others, we ventured to read : " In the beginning God *had* created the heaven and the earth, but the earth *had become* without form and void (Tohu Vabohu), and darkness was upon the face of the deep," the matter would be as good as settled. For it would then have been the distinct teaching of Revelation, that a great change had taken place upon the earth, a catastrophe, which would naturally direct the mind to a catastrophe in the spiritual world, as a presupposition of that in the natural world. But we dare not trust so disputed a rendering, and, therefore, we abide by the old : " The earth *was* without form and void " (Tohu Vabohu). The most accurate interpretation, then, seems certainly to be that which is the general one in theology,—that the earth had been, from the very first, in an unformed condition, had been a chaotic mass, " in primâ materiâ," which, in itself, was spiritless, and needed to receive life from the Spirit; and that the Creator, who willed to develop His work from the imperfect to the perfect, and whose Spirit brooded over the face of the waters, fashioned and finished this formless matter through a series of creative periods, until it had attained the perfection for which it was destined. On this interpretation, the only question is that of a primal creation, which proceeds quite normally.

A closer consideration of the remarkable second verse in the Bible: "And the earth was without form and void, and darkness was upon the face of the deep," may, however, excite doubt as to the correctness of this view. "Tohu Vabohu,"—and it is obvious that this mere verbal sound contains something sinister and terrible,—means not simply the imperfect and the as yet undeveloped ; but, when this expression occurs in other parts of Holy Scripture, it includes the idea of the disturbance and destruction of a previously orderly condition, with the implied notion of the wrath and punitive righteousness of God (Isa. xxxiv. 11 ; Jer. iv. 23 *). It is by no means unjustifiable to ask: *Can Tohu Vabohu be an immediate product of creative activity?* Is it not, on the contrary, the expression for a "turba" which has entered in ? If it is an immediate product of creative activity, why, then, is not Tohu Vabohu reckoned among the creative days themselves as the work of the first day ? Why do we not read : "And God said, Let the

---

* Delitzsch, "Commentar über die Genesis," S. 104.

earth be without form and void; let there be Tohu Vabohu"? But to this is added the sentence of Scripture: "There was *darkness* over the face of the deep, and the Spirit of God moved upon the waters." Again, then, we must ask: Is the darkness an immediate product of the creative activity? To assert this is equally discordant with Scripture. Darkness, in Scripture, signifies Evil. It makes its appearance with sin, and the physical darkness is the counterpart of the ethical. In so far as darkness, in Scripture, is traced back to God, it is as a manifestation of the wrath of God. The judgment day is depicted in the Bible as a dark day. Darkness and Death, Darkness and Hell are closely cognate conceptions. Nor do we read: "God said, Let there be darkness!" but "God said, Let there be Light: and He divided the light from the darkness." That God divided the Light from the Darkness implies that both, the Light and the Darkness, are realities; for only realities can be divided. It is a great and an unscriptural error to treat the Darkness as a mere deficiency, an absence of Light. According to Scripture, Light and Darkness are contradictory principles, conflicting forces; Darkness is the power which is hostile to Light. We also read that God called the Light good, while He did not say that the Darkness was good. That God divided the Light from the Darkness shows that the Light must have been imprisoned in the Darkness, and overwhelmed by it; and we recollect that the Apostle says, with a manifest allusion to the history of Creation: "God, who commanded the light to shine out of the darkness, hath shined in our hearts " (2 Cor. iv. 6). The creative days advance from light to light, until at length Paradise appears as a home of light, destined for the Light-creature, who is made in the image of God, viz., Man. The more attentively we study the darkness, the Tohu Vabohu, the "deep," which betokens a bottomless abyss, and the "waters," which seem to denote the troubled agitation, or "turba," in which the earth was placed, the more are we strengthened in the conviction that all this cannot have belonged to God's original creative order ; but that it represents a state in which the earth, created of God, became the scene of a·catastrophe, a revolt in the spiritual world, which had transplanted itself to nature as an appalling tempest in the morning of time. And whether Lindberg's rendering, "The earth *had become* without form and void," be philologically defensible or not, this is, nevertheless, the conception to which we are led back.

If we ask what Natural Science teaches us with regard to the history of the earth's development, we naturally abide by the simple facts which those, who are conversant with nature, believe themselves to have discovered, reserving our own opinion as to the metaphysical or supersensuous aspect of the subject. Moreover, we can cite here only the barest generalities ; they are, however, sufficient for our purpose. It is unanimously stated that the fashioning of the earth did not proceed by the path of peacefully progressive *evolution*, but by that of the most violent and tempestuous *re*volutions, as a contest between creation and confusion, between the powers of life and death. It is stated that a power of Death, bordering on the incredible, exercised a widely-extended dominion in the antediluvian world. We hear of destroyed fauna and flora, perished worlds of plants and animals; multitudinous swarms of living creatures, which made their appearance contemporaneously with the formation of the mountains, surged forward in all heights and depths, but suddenly met their death, some by floods and deluges, some by precipitated masses of the self-shaping mountains, by which they were buried, others by torrents of fire that burst forth with fury from volcanoes, all of which reminds us irresistibly of Böhme's three first Natural Properties, his Negative Ternary, which is here conspicuous in its utmost ferocity. And a similar experience repeats itself in subsequent geological periods, an emerging world of living creatures, animals, and plants, and, almost instantly, the whole transformed into a huge field of death, with desolation and silence, and the doom of petrifaction.[*]

With regard to the animals of these early worlds, we are informed that many of them, especially the so-called Saurians,—Ichthyosaurus, Megalosaurus, Plesiosaurus, etc., etc.,—were enormous monsters; and that the joy of rapine and murder, coupled with the most exquisite torments, such as human imagination were scarcely able to invent, was an essential feature of this animal world. Unless one were well aware that naturalists aim at the

---

[*] Wagner, " Geschichte der Urwelt," i., 376; Keerl, "Der Mensch das Ebenbild Gottes," 531.

utmost possible exactness of research, one would be tempted to regard many of their descriptions as visionary and romantic. It is said that the mouth of the Megalosaurus, a colossal lizard, whale-like in size, was furnished with teeth like razors and saws ; that its head was so huge, and its jaws could open so wide, that with a single bite of its teeth it could crush an animal of the size of an ox. Of the Plesiosaurus Cuvier says : " If anything could justify those hydras and other monsters whose shapes recur so frequently in the monuments of the middle ages, it would undoubtedly be the Plesiosaurus." These descriptions also remind us of the mythological Dragon.* Keerl, whose acquaintance with physical researches in this domain is acknowledged by naturalists, writes concerning the Saurians : " At the sight of these incredible remains and these gigantic weapons, one can hardly refrain from imagining the appalling battles between these sea-serpents, who inhabited the same waters, pursued the same prey, and were forced by their growing multitude into ever closer proximity. What a moment when these scaly masses clashed against each other, and when their furious wrathful movements troubled the ocean depths!" Again: " This enmailed race of Saurians not only occupied the great waters ; even the air was allotted for the extension of their dominion. Flying serpents swept hissing through the air, and fed upon fish and insects, on which they pounced like swallows. Swarms of such winged creatures in the air, hosts of such monstrous Ichthyosaurians

---

* Steffens, " Religionsphilosophie," i., 213.

and Plesiosaurians in the ocean depths, and giant crocodiles on the banks of the lakes and rivers of that epoch composed the marvellous population of our earth." These monsters were swept away, and were compelled to make room for a Creative Work of which God said that it was good.

We will not venture further into these dreary regions, where, for naturalists themselves, there is a chaos of uncertainty and doubt amid an infinity of hypotheses. We are well aware that many of the hypotheses of natural science have already experienced, and that others are destined to experience, the same fate as the destroyed and buried fauna and flora. Accordingly, we hold fast simply to that which is generally acknowledged. No one denies that in the antediluvian world death ruled as a destructive and disturbing power, or that the animal world was full of horrible monstrosities. And now we ask, Is this in character with a creative history that unrolled itself along normal lines ? Can this be in harmony with that God whose essence is Holiness, Wisdom, and Love ; who has Omnipotence as His instrument ? Must it not rather be founded in the condition of a nature which is not of that God who is a Lover of Life, while these revolutions would force us to the conclusion that He takes delight in death and in the ruin of the creation ? It is quite inadequate to seek to explain this by saying, that God, in His creative work, advances from the less perfect to the more perfect ; that the Creator Himself was obliged to undertake certain crude and tentative experiments, before the perfect could appear ; that these races of living creatures, so quickly and

suddenly destroyed, these perished fauna and flora
are the postulate for that which was intended to be
permanent; and that, without this postulate, the latter
could not have come into being. This assertion,
that a life that was to be permanent could not arise
without the postulate of Death, is precisely the
assertion which requires proof. No necessity for
this, no definite creative purpose therein has been
even faintly indicated, or can be indicated. We
ask: Why, then, was God unable to allow His
creatures to advance in calmly progressive evolution?
Whence the necessity for all this revolution? We
can readily understand that God, whose Will it is
that the Creation shall develop itself, and, in a
certain sense, produce itself, suffers the Creation to
advance from the imperfect to the perfect. But
these monstrosities, this violent and destructive
death, this reciprocal murder and poisoning are not
simply imperfection, not merely contrast, but contradiction of life ; they constitute a hostile principle
within Nature itself. There are naturalists who
deny God and creation, and start from blindly-
working nature. But since even these affirm that
this nature is the highest (although unconscious)
reason, it is incumbent upon them to explain how
all this irrationality, the presence of which in nature
they cannot deny, came about ; and why this reason
was compelled first to produce these worlds destined
to death and destruction, these " crude experiments,"
as they call them, and why it did not at once
produce the normal. They do not attempt to
explain this, but are accustomed to point, with a
kind of blind credulity, to the actual facts as that

which, as a matter of course, must be rationally necessary. We who believe in God and Creation, and acknowledge a Divine revelation in the Mosaic record of creation, cannot, and dare not, deduce all this confusion, all these graves, and all this murder from God. The disturbance must have originated in the Creation itself, in the free creation, in the created spirit-world. Only in Spirit can Evil originate; and who will undertake to prove that spirit cannot also introduce disturbing energies into nature, seeing that nature is the extended body of spirit?

We cannot but hold that God has established His Creation upon a double possibility,—the possibility of a sinless, peaceful, harmonious evolution; and an evolution through sin and death. In this latter evolution, a multiplicity of potencies and forces which, in the normal development, would have remained in latency and concealment, in mere possibility, are liberated into reality and destructive energy; and this explains why nature bears the stamp of mixture and struggle, because now the forces, as Böhme phrases it, have passed "out of temperature." We are very far from supposing that the demoniac powers can create; this would be a Manichæan admission: but it is not Manichæan to admit that the forces, working in false isolation, can produce deformities, both by false admixtures and by false separations and divisions, and that these phenomena presented themselves in the ante-diluvian world upon a colossal and gigantic scale.

LXIII.

IF we combine what has here been set forth, what we have stated above on the subject of Tohu Vabohu, Darkness and the Deep, the Mosaic history of Creation must be regarded as the restoration of a world which was sunk in ruins, in Tohu Vabohu, as a progressive contest between God and the powers of darkness that sought to check and hinder the work of God, where every Light-Creature that God produces must be regarded as a prey which is snatched away from the hostile powers. This, indeed, says Steffens, is enigmatical; this struggle is the very history of nature and the earth. The thought occurs in almost all the writings of Steffens that the creation of the earth must be apprehended as a progressive manifestation of the Divine Will during its contest with an arresting and obstructing principle, which arresting and obstructing principle must itself be a Will.

The World which thus comes into being cannot but bear the stamp and signature of conflict, cannot but possess, as Böhme says, the stamp of Love and Wrath; or, as Steffens expresses it, it must be a mixture of Glory and Terror. When, therefore, it is often repeated in the history of the Creation that "God saw what He had made, and it was good," the word "good" is not to be taken absolutely, but simply in a relative sense, viz., that it is good as a means of attaining the design of the new Creation. It is at the conclusion, when God looks upon the whole, that He first pronounces that it is *very good.*   Consequently, the creative days advance from light to light by the continuous conquest of the darkness until at length the goal is reached in Eden, in Paradise, as the perfect abode of light for the creature of light, whom it was the will of God to fashion in His own image, and for whose sake the entire conflict is sustained, and the whole work undertaken, namely man.

In Paradise there is nothing mixed, nothing impure; all stands in " temperature."   But one must not imagine that all the rest of the earth was also a Paradise.   The old serpent still sits in the midst of the Creation ; how otherwise could he have entered into the Paradise which man was appointed not only to till, but also to guard ?   Outside Eden, there was confusion, there were wild and venomous beasts and destructive forces.   But it was the vocation of man to spread Paradise over the whole earth by subduing and overcoming the hostile and restrictive, and finally, as if by a kind of exorcism, to expel the demonic powers themselves.

It must certainly be acknowledged that this series of revolutions, which is brought to light by geology, is not mentioned in the Mosaic account of the Creation.   But on this point of the silence of the Bible there is room for the often-misapplied maxim, that it is not the purpose of the Bible to give us instruction in natural science ; it simply aims to represent, in brief and sharp outlines, God's advancing work of creation, in order to point to what, for Scripture, is the chief consideration,—Paradise and Man.   On the subject of the Fall and Confusion of the Devil, and the struggle between the

Light and the Darkness, it confines itself to obscure allusions, which can only be understood when the work of Redemption is studied as a whole.

However many enigmas may remain before we can comprehend the history of Creation, the interpretation here given serves to strengthen a postulate which is essential to the Christian view of the world, viz., the indissoluble connection between Sin and Death. ("Death entered into the world by sin," that is, the Death which is not merely a change, a transfiguration into the higher, but Death with its bitter sting.) The chief enigma, which also confronts us elsewhere, is the wide scope, the immense range that God has conceded to the power of the creature ; for it sometimes appears to our feeble vision as if God had endowed His creatures with an overmeasure of freedom and independence. To this we can only reply, as the Christian Theodicy formally replies, it was the will of God that there should be a kingdom of freedom and love, and that this should be effected along the path of freedom. God was, accordingly, compelled, so to speak, to agree to the double possibility, to consent to all the misuses of freedom, assured that, through the whole process, He would bring to victory the kingdom of light and love, because, in relation to the misuse of freedom, Omnipotence reserved to itself its " Thus far, and no farther ! "

LXIV.

THIS interpretation of the Mosaic history of Creation as a history of renovation and new creation is met with prior to Jacob Böhme, although it is far from being universal. We find it, in the Middle Ages, among the Anglo-Saxons. It is said in a document of King Edgar, in the tenth century, that, because God had banished the angels from the earth after their fall, which had reduced the earth to chaos, He has appointed kings, in order that righteousness may reign. And in the seventh century, the celebrated Anglo-Saxon poet Cædmon begins his Scriptural poem by describing the earth as having become formless and void, in consequence of the fall of the angels. He must here have had some tradition to guide him; and this doctrine cannot have been so strange to the Church as many suppose. But in Jacob Böhme we find it stated with the greatest profundity and force, for the precise reason that in him it forms part of a rigorously coherent system. Through him and after him it has gained no small circulation, not only among theologians, but also among philosophers and naturalists.

In imitation of Cædmon, Grundtvig has given expression to this view in a Biblical-historical poem.*

It may be safely said that, as the relations between theology and natural science become more intimate, the question here stated will rise into prominence by an internal necessity. We recall a controversy maintained in our own Danish literature, between

---

* I can only venture on a rough literal rendering of Grundtvig's lines : "World dead ; empty and desolate ; Hell-wilderness ; Gloom and darkness ; the Shadow-kingdom ; the World's corpse ; Winter night ; rocks bare ; goblins cold ; dead forces ; Work thereafter ; Angels fell ; confusion all ;— Spirit brooded over the deep."—*Tr.*

Mynster and H. C. Oersted, on the subject of the treatise of the latter on "Mind in Nature." In opposition to H. C. Oersted, who had asserted that the laws of nature are eternal laws of reason, Mynster laid stress upon the irrational element in many natural phenomena, and affirmed the old Scriptural text, "Death entered into the world by sin." Oersted retorts that this proposition conflicts with our "definite knowledge" :—

"Our numerous researches into the internal structure of the globe and the laws of its development have proved that, long before man made his appearance upon earth, there occurred a multiplicity of great and startling changes, during which entire species, and indeed generations, of animals perished ; that, during these times, many creatures devoured others ; moreover, distinct traces of disease have been found in the bones of animals of the antediluvian world. And, thus, there is clear proof that physical evil, destruction, disease, and death are older than the 'Sinful Fall'" (in which expression, however, Oersted is only thinking of the Fall of Man).

To this Mynster replies:—"We shall, on no account, permit ourselves to attack the rights of natural science, nor will we question results that have been established with adequate validity ; but since an attempt is made to lead us back into these Pre-Adamite regions, we have already observed that we recognize an Apostasy anterior to that of man ; and, disinclined as we are to riot in hypotheses, for which there is a wide field in a darkness which is illumined by so few rays, still we are at a loss to know what can prevent us from maintaining that moral evil, which we cannot accept as original,—that is, as ‘concreated,’ or as a necessary path of progress for spiritual beings—has also introduced disorder into the physical world.”

We have quoted these utterances of two men, so eminent in our Danish literature, because they briefly and plainly indicate the very kernel of this great controversy. From Mynster’s remarks (rendered . with extreme generality) it would certainly not be legitimate to infer that he absolutely accepted Böhme’s view. He was not fond of “rioting in hypotheses.” But it is undeniable that his expressions tend in this direction, and a further development of the thought which he formulates would necessarily end in this, although perhaps with some modifications. Mynster confined himself to the apologetical and practical part of the subject, viz., that natural science is unable to refute the Scriptural proposition that Death entered into the world by sin ; but that, on the contrary, this proposition is confirmed, throughout its whole extent, by the facts which natural science has disinterred from the shadowy and uncertain regions of the ante-diluvian world.

LXV.

ADAM AND THE FALL OF ADAM.

MAN is a microcosm, a little world, an epitome of the great universe ; a “microdeus,” a little God. Man is created in the image of God, and consists of three principles, soul, spirit, and body. The soul descends from the dark fire-principle, and points back to the Father as the Bearer or Conveyer of this principle. The spirit descends from the light-principle, and points back to the Son. The body descends from this world of the senses, which is the third principle. Böhme also accepts this third principle in another sense, viz., as the Union of Fire and Light in God, which is fashioned by the Holy Spirit, and perfected in the Corporeity of God, or His Uncreated Heaven. But he most frequently means by the third principle the created, visible, physical world, which is destined to become a copy of the Heavenly Glory of God. Occasionally, also, he interprets the whole man from the standpoint of the *Soul.* The soul is tripartite, although there are not three souls, but only one soul. The soul, in its strictest and most literal sense, is the *Man* himself, the individual, the contrast to Spirit as the universal. The Soul, viewed apart from the Spirit, is darkness and fire, natural " Self-ness." In the Soul is the glowing Triangle, the Worm, the restlessness of the Ego, with its passions and lusts, and the dark torture-chamber. But there is also in the Soul a yearning after the light, after the idea, or God. The Soul has an aptitude or native turn for the idea, and is destined to receive into itself the idea and God. So far the Soul is Spirit, angelic. When the Soul, which is endowed with free-will, sets its desire and imagination upon the Light, and wholly surrenders itself to it, it is truly spiritual. The austere and savage elements are appeased and tranquillized by the Light ; the Ego sacrifices itself in love, and the soul is blessed.

Truth or falseness of spirituality depends upon truth or falseness of imagination. For Böhme, spirit and idea, spirit and eye, spirit and vision, are inseparable. So also are spirit and word, spirit · and voice. Dumb spirits are half-dead spirits. The body of man is destined to become the temple of the spirit, the spirit's instrument for its activity in the external world. In so far as the soul is the principle of corporeity, it is designated as the "rational soul in the bestial life," or as the "bestial soul." *

Thus, there are three Principles in Man, and three Kingdoms. "When thou seest a man stand before thee, thou mayest say, 'Here stand now the three worlds!'—the dark Fire-World, the heavenly Light-World, and this World of the Senses. With the soul, man stands in the abyss of Hell; with the spirit, he stretches upward into Heaven; and in his body he has an *extract* of this whole world of the senses. To whichever of these three worlds thou dost surrender thyself, this comes to rule in thee; and thou takest on (or dost receive) its properties. Take heed to thyself, therefore! for what we make of ourselves, that we are; what we awaken in us, that lives and moves in us." †

LXVI.

IF we now return from these psychological elements to the first man, Adam, whom God had fashioned out of the dust, into whom He had breathed the breath of life, and who had become a living soul;

---

* "Mysterium Magnum," xv., 15.
† "Sex Puncta Theosoph.," viii., 21.

in him the three principles stood "in temperature," in perfect concordance. Certainly, he had in himself the dark Fire-principle, that principle which had become enkindled in Lucifer, and for which Lucifer had sought to procure the supremacy; he had also the principle of the sense-world; but neither of these was independent. They were both, so to speak, quenched and illuminated by the Light-principle, and were in unqualified subordination to it. He had a clear apprehension alike of Divine, human, and natural things. He understood the speech of God and of the angels, just as he understood the language of nature, as is shown by the fact that he gave names to the creatures. He beheld the sense-world in quite another manner than we do; for, for him, all the visible was illuminated by the invisible. In animals, trees, and plants he discerned the figures (signaturæ) of their internal properties, and the outward did not reveal itself to him, as it does to us, in a false independence, but always in unity with the inward.* His body had not the gross and coarse materiality of ours. It may rather be compared with the corporeity of Christ after the Resurrection, when He passed through the closed doors. His dominion over nature was not mechanical, but magical. In this paradisiacal state, Adam knew nothing of time.

LXVII.

SINCE Adam's life was a disintegrable life, it was needful that he, like the angels, should be tempted

---

* " Signatura Rerum," vii., 2.

and tried, in order that by the conquest of temptation he might acquire indissolubleness, imperish-
ableness, and blessedness.   It was a severe conflict ;
for all three principles contended for mastery over
him.   Each of them sought to have dominion and
to exercise government over him.   The Heart of
God desired to have him in Paradise and to dwell
in him, for it said, " This is My likeness and
similitude ! "   Likewise, the kingdom of cruelty and
darkness (the principle of Lucifer) sought to have
him, for it said, " He is mine, and has issued forth
out of my fountain-source, out of the eternal temper
of darkness (out of the three first Natural Properties) ;
I will be in him, he shall live under my dominion,
I will display through him great and mighty power!"
Finally, the kingdom of the World said, " He is
mine, for he bears my likeness, lives in me, and
I in him; he must obey me!   I have all my
members in him, and he in me ; and I am stronger
and greater than he.   He shall be my steward, and
shall display my strength and my marvels." *

Then Adam permitted himself to be excited by
the devil into false lust, and set his desire and
imagination upon the great world.   He became
foolishly fond of the world of the senses, and its
glory.   The World and the Spirit of the World
(*spiritus mundi*) grew mighty in him.   And as he
became foolishly fond of the earthly visions, he went
back into a false reflection.   For he desired to
ascertain how it was when the " temperature " was
dissolved ; how the properties, the wet and the dry,

---

* " De Tribus Princ.," xi., 33.

the hard and the soft, the bitter and sweet, tasted in their diversity from each other. He fell ; and the temperature was dissolved. Then the Maiden, the heavenly Idea, departed from him. The Divine Image in him grew pale ; and he became earthly.

The Fall of Adam, however, is very different from that of Lucifer. Lucifer placed himself in *direct* opposition and hostility to God, man only in *indirect.* Man did not wish to oppose himself to God, he only wished for earthly enjoyments and possessions ; but, in order to secure these, he certainly was compelled to yield to the devil, and became disobedient to God. But, precisely because his opposition to God was indirect, he can be saved. In comparison with Lucifer, the sinful fall of man is simply an *indecision ;* and we note here the prelude of that indecision which is a peculiar characteristic of man, whether we study the history of the world or of the individual. Man's relation to God and to the devil is that of indecision ; for man is inclined to serve two masters. Certainly, he inevitably ends by wholly surrendering himself either to the Light or to the Darkness. But no man goes to Hell in a straight and vertical line. He is attracted on two sides ; but the tendency towards hell or towards heaven becomes increasingly predominant.

LXVIII

THE CREATION OF WOMAN. ANDROGYNY.

ANOTHER feature of Böhme's doctrine of the Sinful Fall is that this takes place in several different momenta, and is not limited to the fact that man ate of the Tree of Knowledge.

According to Böhme, Adam had already sinned prior to the creation of Eve. Namely, Adam was originally androgynous, or the unity of man and woman, which does not imply that he was hermaphrodite (hermaphrodism being the caricature of androgyny, the merely outward junction of the already separated masculine and feminine). Adam was a higher unity of man and woman,—a union of severity and gentleness, strength and beauty, which union was subsequently sundered into the contrast between man and woman. Certainly, he had a bride. But this bride, this wife of his youth, to whom he became unfaithful, was the pure, chaste maiden, the heavenly Sophia, Wisdom, that dwelt in him. For, as Theosophy so frequently re-iterates, Wisdom, the Idea, can, at the same time, diffuse itself throughout all created space, can pervade, and most subtilely permeate all things, and can also concentrate itself, and dwell absolutely in one individual soul. In union with this heavenly spouse, Adam was to have multiplied himself in a supernatural way, and was to have produced out of himself beings like himself, in whom the maiden could dwell. But when Adam assembled the animals and gave them names, he saw that they were paired; he was then seized with an earthly lust to propagate himself in a "bestial" fashion. Then the Sinful Fall had already commenced; for he had now set his imagination upon the natural world and the nature-spirit, "spiritus mundi," over which he was to have been highly exalted. The heavenly, pure, modest, and chaste Virgin departed from him, and returned into the æther ; the Divine Image grew pale; and Adam became absolutely powerless.· Then the Lord caused a deep sleep to fall upon him. For God saw that, if a greater calamity and crime was to be averted, if Adam was not to sink still lower, there was no other expedient than that of giving him a woman as his helpmeet. Thus, Adam slept away from the heavenly world, and awoke in the earthly.

During his sleep a great change had occurred.' The woman had been taken out of his side, out of his rib. God had closed up the place with flesh, which flesh leads us to think of the belly, which is the most fleshy part of the human body (Κοιλία 1 Cor. vi. 13), where the difference between male and female is specially localized. During the slumber, He had made hard bones, and had brought into separation the organs that belong to sexual distinction as well as those that belong to the vegetative processes. When Adam awoke from sleep, the heavenly maiden had vanished. But there stood beside him the woman, the wife, Eve. Eve was lovely and graceful, but she was a " cagastric " person, *i.e.*, she was subject to the influence of the stars, the elements, and the spirit of nature ; she was an earthly woman. Adam also had become earthly, and she suited him. They mirrored themselves in one another. He set his imagination upon her ; she set hers upon him. They did not, however, notice as yet that they were naked ; this they did not discover until the sin was complete. Eve allowed herself to be deluded by the serpent, into which creature the devil had insinuated himself, in order to be able to tempt and seduce her. She ate of the fruit of the forbidden tree, and gave her husband thereof. When they had tasted this fruit unto death, and now both of them had death in their life, they could no longer remain in Paradise.

From this time forth, they begat children, and lived in manifold earthly miseries and troubles in this great world, to which they had surrendered themselves, and by the spirit of which they were now constrained. They consoled themselves, however, with the promise, as yet dimly understood, " The seed of the woman shall bruise the serpent's head ! " Nor was the relation to the maiden, the heavenly Sophia, in every sense abolished. For she, the heavenly, chaste, modest, and pure maiden, could not forget her favourite, her Adam. Sometimes she displayed herself to him by night as a constellation shining before him at an infinite distance, reminding him of the eternal, heavenly, paradisiacal regions, stirring in him wondrous yearnings and mighty thoughts. Sometimes she sought him at lonely hours, and met him in solitary paths ; just as even now she seeks those true lovers who are willing to prepare for her an abode in their hearts.

LXIX.

THIS is a brief abstract of the theosophic doctrine of Androgyny. It will naturally be regarded by many as romantic and visionary. It deserves, however, very careful inquiry what it was that could have led profound thinkers into a conception which, at the first glance, is so visionary. The conception

occurs as far back as the Jewish Kabbala. It is also found in Plato, albeit only in jest and in heathen vagueness ; for it is said, in the "Symposium," that our human nature was not constituted of yore as it is now, but quite otherwise : that there were then men-women, who united in themselves the male and female sex. They had a highly ambitious spirit, and in their arrogance attacked the very gods themselves. Zeus, however, would not destroy them, but resolved to make them into weaker beings. So he cut them in two, just as one slices a fruit. As men were now severed into two pieces, each ran lovingly towards its other half; they missed one another, embraced one another, and aspired to grow together again. So far Plato. But turning from this jest to Christian authors who have viewed the matter seriously and from the standpoint of revelation, we may mention, in the middle ages, the great John Scotus Erigena. He says explicitly that on account of man's guilt, because he would not abide by the order decreed by God—in which case he would have multiplied himself according to the angelic manner, magically—his nature was divided, halved into man and woman ; and he sank into this " bestial mode of propagation, like the cattle." *
Visionary as this may be thought at present, yet,

---

* "Homo reatu suæ prævaricationis obrutus, naturæ suæ divisionem in masculum et feminam est passus, et quoniam ille divinum modum multiplicationis suæ observare noluit, in pecorinam corruptibilemque ex masculo et femina numerositatem justo judicio redactus est. Quæ divisio in Christo adunationis sumpsit exordium, qui in se ipso humanæ restaurationis exemplum veraciter ostendit, et futuræ resurrectionis similitudinem præstitit."—" De Divisione Naturæ," II., 6.

with a little meditation, it will be perceived that the
problem of sex,—the question why the human being
must be man and woman,—is not so easy to solve as
it appears to the majority of people, to whom it
seems absolutely self-evident.   Neither Erigena nor
Böhme was able to free himself from the idea that
the sexual relation, " with its bestial propagation," is
degrading to man, who is created in the image of
God ; that man, who, as the image of God, provides
a contrast to the rest of the creation, must also
have been intended to furnish a contrast to
the whole of nature and to the " bestial propagation."   And is it so absolutely gratuitous and
unreasonable on the part of these thinkers, and of
those who have attached themselves to them, to
inquire whether they may not, at root, claim as on
their side all races of men, since they are all
ashamed of, and blush at, the " bestial " element in
the sexual relation, and strive, in every possible way,
to throw a veil over it ?   Is the supposition to be
at once unceremoniously branded as visionary, that
there is something in the sexual relation that by
rights ought not to have been in it ?   How comes
it, then, that not only in Christendom, but also in
heathenism, peculiar sanctity has been ascribed to
pure virginity ? that celibacy, notwithstanding the
many errors that have attached themselves to it,
presents itself again and again as something that
harmonizes with a higher order of things, because
it liberates man from a relation of thraldom that
binds him to a lower world ?   Why do we see in
the child an emblem of purity and innocence, if not
because the child is sexless, because this contrast

between man and woman has not yet distinctively appeared ? Why does the Bride, in her glowing passion for her lover, cry (Solomon's Song, c. 8): "O that thou wert as my brother!" unless because she has some suspicion that sexual contrast is a barrier to true love ? And does it not indeed happen that natural selfishness, egoism, and lust are excited by the sexual inclination, even if manifoldly disguised ? What, then, becomes of innocence ? Both Erigena and Baader refer to a saying of Christ, which certainly includes a whole world of metaphysics, "They which shall be accounted worthy to obtain that world, and the resurrection from the dead, *neither marry nor are given in marriage*, neither can they die any more : for they are equal unto the angels" (Luke xx. 36). That they are equal to the angels in no sense implies that they cease to be human beings, but that they, *as human beings*, shall be equal unto the angels. They are to be sexless, raised above the contrast of sex ; like the angels, who are not men and women, do not propagate themselves by procreation and birth, like ourselves ; which recalls to us the saying of an old Thibetan myth, "Those who do not die have no need to beget children!" But how, then, are we to picture to ourselves this exaltation above sexual contrast, if they are still to continue to be human ; are not to be transformed into angels, but reach precisely that perfection for which they were destined as human ? The answer is : Sexual contrast is not simply to vanish, but is to be transfigured into a higher unity. Each of the saved is to be androgynous, is to combine the essence of the male and female nature, and is to attain therewith the true complete human being. Now, if it is the destiny of man to become androgynous, and, by his exaltation above sexual contrast, to become equal to the angels, he must also have commenced by being androgynous. For that which is the goal of a process of development must be somehow already present at the beginning of the development. Man, accordingly, must begin in sexual indifference. The differentiation, or separation into sexual contrast in man and woman, is a secondary and subsequently introduced process, and one belonging to an intermediate stage. Men did not begin as the only natural creatures characterized by sexual distinction; the animals made their appearance in pairs, as a plurality of *hes* and *shes*. Man was created, at the outset, as a unity, as one single human being, who included in himself all humanity; and it was at a subsequent moment that the severance took place. This is the line of thought which lies at the foundation in Erigena and Böhme, and, according to them, and also according to the old Jewish tradition of the Kabbala, this severance was conditioned by a Sinful Fall.

LXX.

NOTWITHSTANDING this, we have one cardinal objection to make against this doctrine. What we are doubtful of is this, whether the severance into man and woman, and consequently the entire racial life, is to be viewed as conditioned by a sinful Fall? We are unable to harmonize this with Holy Scripture. We are well aware that the concession must be made,—and it is a concession often overlooked by theologians—that man does not begin as a pair, like the other animals; and that Adam, prior to the creation of Eve, was androgynous, or man-woman. For whence came the woman? Here we must abide by Scripture, taking no notice of those who hold that not only Theosophy, but Scripture itself is in many places visionary, but being well assured that these things can be dealt with only upon a Scriptural basis. Whence came the woman? She was not created out of the earth ; still less did God create her out. of nothing ; but "God took one of the ribs of Adam, and closed up the flesh instead thereof." In whatever way this is interpreted,—and no one will interpret it in a purely sensuous fashion, for it evidently contains a mystical meaning,—the main point is this, that she was taken out of Adam. This was not the mode of procedure in the animal world ; for, from the very outset, the animals made their appearance in pairs. Here, on the contrary, the first human pair makes its appearance by a severance out of the one Man, the primitive man ; for the man also first becomes *Man*, in the more rigid sexual sense, when the woman appears. Consequently, before the creation of the woman, Adam had the woman in himself; *or*, he had in himself that out of which the woman was fashioned. When Adam gave names to the animals, he must, as yet, have been androgynous ; must have possessed, both in a corporeal and spiritual sense, the contrast between the male and female ; must, in Böhme's phrase, have possessed the two "tinctures," the masculine and the feminine, the stern and gentle, the fire-Spirit and the water-Spirit, strength and gracefulness in combination. He was the whole complete human being. It is needless and useless to tell us that we can form but a very abstract conception of this first man. That cannot be helped ; we must, nevertheless, think of him as the postulate of the race, and not allow him to be etherealized into an idea. If we picture to ourselves the creation of the animals, we can conceive that the whole earth lay in travail-pangs ; and that everywhere, north and south, east and west, under the poles and under the equator, animals swarmed forth. *   But in Paradise, according to Genesis ii. 7, there appeared only one being, a royal being, destined to rule over the whole of nature. At this point, Scripture is not against Böhme, but is on his side. But we cannot discover his Scriptural authority for permitting the severance which now took place to be occasioned by a sinful Fall, and for viewing the creation of woman as, at best, a counter-active measure, a remedial provision against a disturbance which had taken place. Scripture does not give us the remotest hint that Adam was intended to propagate himself "magically," but points out the sexual relation, with which we are acquainted, as the original one. Indeed, God blesses it, and says, "Be fruitful and multiply, and replenish the earth !" Nor do we find the faintest suggestion that Adam was tempted and had fallen into sin when he gave names to the creatures. It is true that Böhme and Baader have supposed that they find such a

---

* Keerl.

suggestion in the word of the Lord, " It is not good that the man should be alone ! " " God had previously said that all was very good, as He now says that there is that which is not good ; something must have meanwhile entered in, which ought not to have entered in, and which must now be counteracted." *

We cannot, however, admit that this argument is satisfactory. In the words quoted we can find only this meaning, It is not good that the work of creation should pause at this stage. If man is to attain his perfection, the severance must take place. Man requires a helpmeet, stands in need of society and sympathy. There must be man and woman.

Nor does Scripture give us the slightest indication that Adam's sleep was the result of a sinful Fall. We see nothing to prevent us, in company with many church teachers, from considering this sleep as a blessed sleep, an almost ecstatic absorption into the bosom of the eternal love. It was God who caused the sleep to fall upon Adam. And we understand that, if God was to effect a new creation with regard to him, it was necessary that he should be placed in an unconscious state, in order that this creation might take place. The words of Psalm cxxi. were fulfilled in Adam : " God giveth His beloved sleep ! " We cannot but imagine that Adam had an unconscious yearning and longing after something, he himself knew not what, but which was in reality a yearning after an Alter Ego, a *Thou.* In his slumber, God gave him this good gift ; and

---

* Baader, " Ueber das Zweite Capitel der Genesis."

when he awoke, the corporeal Alter Ego stood before him, destined to become the mother of the living; and he himself had become another, felt himself to be another, and exclaimed in rapture: " This is now bone of my bones, and flesh of my flesh!" Eve was no "cagastric" person, neither was she "iliastric," or semi-paradisiacal; she was wholly paradisiacal, even as Adam was. It was not until they had eaten of the tree, that they both became " cagastric," or earthly.

And, in reference to the sexual relation itself, it is quite clear that there is something here which ought not to have been. But the question is whether, but for the entrance of sin, the "bestial" element would not have been absolutely quenched by the higher and spiritual elements of the relation. This is Augustine's view,[*] which is shared by many of the great scholastics, especially by Thomas Aquinas. It is obvious that, at the Fall, the sexual relation must have assumed another character than that which it previously possessed, must have become materialized, inasmuch as man sank, by the Fall, into a false dependence upon natural instincts, and became the slave of nature. That we are a fallen race is peculiarly and precisely demonstrated by the sexual relation, with its accompanying disgrace and shame.

---

[*] Augustinus, " De Genesi," ad litteram lib. ix., c. 3, 6. " Non video quod prohibere potuerit, ut essent eis etiam in paradiso honorabiles nuptiæ et torus immaculatus: hoc Deo præstante fideliter justeque viventibus, eique obedienter sancteque servientibus, ut sine ullo inquieto ardore libidinis, sine ullo labore et dolore pariendi, fetus ex eorum semine gignerentur"—Migne, " Patrologia Latina," xxxiv.

LXXI.

BUT why, then, must the separation take place? why must the woman be created, unless a Sinful Fall had made it necessary? We have no other answer than this, Man was destined to have become equal to the angels, as was pointed out above; and man, at the outset, was androgynous. But he was to attain his eternal goal through an ethical development. Now, an ethical development is the more complete the richer it is in contrasts, to which truth belongs also the contrast between nature and spirit. But the development of man from nature to spirit is impossible without woman, and the birth of children. We can imagine no more complete ethical development than that from the helpless and nature-fettered condition of childhood to the highest spirituality under the educating guidance of grace, so that the most extreme contrasts in existence may finally be harmonized in man. A moral world, furnished with the richest contrasts, can make its appearance only with woman, or with the contrast between man and woman, to which we add the third, the *child.* Without the woman, the family cannot arise; and the family is the basis of the nation, of society, of the state with the whole infinity of contrasts which this embraces; the family is also the basis of the church and congregation. The contrast between man and woman is reflected in all the moral circles of life. We may also say, Man is to reach his ethical goal through *history*, through a social evolution of successive generations; and, so long as there is time and history, children must be born, there must be sexual life, family life, man and woman. But sexual life is at home only in this earthly intermediate sphere, which lies between the two extreme points: Adam in his androgynous relation and the resurrection, when those who are counted worthy become equal to the angels, and are again restored to the androgynous state, enriched with the harvests of a previous history which is far richer and more copious than that of the angels. For it is only in a very circumscribed sense that the angels possess a history. They have to undergo a test of obedience, and the good angels participate in the history of man as ministering spirits. But the paramount conception we form of them is as existing in the blessed circles of a derived Eternity. To those blessed circles of eternity man also aspires, but he has previously to undergo development *through time*, in which there must be sexual life, and in which human beings must marry and be given in marriage. For this reason, woman must be created. Consequently, if we view man from the standpoint of sexual life, we have to distinguish the following momenta :—

1. Adam as androgynous.
2. Sexual life in paradise after the creation of Eve.
3. Sexual life after the sinful Fall.
4. Death.
5. The androgynous condition in the resurrection, where sexual life has ceased, but where the type of the masculine and feminine is still preserved.

LXXII.

ALTHOUGH we cannot accept the doctrine of Böhme and Baader as to the *reason* for the creation of woman, we are in absolute harmony with their demand that the sexual relation shall be viewed in the light of androgyny, and ethically treated in accordance therewith. This does not involve the recommendation of celibacy and false asceticism. But it does mean that the relation between man and woman is not exhausted by the act of propagation, whereby one does not rise above the man-animal and the woman-animal. It means that man and woman, in their relation of love, are to aid one another in becoming whole and complete human beings, seeing that each of them, apart, is only semi-human. The man is to assist the woman by liberating her from one-sided womanhood, and she is to assist him by liberating him from one-sided manhood, both of which are swayed by egoism and egoistic lusts.

But this will be possible only when both of them are combined in the maiden, in the heavenly Idea, which displays to them the ideal of man, and which will wed itself to each of them ; or, as it may be expressed in a manner universally intelligible to Christians, they must both be united in Christ, who has restored to us the heavenly Idea which had departed at the Sinful Fall, and who has once more introduced into our souls the true human ideal. In marriage, the united ones are not simply to propagate themselves and to continue to beget children, are not to continue to bring unsolved problems into the world,—every child is an unsolved problem—while they absolutely fail to solve their own problem, but remain unchangeably what they are. But marriage is to produce in them this transformation, that they assist one another to beget the child of God in themselves, to become themselves regenerated as children of God, and thereby to be ripened for eternity and for their higher form of existence. Every human being is destined to become androgynous, and can be developed into this even in the unwedded state, if he or she is married to Christ, in whom the ideal existence of the man and woman is combined. The Apostle says, "Whom (Christ) we preach, warning every man and teaching every man in all wisdom ; that we may present every man perfect in Christ Jesus" (Col. i. 28). Christ will make us perfect and complete men. But a combination of the essence of the man and of the woman is necessary for human perfection.

LXXIII.

THE doctrine of androgyny has not simply an ethical meaning ; it has also its significance for poetry and art. The highest human beauty must be androgynous. Certainly, we cannot picture to ourselves the human being unless in masculine or feminine form, and must conceive of Adam himself, in his androgynous condition, as *man*. But if the masculine or feminine form is to be beautiful in the highest sense of the term, it must rise above the sexual contrast, and express a combination of the nature of the man and woman. Franz Baader has affirmed that Raphael's Sistine Madonna is androgynous, and that in this creation the artist has achieved his supreme victory. We leave the question open whether Baader is right in his assertion that Raphael here won his supreme triumph. But Baader's meaning must be, that in this woman we behold the contrast between the masculine and feminine harmonized ; that we are impressed with unqualified self-surrender and world-conquering strength, gentleness, and severity, blessed joy and holy solemnity ; that in this figure every trace of female animalism is extinguished, and that every sensual lust and craving is silenced in the spectator, while, at the same time, the figure reveals to us a transcendent loveliness before which we stand enraptured as if in a vision.

And on this subject one must undoubtedly assent to Baader's remark that the artists and poets whose art is centred in sexual love have been quite too little alive to the fact that sexual love ought to be lifted above itself into the androgynous, ought to be transfigured into the true and complete human ; and that they devote their artistic and poetical resources far too exclusively to the delineation of the man-animal and woman-animal with their appetites, sufferings, and passions—a course which fully satisfies the taste of the great public, itself consisting, in a preponderant measure, of simply man-animals and woman-animals.

And now let this be sufficient upon so difficult a subject. We end by quoting a sentence of Steffens, uttered in another, but a kindred sense: "The time has not yet come, language has not yet acquired the requisite purity, clearness, and depth to permit us to speak freely, and without, in some respect or other, provoking misunderstanding, upon a subject in which the deepest enigma of existence is concentrated."

LXXIV.

THE PRESENT WORLD.

AND now for the first time, after all the preceding discussions on themes that lie beyond the region of experience, we have reached this present world, of which we have experimental knowledge, this world with men and women, with sin and death and all kinds of miseries, but the world also into which Christ has come to redeem us. Böhme, in harmony with the Apostle (Romans viii.), teaches that the creature is subjected to the bondage of corruption, and sighs after redemption ; and that this is a consequence of the Fall both of Lucifer and of Adam. By the dissolution of "temperature," Nature has become materialized. The physical world has assumed the character of the gross, coarse, and material, the hard and impenetrable, rigid and stiff ; and, on the other hand, it has assumed the character of the fluid and volatile, of that which evaporates and vanishes like smoke ; and this contrast has not been brought into actual harmony. The four elements, Fire, Air, Water, and Earth, which, previous to the Fall, were only one element (" quinta essentia "), and which then appeared only in harmonious contrasts, now stand against one another in painfully eager desire. They anxiously desire to return to unity, but are compelled to struggle and fight with each other in an empty resultless circle ; while, at the same time, God sustains them by a powerful bond to which they are subjected,— natural law. Everything in this earthly nature is exposed, by the influence of the stars, to great changefulness. Now there are storms of rain and snow, now there is dead calm ; at one time it is hot, at another cold ; now there is sunshine, and now there is cloud ; but nothing is permanent.

" The whole of Nature is pervaded by anguish, a birth-pang, a death-pang, an agony of silent expectation, and everywhere thou dost find thyself in a world of unreconciled contrasts. Throughout all nature runs a discord between life and death, fire and light. We behold at once the manifestation of the wrath of God and of the love of God. Thou dost behold huge, monstrous, and desolate rocks and stones, which testify to the power of death and darkness and the might of the kingdom of death ; but thou seest also noble and precious stones, carbuncles, rubies, and emeralds, which cannot but have descended from the kingdom of Light. Thou beholdest in the vegetable world curse, decay, and corruption, but dost also behold the power of blessing, which brings forth the most beautiful verdure and the most delicious fruits. In the animal world thou seest venomous and savage animals ; seest also useless fantastic beasts, which the nature-spirit, ' spiritus mundi,' has fashioned out of the kingdom of phantasy, monkeys and strange birds which do nought else but torment and vex other creatures ; but thou seest also friendly, gentle, tame, and useful animals." *

When simple men regard this nature subjected to vanity, they say : " All this has God created out of nothing, the one thing with the other ! " But they know not what occurred before all this came into being.

LXXV.

WHAT has been said of nature repeats itself in the world of man. Man has sunk, through sin, into a false dependence upon nature, and the human body has become materialized. It is not a simply and willingly obedient instrument, but is, in many respects, a burden, which occasions us many sufferings and troubles. With this immersion in nature and dependence upon natural instincts is closely connected the fact that the animal world, in a certain sense, projects itself, so to speak, into the human world. For, by Adam's most lamentable and terrible Fall, man has become the property of the nature-spirit, "spiritus mundi," and has acquired a tendency towards the bestial, which presents a glaring contrast to the dignity for which he was designed. Every man has, as it were, an animal in his life, a lion, wolf, dog, fox, serpent, toad, ape, or vain peacock, or such-like. There are also men who have within them some good and upright animal or other. The animal form does not manifest itself in their body, but is figured in their disposition. Böhme

* " Drei Princ."

can here appeal to Holy Scripture, inasmuch as Christ calls Herod a fox, and the Pharisees vipers ; the prophet Daniel and John (in the Apocalypse) call the tyrants and the kingdoms of this world by the names of wild animals, bears and leopards. They thus suggest to us that, in this world, the human is strongly tainted with the bestial, and, indeed, that it sometimes totally assumes the character of bestiality, as will be particularly seen in the times of the Antichrist, when the beast will arise from the sea and the abyss. But we are all to take heed lest the beast-image in us (the greedy hound, the crafty fox, the lustful goat, the deceitful cat, the venomous toad, the foolish monkey, etc.) gain the mastery, and wholly quench the human in us ; and are to make it our aim that the beast-image may be brought to vanish entirely in penitence and conversion, and may thus give place to the Divine image, the maiden.

For we are to give good attention to this fact, that all three principles are active in this world, and that what every man is and how it will fare with him in the life to come depends upon which of the three principles it is that has dominion over him. The majority of men are ruled by the third principle, by this phenomenal world, which wholly engrosses their ambition, and in which they live for their daily provision, for enjoyments and luxuries, honour and distinction. Some devote themselves to worldly arts, and sciences, and politics, and are enabled hereby to win great power, reputation, and celebrity. Still, this great world is, in comparison with the heavenly light-world which is behind it and shines into it, only like vapour and mist. Other men have entirely surrendered themselves to the dark Fire-principle ; they live in arrogance, envy, and pernicious scheming, and some of them aspire to become tyrants, who exercise a fire-government. Others again, but by far the fewest, stand in the Light-principle. For although man, by the Sinful Fall, lost communion with the Light, there is still in the human heart a yearning for the Light, a hunger and thirst after the Living God. The law is written upon man's heart, and there are pagans who have striven to live in purity ("Aurora," 20, 22, 23). Böhme has conceptions of heathenism which are far higher than those current in his time. Mythology is not to be unceremoniously regarded as the work of the devil, as many regard it who incessantly say "Devil! devil!" and know neither what God nor devil is ("Mysterium Magnum"). It is true that the heathen worshipped the powers of nature, and adored natural properties, fragments of the Glory of God, since they forgot God Himself ; but when they were animated by strong faith, God sometimes spoke to them through nature.

LXXVI.

As Time begins with the dissolution of "Temperature," so must it end with its restoration. Consequently, the essential import of history is that it is a history of redemption. That it is the will of God to redeem and regenerate the world was manifested immediately after the Fall in the promise, "The seed of the woman shall bruise the serpent's head!" it was manifested in the covenants with Abraham and Moses; and by the fact that "God spoke at sundry times and in divers manners by the prophets." Moreover, a succession of children of God and of the Light passes through time from the beginning, and has its contrast in that succession of children of the world which began with Cain. But when the fulness of the times had come, God sent His Son, born of a woman. In Christ, the Word which was in the world from the beginning, and which spoke to Adam and Eve concerning that Bruiser of the Serpent who was to come, has become *man.* The Lord has entered into the form of a servant, whereat all the angels marvel; and this is the greatest miracle that has happened from all eternity; for it is against Nature: it must then indeed be Love.*

LXXVII.

BÖHME'S view of the world is thus conditioned by the Sinful Fall. His pessimism and optimism depend upon this contrast. We must particularly emphasize his conception of man's lofty destiny, and of man's significance, not only for the earth, but for the universe, for the whole creation. For Böhme, man is the central creature in God's world, the all-concluding creature, at whose advent the whole creative work first reached its goal; the being who ideally and in design is the *first*, although in the order of execution he comes last. It can, therefore,

---

* "Three Principles in Man," xviii., 43.

be viewed as merely accidental when it appears from some isolated passages as if it were Böhme's opinion that man was created only to fill the place that had become void by the Fall of Lucifer. Böhme's fundamental view is obviously that which is also found in other theosophists, especially in St. Martin and Baader, that man was destined to be the mediator between heaven and earth, between spirit and nature, the creature in whom, after the completion of the creative work, God might find His Sabbath rest, and into whom God might enter with His whole $\pi\lambda\acute{\eta}\rho\omega\mu a$, for which reason the conception of man points forward to the conception of the Incarnation.

It is true that this exaltation of man was not yet firmly established in the first Adam ; he was to be developed into it ; it was possible for him to lose it,—and he lost it ! It is in consequence of this that the whole present world, not only the human world, but nature, which by the Fall of Man became subject to corruption, reveals so painful a contrast to its true destiny. And man, when his eyes are opened to his actual state, cannot but view himself as a dethroned king, who by his fall has drawn his whole kingdom with him into misery, a king in exile. It is in Christ, the new Adam, that man's dignity is first re-established, and this completely. For Böhme Jesus Christ has not simply an ethical, but a *cosmical* significance. Christ is not only the Head of the human race, but of the whole creation, by whom and for whom all things are created, that in Him they may all be gathered together in one ; to whom also the angelic world is made subject

(Col. i. ; Eph. i. ; Heb. i.). By Him not only the human world but nature also is to be redeemed ; for, through Him, at His second coming, shall arise new heavens and a new earth, wherein dwelleth righteousness.

Certainly, Böhme represents Christ essentially only as the Atoner and Redeemer, whose coming is occasioned by sin. Böhme lives and breathes in the Reformation-period consciousness of sin and grace. But his conception of Christ's cosmical significance, which is his all-pervading postulate, leads necessarily to the theory that, even if sin had not occurred, Christ would yet have come, not indeed as the Saviour who was crucified, but as the Consummator of man and of the whole creation.

This ancient theologoumenon, occurring as early as Irenæus, and more copiously developed by many of the mediæval theologians, is repeated by no small number of modern thinkers, although many, with great inconsistency, as it seems to us, decline to accept it.[*]

But how does this view of the cosmical significance of man and of Christ, which is also, in the main, the view of Scripture, and the recognition of which no theologian will be able to evade without doing violence to Scripture (Eph. i., Col. i.),—how does this view stand against the so-called modern view of the world ? How is it consistent with the Copernican system, which is said to be so dangerous to the Bible and to the Biblical view ? With regard

---

[*] Cf. Baader's Letter to Molitor, " Über das Versehensein des Menschen im Namen Jesu vor der Welt Schöpfung." Werke, iv.

to Böhme, we remark that he is acquainted with, and accepts the Copernican system. " The Sun," he says, " has its own royal place to itself, and does not go away from that place where it came to be at the first, although some suppose that it runs round about the globe in a day and a night. But this opinion is false" (" Aurora," xxv., 65). He is not, however, in the slightest degree affected by this, as if it imperilled the Biblical view of man's central position in the universe. Nor is there really any contradiction between the Bible and the Copernican system. But there is a contradiction between the Bible and a certain application which has been made of this system, a certain argument which some have fancied that they could construct upon it, but of which the system itself is absolutely innocent.

LXXVIII.

BECAUSE the Copernican System has given us a view of the world, and opened to us the vista of an outward infinity, there are those who have supposed that they could prove, from the insignificance of the earth, the untenableness of the Biblical view. This earth, and with it also man and Christ, is only a vanishing point in this immensity ; and it is highly immodest of man to ascribe such importance to himself and to the earth. The revelation which confirms man in such immodesty cannot, therefore, be true.

The retort, however, is obvious, that this rationalistic-fantastic argument from the insignificance of the earth depends upon a confusion between the quantitative and the qualitative, between external and internal greatness, outward and inward infinity. The fact is overlooked that, although physical centrality does not belong to man and to the earth, it is very possible that metaphysical and invisible centrality may. In so far as we are capable of tracing the wisdom of God in Nature and Revelation, we return to the discovery that God pre-eminently reveals His glory, not in the outward infinity, but in the inward ; that His path proceeds from outwardness to inwardness, from the externally great to the small and outwardly insignificant, which, in internal respects, is the fullest of meaning, and has the whole $\pi\lambda\dot{\eta}\rho\omega\mu\alpha$ intensively concentrated in it. That which is despised by the world, by those who judge everything according to the outward appearance, that hath God chosen. These words may also be applied to the earth, this Bethlehem of the universe. But, because man has sunk into false dependence upon nature, he is readily disposed to estimate the spiritual according to an external and material standard. He allows himself to be overawed by material mass, by that which is great to the man of the senses. He forgets that when the question arises as to that which is the greatest in value, the world of thought and speech is infinitely higher than the silent and unconscious natural worlds ; and hence he falls into self-depreciation by reason of his false modesty and servility to nature. With great truth does St. Martin say to man : " Dost thou dare to measure thy being and thy destiny with thy bodily eye ? Beware, lest this admiration-rousing, seductive, terrible spectacle of immeasurable space and the countless bodies that float in it crush thy thought, which shows thee thy body as wholly vanishing! Step into thy rights, and separate thyself from these over-awing but dumb existences by the superiority of thy thought and speech!"

This same view of the centrality of man and of the earth is also to be found, although discussed along different lines of proof, in thinkers like Schelling, Hegel, Steffens, Schubert, etc.[*]

After the famous treatise of Fontenelle, "Entretien de la Pluralité des Mondes" (Paris, 1686), the idea that the heavenly spheres must necessarily be inhabited by rational beings gained wide acceptance ; and arguments were drawn from it against the dignity and centrality of man. This whole assumption, however, depends upon a purely subjective speculation as to what must necessarily have been the purpose of God in creating this infinity of spheres, viz., to people them, as, in the contrary

* "Astronomy," says Steffens, "is rapidly approaching the time when our planetary system will be recognized as the most highly organized point in the universe; and the time is not distant when our earth will be recognized, not, indeed, as the phenomenal but as the internal spiritually-viewed central point in the planetary system, just as man is in the Total-Organism." Hegel expresses the same thought, certainly in his own peculiar method. On this whole question, see Lutterhed's "Baaders Lehre vom Weltgebäude," 1866. A closely associated question is whether the earth's physical position in the universe was at the beginning the same as now, or whether a displacement, an expulsion from the central point has occurred, to which Schelling alludes, as well as Schaden in his "Orion." For the rest, I refer the reader to my treatise in Heiberg's Urania, "The Church-Year and the World-Year."

case, He would have made something wholly super-fluous. We will not enter into barren prolixities, but will limit ourselves to the observation that, when it has been experimentally proved that these star-dwellers are not creatures of imagination, such as one reads of in romances, but that they actually exist, we shall be prepared to enter upon the dis-cussion of their ability to affect the centrality of man. Of this there is not the remotest prospect. Revelation speaks of only two classes of created spirits : angels and men. We shall continue to abide by this postulate,—One earth, one human race, one Christ to whom also the angels are subject ; who is the image of the visible God, and the first-born of every creature ; for by Him were all things created that are in heaven and that are in earth, visible and invisible, whether they be thrones or dominions or principalities or powers ; all things were created by Him and for Him (Col. i. 15, 16).

LXXIX.

RECONCILIATION AND REDEMPTION BY CHRIST— THE NEW ADAM—THE INCARNATION—THE NEW ADAM.

BÖHME expresses a firm belief (in harmony with the creed of the Church) in the historical Christ, who was revealed in the fulness of the times.

" Beloved mind ! we write no conceits and tales ; it is earnest, and it is as much as our bodies and souls are worth : we must give a strict account of it, as being the talent that is committed to us. If any will be scandalized at it, let them take heed what they do : truly it is high time to awake from sleep, for the Bridegroom comes.

I. We Christians believe and acknowledge that the Eternal Word of God the Father became a true self-subsisting Man (with Body and Soul) in the body (womb or life) of the Virgin Mary, without man's interposing. For we believe that He was conceived by the Holy Ghost, and born of the Body of the Virgin, without any blemishing of her virgin chastity.

II. Also we believe that, in His human Body, He died and was buried.

III. Also we believe that He descended into Hell, and has broken the bands of the devil, wherewith he held men captive, in pieces, and redeemed the soul of man.

IV. Also we believe that He willingly died for our iniquities, and reconciled His Father, and has brought us into favour with Him.

V. Also we believe that He rose again from the dead on the third day, and ascended into Heaven, and there sits at the Right Hand of God.

VI. Also we believe that He shall come again at the Last Day to judge the living and the dead, and take His Bride with Him, and condemn the ungodly.

VII. Also we believe that He has a Christian Church here upon earth, which is begotten in His blood and death, and so made one Body with many members, which He cherishes, and governs with His Spirit and Word, and unites it continually by the Baptism of His own appointing and by the Sacrament of His Body and Blood, to be one only Body in Himself.

VIII. Also we believe that He protects and defends the same, and keeps it in one mind."

We find in Böhme no thorough-going Christology. He lays especial stress upon the points which possess for him a metaphysical, but assuredly, at the same time, a most profound religious interest. He sees in Christ the great mystery of godliness, God manifest in the flesh. By the Incarnation, there has arisen one Person of Deity and Humanity, of the essence of Mary and the essence of God. The Being of God and the human being has become one being, one Fulness ($\pi\lambda\dot\eta\rho\omega\mu\alpha$) of God. It is one of Böhme's most characteristic features, that he predominantly conceives of Christ as the New Adam, who has restored what was lost and flung into confusion by the first Adam.

LXXX.

THE Virgin Mary was the daughter of Joachim and Anna, a pure Virgin. She was not, however, an ordinary woman, like other daughters of Eve. She was the " daughter of the Covenant." The whole of the ancient covenant pointed to her, when it pointed to Him who was to be born. In Nazareth, she received the Annunciation ; and when she said to the angel: " Be it unto me according to thy word !" she conceived. The Eternal Word passed into her flesh and blood, together with the heavenly Virgin Sophia, by the power of the Holy Ghost ; and the Divine Fiat stood in her matrix. The Eternal Word, who passed into her to become flesh, did not, on that account, cease to abide in the Father, without any separation. But the Word was in the heavenly Maiden, and drew Mary's essences to Itself, and arrayed Itself in her flesh. For nine months Jesus was shaped in her womb, a complete man, with soul, spirit, and flesh. The child possessed, at one and the same time, the essence of His Mother Mary, the essence of the Word, and of the Heavenly Virgin. But this whole conception and birth was without sin. It was by this very conception and birth that Mary first became an absolutely pure maiden, attained perfect virginity, because she " put on " the Heavenly Virgin, who penetrated her essences. She achieved perfection as a shining morning-star. But we must not forget, that, notwithstanding this her exaltation, she was yet only able to become righteous and to be saved through her Son.

There are those who have supposed that the Eternal Word, who entered into Mary in order to become flesh, brought with It not only the Heavenly Virgin through whom Christ became a Heavenly Man, but also brought from heaven the *soul* of Christ. But this is false. The soul of Christ is of the essence of the Virgin Mary, but this human soul became absolutely penetrated and pervaded by the Eternal Word and the heavenly Virgin. What better should I be if Christ had brought His soul with Him from Heaven ? What would then become of the promise concerning the seed of the woman, the Bruiser of the Serpent ? For then, indeed, He would have been unable to be like us, and to be tempted at all points like ourselves, would have been unable to suffer in our stead and to bear our sin.

Then He would not have become our Brother, would not have become the Son of Man.*

LXXXI.

CHRIST is thus, in a double sense, the Son of the Virgin. He is the Son of the earthly Virgin Mary, and He is the Son of the heavenly Virgin, who united herself with Mary. But, from another standpoint, we may employ another metaphor, and say that the heavenly Virgin is wedded to Him, is indissolubly joined to Him. It was this very heavenly Virgin or Idea who departed from Adam when he became unfaithful to her, the bride of his youth, when he fell and the Divine Image grew pale in him, and who, subsequently, revealed herself to him in far-off visions that awoke his longings. This heavenly Idea has absolutely entered into the Second Adam, who is to restore her to us.

It has often been described as one of the most obscure points in Böhme, how the relation between Christ and the heavenly Virgin is to be apprehended? Some have supposed that in reality, viewed in the proper light and apart from poetic colouring, the Virgin is not distinguishable from Christ, and that she is Christ Himself, who in Scripture is certainly called Wisdom. We, however, do not thus read Böhme. It is, indeed, undeniable, that Christ designates Himself as *Wisdom* (Luke vii. 34), and that Christ " is of God made unto Wisdom." But the personal Wisdom, the Word, the Wisdom that expresses and

---

* " Three Principles in Man," xviii.

reveals itself, and the Father is one thing; the impersonal, objective Wisdom, the Idea, which is the servant of the Word, is another thing. And if we are to indicate more precisely what significance the latter has for Christ, we must formally construe it as a Spirit-being, a Light-being, which is united with Him, is the shining spirit-image always hovering about Him, and wherein, as in a mirror and inward heaven, He beholds the visions of the Kingdom of God, beholds the true world-ideal, the ideal of man and of the Church, beholds His own ideal as the Head of the human race, which He is to realize. An analogy of this is often found in the life of the regenerated, into which also Böhme introduces the heavenly Virgin. The Virgin is the ideal of the Kingdom of God, and, therewith, of man, which Christ introduces into our souls. It is noticeable that what Böhme, speaking of the life of the regenerated, attributes to the Virgin, Christians, as a rule, are wont to ascribe to the Holy Ghost. But, together with this, it must be observed that, for Böhme, the Virgin is not the Holy Ghost, but the gift of the Holy Ghost, of which Christ and the Holy Ghost certainly constitute the principle. This is the gift of Grace, in its most general and comprehensive sense, which pervades all special gifts of Grace, and places the special gift of Grace in its right relation to the Kingdom of God. The more completely the heavenly Idea is wedded to a man, and gains life and power in his personality, the more possible will it be to say of that man, that Christ through faith dwells in his heart, and that he has put on the wedding-garment.

When Böhme speaks from his own personal experience, he describes the Eternal Sophia as his heavenly Genius, given to him of the Lord to lead and direct him. He laments that he cannot always embrace and hold the Virgin, that his heart sometimes falls into sins. " But the Virgin has promised to be faithful to me, and never to forsake me in any adversity ; she will come to my succour in her Son ; I am to cleave fast to Him ; He will bring me back to her in Paradise. Therefore, on these terms, I will venture it, and I will go through thorns and thistles, through all kinds of jeering and infamy as well as I can, until I find again my fatherland, where my dearest Virgin dwells. I rely upon her faithful promise, when she appeared to me, that she would turn all my mournings into great joy; when I lay upon the mountain at midnight, so that all the trees fell upon me, and all the storms and winds beat upon me, and Antichrist gaped at me with his open jaws to devour me, then she came and comforted me, and married herself to me." [It is the ideal that went forth from Christ, and includes his own personal life-problem, which has wedded itself to him.] " Therefore, I am but the more cheerful, and care not for Antichrist ! " *

It is asked whether any parallel to Böhme's doctrine of the Virgin is to be found in philosophy. We might refer to the *Logos* in Philo, which is not a personal Being, as God is, but the fulness of thought, the world's ideal, which makes its abode

---

* "The Three Principles," xiv., 52.

in a man's soul, and is a guide and conductor to God; to the *Universal Idea* in Plato, which embraces all models and archetypes of that which makes its appearance in the actual world; to the *world-soul* in the Stoics; to the *ideal-world* in the Neoplatonists, which is an effulgence of God, and which, as Wisdom, has entered into the human soul, in order to lead it to purity and to that higher vision in which it wholly absorbs itself in the Divine depths.

All these, however, are but faint analogies; for the Maiden, in Böhme, has quite other postulates and surroundings. She is, as we have seen, the World's idea, which is not different from the idea of the Kingdom of God, and which, prior to the creation, played before the Face of God, wedded itself to man, who is created in the image of God, departed from him because of sin, was restored to him in Christ, and now variously individualizes itself in different human personalities.

LXXXII.

As the first Adam, before the Sinful Fall, was androgynous, so also must the second Adam be. Not, however, in a physical sense, for this would conflict with Luke ii. 21. After the fashion of the external world, Christ was a *man*. When the Word was to be arrayed in flesh, one of the two forms had to be selected, the masculine or the feminine. Christ was to be a *hero*, a warrior, the Bruiser of the Serpent; therefore He assumed masculine features; but it is clear from Böhme's whole delineation that Christ, in a spiritual sense, that the Love of Christ, was androgynous ; for He was destined to restore the sundered properties to " temperature," and to conduct us to that grade of life " where there is neither man nor woman " (Gal. iii. 28). And with this view we must certainly coincide. The Love of Christ would not be the complete Divine-Human Love if this Love had simply the properties of the man, and not those of the woman also. Although we cannot fail to recognize in Christ the highest excellencies of the masculine character, a world-subduing, world-conquering heroism, still, we cannot call Him a masculine character, in so far as this presents a contrast to the feminine. For we also find in Him the highest attributes of feminine virtue, infinite self-devotion and affec-tionateness of disposition, the incorruptible ornament of a meek and quiet spirit, purity and chastity of sentiment, the observance of the most delicate fundamental moral conditions, and the woman's characteristic capacity for passive obedience, strength of endurance, and self-abnegation full of unspeakable fidelity.

The Divine Love to man is pictured in the Bible not only as a father's love, but also as a mother's love. " Can a woman forget her sucking child, that she should not have compassion on the son of her womb ? Yea, they may forget, yet will I not forget thee, saith the Lord " (Isa. xlix. 15). And Christ says to Jerusalem : " How often would I have gathered thy children together, even as a hen gathereth her chickens under her wings ! " (Matt. xxiii. 37). Here most assuredly we have the metaphor of the mother's love in its infinite solicitude.   And if we think of the Crucified Christ, it is not enough to see in His Love simply that of the hero, the King, who sacrifices Himself for His people, for all races; we must also see in it the mother's love which vainly seeks to gather her rebellious and wandering children under her wings, and now leads Him to pour forth His blood in order to save them, and to draw them to Himself beneath the Cross.

The Apostle Paul, who was undoubtedly a heroic character, and one in whom the principle of strength, the fire-principle, was powerfully energetic, compares himself, in the Epistle to the Galatians, to a travailing mother: "My little children! of whom I travail in birth again, until Christ be formed in you!"   In 1 Thessalonians, he compares himself to a nurse who cherishes her children.   In ancient Christian art, androgynous pictures of the Crucified One are to be met with.   These, indeed, may be regarded as very naïve and paradoxical, and, if one please, lacking in taste.   Archæologists and art-critics have here attempted manifold historical and learned elucidations, but with total failure to arrive at unanimity.   But we ask the question whether any meaning can be found in these symbols, except in virtue of the conception alluded to above?   It will scarcely be doubted by any one that Christ, after the resurrection, was androgynous, even in a physical sense.

LXXXIII.

THE PROCESS OF CHRIST.

THE central point in the work of Christ is the Atonement and Redemption. It would have been of little benefit to us if, without the occurrence of any actual change in the world, God had simply proclaimed that He is gracious and merciful to us. Life in the creation is veritably disturbed, and " Temperature " has been lost. Thus, then, a new process of life and suffering must be initiated, in order that actual healing may take place, and " temperature " be re-established. In the " Process of Christ," Böhme lays special stress upon two points : the Temptation and Death, with the history of the Passion. All three principles are present in Christ, precisely as in Adam : the Light-principle, the dark Fire-principle, and the principle of this world ; but in Him the last-mentioned is in proper subordination. He must, however, be tempted of the devil, in order that He may be able to prevail in that trial in which Adam did not prevail. During this struggle, Christ wholly fixed His imagination upon the Father and the Kingdom of Light, vanquished the temptations of the senses and those of arrogance and ambition, and fulfilled the law in our stead. But this is not sufficient. He must bear the wrath of God in our stead, must bring the sacrifice of propitiation, must quench wrath with love. It must here be repeated that Böhme interprets wrath not merely on its ethical side, but also, and quite as fully, on its material side. The material side of wrath consists of the first three natural properties which are released into independence. All the disturbing and destructive forces, all sufferings and pains which have been evoked by the sin of man, and which men have to bear as the penalty of sin, pour in upon Christ, and He conquers them, and quenches wrath by His voluntary self-devotion in the Passion.

"He said that He was a King of Love; then the worldly magistrate thought, 'He will take away our might!' and the priests thought, 'This man is too mean for us; we will have a Messiah who may bring us to worldly dominion; we will not receive him; he is too poor for us; we will rather abide in our power, respect, and authority, and abandon this beggarly King with his love-kingdom.'"[*]

Thus, then, they made Him prisoner; and in every momentum of the Passion-history—which Böhme treats with great minuteness, and often allegorically,—some form of wrath came into manifestation, and was always vanquished by love. The aim of the "Process of Christ" is, "that Self might cease in the humanity, and God's Spirit might be all in all, and the Self only His instrument."[†]

For this reason it was necessary that Christ should surrender Himself unto death, in order that He might vanquish it from within. His outward body, which was in the likeness of sinful flesh, must die upon the Cross, to the end that the power

---

[*] "Signatura Rerum," x., 79.
[†] *Ibid.*, xi., 10.

of His heavenly Blood, the power of eternal life, might come to rule in inward and outward humanity.

"And when Christ was upon the Cross, it came about thereby that God's speaking Word stood still now in the human property; and the new-born Essentiality, which was dead in Adam, but was again quickened in Christ, cried out with the same, ' My God, my God ! why hast Thou forsaken me ? ' For the anger of God was by the soul's property entered into the image of the Divine Essentiality, and had devoured the image of God, because this image was to bruise the head of God's wrath in the Fire-soul. Thus must not only the selfishness of the human property, viz., the soul's own self-will to live in the Fire's might, die and be drowned in the image of Love, but also the image of Love itself must resign and give itself in unto the wrath of Death. All must fall down into Death, in order to arise in God's will and mercy through Death in the Paradisiacal source in the resignation, that God's Spirit might be all in all."*

When Böhme says that the *Essentiality*, which was dead in Adam, and was again quickened in Christ, cried, " My God, my God ! why hast Thou forsaken me ? " we believe that we can approximately understand this marvellously profound but obscure expression, if we take "Essentiality" to mean the Spirit in distinction from the soul, that which is, in the most rigid sense, the Divinely-imaged in human nature, that which makes it capable of love, and of union with the Idea, the Virgin.

---

* " Signatura Rerum," xi., 28, 84.

It is not only that the body must die upon the Cross, and not only the soul-element which craves self-preservation and earthly enjoyments, but also the spiritual Ego, the Will of Love, the Will towards the Kingdom of God, which He is to establish. This also must die as Egoism, as something which was Christ's own, because Love is to have nothing as its own, as its possession. It was necessary that even His Work and His Kingdom should sink into death before Him, when God's speaking Word stood still. It may be truly said that Christ, during the whole of His active Life, sought to have nothing as His own, but all as the Father's, that He did not seek His own Glory, but the Father's. But it is precisely this which is now, in the Passion and Death, to constitute His trial, when He has to sacrifice everything. Christ's Soul-life and Spirit-life were not, however, annihilated in this sacrificial Death ; only the humanity in Him had wholly surrendered its own Will. But this was absolutely merged in the First Will, in the Father's Will, as in the First Root. When He had absolutely surrendered everything into the hands of the Father, Love had swallowed up wrath, and wrath itself was sunk in death. " Temperature " was restored in Him, who had acted vicariously for the fallen creation.

" Thou dear, seeking Heart, that floatest about as in a dark pool, where thou canst not see in or out, cleave fast to the Crucified Christ ! Forgive them that trespass against thee (thy debtors), and entreat God that He, for Christ's sake, will forgive thee thy trespasses ; then He will hear thee, and thou shalt be led into the ‘ Process of Christ,’ which ends in Light and the Kingdom of Light.”

LXXXIV.

THE EXALTED CHRIST.

THE Saviour rose from the grave, at the midnight hour, in a paradisiacal body, in which His earthly body was, as it were, swallowed up, on which account, moreover, He was able to manifest it to His disciples, as a testimony that it was He Himself. That the stone was rolled away from the sepulchre was only for a sign to the disciples and to the Jews ; for Christ Himself it was unnecessary. He was able to pass, in bodily shape, through closed doors, through all things.

By the Resurrection of Christ it is demonstrated that He is true Lord over Heaven, Earth, and Hell ; and that all power is given to Him in heaven and upon earth. “ Let this be told you, all ‘ye Jews, Turks, and heathen ! it profits you nothing that you expect another. Beware only, lest the Fire of Wrath and Judgment descend upon you ! ”

During forty days, He manifested Himself to the disciples at various times, and became visible to them ; and finally He ascended into Heaven, and sat down at the Right Hand of the Father. Heaven is the inward basis and foundation of this visible world, and the Right Hand of God is the Might of His Omnipotence.

LXXXV.

WHERE then is Christ, and *where* is the Right Hand of the Father? Böhme is in absolute agreement with the old Lutheran dogmatic which teaches that "dextera Dei ubique est," and that Christ is in no definite place. Luther combats the mediæval scholasticism: "They invent a phantom Heaven, where stands a golden throne, and Christ sits at the right hand of the Father in a chorister's mantle and with a golden crown!" "They talk childishly about heaven, and want Christ to have a *place* in heaven, like a stork that has a nest in a tree!"

But, however correct it may be that all material space-limitations, borrowed from this world of the senses, must be rejected, and that Christ is not circumscribed by any definite and fixed place in heaven, this Lutheran definition is, nevertheless, inadequate, and it must be regarded as a defect in Böhme, that he did not pass beyond Lutheran idealism, and that he did not here maintain his own realism. We cannot imagine any actual existence, cannot conceive of the heavenly individuality of Christ, without some relation to space, a fact, however, which by no means implies that these material space definitions, under which we are held, are the only ones possible. Even although the Right Hand of God, His Omnipotence, is everywhere, does it follow from this that the *seat* at the Right Hand of God is everywhere? When Luther says that Christ is not in a single spot, but that He is everywhere, this ubiquity becomes a diffused and indefinite extension throughout the whole creation, not visibly distinguishable from a pantheistic Immanence with a pantheistic nature—Christ—although this is very far from Luther's thought. We maintain, notwithstanding Luther's polemical utterances, that which was perfectly true in mediæval realism, although it may have been arrayed sometimes in puerile forms, that there must be a *Central Place* for the Omnipotence and Glory of God, a Holy of Holies in Heaven itself, wherein the perfect Presence dwells ; and that we cannot imagine the omnipresent Power of God, unless this be also centralized in itself. Oetinger, indeed, goes farther than Böhme, when he speaks of a concentrated ubiquity. We do not hesitate to say that Christ is where the *Throne* is, and where the seven Spirits or Lamps stand before the Throne. The Throne is precisely the central place in the inmost sanctuary. But He is not circumscribed there as if in an earthly space. From thence He can penetrate all things with His powers and gifts ; can make Himself actually present where He wills ; can "be with us unto the end of the world ;" can, by means of the Word, the Sacraments, and the Holy Ghost, come with the Father and take up His abode with us ; and can walk in the Church in the midst of the seven golden candlesticks, that is, can be the centre of His Church. The higher region can penetrate the lower, while the lower cannot penetrate the higher, although the higher region is quite close to us, hovers around us, and encircles us. For there can be no question here of material distances. As the One who is in the midst of the Uncreated

Heaven, He is also the centre of the whole creation, He is the centre of the Church.

LXXXVI.

IN his interpretation of the incident of the Ascension itself, when " He was taken up, and a cloud received Him out of the disciples' sight," as Scripture relates, Böhme opposes the scholastic view which " counts and measures how many hundred thousand miles it is to the Heaven whither Christ is gone " ("The Three Principles," xxv., 101). Because Heaven is the internal ground and basis of the outer world, Böhme teaches, in harmony with Lutheran theologians, that Heaven is quite near us, and that (as has been expressed, for instance, by old Philip Nicolai) one does not need to undertake a journey after death in order to reach Heaven, but that those who are counted worthy to enter in simply require to open their eyes. It may be regarded as a view of the Ascension of Christ, which has become more and more general among Protestants, that the way to Heaven does not lie through infinite expanses of starry space,— a mediæval conception which many opponents of Christianity in our days give themselves the trouble to confute, as though it were the only conception possible. The old dogmatists rightly interpreted the Ascension of Christ (which, in so far as it was visible, scarcely requires to be considered as a movement persisting over a longer time) as a sign, a σημεῖον (δεικτικῶς), which was necessary for the disciples, in order to acquaint them with the fact that the Work of Christ was now concluded, and that He had now exchanged life in the earthly sphere, wherein is sin and death, darkness and heaviness, for Heaven, the imperishable Kingdom of Light, where He will henceforward exercise His invisible activity. For Christ Himself this visible uplifting was unnecessary. It is scarcely too bold to suppose that He, whose corporeity was now wholly transfigured in order that He might enter into Heaven, might have remained where He stood, have become invisible to the disciples, and might then have been in Heaven, as a movement *ab extra ad intra*, a return to the mysterious regions that lie behind this world.

And yet, although we thus reject material space-determinations with their measures of length and miles, we are again compelled to posit, even in Heaven itself, space-determinations of another and a higher kind. For it is expressly stated in Scripture that " He has passed into the *Heavens*, and has entered into Heaven itself," which latter can only be the Heaven of Heavens, where the throne stands. Indeed, it is said of the beggar Lazarus that the angels carried him into Abraham's bosom. Here, consequently, we have both movement and space-relation, which, for good reasons, we are incapable of apprehending more closely, so long as our eyes are shrouded by the veil of materiality. We may say, There is a cloud which conceals these regions from our sight, and this cloud is essentially our flesh, our own material nature. We can only affirm : What is here corporeity must there be extension and extended relation. A single question then remains : Whether this material corporeity which continually dies and passes into corruption is the only corporeity which is possible and real ? Scripture tells us that there is a spiritual and heavenly body, from which it follows that there must be for this appropriate space-relations. If Christ has a transfigured and glorified corporeity (which is an *articulus fidei stantis aut cadentis*), there must also be a region that corresponds with this. Now, although this region or these regions must, in comparison with our material region, be called spaceless, super-spatial, yet absolute spacelessness cannot be attributed to them. For, if it be true that in the Father's House there are many mansions, and that we must picture to ourselves in Heaven the Throne with the seven Lamps, then also quantitative and phenomenal relations must prevail in Heaven. Upon this point, the necessity of a Locality in the other world, Böhme has not entered more minutely, although, as he so energetically maintains the Uncreated Heaven, this is the very point on which he might be expected to dilate. He has not gone farther than the old Lutheran dogmatic, which, in its struggle with mediæval scholasticism, the essential contents of which are embodied by Dante, sacrificed the substance with the accidents. We shall return to the subject in discussing Böhme's Eschatology

LXXXVII.

THE APPROPRIATION OF GRACE—REGENERATION.

"ON the day of Pentecost, the Holy Spirit was poured forth from the centre of the Trinity, and all the doors of the wonders of God were opened, for the Spirit of God passed into the essences of men, into their inmost basis of life, filled them, and spoke out of all the centres. Hearts, mouths, and ears were opened, and the Apostles spoke in the tongues of the peoples. Then the 'Process of Christ' began to repeat itself in human souls, for all that Christ has done outside us is to repeat itself within us, and we ourselves are to return into 'Temperature,' and pass out of the 'Turba' in which we are buried."*

Regeneration is accomplished by the Spirit of Christ and the means of grace, the Word and the Sacraments. But however high a place Böhme may assign to the Word and the Sacraments, he repeatedly insists that the object and matter of chief importance is what is to be effected by these means, viz. : Regeneration, the new man after the similitude of Christ. For this reason he contends so strongly against Babel, the existing Church, in which the Sacraments are only outwardly used, the Word is only outwardly preached and heard, without the true dispositions of the heart, without the inward doors being really opened.

"It profits nothing," he says to the clergy, "that

---

* "The Three Principles," xxvi., 4, 5.

you shout and bawl from the pulpit; if you have not the right hammer to strike the clock that awakens the hearts, you are really dumb for those who hear you. The spirit and power of Christ must be in your words, so that your hearers may be able to observe Christ in your words, and to hear the Voice of the Good Shepherd. In Babel one finds only the historical faith. It is mere childishness to think to be saved by a simply historical faith, as is heard every Sunday in the churches. They suppose that it is enough to admit and agree that Christ died for our sins, and that His righteousness is imputed to us, and that then they may continue as they are, and go on in their old worldliness and sin." In many parts of his writings, Böhme is exceedingly violent against Babel. He strives against all these nominal Christians, sham Christians, Christians of habit, all these clergy, who are only sounding brass and tinkling cymbals, slow-bellies, etc., etc. Similar lamentations are well known in every period of earnest Church-revival.

There is no use in Babel. You are not saved by a merely historical faith by which you imagine that you can throw the robe of grace around you, while, within, you continue to be a wild beast. Consider, O man! that we can stand in three principles, the dark fire-principle, or the devilish principle, the principle of this world, with the world's lusts and appetites; but that it behoves us to enter into the Light-principle and into the Kingdom of Light, which we lost by Adam's fall, and which Christ has brought back to us. The important matter is that the Light and the World of Light should be kindled in you. Consider that we in this world are as if in a field. We all grow in secret, and when our hour-glass has run out, and this outward body becomes a corpse, and this outward world is taken from us, then it shall be made manifest whether the new man has been born and has grown in you, or whether it is only the old man that has been growing, with his old attributes, pride, envy, covetousness, and wrath. Then shall it be seen whether you belong to the children of the Spirit of God, or to those who have comforted themselves in stone churches with an imputed righteousness, and still have continued to be greedy dogs, vain peacocks, lustful goats, and other such pernicious beasts. A great change must take place in you. You must die with Christ, die away from your sinful egoism and selfishness, your evil propensities, that Christ may arise in you. There must be a violent transition into the fourth natural property, into the Lightning, so that you may come out of the wrath of God, out of the torture-chamber, in which you are secretly a captive.

"Per ignem, per crucem ad lucem!"

LXXXVIII.

PERHAPS there are some who will ask here whether Böhme has forgotten that Regeneration takes place at Baptism, that Baptism is a bath of Regeneration. He has not forgotten this. He teaches that God, by baptism, introduces His Covenant of Grace into humanity, that the whole man, both soul, spirit, and body, needs to be baptized, needs a fresh unction, a new "tincture," so that a new life may bloom and flourish. The heavenly element is imparted through the element of water, by means of the Word, and it is the whole Trinity that baptizes. The Father baptizes with Fire unto repentance and conversion, and assails the soul with the Law, with His severe righteousness, whereby the foundation is laid for repentance and sorrow over sin.

The Son baptizes with Love and Grace, with the gentle Light, quenches the Father's wrath, and heals the soul by the Forgiveness of sins.

The Holy Ghost baptizes with a new Life, and bestows the right understanding and the true belief, which we recognise and accept as such.

And all this is not metaphorical. An essential operation takes place, a union of the essence of Grace and the essence of man. The sinful human nature acquires a new tincture, a new life stratum, which, however, cannot unfold its power until faith is added.

But what does it avail us that there is preaching in Babel concerning Baptism and the Covenant of Baptism, when there is no regular preaching concerning Faith ?

"We are taught an imputed righteousness and an imputed grace ; but what Faith is, how it is born, what it is in its essence and nature, and how it appropriates the merit of Christ,—these are points on which the majority are absolutely dumb ! Therein are they blind ; and there remains a simply historical faith, which gives us only nominal Christians. To believe is not merely to accept as true, to agree that the matter stands thus and thus ; it is not simply a thought, a knowledge, which even devils possess ; nay, to believe is to partake of grace, to partake of the being of God ; and in order to this a great and mighty earnestness is requisite. Faith is a strong desire, a hunger and thirst after Christ and the Spirit of Christ, and the setting of the whole imagination upon that which one desires, the introduction of it into, and the embodiment of it in oneself. In Faith, the soul leads its will out of this corrupted flesh, with all its perishableness, and leads it into the Gate that is opened in Christ. Christ then draws my will, which I surrender to Him, into His Will : He 'tinctures' my will with the highest tincture of the Divine Will, and guides it to God. Then steps He forward with His Will before God, and in His Will is my will, and I become accepted as a child of grace" (" Epistles,"46).

For Böhme, Faith is, consequently, the most profound act of the will ; still, no one can believe simply by his own power. If I am to believe, the Spirit of Christ, the desire of Christ, the Will of Christ must believe in my desire and will. Not that this is to be understood as implying a fatalistic election of grace. Although faith itself is an effect of grace, yet the natural man has the choice whether he will surrender himself, and let himself be grasped by grace, or whether he will resist grace. Böhme frequently repeats the Lord's words to Jerusalem : " *Ye would not !* "

LXXXIX.

THE objection has been raised against Böhme that he does not assign its due place to the doctrine of justification by Faith, that kernel of the Lutheran Creed, because he does not establish a thorough-going distinction between Justification and Sanctification. This distinction is undeniably of great importance, when the question is asked : Upon what do I base my assurance that I am admitted into the grace of God? If I base this assurance upon my sanctification, I base it upon an insecure foundation ; for my sanctification is an unfinished fragment, in which there is both progress and retrogression. I can have firm assurance only when it is built exclusively upon the Grace of God, who, for Christ's sake, is willing to forgive me my sins and to accept me as His child. I am then recognized as just before God, not on the ground of any merit or work of mine, but because I appropriate in faith the merit of Christ, which God, in His Grace, imputes to me. This faith is not, in the remotest degree, my own merit. It is simply the organ by which I receive grace : it is, so to speak, merely the hand with which I reach after and grasp grace. This is the only source from which sanctification can first proceed, as an endeavour after righteousness and perfection of life.

It must certainly be admitted that Böhme has not deemed it of great consequence to develop this distinction. And it must also be granted that his doctrine of an indwelling grace, an indwelling righteousness, is open to misconception, unless close attention be paid to his precise meaning. But it must not be overlooked, on the other hand, that he really wishes to supply a corrective against an abstract and mechanical distinction, a false separation and illegitimate severance of Justification and Sanctification, which had become very general. For it was supposed by many that if one simply accepted justification by Faith as an axiom to which one gave one's assent, one could then array oneself in the robe of grace, without the necessity of any earnest spiritual desire for sanctification, and without coming into any really living fellowship with Christ. The inmost meaning of Böhme's polemic is this: that it is unavailing so to distinguish between Justification and Sanctification as thereby to deny their necessary connection, and to make Sanctification appear as an accidental appendage, which, at a pinch, may be dispensed with.

For Böhme, justifying Faith is no external dogma, but a life-momentum in the soul, which must not be separated from the other life-momenta, but must continue to form an integral part of the " process of life." His meaning is : As truly as Faith is a will, which grasps Christ, so truly must the whole Christ and communion with Him be the object of this will. I cannot earnestly will to participate in the atonement of Christ, the restoration of the broken covenant, and the removal of guilt, without also wishing to participate in His redemption, in the actual cleansing and liberation from sin and sinful propensities, and without also setting my will upon the new life. I cannot believe in Christ as my Justification, and set my imagination upon His glorious Light-image, without also forsaking the devil-image and the world-image, and banishing these false images from my soul.

It is thus, as it seems to us, that Böhme must be understood, when his main intention is regarded, and when isolated and unguarded expressions in the course of his polemic are not unduly pressed. He has never denied that the whole fountain-spring of our justification is Christ, the Crucified and Risen (*justitia extra nos posita*). He shows most clearly, in many passages, that he builds his salvation, his assurance of the grace of God not upon anything in himself, but exclusively upon the compassion of God in Christ, upon the Sufferings and Death of Christ (the central point in his Christology), in which we are wholly to absorb ourselves, and absolutely to develop our will. And he proved this, even in his dying hour, by praying: "Thou Crucified Lord Jesus Christ! have compassion upon me, and take me into Thy Kingdom!" But he demands that Faith shall be regarded as an earnest and serious thing. Without saying so, and perhaps without being fully conscious of it, he thus points back to the original doctrine of Faith, held by the Reformers and by our Church, viz.:—that it is not simply knowledge and assent (*notitia, assensus*), but a hearty reliance upon the Grace of God in Christ, a grasping of grace as it is also a grasping of Christ. But if Faith be this, there must also in Faith be an actual union with Christ. Nor is it astonishing that Böhme was unable to rest satisfied with the position that Justification is only an external act of judgment, by which man is *declared just*, without the occurrence of any kind of inward change, without any real communication of the Righteousness of Christ, were it only in a small beginning, like a grain of mustard-seed, what Luther, in his preface to the Epistle to the Romans, calls " the beginning of the Gifts or of the Spirit." This is what Böhme expresses by saying that Christ "tinctures" our will and, in order to lead it into a higher form of life, imparts to it a living power, which, during the progress of life, may become an indwelling grace. If the will is tinctured by Christ, justifying Faith must contain the germs of Sanctification, must be, not only a living, but also a vitalizing, sanctifying Faith, containing in itself the new principle of obedience. Then must there subsist between Christ and the believer a *unio mystica*, which is to grow and increase during the development of life.

Böhme's leading idea is *life*. What he is urging in the present connection is, that Christianity in the individual man must be *life*, in its complete movement, in its "process." It is the living Christian personality, the whole Christian man that he brings before us in his doctrine of Regeneration, the scope of which he regards as stretching through the whole life.

XC.

IT is for this reason that he returns so often to the conflicts of the Christian life, which continue until this life's end. We have in our nature two wills, the one, the quiet gracious will, which is the will of the new man ; and the other, the restless pernicious thistle, which is the old Adamite will : and these are always at strife with each other. We have a lily-child and a thistle-child within us, and the storms of this life sweep often so tempestuously over the lily, that it might seem at times as though the lily must utterly perish. But, by the grace of God, it grows and becomes green, so that, at last, it may blossom in eternity, when this body falls off like a husk. It is simply a question of perseverance in the conflict, and of resistance to temptation, in the name of Jesus. For we are tempted now by our own proud ego, which is veritably a thistle, now by the devil, and now by our flesh. As a resource against everything that would hinder our salvation, he recommends prayer in the name of Jesus. For the name of Jesus is a gate, and whatever is spoken through this gate reaches the ear of God ; He hears it. By means of prayer, the soul soars up above the *centrum* of anxiety, the abyss of hell, the spirit of this world, and penetrates into the other principle, into the Light, into Christ, into the Heart of God. But if you would pray, you must first cleanse yourself of all your abominations, and must next examine yourself, whether there be anything you more highly desire than God's compassion. But if God's compassion is the highest thing to you, and if your prayer is earnest, you shall prevail. For to pray is not only to desire, but to *work* in the strength of God. In true prayer the soul becomes a hungry magical fire which draws the Being of God out of the Incarnation into itself, and the soul becomes clothed with a Light-body, in which it can find rest, while in the world it has only anxiety ("Epistles," xi., v.).

Böhme often returns in his meditations to those states of anxiety in which the soul falls into doubt of its salvation, when sins oppress, and the soul is disconsolate, when the devil and hell storm in against it, and would tempt it to despair. His own experience has made him acquainted with such conditions, for he himself is in a perpetual process, in order that his gold may be refined, that the hard rocks in which it is imprisoned may be burst asunder, and that the lily within him may succeed in growing. We have already heard him concerning the hour when he lay on the mountain at midnight, when all the trees fell over him, the storm swept about him, and Antichrist opened his jaws to devour him, and when, finally, the Sophia came, and comforted him. He advises to all men the course that he himself pursued : on no account to lose faith, on no condition to relinquish the strong resolution to be saved. " Even if thou hast no strength in thy heart, and the devil binds thy tongue, thou shalt yet let God's promises to thee be more certain to thee than thy own heart. And even if thine own heart says nay! that shall not appal thee. Thou shalt hold fast to this resolve : ' Lord ! I will not lose Thee ! Do with me as Thou wilt, I will be Thine ! ' Then will He have compassion upon thee, and thou shalt enter into the will of God, and then thou art God's child, and Christ's goods belong to thee, and His merits are thy merits. His Life, Death, and Resurrection are all thine, and thou art a member of His Body, and His Spirit is thy spirit. He leads thee in right paths, and all that thou doest, thou doest unto God " (" Incarnation of Christ ").

To Böhme's teaching with regard to despondency, on which subject he displays a profound knowledge of the human heart, belongs his "Treatise on the Four Complexions," written as a direction to an ever-sorrowful and anxious heart. By the Four "Complexions" he understands what we call the Four Temperaments, which he compares to the four elements : the sanguine to air, the choleric to fire, the phlegmatic to water, the melancholy to earth, which is cold, dry, dark, and hungry after light. The complexions do not belong to the eternal essence of the soul, but possess a merely temporal significance. They are only inns, places of abode, in which the various souls must dwell during this outward life. They are given to man at his conception and birth, and it depends upon the influence of the stars and the nature-spirit which temperament one receives. Böhme now especially applies this to consolation and advice for the melancholy temperament. The melancholy temperament is dark and dry, and is prone to consume itself inwardly in its own being. It abides always in the House of Sorrow, and is continually afraid of the wrath of God and the power of wrath. Souls that dwell in this inn, where they often lament that God has forgotten them, that they are forsaken, without comfort, and cannot receive grace, are to take note that there are many anxieties which do not come from the devil, but from the natural temperament. They are to know that in this dark chamber they certainly have the devil for a neighbour, since he dwells in darkness, but that he cannot hurt them, if they only hold fast to the promise of God, and believe although

they do not see. They are to know that it is the
will of God to try them in this dark chamber, and
that they are to fight and wrestle with themselves,
reflecting that this is for their profit ; and that while
the soul dwelleth in the House of Sorrow, it is not
in the House of Sin, but that it is a great sin to
yield to false imaginations, such as delude us into
the idea that God will not be gracious to us.

As remedies against the anxieties of the melancholy nature, Böhme advises industry, for idleness
only nourishes sorrow. Nor should a soul in the
melancholy chamber give itself up too much to
solitude, but should seek the society of men, and
converse with them, in order to lose its heavy
thoughts. It ought not to read too many books,
least of all such as treat of election by grace ; but
in all questions of this character it should attach
itself simply to Holy Scripture. It is not to
surrender itself to speculations and inquiries. But
if a soul in the dark chamber is naturally endowed
with a mind and thoughts that are deep, so that
it *must* search and cannot avoid inquiry, then let it, in
the fear of God and with constant prayer, seek for the
opening of the centre of nature in itself, for it will
see therein its own ground and cause ; and then all
fear and sorrow will vanish away from it, and it will
find rest. This testimony Böhme gives from his own
experience ; for he himself, in this world, dwelt in the
melancholy inn.

XCI.

WE will close this description by recalling a simple
picture of life under sin and wrath, and life under

grace, in the following of Christ, which Böhme has sketched in a " Dialogue between an Enlightened and Unenlightened Soul," in a letter to a soul that hungers and thirsts after the love of Christ.

There was a poor soul had wandered out of Paradise and come into the kingdom of this world ; and there the devil met with it and represented to it that, if it would break its will off from the Will of God, and from God lead its will into nature and the creatures, and open its *centrum naturæ*, it would be able to know all things, and become its own lord upon the earth, and rule in the world with great might. The devil showed it a serpent biting itself in the tail, which had precisely the appearance of a Fire-wheel (a symbol of the *centrum naturæ*, the *Worm !*), and said to it, " Thou art thyself such a Fire-Wheel, such a *Mercurius in Vulcano ;* if thou only wilt arouse it in thee by breaking off thy will from the Will of God, thou shalt bring all things into thy power." The soul let itself thus be seduced, opened its *centrum naturæ*, and went out of " temperature " ; and now awoke in the soul all the properties of nature, and each of them introduced itself with its own lust and craving. The Wheel of Birth burst into flames, and there arose a desire to uplift itself over all, to rule over all, and to despise humility, viz., *Pride and Haughtiness.* There arose a desire to draw all things to itself and to possess all, *Covetousness.* There was kindled a stinging, thorny lust in the fiery life, a poison of hell, *Envy.* And there awoke a torment like fire, which would murder and destroy all that which would not be subject to this pride, viz., *Wrath.* The whole Foundation of Hell was manifested in this soul, the devil brought it on from one vice to another, and the soul lost God, and Paradise, and the Kingdom of Heaven, and became a Worm, like the Fire-serpent which the devil had shown it.

In this plight, it met our dear Lord Jesus Christ, who was come into the world to destroy the works of the devil, and He looked upon it with His compassion, and called it back. It was to repent and be converted, and then He would deliver it from the monstrous deformed shape, and bring it into Paradise again. Then the soul considered itself, and was affrighted with the greatest possible anguish, for God's righteous judgment was manifested in it. Then said the Lord Jesus Christ, with the voice of His grace, " Repent, and forsake vanity, and thou shalt attain my grace ! "

Now, therefore the soul went before God, and intreated for grace, and was strongly persuaded in itself, that the satisfaction and atonement of the Lord Jesus Christ did belong to it. But since the serpent-symbol was not abolished, and the soul did not observe that it was still monstrous, and that it had preserved all its old evil inclinations in their false natural right, it could not attain peace. For, when it sought to pray and lead its will into God, then all its thoughts fled away from God, and went into earthly things. The devil tempted it in all manner of ways, and said to it in its restlessness, " Why dost thou torment thyself ? Behold the world, how it lives in jollity and mirth, yet it will be saved well enough for all that ! Hath not Christ paid the ransom and satisfied for all men? Thou needest only to comfort thyself that it is done for thee, and then thou shalt be saved. Thou canst not possibly in this world come to have any feeling of God; take care for thy body, and look after temporal glory. Salvation comes well enough at the last!"

But with all this the soul could not find rest. And it knew not that itself was a monster. Now would it betake itself to the pleasures of the world, and now it yearned after God, and did not know that this its longing came from God, from Christ, who sought to lead it from the world unto Himself. Then it resolved to be free from all business cares and the hindrances of the world, and betake itself to some private solitary place, to perform true repentance ; and it thought also to be bountiful and pitiful to the poor. But neither in solitude could it find rest, but sank down into the deepest misery, became sick with apprehension and anxiety, and could not find a single consolation.

Then happened it, by the providence of God, that in the solitude an enlightened and regenerate soul came to it, and thoroughly acquainted it with the fact that it bore the monstrous shape of the devil, and that its error was in fancying that it could believe without forsaking its own will and dying. And when the Unenlightened Soul asked, "What, then, am I to do, so that I may attain peace?" the Enlightened Soul replied, "Thou shalt do absolutely nothing, but thou shalt wholly forsake thine own will ; and then, thereby, all thine evil propensities will grow weak and faint, and ready to die, and thou wilt sink down again into that one thing from which thou art sprung originally. For now thou liest captive in the creatures, and if thy will forsaketh them, the creatures, with their evil inclinations, will die in thee, which, for the present, stay and hinder thee that thou canst not come to God. We must not allow ourselves to be held captive by the creatures, whereby we are unable to follow Christ. For this reason also we must forgive our enemies, for, so long as we hate men, we are held captive in hostile creatures, and our will is not free."

And when now the soul began to practise this course with much earnestness, when it wholly absorbed itself in Christ's Suffering and Death, in deep repentance and off-dying, yet it did not all at once come to peace; but at last God let His face shine upon it, and it was enabled to pray and to rejoice exceedingly, because it was released from Death and Hell. And although it fell subsequently into great contempt, and was assaulted by the shame and reproach of the world, and although the devil tempted it, and said, " It is only an imagination that thou hast partaken of the grace of God ; it is not of God ! " nevertheless, the soul, without letting itself be captured by the creatures, went its way through inward and outward tribulation, through joy and anxiety; and the Lord Jesus Christ went with it, until at last it entered into the great Kingdom of Grace.

We see that Böhme has sought to indicate, in this simple sketch, the difference between a spurious and a real conversion, between an outward appropriation of the Righteousness of Christ and that faith in the atonement of Christ which is inseparable from a thorough resolution to forsake sin, and to enter upon the new life.

XCII.

THE LAST THINGS.

AS we now proceed to notice Böhme's doctrine of the Last Things, we cannot refrain from wishing that he had, on this subject also, supplied a corrective to the church theology of his day ; for he does not essentially pass beyond the old Lutheran dogmatic, the eschatology of which has well-known defects ; still, his detailed development of the subject has its own peculiar character, and leads us back to the depths of his fundamental view.　　　　　　　　.

XCIII.

HEAVEN AND HELL—THE UNCHANGEABLE WILL AFTER DEATH.

WHITHER does the soul go when it is separated from the body ?　He who rightly understands the three Principles has no need to ask this question. In this life man can stand in three principles. The first principle, the dark Fire-principle, is eternal, because it has its root in the eternal *centrum naturæ*, in the Wrath of God. The second principle, the Light-principle, is also eternal, because it has its root in the eternal Love of God. The third principle, this external world, is temporal ; and when the body, which attaches us to this external world, is broken asunder and becomes a corpse, the soul must stand in one of the two eternal principles, in Heaven or Hell.

Here, during this present life, the soul has still a choice, and can let itself be born again. Here it can still change its will ; but after the death of the body it has no longer *anything* in *which* it can change its will. *Here* it can break its images in pieces, and set its will upon another ; but after death this is no longer possible. For it must then retain what it has taken along with it in its desire and imagination. That wherein it has developed its will during this life, that does it retain, nor can it be released therefrom. It has entered into the still Eternity ; it dwells in a "*Magia,*" and gains a simultaneous view of its whole life and of all its deeds, not indeed in reality, but in their figures or images in the magic mirroring. The quality which was strongest in the soul during this life grows even stronger yonder. This is a great consolation to believers ; for if thou here dost struggle earnestly against thine evil habits and subdue them, thou hast still to lament and sigh that thou canst not always accomplish what thou willingly wouldst ; so thou art to know that much that here was only smoking flax becomes a mighty flame yonder, when this corruptible body is laid aside with its evil vapours.

But, in the ungodly, the evil quality which was strongest here becomes even stronger yonder. Anti-christian Souls do not ask for the Gate of Christ, but only sink deeper in their false opinions. They wrap themselves up in these, and again unwrap themselves, because they have nothing to hold fast by.

The ungodly grow into the shape of their ruling passion (*e.g.* : a hound-temper, a serpent-temper, and so forth).

The ungodly have no light, neither the light of this world nor the light of God. Their own ever-mounting fire is their light. God is with them only according to His wrath, with terrible lightning.

All their sins stand before them, and produce in their essences remorse, eternal despair, and a hostile will against God. For such a soul there is no remedy. It cannot come into the light of God, cannot come into Heaven. And even if St. Peter had left many thousand keys upon earth, not a single one of them could open Heaven for it. For the soul is separated from the Bond of Christ, and there is a whole birth between it and God, as it is said of the rich man in the Gospel, " There is a great gulf fixed : so that they which would pass from hence to you, cannot ; neither can they pass to us that would come from thence" (Luke xvi. 26). Such a soul after death is like one who lies and dreams that he is in great agony and dread, and everywhere seeks help, yet no help can find. Finally, it despairs and surrenders itself altogether to the devil. Then it reverts to the three first natural properties, and is as if in a dark torture-chamber. It is in continual apprehension of the final judgment of God, "like an imprisoned malefactor who continually listens when anything stirs, as if the executioner should come and execute judgment." Those souls, on the contrary, that have died in the Lord, are in blessed rest, in ever-increasing gladness and refreshment, and in delight-ful expectation of the future. Their works do follow

them in a figure and shadow ; and although they
also have sinful deeds, yet these are forgiven them,
and are blotted out by the atonement of Christ ; and
they realize that there is greater joy in Heaven over
one sinner that repenteth than over ninety-and-nine
just persons who need no repentance.   Such a godly
soul, fallen asleep in the Lord, is like one who lies
in sweet slumber, surrounded by heavenly images,
and rests peacefully.   It is in the bosom of the
Virgin ; and from the Virgin the splendour of the
Holy Trinity shines forth into it.   Its lily grows
green, and blossoms in expectation of the Resurrection.

XCIV.

THE matter, consequently, rests thus :—After death,
when we have done with this outward world, when
our sæculum and our constellation, the time allotted
to us, our hour-glass, has run out, we stand in one
of the two eternal principles.   Not that we are to
suppose that there is need of any long journey when
we part company with this world.   " For far-off and
near is all one and the same thing with God.   And
at that place where the body dies, there is Heaven
and Hell.   God and the devil are there, yet each of
them in his own kingdom.   When the body comes
to be broken, then the holy soul is already in Heaven,
the damned soul in Hell.   It needs no going out or
in " (" The Three Principles," xix., 62-67).   Even
here upon earth, believers roam in Heaven ; but their
eyes are held by this flesh, and they do not see the
heavenly, but, as if with blindfolded eyes, they hold
fast in faith by what they do not see.   And here

already do the ungodly walk in Hell, although they do not see it ; for their eyes are holden and blinded by the distractions of this world and the many things in which they take delight.

There are, however, souls that have only attained a half-regeneration, whose faith is mixed with doubt, or whose faith is like tinder which has been unable to be kindled, because of the damp and moisture which comes from sin and the world, from worldly affairs and distractions, so that it has never been properly lighted.

Some of these come at last to repentance, and in their anxious apprehension they hang by a thread, and seek to lay hold of the Kingdom of Heaven. These stand neither in Hell nor in Heaven. They stand in the Gate, where Fire and Light sever themselves, and are held by their *Turba*, that always seeks the fire. For such souls, clinging to Christ by a feeble thread, Heaven may finally be opened. But what it is thus to stand at the Gate and in a Turba, I leave it to him to try who wilfully persists in sin until his end, and then first desires to be saved. What such souls must undergo, how they are held and tormented, tempted and afflicted, and how woefully they groan, is utterly indescribable. The world does not believe it ; it is far too clever, and understands nothing. Would God that no one experienced this ; I would willingly keep silent about it ! *

We have here attempted to give a very high abstract of Böhme's doctrine of the Intermediate State. We will now submit the doctrine to criticism, and inquire how far we can accept it.

---

* " Answers to XL Questions on the Soul," c., xxiv.

XCV.

THE MAGICAL CONDITION AFTER DEATH.—THE REGIONS BEYOND.

IF we first take a general view of the physical aspect of the subject—the doctrine of Böhme concerning the form of existence in which souls abide after death—one must certainly agree with his description of the state after death as a *state* of *Inwardness* and of the kingdom beyond as a *Kingdom* of *Inwardness*, in which there is not this outward corporeity, in which, indeed, there is no real corporeity, inasmuch as this does not make its appearance until the Resurrection and final Consummation. But in so far as it may be urged, however, that an absolute non-corporeity is unthinkable, because spirit and nature, the inward and the outward, cannot be entirely separated, Böhme teaches, in many places, that there is an inward and finer corporeity imperceptible to our senses,—a corporeity which we do not acquire beyond, but take with us from this world. He teaches, in fact, with Paracelsus, that behind our material body,—which he calls the *elemental*, because it is taken from the four elements, —there is a finer body imperceptible to sense, which he calls the *sidereal;* and, indeed, that behind this sidereal body, which we retain for only a brief period after death, there is a *Light-body*, which the pious and blessed develop into greater perfection as their heavenly attire. We will not venture to plunge farther into these surmises, because they lead us into obscure subtleties. We simply maintain the unavoidable necessity of agreement with Böhme on this point, that the soul may exist hereafter in a certain intermediate corporeity,—a figure of corporeity, as he often terms it—or, as modern students have called it, a *symbolical body*, which can only make itself known by shining and sounding, and which is destined to be succeeded by an actual body, when the hour of the Resurrection arrives.*

So also must we agree with the description of the form of consciousness which belongs to the departed. They are in a "*magia*," that is, they are self-conscious in a condition of relative non-corporeity ; they perceive and comprehend, independently of a material sense-apparatus,—a view which, un-doubtedly, stands in diametrical opposition to the materialistic view which affirms that there can be no other form of consciousness than that which is con-ditioned by these physical organs, this brain-con-sciousness, and the therewith-associated, discursive, fragmentary, and lacunated knowledge with which we must be contented upon earth.

As a symbol of this "magical" consciousness, Böhme refers us to the *Dream.* He teaches that blessed souls rest in sweet slumber, encircled by blessed images, and that the ungodly are in anxious and disturbed dreams, seeking help, but unable to find it. We are here reminded of Hamlet's words in the famous monologue :

> " To die, to sleep,—
> To sleep : perchance to dream :—ay ! there's the rub !
> For in that sleep of death what dreams may come,
> When we have shuffled off this mortal coil,
> Must give us pause."

---

* J. B. Fichte, " Anthropologie."

Both Böhme and Shakspeare have, with profound divination, alluded to the Dream, this natural contrast to our day-consciousness, as a symbol of the form of consciousness that awaits us after death. In dreams we are relatively independent of the material senses. In a wider sense, we may give the name of Dream to every state in which perspicuous images rise before us with the stamp of reality, without the co-operation of the material sense-apparatus, and in which, instead of sense-perception, another faculty is prominent, viz.: the faculty of imagination. It matters not how many empty, meaningless, and confused dreams may now occur ; no one will deny the possibility of visions that are fashioned by objective, plastically-working imagination.

This view, moreover, is corroborated by Holy Scripture, in so far as Scripture alludes to the night and to sleep. Scripture refers us to night ; when it speaks of things beyond, as to a quiet midnight hour, moonlight, or starlight, or lighted by a faintly-glowing midnight sun, it does not tell us. The Lord speaks only of a night when no man can work. And this means work in an outward direction ; for the fundamental character of the night is that of inwardness. In Scripture, moreover, the dead are called "those that are asleep" (1 Thess. iv. 13). Seeing, then, that this state of sleep is a sleep accompanied by consciousness, we cannot but be led to the dream, as the form of consciousness, which includes the religious and ethical content of Eternity. The dream, however, is but an imperfect symbol of the future. The future is not a one-sided dream, such as we are acquainted with, and which stands in contrast to the awakened understanding. On the contrary, the future dream is characterized by the most alert wakefulness. We can here only recall the Gospel narrative of Dives and Lazarus. Each of the conspicuous personages, the rich man, Lazarus, and Abraham, we must conceive of as in a relative non-corporeity ; and yet we must suppose them to be most intensively conscious, inasmuch as everything stands out in bodily shape, in lifelike distinctness, which is precisely the definition of the " magical." In the rich man, desire and imagination display themselves as the source of his torment. Instead of speaking of the state of the departed as a dream-state, it would be more correct to speak of it as a " magical " state. The departed are in a " magia," even although we must admit that our conception of this state can be only imperfect and approximate.

XCVI.

As a symbol of the " magical " condition after death, modern inquirers have pointed to the dream which takes place in the Mesmeric sleep, to the so-called clairvoyant and ecstatic states, in which the soul is, as it were, rapt from the body. Although there is no slight dissimilarity between these states, it is, nevertheless, true of the highest clairvoyance, that the soul lives an inward life, and that everything in these clairvoyants betokens the most inward and intense consciousness. The limitations of time and space are here abolished in the most unusual and extraordinary manner. So far are these clairvoyants from losing their memory, that a more distant past is illuminated for them, and a not-immediate future is unrolled before them. Moreover, the contrast between *near* and *far* is extraordinarily abolished for them. It is as though their whole being were concentrated into a single focus, in which past, present, future, near and remote are blended. In this condition, their attitude towards the external world is, in the strictest sense, like that of the dead. Although, at the outset, before they fall into this state, they are sensitive to the most delicate sounds, and even to distant tones inaudible to others, they cannot now be aroused by the rumbling of wagons or the thunder of artillery. Nor can any human voice reach them, except that of the person with whom they are *en rapport.**

We are compelled to postulate in them an inward sense, a sensorium which must be supposed to exist in us all, although in a fettered condition, and not destined to be liberated and to gain power until death, on which account these clairvoyants are described as anticipations of the state after death. Thus, for instance, by Franz Baader and Schelling. Of the condition itself after death, it is said, in Schelling's " Clara," that the blessed are " in a sleeping wakefulness and a wakeful slumber." In their very slumber, the departed are attracted into a wakeful state, in comparison with which this our earthly consciousness is but as a sleep and a vague dream. And while our earthly life is in a continual

---

* Schelling's Werke, i., 9, 67; Passavant, "Über Lebens-magnetismus;" Haddock, "Somnolismus and Psycheismus."

change between day and night, the externality of
the day and the inwardness of the night, it is only
the saved who are received yonder into "a night-
like day and a day-like night." Is this the reason,
asks Clara, why the moonlight so sweetly touches
our heart with its tremulousness, and fills us with
surmises of the nearness of the spirit-world ?

When magnetic and mesmeric states are designated as anticipations of the future condition, it is not
superfluous to observe that these states, viewed in
and for themselves, ought by no means to be over-
valued. For the very reason that an organ, the
proper function of which lies only in the world
beyond, becomes active here, these states are not
only extraordinary, but abnormal. Stress, moreover,
must be laid upon the fact that in the magnetic
conditions with which we are acquainted, the
essential contents of Eternity are absent. The
clairvoyant looks only into the present world. When
anything of an ethical and religious character occurs
in magnetic states, it is very frequently turbid, confused, and uncertain. The resemblance is thus only
formal ; it applies simply to the *form* of consciousness. It is a resemblance which has at the same
time its obvious limitations.

XCVII.

WE are certainly very far from being able to comprehend the " magical " conditions ; nor ought we to
expect to be able, by any kind of mental effort here
upon earth, to gain any adequate knowledge of the
Life Beyond. Nevertheless, we must maintain, in

accordance with what reflection and Scripture teach us with regard to those regions, that the material relations of Time and Space are abolished, even although these may be conceived in various degrees and stages. For those who have exchanged time for eternity, the successive, the incessant sequence, the constant severance and separation, the lacunated, tardy, and protracted, the intolerable delays and restraints, which are the cardinal features of our development in time, must be replaced by circularity and simultaneity, where everything exists all at once, whole and complete. Those beyond live in a derivative eternity, be it blessed or unblessed. But although the *form* of Eternity is paramount, there is still time. For the intermediate state is a period of expectation, during which all souls await the last and final Judgment with the Resurrection of the Body, a state in which the "magical" is to become the most perfect reality.

XCVIII.

AND the same thing applies to the relation to space. Even now, when we speak of the relation between this world and the world beyond, the relation beween earth and heaven, material space-limitations must be abolished, and we are compelled to admit objectively magical relations. The higher heavenly regions must be presupposed as encircling and penetrating the lower, in a supermaterial manner. Nor can one avoid agreeing with Böhme when he says that the distance between heaven and earth cannot be defined by miles or by any kind of earthly standard of measurement, and that we are not to suppose that we need to take a long journey when we go hence, because everything is near us. This abrogation of space-relations is also shown in those to whom it has been granted, according to Scripture, to gaze into heaven even during their residence upon earth. They were in a " magia " ; and, although they were still in the body, they were rapt away from the body.

In order to gaze into heaven, they did not need to change their place, to surmount opposing barriers, or to traverse intervening distances.

Thus Stephen, who in his dying hour saw the heavens opened and the Son of Man at the right hand of God, did not need to gaze through vast expanses of sky ; but what he saw, he saw immediately at hand.

Thus Paul, who was caught up to the third heaven, did not know whether he was in the body or out of the body ; but he did not require, in any material sense, to change his place.

The disciples stood and gazed into Heaven when Christ was taken up, and the cloud had hidden Him from their eyes. But the essential veil which prevented them from seeing Him was their own flesh, this material body. If this veil could have fallen aside, or if its limiting, oppressive, and darkening power had been only momentarily suspended,—as in the case of Stephen and Paul—they would have been enabled to gaze into Heaven.

A passage in the Old Testament, which shows that the heavenly is not separated from us by material distances, is 2 Kings vi. 15, where it is narrated that the prophet Elisha sent his servant out of the city, and that this servant, when he beheld the city, compassed by a host with horses and chariots, was afraid, and said, " Alas ! my master, how shall we do ? " Then said the prophet, " Fear not : for they that be with us are more than they that be with them ! " and Elisha prayed and said, " Lord ! I pray Thee, open his eyes, that he may see ! "   And behold, the mountain was full of horses and chariots of fire round about Elisha !

This passage shows that heavenly forces and powers may be quite close to us, but that our eyes are holden.

XCIX.

BUT if it applies to the relation between earth and Heaven, so no less does it apply to Heaven itself, that material space-relations have no validity there. On this subject we will limit ourselves to the consideration of Heaven, because it is the perfect and normal, and is far more accessible to our thought than Hell.   It is to Heaven that those words of Böhme, " Far off and near is all one and the same thing with God ! " have their closest application. As we must imagine existence in Heaven to be absolutely free from time, seeing that, as Master Eckart says of eternity, " everything stands in a present *now*," so we must also say that everything in Heaven stands in an immediate *here*.   In Heaven this is perfectly true : " quod petis, hic est ! "   The separation between *near* and *far*, under which we so often sigh, is abolished ; all that belongs to the consummation and fulness of life must be conceived as being together. Separation, impenetrability, insuperable distances cannot be imagined in Heaven ; for although the existences are outside one another and beside one another, they are no less *in* one another. An analogy to this is found in the healthy organism, where indeed the members are outside one another, and yet are not in abstract separation, but are also in one another, as is plainly evidenced by the fact that when one member suffers, the whole body suffers.

Nevertheless, however true this may be, when we speak of Heaven in general terms as the perfect place, Scripture compels us to recognize in Heaven itself a contrast between *near* and *far*, *here* and *yonder*. For Scripture teaches us of many heavens, and, consequently, of higher and lower regions in Heaven itself.

And here we must complain, as an essential defect in Böhme, that he construes Heaven only in general terms, without noticing the contrasts and varieties which Heaven includes, or heeding the glimpses and suggestions afforded by Scripture on this subject. We shall see very shortly that this defect in the physical is accompanied by a remarkably significant defect in the ethical. Here, however, we will simply lay stress on the fact that Paul speaks of the third heaven to which he was caught up ; and that it is said of Christ, our High Priest, that He has passed through the heavens into Heaven itself, which can be interpreted only as the highest, the Uncreated Heaven ; and that, in the Lord's Prayer, we pray not merely to our Father in Heaven, but to our Father *in the Heavens.*

It is true that we are not now to attempt to frame a topography and, as it were, to design a map of the regions beyond, as some have attempted to do, whose efforts may be easily shown to be fruitless, and may indeed easily provoke our ridicule. But just as it is wrong to desire to know more than can be known on these subjects, so it is no less blame-worthy to desire to know less than, on the basis of revelation, *can* and *must* be known. We are, there-fore, not to slight the intimations that are afforded us by revelation, even though our comprehension of them may be but fragmentary, and even though these very intimations should compel us to modify our preconceived views. Thus, we are not to reject the suggestion which Scripture gives us with regard to what has been called the " Configuration of the Universe," the World-Edifice, the situation and rela-tion of the circles of creation, which remains so incomplete in Böhme, notwithstanding the great and solid foundation which he has laid.

Scripture refers us to the tabernacle in Israel, which Moses made " according to the pattern which the Lord showed him on the mount," and in which we, in common with more ancient teachers, discern a symbol of the whole creation in its relation to God. In the tabernacle was the Holy of Holies, with the perfect presence of the grace of God ; next, the Holy Place ; and finally, the Fore-Court. To the Fore-Court then corresponds this earth, with its encircling, visible, starry heaven. To the Holy Place correspond the created, but to us invisible Heavens, which form a habitation for the blessed Spirit-world, holy angels and men, who, in harmony with their nature, and in relation to their communicated perfection, gaze adoringly into the Holy of Holies, where is the throne of God, the central seat of His self-concentrated glory, the innermost centre of that Glory itself. And, according to the intimations of Scripture, there are also created spirits who are allowed to dwell in the Uncreated Heaven.

We add that, outside of the Heavens, Scripture speaks not only of hell, but also of Hades, which it places under the earth ($\kappa\alpha\tau\alpha\chi\theta\acute{o}\nu\iota o\iota$); and from this also we must exclude material space-determinations, and must, consequently, conceive of it as a non-material cosmical "*Below.*" And the fact must be emphasized that, according to Scripture, there is in Hades also a Paradise, which, in a certain sense, may be ranked as *heaven.* It is this which is also called "Abraham's bosom"; this which the Lord promised to the penitent thief, and to which He Himself descended, according to His words: "This day shalt thou be with Me in Paradise." Many ancient church teachers hold that Christians who are saved must first enter this Paradise, in order that they may traverse absolutely the same path which the Lord Himself has trodden.

Thus, there are both lower and higher regions; and a distinction between *near* and *far,* *here* and *there* will be valid even in these regions. For the inhabitants of the lower heavens, there must thus be an appointed limit, a "thus far!" in relation to the higher and the highest Heaven. We can but suppose that this limitation depends upon the degree of their own spiritual perfection. By this their dominion over *near* and *far* is conditioned. Their *here* and *yonder* is defined in accordance with the limitation of their spiritual attainment, in accordance with what they still lack. It is only thus that we are capable of understanding our Lord's words with regard to the " Father's House, and the many mansions."

But on this whole subject of the Created Heavens, the many mansions, and the intermediate regions, Böhme gives us nothing, or tantamount to nothing. He is aware of only two regions beyond : Heaven and Hell ; and this is in entire correspondence with his doctrine that, after death, there are only two states,—Salvation and Damnation. This latter doctrine, again, harmonizes with his assertion that, after death, the soul can no longer change its will. This assertion must be examined more closely, for it leads us back to a highly important article of our Christian Faith, to which Böhme has not done justice.

C.

DOES IT APPLY TO ALL SOULS AFTER DEATH THAT THEY CANNOT CHANGE THEIR WILL ?—THE MULTIPLICITY OF THE FUTURE WORLD.

BÖHME bases his doctrine that the soul cannot change its will after death upon the argument that, after death, it has nothing in which it can change its will. Everyone is there entangled in the spiritual contents, the imaginations that he brings with him from this lower world ; and he can only roll and unroll these among themselves. Böhme thus seems to assert that no new problem can be presented to the soul in the world beyond, that after the laying aside of the body it can acquire no new material for its energy, and that it must, therefore, continue in its then existent state.

But it appears that weighty objections can be urged against this view. However true it may be that the soul takes with it its will-contents from this lower world, and that this fact must decide its immediate destiny, how does he know that the world and the scenes that surround the soul may not set it new tasks, inasmuch as time is not, in every sense, excluded; and on this account something of the third principle may still be active in the world above? How does he know that, in that higher world, there may not be new manifestations of the Divine Will, with regard to which the soul may have to determine itself? And how does he know but that fresh problems may arise out of the native depths of the soul itself? The spiritual contents we bear within us are far richer than those which are absorbed by this lower world; and the distinction between the day-side and the night-side of the soul is very correctly drawn. Why, then, is it inadmissible that there should be that in this nocturnal depth which in the world above will burst into clear consciousness, with new and unsuspected problems, which most certainly must be viewed in connection with the state of consciousness in which the soul then finds itself?

Meanwhile, we need not sustain ourselves by our own conjectures and arguments; we may decide the matter by an authority which is unimpeachable by Christians, viz., the article of Christ's descent into the regions of the dead. If the Gospel is preached to the dead, who had been unable to hear it as an effectual call, and if there are those who received the joyful message beyond the grave, there must be souls there who have changed their wills, have been converted, and have become believers after death. And since the energies that issue forth from Christ in the kingdom of the dead cannot be conceived as simply momentary and limited to a single group of those who were unable to know the Gospel upon earth, the possibility stands open that many souls may change their will after death. Although Böhme confesses the descent of Christ, according to the Apostles' Creed, he has absolutely no comprehension of this article,—a defect which he shares with the general dogmatic of his period.

The old orthodox view in the Lutheran Church ascribes to the descent of Christ a judicial, but no redemptive significance. He descended in order to vanquish the devil, and to shatter the power and kingdom of the devil (Hase, " Libri Symb. F. C.," 788). Böhme rejects this doctrine without suggesting an alternative. He calls it erroneous to suppose that the Soul of Christ, apart from the body, descended into Hell ; and that He there, in His Divine strength, sustained a conflict with devils, bound them in chains, and thus shattered Hell. He teaches, on the contrary, that, at the moment when Christ laid aside the kingdom of this world, His Soul penetrated into death and the wrath of God, and wrath now became reconciled in love. Thus, then, the devils were held captive in the wrath in themselves, together with all wicked souls, and death was destroyed, and life sprang up through death.   Here there is really no Descent ; but Christ's victory over the devil and hell takes place at once upon the Cross.

The profound eschatological meaning of the Descent is wholly hidden from Böhme, and his doctrine of the Intermediate State could not fail to be unsatisfactory, because it lacked this important foundation.   From this indistinctness spring also many strange and baseless utterances on the subject of the salvation of heathens, Turks, and Jews. Böhme says in many places that heathens, Turks, and Jews can be saved, even although they have not known the Christ who has come in the flesh, provided they have only stood in the *other* principle, in the Light-principle, and have sought God with earnestness.   God, then, considers them as children, who know not what they say.   It does not depend on knowledge, but on the will.

We would not depreciate the deep human feeling that expresses itself in these utterances.   But, from an eschatological standpoint, they are altogether inadequate.   If it be sufficient for salvation to stand in the Light-principle (in the non-incarnated Logos), the question arises : Why is the Incarnation neces-sary ? a necessity which Böhme, in accordance with his fundamental view,. most vigorously maintains. The difficulty is removed only by the Article which he did not understand, and which both asserts that no man cometh to the Father except by the Son, Christ come in the flesh, and also embraces Jews, Turks, heathen, embraces all men who have lived here upon earth in innocent ignorance of the way of salvation.

CI.

BÖHME'S one-sidedness upon this article has found its corrective within Theosophy itself in Oetinger. Oetinger apprehends the Descent of Christ not only in its judicial, but in its redemptive aspect, teaches that Christ has conquered the devil and death, and brought all to its consummation, that He has revealed Himself in the invisible Kingdom as the Vanquisher of the devil, and has preached the gospel and life to the captives.

Oetinger often refers to the three first centuries, when Church teachers held the correct view. Upon this presupposition he founds his Scriptural Meditations on the subject of the Intermediate State, in which he is also influenced by Swedenborg, the Northern seer, who alternately attracts and repels him, and in whom he is resolute to accept only that which is good and consonant with Scripture. He thus succeeds in formulating a doctrine which furnishes a counterpart to Böhme's, viz.:—the doctrine of an infinite multiplicity and variety of states after death, although the contrast between believers and unbelievers, saved and unsaved, remains the fundamental contrast.

He agrees with Böhme in the view that souls take with them from this world the plastic image and form-fashioning imagination, and that unbelievers and the ungodly suffer from appalling penal fantasies, generated by themselves. The souls are certainly outside the body. But all the organs of the body, the ears, the eyes, the tongue, etc., have bequeathed their form to the souls, which, conse-

quently, are surrounded by things that belong to
these physical organs. Colours, words, sounds, fire,
and other physical forms are round about them.
They behold mountains and hills before them,
forests and fields around them, after the pattern of
those that they were acquainted with in this world.
In short, they take with them the *form* of their
previous condition, precisely as they have surrendered
themselves to this with their whole appetite, or, as
Böhme would say, with their imagination and desire.
But, in contrast to the orthodox monotony,
Oetinger teaches that there exist, after death,
innumerable varieties of souls, conditions, abodes,
and shapes, torments and horrors, countless varieties
in fancy and imagination, in understanding and conceptions, and that there are many kinds of *Schools*
after death. This view of schools after death
Böhme utterly rejects. Oetinger, on the contrary,
preached a sermon on the sorrowful school of the
ungodly, and the joyous school of believers after
death. The idea of a school suggests not simply
better instruction, but, above all, the purification and
amelioration of the Will.

On the subject of the possibility of Repentance
after death, Oetinger teaches: There are amongst
the dead those who have never heard the Gospel;
next, such as have heard it, but became indifferent
and never formed a decision; but there are also
others who in every possible way disregarded the
call of the Gospel, and rejected it with contumely.
For the two former classes, there is a possibility of
forgiveness and salvation in the world beyond, but
the last must endure their punishment, and must

pay the uttermost farthing. Moreover, the first also, the indifferent classes, must bear the judgment of which Jesus speaks (John iii. 19) for a considerable period after their death.

With regard to the ungodly, Oetinger teaches that their soul is a "Wheel of Birth" which has been set on fire, or, in other words, it is a Worm that dieth not. That the Soul is called a Worm implies that it is nothing but an indescribably restless self-torturing energy (Böhme's third natural property, or desire), which burns like a fire, and yet is never reduced to ashes. But this restless self-torturing energy of the soul receives countless modifications, according to the sins and vices of men during this life.

Concerning the saved, who take with them what God has here bestowed upon them, the grace-gift of eternal life ($\pi\alpha\rho\alpha\theta\acute{\eta}\kappa\eta$, 2 Tim. i. 12), he teaches that they advance from class to class, from grade to grade, from Abraham's bosom, or the lower Paradise, to the higher heavenly region. After death we shall most certainly not at once be at home with the Lord, but there are many degrees of progress. Jesus guides us from station to station with His shepherd's staff. Oetinger agrees with Swedenborg that one does not come into the arms of Jesus immediately after death, but that one is first grasped by His mighty Hand. He censures the clergy, because in their sermons they cut off all development and progress in the Intermediate State, and thus make this into a wilderness; and he thinks it perilous for the clergy to beguile the common people with the error, that they are to enter into complete salvation immediately after death, and that they are at once to embrace Jesus, whereas they ought to remember that the Lord Himself, who has left us an example, ascended from the lowest to the highest. The clergy are indisposed to form a proper conception of the state after death, and most of them are silent on the subject, because one exposes oneself to odium by stating any other doctrine of the Future State than the one commonly received.

But the currently-accepted doctrine is that, immediately after death, one passes either into Heaven or into Hell, without successive transitions. It should, however, be observed that those who came next to the Apostles, Irenæus, Tertullian, Cyprian, Chrysostom, etc., hold quite another view ; for they all teach the doctrine of gradual transitions.

It must be added that, although Oetinger teaches a general Resurrection in a transfigured corporeity at the end of the world, he, nevertheless, supposes that there are some souls which attain the Resurrection of the body prior to the general Resurrection, and, at the same time, attain perfection, because they are ripe for it, souls which may be compared to fruit which the gardener is able to pluck from the tree before the harvest, before the time of the general ripening.

This first resurrection goes on throughout the centuries, and there are, even now before the time, many souls that are made perfect.

Whether this idea can be reconciled with Apocalypse xx. 5, we simply suggest for closer consideration.

CII.

As a special argument in favour of his doctrine of the great diversity of souls and of spiritual states after death, Oetinger adduces the many spiritual manifestations from the other world which were accepted in his time as well-authenticated, and in which he sees a sign and testimony against the negligent silence of the clergy with respect to the Intermediate State, on which account he very frequently alludes to such manifestations in his sermons. He leads us here into a domain into which we are also led by Swedenborg, and, after Oetinger's time, no less by Jung-Stilling's well-known treatise, " Theorie der Geisterkunde," as well as by the book that caused so much excitement in its day, " Die Seherin von Prevorst," and also by the so-called spiritualism of our own period. For our own part, we are not disposed to resort to these arguments. But, seeing that Böhme also accepts manifestations and phenomena of spirits that move about houses or show themselves in churchyards,—although Böhme does not deduce from these what Oetinger deduces, —we will, as it were, in the form of an appendix, examine the hypothetical meaning that can be ascribed to this argument in favour of Oetinger's doctrine.

When one speaks of spirit-manifestations from the other world, one is usually met by the uncritical cry that such things are absolutely impossible ! But one must not allow oneself to be overawed by this cry. Unless one professes pure materialism, and denies the conceptions of spirit and the spirit-world, one cannot deny the possibility that spirit may be able to manifest itself to spirit; nor is it possible to perceive what natural laws can prevent a purely spiritual " commercium."

Kant—whom no one will describe as a credulous or uncritical man—expresses himself (within the limits of his philosophy) upon this subject in a manner that merits great attention.

He confesses that he knows just as little how a man's soul goes out of this world (that means, what its condition is after death), as he knows how it comes into this world (that means, its precise relation to generation and propagation); indeed, that he does not even know how a man's soul is present in this world, that is, how an immaterial nature can be active in, and by means of, a body. Then he goes on to say: " In consequence of this ignorance, I do not presume to deny all truth to the many kinds of spirit-manifestations, although with the usual, if somewhat remarkable, reservation of challenging each single instance, according, nevertheless, some credence to spiritual manifestations on the whole."

This modest, but by no means uncritical standpoint is precisely the one which it would become others also to accept.

The hypothetical meaning which belongs to Oetinger's argument is thus the following: If the facts are correct, and the manifestations in question, or even some of them, are adequately substantiated, this supplies additional evidence in favour of the theory that there are many kinds of spirits in the other world, that there are various degrees and stages in relation to Light and Darkness—a contribution to the establishment of the conception of non-finality in the Intermediate State. The kinds of spirits or souls which manifest themselves upon earth after death belong,—if one analyses the dominant impression one receives from what is related of them in the above-mentioned books,—neither to Heaven nor to Hell, neither to the perfect Light nor to the perfect Darkness, but to the twilight ; the predominant impression that we gain from most of the descriptions is that these souls are homeless, that they have not succeeded in finding their abode in Heaven or in Hell ; that, upon the whole, they cannot properly establish themselves in the world beyond, where their condition may be compared, metaphorically speaking, to that of those who roam about in a dark valley from which no exit is discoverable, or to that of wanderers in a forest where they cannot find the right path, but seek it while they feel the impossibility of finding it.

An explanation of the fact that they find themselves again attracted to this earth must be sought in the impurity that oppresses them, in the law of moral gravitation which drags them back to the earth and to earthly concerns, as that in which they feel themselves at home, and which is their proper element. A striking feature in many of them is that they experience a necessity of confessing to earthly beings this or that sin or misdeed which particularly burdens them, as, for instance, it is related of Czar Peter that he manifested himself to Dr. Dippel, and self-accusingly bewailed the perennity of his murderous crimes.

Nothing is more preposterous than to suppose

that by coming into closer relations with these souls
one would be able to gain deeper insight into the
mysteries of the world beyond, and perhaps even to
apprehend eternal truths, which one cannot already
know from Revelation.   These spirits are incapable
of divining mysteries, they reveal themselves most
frequently as beings totally adrift, full of ignorance,
folly, and error with regard to the means that can
promote their own amelioration, and they often say
things that cannot but strike us as ridiculous.   If
any reliance can be placed in the information which
the spiritualism of our day gives on the subject of
spirit-manifestations, one can arrive at no other
conclusion than that these spirits are, as a rule, what
we are wont to call *spiritless*, that they are cha-
racterised by " poverty of spirit " in the worst sense
of the term.

If one would draw inferences, one cannot but
suppose that there are in the other world peripheral
regions, which form the habitation of a multitude of
spirits, whose imagination, in so far as it is not
pre-occupied with sins, is filled only with trivialities,
finite, temporal, subordinate interests which they
cannot let go.   And, at bottom, this can excite no
surprise except among those who have established
themselves in the idea—so often found in funeral
hymns—that the spirit of every one who departs
this life is lifted in ethereal clearness to the blessed
regions.   It is unreasonable to seek the spirit after
death where it was not before death.   But it must
arouse great astonishment, that there should be those
who suppose that these spirit-phenomena, with which
spiritualism makes us acquainted, are to be regarded

as a consoling substitute for that Christian faith in immortality which many have lost. To have the prospect of joining such society is a miserable consolation !

We have been somewhat minute in our account of Oetinger's view, because it contains so important a corrective of Böhme's, and betokens a new momentum of development in Protestant eschatology, which has attained wider expansion only in the dogmatic of the present century. Personally, we base nothing upon the phenomena in question, but let them stand aside altogether. We build only— and advise others to do the same—upon that authentic Word of the Lord wherein one cannot go wrong : " They have Moses and the prophets : let them hear them ! "

CIII.

THE CONSUMMATION.

WE return from this digression to epitomize Böhme's doctrine of the Consummation of all things. Of the history and fortunes of the Church in the Last Times, Böhme says but little ; he is here far surpassed by Oetinger, who is influenced by Bengel's meditations on the Apocalypse, and has a keener eye for the ways of God throughout the ages. Böhme has an eye only for the conclusion. His doctrine may thus be briefly summarized. God has from eternity moved Himself twice : the first time to the creation of the world, which belongs to the Father ; the second time to the Incarnation, which belongs to the Son ; but, at the end of the world, He will move Himself for the third time, in the nature of the Holy Ghost, when the Holy Ghost is to reveal Himself not only as the Spirit of the Church, but as the Creator Spirit with the seven spirits or lamps, and then the third principle or this world shall be abolished and return into æther, and the dead shall arise. After the world has enjoyed a spring-tide in the " thousand years' reign," a season of " peace upon earth " during which all religious dissensions are to cease, and when Christ is to rule over the Church like a shepherd over his flock, the Philosopher's Stone, by which we shall be enabled to know all things and to extract from the metals their spirit and heart, will be discovered, and the world will perish by fire. This fire is not an ordinary fire ; it is Fire from the " *centrum naturæ,*" which sets the world on a blaze from within, and bursts forth at every point.

And now occurs the Last Judgment, the Final Crisis, sundering, and separation. The mixture of good and evil, love and wrath, which is the fundamental characteristic of the present world, is now to be abolished. The twilight is to cease ; everything is to be sharply separated into light and darkness. Out of this crisis, in which everything that cannot endure the ordeal by fire must sink into the darkness, the new world arises in unspeakable glory. Heaven and earth are united, and believers ascend to perfect blessedness. Everything is penetrated and filled with the Light of God.

When Christ is revealed in His majesty, as the Judge, the devil and the ungodly are seized with indescribable despair ; and, as being eternally condemned, must sink, with their character and with all their deeds, into the deepest darkness. But believers arise in a transfigured corporeity after the likeness of the Risen Christ. They are now no longer—as in the Intermediate State—in a mere "magia," but in a spiritual-corporeal reality. Their bodies are palpable, and yet spiritual and incorruptible, free from time and space, like the Body of Christ, in which He passed through closed doors. The risen are androgynous ; the earthly relations of sex and family endure only in recollection.

In reality, each one—man or woman—has in himself or herself the perfect combination of masculine and feminine. They are now, for the first time, perfect human beings, who neither marry nor are given in marriage, but are equal to the angels. They live under Christ, who has now delivered up the Kingdom to the Father, and is no longer our Redeemer, but continues to be our Head and Brother. The whole of this blessed world now abides in perfect and unchangeable "*temperature*," in indissoluble harmony of spirit and nature. And all spirits, angels and men, are now the willing instruments and ministers of God, in complete unison with God and each other.

CIV.

BÖHME'S doctrine of the conclusion of the world is often met by the objection that his doctrine of eternal damnation conflicts with his premises. The idea of Redemption certainly suggests that the creation, disturbed by sin, is to be restored to "temperature." It seems quite natural to expect that, at the close of the system, Evil, *as evil*, must be annihilated, must be reduced into a mere possibility as a ministering basis for the Kingdom of God, just as the dark nature-principle in God Himself is only the ministering basis for the manifestation of the Light. But, according to Böhme, who is here in harmony with Church doctrine, the devil and the damned remain out of "temperature," and cannot be restored to it.

However the case may stand with regard to scientific consistency, Böhme holds very deliberately by his doctrine of the eternity of Hell. Whenever the question is presented to him whether Hell must not, at some time or other, come to an end, and Salvation become universal throughout the whole creation, he replies that this is not to be thought of, and that it is totally in conflict with the Foundation of Hell. If the devil were again to become an angel, he must again draw out of God's unity and love ; his fire-life, his life of pride must be transformed into humility. But this the devil and the devils will not, cannot do ; for there is no inclination in them and no desire for repentance and humility. Their whole life is nothing else than a "Nay!" against God's "Yea!" is nothing else but poison and stench ; and when they hear of love and humility, they flee away, for love is death to their false life. And what is here said of devils applies equally to ungodly, condemned men.

Böhme thus essentially takes his stand upon a basis which goes back into the mystery of free-will. He maintains that the free-will of the creature can attain such a degree of obduracy and darkness that a change of the will is no longer possible, because freedom of choice is lost, since the divine image in these creatures has absolutely paled, and has become a lifeless, powerless, inoperative " Figure." They cannot will anything but evil ; their free-will has become an unalterable necessity ; and this self-darkened will, in which freedom of choice is irrevocably lost, Böhme regards as the Foundation of Hell, just as the Foundation of Heaven is the good will, in which Love is a holy necessity. Both to heaven and hell there belongs, in the strictest sense, a fixed, fortified, and no longer changing Will. It is not God who arbitrarily assigns the eternal punishments of Hell. The ungodly have themselves unlocked Hell, have kindled the fire of Hell within themselves, and must now abide by their choice as irrevocable. They *will* not be in Heaven : *will not* have fellowship with God and be saved.

Leibnitz states essentially the same thought in his observations on the possibility of an eternal Hell. He combats the usual conception that the ungodly are placed in Hell by an arbitrary fiat of God against their own will, and that they suffer a punishment which is regarded as too severe by those who deny the eternity of Hell,—a punishment which the ungodly would eagerly flee from were it possible, just as a criminal would flee who, against his will, has been placed in rigorous, perpetual captivity as a punishment for his crimes.

It must be maintained, on the contrary, that it is the ungodly themselves who build the prison, from which there is no exit, because they themselves are never willing to leave it. When a soul, says Leibnitz, dies in a temper of hostility against God, it falls of itself, by a kind of voluntariness or spontaneity, into the abyss of destruction, just like a weight that has torn itself loose, and no longer has any support. It will no longer have anything to do with God. It desires to be damned. He adds that, according to the view of many pious men, the hatred borne by the damned towards God is so great, that they absolutely *will not* implore His grace; and it is precisely thus that they adjudge themselves to eternal misery, and abide in it.

As a consequence of Böhme's conception of the will of the creature, eternal damnation consists in this: that the damned certainly perceive that after the last catastrophe (the final Judgment or Crisis) it is absolutely hopeless to contend against God, but that they are, nevertheless, compelled incessantly to contend against Him, even although this is not an actual struggle, but a hunger after it, a yearning to give themselves a reality which they can never attain. They cannot be annihilated, because a spirit cannot die. A spirit must incessantly move and energize, but, because the damned cannot acquire motives for a new movement of the will towards humility and love by means of repentance, they must continue endlessly to prosecute and repeat their false movement of the w'll.

A question that may be proposed here, and which has its significance, even on the assumption that Hell has an end, is this: *Where is Hell*, when the new order of nature is established, when all has become Heaven, and the Kingdom of Glory has arrived? There appears to be no room for it, and the quest after a locality seems vain. Böhme does not enter more closely into this subject. But we may refer to Schelling, who proposed this question to himself, and answered it in a manner which is in constructive harmony with Böhme's view. Schelling affirms that Hell is in the most utterly deep abyss, below or under nature, so that Hell is the *substratum* of nature, just as nature is the substratum of Heaven, of the world of the blessed spirits. According to Schelling, evil no longer exists in actual relation to God and the universe; it continues to exist *only in itself*. It has now what it wants—absolute isolation, and, consequently, separation from the general and Divine World. It is delivered over to the agonies of its own egoism, to the hunger of selfishness.

CV.

WHEN Böhme, in order to support his doctrine of eternal damnation, points to the mystery of the created will and to that self-darkening in which freedom of choice is lost, it immediately occurs to us to point, in contrast, to the mystery of Divine love, to the Fatherly power of God, and to ask whether that which is possible for the creature may not be possible for God; whether God is unable to change the will of the creature, not, indeed, by physical means, but along the path of freedom and educating development, which does not exclude, but includes, the most serious and severe punishment and chastisements. One naturally asks whether the Divine image, which lies in these lost spirits like a lifeless corpse, may not once more be recalled to life by these chastisements and by the influences of Divine grace, and freedom of choice be restored to them, so that they may rediscover the motives of humility and love.

A *human* teacher, it is true, may come to the conclusion that he must give up some of those who were entrusted to his care, and confess that all his toil for them has been fruitless and wasted. But is God to be conceived of as a Teacher who is unable to overcome the will of the creature, and must partially abandon His object, the universal, all-embracing Kingdom of Love? This is the thought which forms the starting-point of those who deny the doctrine of eternal damnation. However inadequately they may be able to explain how the restoration of the devil and of ungodly men to God is to be effected, yet this restoration is an assumption, a postulate, and, so to speak, an article of secret hope, which they hold in virtue of the power of the eternal Love of God.

CVI.

WITHIN Theosophy itself, we first mention Oetinger as having laid down a doctrine which contrasts with Böhme's. His starting-point is, that God's essence is Love; and that the Wrath of God, in comparison with His Love, endureth but for a moment. Undoubtedly, everything must be fulfilled which Scripture teaches with reference to the Lord's second coming, the Final Judgment, and the separation between believers and unbelievers, saved and unsaved.

Oetinger does not deny the reality of hell, but teaches it in the most definite way with all its terrors. Still, he emphasizes, with his utmost power, the idea that this reality must some time come to an end. He imagines that the catastrophe which we are accustomed to regard as the final one (when Christ comes to judge the quick and the dead) is the beginning of a series of æons, in which also run the æons of the damned, which for us stretch into the infinite distance, and which are closed by the fact that Christ delivers up the kingdom to the Father. Then, for the first time, the words will be completely fulfilled: "The last enemy that shall be destroyed is Death." So long as Hell endures, these words remain unfulfilled. For Hell is precisely this Kingdom of Death, and Death is very far from being merely physical death.

Oetinger lays stress on the point that the word αἰώνιος (eternal) also means, in Scripture, that which is indefinite in duration, *e.g.*, a "mystery hidden from the eternal ages;" and that in the expression "eternal damnation," the word "eternal" must not be construed in the same sense as when one speaks of eternal life. Eternal life must be without end, because it is grounded in God Himself, who has no end ; but "eternal" damnation can only mean *that* of which the end is undefined ; for sin and death have not their ground in God and in communion with God, but have only a temporal beginning in the will of the creature, and must consequently come to an end at some time or other.

An important passage in Scripture to which Oetinger appeals is Psalm cxlv. 10: "All Thy works shall praise Thee!" These words are not fulfilled until even the damned offer praise in Hell, thank God for their punishment, and recognise and confess all their unrighteousness and all their falsehoods, and that God alone is right. They are not fulfilled until this cry goes up from the whole creation: "Blessing and honour, and glory and power be unto Him that sitteth upon the throne, and unto the Lamb for ever and ever!" (Apocal. v. 13).

Oetinger is well aware that he is here at issue with the Augsburg Confession, but believes that Scripture is entirely on his side. He thinks that the Church doctrine upon this point rests upon a misinterpretation of the word *Eternity.*

In a similar manner, Franz Baader opposes Böhme's doctrine upon this subject. No one has ever expressed himself more strongly than Baader in favour of the reality of Hell; no one has more vividly depicted the infernal state. He is vehement in his opposition to those who shrink back effeminately from the reality of Hell, and change the conception of Hell into that of Purgatory. But he considers the conception of an endless Hell to be wholly untenable, and is, indeed, of opinion that it leads necessarily to Pantheism and Atheism. He specially accentuates the fact that in Hades much can again be made good, and that here grace still goes before justice. But in Hell, justice goes before grace. And here it is true, that no one escapes before "he has paid the uttermost farthing" (a passage also quoted by Oetinger), and before the severe judgment of righteousness has been accomplished. Here all the deeds of the wicked are burned in the fire, and the ungodly must pass through the sulphur-pool and the stifling smoke, that ascends throughout the æons. But the Divine Righteousness is not without measure or without limits. The punishments of Hell are not *infinitæ*, but *indefinitæ*. Their duration is indeterminable. But Death and Hell must be absolutely vanquished at some period or other ; or else the last enemy is not destroyed, and Scripture remains unfulfilled. How the restoration is to take place he certainly does not tell us. Hamberger represents the transition in such a way as that the hosts of Lucifer will gradually rebel against him, and stretch out their hands for mercy ; and that, at length, Lucifer will find himself left utterly alone, and will then, as the last creature, entreat mercy. He will then acquire a place un-determinable by us in the Blessed Kingdom.*

For our own part, we cannot but hold that each of the views here brought forward presents us with unsurmounted difficulties, especially on careful investigation of all the declarations of Scripture that bear upon this subject. We shall not, however, discuss the matter more fully here, as we have lengthily and explicitly stated our view elsewhere ("Dogmatics").

But, in so far as concerns our old theosophist Böhme, it is unquestionable that, whenever he hears of a general and universal restoration and an end of Hell, he shakes his head, and says : "This is not to be thought of! It is at variance with the

---

* Hamberger, "Gott und seine Offenbarungen," 479.

Foundation of Hell. The devil cannot, and will not, become humble. Never, to all eternity, will he betake himself to repentance and conversion. Neither he nor any of his adherents will be saved!" When the agonies of the ungodly are dilated upon, he repeats the words of Christ to Jerusalem, "Ye *would* not!" The Lord does not say, "Ye *could* not!" but "Ye *would* not!" and, because they continue in the evil of their sins, they *cannot.*

But by way of admonition to himself and others, and in order to excite rejoicing over the Gospel of Christ in this world of troubles, where everything depends upon grasping the proffered grace, he ofttimes repeats: "A Lily blossoms upon the mountains and valleys in all the ends of the earth. He that seeketh findeth! Amen."

L'ENVOI.

As I have now completed this sketch, which is certainly rather of an introductory than of a conclusive character, the opportunity might now appear to be naturally presented of instituting a series of inquiries with regard to the relations of Theosophy to Theology and Philosophy, of defending Theosophy against its assailants both theological and philosophical, and of proposing terms of accommodation between them. But I have no intention of attempting this. I shall confine myself to a very few words.

With regard to Theology I make the general remark, that in my judgment—a judgment which has been greatly confirmed by these studies,—Church

Theology is not wise in assuming a hostile attitude towards Theosophy and in endeavouring to exclude it altogether (a course, however, which has not been adopted by *all* the representatives of theology).

It is not wise in this course, because it hereby deprives itself of a most valuable leavening influence, a source of renewal and rejuvenescence, which Theology so greatly needs, exposed as it is to the danger of stagnating in barren and dreary scholasticism and cold and trivial criticism.

So far as the charge of a *"non-Scriptural"* element in Theosophy,—that is, its discrepancies with current exegesis,—is concerned, there is certainly no one who is prepared to assert the infallibility of theosophical exegesis. It must, however, be obvious to every theologian who has a more than superficial acquaintance with Theosophy, that it has aroused and attracted attention to a circle of Scriptural conceptions which theology has disregarded or to which it has devoted very slight pains, because it is not in possession of the categories which are requisite for their treatment. As one great instance, among many, may be mentioned the conception of the Glory of God and the Uncreated Heaven. No one will deny that these are fundamental conceptions in Holy Scripture, while in theology they are scarcely even accessory notions, and, indeed, are referred to in many theological systems as "dark points," which it is best to avoid. And yet it will hardly be denied that it is the duty of the theologian to bring to light the fundamental conceptions of Scripture, and to offer some explanation of them.

Next, as to the outcry against the *"unscientific*

element in Theosophy. No one denies a measure of truth in this outcry; for the matter is so absolutely clear as not to require diffuse and tautological repetitions,—repetitions which are very far from proving that the man who takes delight in them is a genuinely scientific theologian. No one denies that mediate or reflective knowledge, and thorough-going analysis and combination of conceptions, or what may be called, in a wider sense, the scholastic element, is indispensable to theology. But it is very illusory to suppose that this scholasticism has any value of its own, when it lacks the emotion of the mystic or the immediate intuition of that new and higher world of experience of the heavenly realities which Revelation unveils for us.

Church history shows also that it is scarcely possible to point out a single important dogmatic work which has been able to restrict its operations within the narrow domain of the School, and to dispense with the influence of a fortifying element either of mysticism, or of Theosophy, or of both combined. Thus it merits attention that the most important, epoch-making dogmatic work of this century—"The Dogmatic" of Schleiermacher—has undoubtedly kept itself free, indeed far too free, from Theosophy, but is remarkable, on the other hand, for an experimental mysticism, the presence of which manifests itself in Schleiermacher as early as his "Reden über die Religion." That Schleiermacher's "Dogmatic" has been enabled to exert such widely-spread and living influence until the present day is due, not simply to its admirable dialectic or to its intellectual standpoint (in which there is so much that must now be regarded as obsolete) ; it is essentially due to the vivid perspicuous image of Christ, the living experimental consciousness of the Grace of God in Christ, and the mystical relation of Love to the Saviour, which are among its strongly-marked characteristics. Schleiermacher's " Dogmatic " was destined—greatly against the author's will, but by an obvious necessity—to lead younger theologians who had studied it attentively to speculative theology and Theosophy, as was evidenced by subsequent dogmatic works. And it must be regarded as a sign of retrogression, not of progress, that there should now be any who occupy a position in which they do nothing else but repristinate the old orthodox theology. It must undoubtedly be admitted as expedient that ecclesiastical tradition should be preserved, and ecclesiastical testimony maintained, in opposition to neo-rationalism and all its cognate systems. But in such circles there can be no real progress in the Christian apprehension of truth.

With regard to philosophers and other disputants, who attack not only Theosophy, but also theology, and even Christianity itself, in the name of modern science, I shall simply confine myself to quoting a sentence from Böhme's doctrine of knowledge or apprehension, which is extremely *à propos* amid existing controversies with respect to Divine things.

" Every spirit," he says, " sees no further than into its mother, out of which it has its original, and wherein it stands ; for it is impossible for any spirit, in its own natural power, to look into another

Principle, and behold it, except it be regenerated therein " (" The Three Principles," vii., 1).

This sentence closely applies to the literature of the present day, in which naturalistic, materialistic, and atheistic spirits continually appear, with attacks and objections against Christianity. One ought to feel absolutely no surprise at this, but to remember that these spirits cannot speak with regard to Divine things otherwise than they do. They can only testify of that which they have seen and heard in their mother, *i.e.*, in blind nature or unconscious reason. All that lies beyond this must necessarily strike them as fantastic and visionary. It is perfectly true that one may sometimes be tempted to impatience by hearing these objections urged with a strong assumption of superiority. Even Böhme sometimes allowed himself to be carried away by impatience, when he had to defend Theosophy against its opponents, whom he designates as sophists, " who butted against his doctrine like cows against a freshly-painted stable door, and rejected all that their calvish understanding could not grasp." Such diatribes, however, are useless ; they convert no one. For the spirits " will continue to gaze into their mother, and, according to circumstances, to speak about, scream, and cackle out of their mother," *i.e.*, out of that principle which for them is the constitutive, the fundamentally-determinant, and out of which they are spiritually born. And thus it is often one's best plan to refuse to enter into any discussion, but simply to place the recognised truth before those who are able to be influenced by it, or, to speak with Böhme, " to write

simply for seekers and for children of God, and for
the rest, to leave the spirits to shout or cackle in the
name of what they call 'science,' which means their
mother, as they will continue to do so long as the
course of this world abides." As this sentence of
Böhme's is not to be construed fatalistically, it must
depend upon the inward leadings and inward deci-
sions of the spirit whether opponents will be able
to accept the one word which sums up the whole
matter: "Ye must be born again;" whether this can
flash in upon them like lightning, or whether they
will persist in regarding it as visionary, in which
case they will remain in their darkness and in secret
anxiety. Böhme's meaning is this : that only those
who are regenerated by the principle of which our
Lord spoke to Nicodemus, who came to Him by
night, can understand one another in discourse
concerning Divine things, and that otherwise, however loudly they may speak or shout, they remain
mutually dumb to one another ; that only those who
speak out of this principle can discourse of the
Wisdom in God, which is a Wisdom in Mystery,
and descends from Him in whom all the treasures of
wisdom and knowledge are hidden,—hidden, not in
order that they may remain secret, but in order that
they may ever increasingly be made manifest, and
appropriated by us.

We shall do well to lay to heart what Böhme
says in all gentleness: "Dost thou not understand
these Scriptures ?   Then do not behave thyself like
Lucifer ! Do not give thyself to arrogance and scorn,
but seek from God the humble heart ! Thereby thou
wilt attain this, that a little mustard-seed of the

growth of Paradise will be brought into thy heart, and out of it will spring a great tree.　Thus it has been with the present author ; for he is a very simple person in comparison with the learned.　But Christ says : ' My strength is made perfect in weakness ' (2 Cor. xii. 9)."

THE END.

Printed by Hazell, Watson, & Viney, Limited, London and Aylesbury.